FORGOTTEN HEROES
A NOVEL BY
DANNY J. BANISTER

For my loving wife Liz,
Without her help I could not have written this.

For my children

| Brian | Paul | Keith |
| Michael | Leah | Heather |

For the Men and Women who served

Many made the journey
Most survived
Few have told their story
None will forget

AUTHOR'S NOTE

A nation should never forget its heroes. For if it does, it will inevitably be harder to find new ones in its next crisis. Unfortunately, this is what America did to her Vietnam Vets. At best they were ignored, treated as if their ordeal never happened, as if their service and sacrifice was never given. But more likely than not, they were treated like criminals, verbally and physically attacked, literally spat upon by strangers, when their only crime was to answer their country's call. Setting aside their personal feelings they served their nation when asked to do so, an obligation we all have.

This book is an attempt to tell a story of a few of those Forgotten Heroes.

PROLOGUE

The huge CH-47 Chinook helicopter was slowly descending to land in the middle of the perimeter made up from the units of the Third Squadron, Fifth Armored Cavalry. It was shortly after dawn and the residue of the battle that had raged most of the night was apparent everywhere. The morning haze was mixed with smoke from the burning vehicles, forming a partially opaque vapor suspended in the atmosphere. There were two Armored Personnel Carriers melted down to half their size still smoldering and two others still in flames. The wreckage of a Bell UH-1Huey Medevac helicopter, easily recognized by the large red cross painted on it, laid on its side. It was one of six that had been called in during the battle. The other five had made it out and took with them nineteen wounded soldiers.

The Chinook's mission was not one of mercy like the Medevac's had been. No, it was there to pick up the dead, the bodies of twenty-six young men. They were lying on the ground, lined up neatly in two rows of thirteen, orderly and precise, a systematic grouping. They were the only thing that seemed to have any comprehensible design. The helicopter set down only forty feet from the bodies. The turbulence of the two large rotors blew the ponchos off some of the dead, revealing the carnage. Soon the bodies would be placed in plastic body bags and tagged with an ID, naming the dead soldier inside.

It was also picking up one passenger, a young Staff Sergeant, who was going home. He had completed his one year tour of duty and was alive and in one piece, but changed forever. He walked up the back loading ramp of the Chinook and was standing in the doorway. His fatigues were torn and sweat-stained from months of continuous wear. Although only twenty-one, he looked older, his face tired and sad, his physical strength and his strength of spirit depleted. He was carrying a mere one hundred fifty-seven pounds on his six foot frame, twenty pounds less than the day he arrived. This last year had taken its toll, especially this last night, this last battle. It had been the worst night of his young life, the worst battle he had ever fought.

He checked the name tag of each body bag as it was loaded on the helicopter. When he found the one he was looking for, he walked along side until the two crewmen carrying the body, placed it on the floor. The young sergeant sat down beside it, gently lifting the upper half of the body still sealed inside the bag, and cradled it in his arms. He was quietly sobbing, rocking slowly back and forth.

So many things had happened. So many things had changed. He closed his eyes and began to play it all back in his mind, back to the day he first arrived.

CHAPTER ONE

The jar of the wheels touching down on the runway snapped Bobby Mitchell away from his thoughts and back to the moment at hand. He leaned forward and looked out the window, all he saw was darkness. The air base was blacked out as it was every night, part of the security procedures. There was an air of anxiety as everyone began moving about, a hum of indistinct whispers filled the plane. The soldiers seemed to be glad that the long flight was over, ready to leave their cramped seats, but leery of stepping into this unknown place - The Vietnam War.

Mitchell traveled to Vietnam with one hundred and eighty other soldiers on a military chartered commercial airliner, Continental Airlines, flight T4E79. He landed at Bien Hoa Airfield, outside of Saigon. The flight from Travis Air Force Base, California, had taken eighteen hours with refueling stops in Anchorage, Alaska, and Tokyo, Japan. The crew of the aircraft were civilians. The flight attendants had been smiling and cheerful during the long flight, but after they had landed and as the young soldiers were deplaning, they looked sad and some had tears in their eyes. It was not unusual for these civilian flight attendants to become emotional when delivering these young men to this place of anguish.

As Mitchell walked through the door of the plane, a strong smell filled the air; it hit him right in the face. It was a combination of smells that he recognized, but never together; the spicy aroma of oriental cooking mixed with a strong pungent odor of raw sewage.

He turned to a young PFC walking behind him, "What the fuck is that smell?"

The PFC answered in what Mitchell thought was a southern accent, "I don't know, but it smells like the shitter's backed up!"

It was July 27, 1968, and Sergeant Robert Mitchell was only twenty years old and just stepped into what would be the longest year of his life.

Mitchell had been in the army for eleven months. He was drafted back in August 1967. Just eleven months and he had three stripes on his sleeve. Normally, it would take four or five years to make E-5, but Vietnam had changed all that. The United States had so many combat troops in Vietnam by 1968 that there were not enough NCO's (non-commissioned officers) to fill all the slots. So the army started a program to address that need. That program was NCO Candidate School at Fort Benning, Georgia. Mitchell was a product of that school. He had taken his basic training at Fort Bliss, Texas, and then he went straight to A.I.T. (Advanced Infantry Training) at Fort Polk, Louisiana. He had finished in the top five percent of his class at Fort Polk and was selected for NCO School. It was a two part program, the first part was three months at Fort Benning, covering tactics, leadership, and self-confidence. The second part was back at Fort Polk for two months as an instructor at the AIT School, teaching other young men his age the same thing he had gone through just three months prior. After the two months at Fort Polk as an instructor, he was offered a chance to be part of a test program that would combine eight weeks of Ranger Training and the three weeks of Jump School into a course eleven weeks long. Mitchell didn't have any great desire to be a paratrooper or a Ranger, but it meant staying stateside that much longer, so he signed up. This training took place back at Fort Benning. That was the extent of his military experience.

During the flight, he wrestled with many unanswered questions that he could not get out of his head. He had just spent the best part of a year being trained on how to lead men into combat, and he wondered to himself, "Could anyone truly be prepared for combat without first having experienced it?" From the day he was drafted, he knew he was headed for Vietnam, and the thought of killing another human being was something he had not yet resolved in his own mind.

From the aircraft, they were led to buses, the same basic olive-drab green army bus he had been shuttled around in since his training had begun. It was a hot, humid night. The combination of heat and humidity was formidable, it was as if a steamy wet blanket had dropped over him. Mitchell felt like it took added effort just to walk through it, let alone breathe it in.. He had only been out of the airplane for a few minutes and already the sweat had saturated his fatigues. All the windows on the buses were up to let the air in. As he sat down he noticed something different, what had caught his attention was the heavy metal screens covering the windows.

One of the other guys, two seats in front of him, was puzzled by the same thing and asked the driver, "Hey buddy, what's with the bars on the windows? This some kinda prison bus?"

The driver was a Spec-4 with bright red hair and a huge handle-bar mustache. You could tell by looking at him that this guy had been here for a while; his face redden from the months spent in the burning sun. He looked up with a grin, "They're not for keeping things in, they're for keeping things out. Charlie likes to throw grenades in the windows when you drive by. Blow your shit away, you know."

Hearing the driver's explanation gave Mitchell a tight feeling in the pit of his stomach. He thought to himself, "This is not training, not make-believe, this is the real thing."

The young PFC whom he had spoken to coming off the plane sat down beside him. He was tall and lanky, with light brown hair and fair skin. Mitchell wondered if the sun would redden this young soldier's face the same way it had the driver's.

"Hey Sarge, what da ya think bout this here place?"

"I don't know, but it sure not like home."

"Ya got that shit right. Where is home?"

"Phoenix, Arizona. How about you?" Mitchell asked.

"Pineville, North Carolina. I know, ya never heard of the place. It's bout fifteen miles south of Charlotte."

"Thought you sounded kinda country."

The bus pulled away as Mitchell turned his head, staring into the darkness. They drove for forty minutes or so through the edge of the city. The roads were narrow, some paved, but most were dirt. Mitchell could see into some of the dimly lit buildings along the way. They seemed to be cramped and congested, poorly constructed, almost as if they had been built out of whatever material that was lying around. He had been across the border into Nogales, Mexico, a couple of times and always thought it was shabby and rundown, but this place was much worse. Everything was strange to him. He thought how he knew nothing about this place, or these people, their culture, and their beliefs.

How different his life was from just a year before, back in Phoenix, eating at Whataburger and going to the drive-in with his high school sweetheart, Maggie. He thought how different things are now even for Maggie. She's halfway around the world from her husband, alone and three months pregnant with their unborn child. It had been less than twenty-four hours since he last kissed her and he was already missing her. He could see her standing at the airport trying to be brave, but betrayed by her tears, as he boarded the plane. This was going to be a hard year for both of them. "How could things have change so fast?" He asked himself.

They arrived at Bear Cat, the replacement center for the Ninth Infantry Division. It was part of the large Saigon, Long Binh, Bien Hoa area of South Vietnam, and the center of the U.S. military complex, the most protected area in the country. Mitchell and a handful of other NCOs were directed to a large open-sided tent, the enlisted men to a similar one fifty meters away.

Inside there were cots lined up and down each side. Some of the cots were occupied, but most were empty. There was no bedding or pillows, just the bare cots.

Mitchell picked out one and put his duffel bag at the head to use for a pillow. He took off his boots and laid down. It was late and he had been awake for over twenty-four hours. Between the long flight and all the time changes, he was exhausted. His head was full of all the things he had seen and thought, but being so tired nothing seemed to make sense anymore. After a time of staring at the top of the tent, he finally fell asleep.

CHAPTER TWO

Mitchell awoke to a loud and authoritative voice. "Up and at em, men! Let's go! The war needs you! Come on, up and at em!" It was coming from an older E-7, a lifer for sure. "There's a water trailer just outside, get shaved and cleaned up. Mess hall's serving breakfast in fifteen minutes. Be ready for assembly at 0630. Let's go men!"

Mitchell sat up and put his boots on, dug through his duffel bag and pulled out his shaving kit. Outside he threw some water on his face, shaved, brushed his teeth, then went back inside the tent and put his kit away. He didn't feel like eating, instead he walked around the immediate area. The sun was up and he got his first real look at this place. It was a bare-bones Army compound, some permanent buildings, but mostly tents. No frills at all. Much more primitive than Fort Polk, a place he had thought of until now as a real hell hole.

During formation, a first lieutenant explained that they would be here for two days, getting papers processed and then off to the Ninth Infantry Division In-Country Jungle Warfare School for ten days, before getting their final assignments. He then called some of the NCOs by name and gave them details to take charge of, Mitchell was no exception.

"Sergeant Robert Mitchell."

"Here, sir."

"Fall out and pick three men for shit burning detail. Report over to Sergeant Langston, he'll tell you what to do."

"Shit burning detail? What the hell could shit burning detail be?" Mitchell thought. He stepped out of formation and turned to face the other men. Out of the corner of his eye he saw the PFC from North Carolina that he had talked to the night before.

Mitchell pointed right at him, "Country, and the two men to your left, follow me."

He went up to Sergeant Langston to find out what shit burning detail was, and to his surprise, shit burning detail was literally that; shit burning! There were eleven latrines in the area. Each one was a four holer and under each hole, instead of a pit, there was a metal fifty-five gallon drum cut in half that the waste would fall into. Their job was to replace the filled drums with empty ones and take the filled ones to an area, pour gasoline in them, and burn the shit.

At the first latrine, using broom handles with metal hooks on the ends, the enlisted men began dragging the fly-infested drums out from under the latrine, and the smell was strong and pervasive.

The PFC from North Carolina turned to Mitchell and said, "Hey Sarge, why did ya pick me for this? Talk about a shitty job."

Mitchell grinned, "Well Country, I just thought you might have a real knack for this kind of work."

"Funny Sarge, real funny."

"Say, what is your name anyway? Can't keep calling you Country."

8

"Hollis Macintosh."

Mitchell was half laughing when he said, "Hollis, maybe Country's not so bad after all."

One of the other soldiers that Mitchell had picked for this detail, a young Mexican kid from El Paso, spoke up, "You guys know each other, Sergeant?"

"We came in on the same plane last night." Mitchell answered.

"So we just got picked for this, cause we standing by him?"

"Right place, right time. Lucky you." Mitchell said with a little smile.

"Oh yeah, shit burning, lucky us. I'm just glad my girl can't see me. Burning shit all day, I don't know if she would respect me if she saw this."

"You don't think your girl would appreciate shit burning for the honorable and productive work that it surely is?" Mitchell teased.

"I don't think nobody would call this honorable!"

"Well, I think this has to be the worst job here," complained the third kid that Mitchell had picked for the detail.

Mitchell didn't respond for a few seconds, then said. "I think all of us may be looking back at this in a few weeks and thinking shit burning wasn't that bad of a job."

They spent the rest of the morning on shit burning detail. That afternoon they exchanged their U.S. greenbacks and coins for Military Paper Certificates, MPC. This funny money as it was called, was all in paper script, even the nickels, dimes, and quarters. The reason for the use of MPC was to prevent the black market trade of U.S.

dollars. Then they were taken to clothing supply, where they were issued two sets of jungle fatigues, a pair of jungle boots, three pairs of socks, three pairs of underwear, three T-shirts, and three towels. And like everything else in the army, they were OD green.

That evening there was nothing for them to do, so they spent the time getting to know each other, and talking mostly about home.

"So Country, you have a girlfriend?" Mitchell asked.

"No, I had one, but not anymore. You have a girl back in Phoenix, Sarge?"

"I have a wife."

"You're married?"

"Yeah, seven months now. Her name's Maggie." Mitchell smiled, his eyes flashed a hint of pride, "She's pregnant."

"You gonna have a kid?"

"Yeah," Mitchell's face changed from pride to pensive, "but when she has the baby I'll be stuck over here."

"Boy, that's a shitty deal."

"You're telling me. So, how is it living in Pineville?"

"Oh it's great. I don't live right in Pineville, we live on a little farm, three miles outside."

"Farm boy, huh?"

"Yeah, all my life. Pineville's just a little pup of a town, but we do have one famous person from there."

"Oh yeah, who?" Mitchell asked.

"President James Polk."

"Polk, huh? Not exactly one of our more famous presidents. He's kinda like Taylor or Garfield, or one of those other guys we don't know much about."

"He still was president. Ain't been no president from Phoenix, has there?"

"Goldwater ran last time against LBJ."

"And he lost!" Country pointed out with satisfaction.

"True." Mitchell said, "But if he had won, maybe we wouldn't be here right now."

Country's face got more serious, "You think?"

"I don't know, but a lot of people say this is Johnson's war."

Mitchell could see Country's mind hard at work behind his naïve green eyes. He had never paid much attention to politics or thought how it could affect his life. He wrinkled his nose and brow like he was forcing a thought. "Johnson's war?"

"May... be."

The next morning Mitchell and Country were back on shit burning detail. That afternoon they were loaded on a deuce and a half (2.5 ton truck) and driven a short distance to the Jungle Warfare School, where they spent the next ten days going over the same things that they had learned back in the States. The difference was the instructors had just recently been pulled from the field and had firsthand knowledge and experience with the most recent types of booby traps and ambush techniques that the Vietcong were using.

They spent hours every day walking down trails trying to locate all the booby traps, but inevitably, they

11

would trip some of them. There were simulated ambushes and most of the time the men walked right into them. Mitchell found himself getting killed several times a day, and thought "At this rate, when I'm out in the real boonies, how long will I last?" But by the end of the ten days, he began to recognize the different dangers and finally made it through a day without being wasted. During this time, they were issued M-16s and spent a day on the rifle range sighting them in and getting use to firing weapons again.

It was August 8, 1968, when Mitchell received his final unit assignment. "A Troop, Third Squadron, Fifth Armored Cavalry." The clerk handed Mitchell his orders.

"Armored Cavalry? I'm Eleven-Bravo."

"MOS don't mean shit here," the clerk answered. "You go to whatever unit that needs warm bodies. The Third of the Fifth hit some shit a few days ago and now they're shorthanded."

Mitchell didn't say anything, but thought to himself, "I'm replacing someone who got killed a few days ago." He didn't know why that surprised him, but it did. After all, this was a war and guys got killed; but now for the first time he saw himself heading straight into it.

"There'll be a truck outside at 1100 hours to take you to the airstrip. You'll be going north this afternoon."

"North!" Mitchell said. "I thought the Ninth Division's AO was the Mekong Delta?"

"It is, but the Third of the Fifth is on loan to the First Air Cavalry. They work north of Quang Tri up by the DMZ."

Mitchell tapped the manila envelope containing his orders on the clerk's counter. "Thanks," he said and walked out the door.

On the front of the processing building, there was a map. Mitchell traced north from Saigon, past Da Nang, and Hue until he found Quang Tri. "Boy, when he said up north, he meant way up north."

"Sarge," the voice came from behind him. "Where they sending ya?" It was Country. He had his gear over his shoulder and a manila envelope in his hand.

"Up here!" Mitchell said, pointing to the map. "A Troop, Third Squadron, Fifth Armored Cavalry."

"Hey, me too, Sarge. Whatcha know bout that!"

"All right!" Mitchell grinned. "I gotta get my shit out of the NCO's tent. I'll meet you back here in a few minutes." It made Mitchell feel good knowing that Country was assigned with him. They had spent a lot of time together the last ten days and had become friends. Mitchell enjoyed Country's easy going, folksy ways and felt a kinship towards him. Having a friend here, even a new one, was better than no friend at all.

Despite all the uncertainties and fears Mitchell had inside him, his outward appearance projected an image of confidence. He had been blessed with a good dose of common sense and the ability to discern most any situation that he found himself in. Country sensed this in Mitchell and it made him feel a little more secure. Being sent to Vietnam was the scariest thing he had been through and being around Mitchell, for some reason, lessened his fears, if only a little.

When the truck arrived, there were four guys in addition to Mitchell and Country going north. The truck dropped them off at the backside of the airstrip. Along with forty-five other soldiers, they were loaded onto a C130 aircraft bound for Camp Eagle. Eagle was a large base located south of Quang Tri, the home of the 101st Airborne Division, one of the most northern bases with an airstrip large enough to land a C130 aircraft.

Mitchell and Country were some of the last to get aboard. There was web seating along each side, but not enough for everyone. They found themselves among twenty soldiers who had to sit flat on the floor of the aircraft. The flight to Camp Eagle would take an hour and a half and the noise inside the uninsulated C130 was deafening. It made it impossible to carry on a conversation and the cramped conditions and rough ride made sleep not an option. When the plane finally landed on the relatively short runway at Eagle, it was forced to reverse its props and brake severely. Of course, the laws of physics being what they are; Mitchell, Country, and the other men sitting on the floor found themselves piled up against the cockpit wall, within half the space they had originally occupied.

The last leg of their trip was made in the back of a deuce and a half, with just Mitchell, Country, and four bags of mail. Driving in front as an escort was a jeep with a M-60 mounted on the back. The E-6 in the jeep told them that during the day nothing ever happened on Highway One, but if Charlie did pull something, lie flat and ride it out.

The trip was sixty-three miles and took two and a half hours. Highway One was the national highway, but it was nothing like a highway back in the States. This narrow, unpaved artery traversed its way from Saigon in the south through Quang Tri in the north, like a little dirt county road through farms in West Texas.

The further north they traveled, the sandier the terrain got. The last ten miles was nothing but rolling sand dunes, but every so often alongside the road would be an oasis of dense vegetation. Some were small, maybe five to six hundred meters around, others larger than fifteen hundred meters.

It was late afternoon when they got to the base camp that A Troop worked out of. It was on the beach, the South China Sea made up half of the perimeter. Mitchell could see ships laying off shore and large amphibious vehicles carrying supplies onto the beach. Triple layer concertina wire (rolled razor sharp barb wire) ran along the inland perimeter. Along this perimeter every seventy-five meters was a permanent bunker constructed of sandbags and corrugated steel sheets. These bunkers were large enough to accommodate a four-man fighting position. In front of the bunker was a network of claymore mines. Inside the perimeter there were very few permanent buildings, it was like a tent city. It was manned by the Second Battalion of the First Air Cavalry. A Troop was assigned to them.

The truck dropped Mitchell and Country off at A Troop's command post, where they were told to report to Lieutenant Neilley on Track One-Six. He was in command of First Platoon.

Locating Track One-Six, Mitchell questioned out loud, "Lieutenant Neilley?"

"I'm Neilley." The reply came from atop the APC. The lieutenant was placing something into turret and had his back to Mitchell.

"Sergeant Mitchell and PFC Macintosh reporting as ordered, Sir."

The lieutenant turned to face them. "Good! I've been expecting you. Got your papers there?"

Mitchell and Country stepped forward and handed up the manila envelopes containing their orders. The lieutenant began to read intently. Lieutenant Neilley was regular army, a graduate of West Point. His father was a career officer and it was his intention to be a career officer also. He was young, twenty-five years old and a big man physically, well over six feet tall. During his years at West Point, he played linebacker for Army. He had been in command of the First Platoon for the past three months; during that time he had won the respect of and was well liked by the men of the First Platoon. He knew the book inside and out, but he also knew when to throw the book away and that was the key to his success as a leader.

Lieutenant Neilley reached for the mike of the PRC-25, "One-One, this is   One-Six, over."

A reply came back over the radio, "This is One-One, over."

"This is One-Six, Steve come over here. I have your new TC waiting here, over."

"This is One-One, roger, out"

Lieutenant Neilley put the mike down, stood up and jumped from the APC to the ground beside Mitchell and Country. I see you're 11-Bravo Sergeant. Have you had any experience in Armor at all?"

"No sir," Mitchell replied. "This is as close as I've been to an APC."

"How about you, Macintosh?"

"No sir, me either."

"Well Macintosh, you are now a gunner on One-One and Sergeant you are its track commander."

"Commander, sir?"

"Don't worry Mitchell, I read your file and I know you can pick up the technical things you'll need to know in no time. Steve is a good man. He's been the acting TC of One-One for the last ten days. He has a few weeks to go before rotating, he'll show you the ropes." As he spoke Spec 4 Steve Lund had join the threesome.

Steve was light complexed with blonde hair and a thin mustache. It wasn't that the mustache was trimmed, but that he was having a hell of a time getting it to grow.

"Steve," Lieutenant Neilley said, "This is Sergeant Robert Mitchell and PFC Hollis Macintosh. Take them to One-One and get them settled in. We're moving out to take our position on the perimeter in twenty minutes."

The lieutenant reached out and shook hands with Mitchell and Macintosh. "Welcome aboard. We'll talk more in the morning."

Steve led the way followed by Mitchell and Country with their duffel bags over their shoulders and their new M-16 rifles in hand, through a maze of armored personnel carriers and tanks. He led them to a dirty gun-metal gray APC, at first glance only distinguishable from the dozen others they had passed by the number eleven painted in red inside a yellow triangle located on each side near the rear of the vehicle. They would soon learn that the two red ones didn't stand for eleven, but was to be referred to as One-One, for number one platoon, number one vehicle.

"Hey Frank! This is our new TC and gunner." Steve was speaking to a young black man standing in back of One-One.

Frank was tall and muscular. He wasn't wearing a fatigue jacket, just an olive-drab towel around his neck. "It's about time man. Now we'll have four guys to pull watch."

Spec 4 Frank Johnson was also recently in-country. This was just his eleventh day in the field. He was from New York City, where eighteen months ago, a judge had given him a choice, jail or the army. Frank chose the army, and ever since then, he swears that he made the wrong choice. He had never been in any serious trouble, just several years of minor things, and finally the juvenile court system got tired of messing with him. Frank was not a special case. There were a lot of guys in the army, in Vietnam, by the same route. Frank was a street-wise kid, a bit of a con-man, a bit of a hustler. He took great pleasure in putting people on, keeping them off balance, so no one would know quite where he was coming from. But from the very beginning, Mitchell would see through his charade and of all the men that Mitchell was to share this next year with, Frank was destined to become his closest and most trusted friend.

"You can store your bags up here." Steve took the bags from Mitchell and Country and placed them in some cargo netting that was along the right side wall close to the ceiling. "We got some empty ammo cans here. You can use them to store your shaving stuff."

The inside of the APC had all of the seating taken out of it. It was open from wall to wall, front to back. The floor was layered with ammunition boxes, two high. Along the left wall up close to the top is where the PRC-25 radio was mounted. It had two CVC helmets connected to it, one in the driver's compartment and one up top for the TC in the turret. There also was a hand-held mike inside the APC by the radio.

The inside clearance was about five feet from floor to ceiling, but with the two layers of ammo boxes, it was decreased to less than four feet. The inside dimensions were seven and a half feet wide, and from the back to the front, nine feet. The driver's compartment was in the left front of the APC and beside it to the right was the engine compartment.

This APC was home for its crew of four or five men. They would eat here, sleep here, and fight from its top. When an Infantry man returns from the boonies, he would have a barrack or tent with a cot that was his, but not for the Armored Cavalry. Even when they were in the rear areas, which was rare, they lived in their APC.

After looking around inside, they climbed to the top through the roof hatch. "This is the TC's turret," Steve said. It was small with one-quarter inch armored plating and was equipped with a fifty caliber machine gun. There was a hatch in the hull which was always kept open.

"This is your CVC helmet," Steve pointed out. "It has a headset and mike built in it. You can transmit and receive and there is also an intercom to the driver's CVC."

"Frank's been doing the driving and I've been acting TC. Do you want to take over as TC?" Steve asked Mitchell.

"No, let's leave it like it is for now. I think it would be best if I just watched you for a day or two. Country and I will just man these guns."

"Country?"

"Yeah, I just couldn't bring myself to calling this guy Hollis."

"Anything you say Sarge." Steve said.

A squelch came from the radio inside the track and then a voice, "All units, this is One-Six, saddle up. Get ready to roll. Out."

"Saddle up," Mitchell thought. "This is the cavalry, but nothing like the Seventh Cavalry at Custer's Last Stand."

An armored cavalry troop is roughly equal in size, as far as manpower goes, as an infantry company, one hundred and twenty men. But it has more firepower than an entire battalion. A troop is made up of three combat platoons and one headquarters platoon. Each combat platoon contained seven APCs and three M48-A1 tanks. Six of the APCs were assault vehicles, M113A1 armored personnel carrier, modified for service in Vietnam. M113's usual complement was one fifty caliber machine gun in the turret and two M60 machine guns, all protected by armored gun shields. It was manned by a crew of five men, the driver, the TC usually manning the fifty caliber, two gunners manning the M60s, and the fifth crewman armed with a 40mm grenade launcher. In One-One's case, the right side machine gun was also a fifty caliber and the left side gun was a M60.

The seventh APC was a mortar track. It also had a fifty caliber mounted in its turret, but no other guns. Instead, it had a four-deuce (4.2") mortar tube mounted in the back. At the time, the M48-A1 was the army's standard medium tank. Its main gun was a ninety millimeter cannon.

Steve climbed into the turret while Frank lowered himself down into the driver's hole. Frank started up the APC's diesel engine and then began to lift the hydraulic lift gate in the rear of the APC.

Mitchell turned to Country "Do you know how to use this fifty?"

"No," Country answered. "I've never fired one."

"How about that M60?"

"Yeah, I did pretty good with it back in AIT."

"Okay, you take it and I'll take the fifty."

Steve keyed the mike on his CVC helmet. ""This is One-One, ready to roll, over."

Each of the other tracks responded in order, One-Two, One-Three, One-Four, and so on, until all the units had reported in. First Platoon pulled out of the parking area heading for the perimeter of the base camp named Joy Beach.

Mitchell found himself sitting on top of an armored personnel carrier for the first time in his life. An armored personnel carrier that technically he was now in command of. He watched as the sun set, sinking into the sand dunes; until darkness had replaced its glaring light, bringing with it a chilling reality. A reality of fear and danger.

CHAPTER THREE

For A Troop, the next ten days were relatively uneventful. Their main assignment was to be a reactionary force for the Second Battalion of the First Air Cavalry. If any unit of the Second Battalion made contact with an enemy force, then A Troop could be called upon to help reinforce that unit. Because of the Armored Cavalry's firepower and mobility, they were very effective in this role and therefore were involved in more firefights than the average unit. However for the past ten days, there had not been any action serious enough to call on them for help.

A Troop spent this time doing convoy escort, perimeter guard, and making night road runs. These activities were good ways for Mitchell to gain experience at being the T.C. of Track One-One and also for Frank as its driver. The T.C. and the driver of an armored cavalry APC needs to have a unique understanding with each other. They need to be able to think as one and to anticipate each other's next move. Mitchell knew that next to himself, the action of his driver would most determine their effectiveness as a fighting unit and even more important, their ability to survive. With that thought foremost in his mind, Mitchell decided that Frank would be the best one for the job. He had known Country from the first day they had set foot in Nam and liked him from the beginning, but felt Frank would be the better driver.

But this decision did not set well with Frank. It wasn't the fact that Mitchell had picked him to be driver, Frank also understood the importance of the job and knew it was a vote of confidence in him. It was being told he was going to do something and not have any say in the matter that bugged him. That and the fact that he was still in a feeling out process to see just how far he could push Mitchell; and to his surprise, he was finding out that Mitchell wouldn't take any unnecessary shit. Frank wasn't sure how he felt about that. On one hand he respected him for it, but on the other hand he liked getting his own way.

"Why the fuck is it always me who has to get down in the driver's hole?" Frank complained to Mitchell. "Why can't Hollis do some of the goddamn driving?"

"Country will drive some of the time," Mitchell replied. "Everyone will be able to do everybody's job. But you're the driver of this track. Now get down in that goddamn hole and start it up. We have to get the hell moving."

Frank looked at him with annoyance and said a few words under his breath, then slid into the driver's hole and started the engine.

A squelch came over Mitchell's headset. "One-One, this is One-Six. You take the point, over."

"This is One-One, roger." Mitchell answered.

The first platoon had been making road runs for the past six nights, but this was the first time that Mitchell and his One-One track was put into the lead position.

To say that a night road run was an interesting experience would be an understatement. The idea was to try and deter Charlie from mining the road during the night time hours. To accomplish this, they would drive a convoy of armored vehicles up and down the road several times a night at irregular intervals to disrupt any enemy activity. The kicker was, in order to make themselves less vulnerable to ambush, they would make the runs without lights and at a high rate of speed. Occasionally the column of tracks would roar by some huts built along the roadside. The people that lived there were used to these convoys, but it was still unnerving. They could hear the rumbling from a distance away, but couldn't see anything until the moment the convoy roared by, and then only a blur of large dark shadows streaking by in the night. The nights in Vietnam were truly dark, nothing like the nights Mitchell was used to living in the city; but the kind of dark you can only experience by getting far away from the city lights. And of all the vehicles, the lead track had the most difficult task. Everyone else could rely on the shadowy image of the track ahead of them as a guide, but the lead track had to stay on the road and keep the speed up for the entire convoy.

With One-One in the lead, the First Platoon pulled out of the base camp and onto Highway Nine. The tracks were in single file and spread about fifteen meters apart.

"One-One, this is One-Six. All right, let's go!"

"One-One, roger."

Mitchell didn't have to say a word. Frank accelerated hard and they were on their way with First Platoon right behind. There was a great deal of pressure on Frank as the driver of the lead track. He was straining to see every curve and turn in the road and to see them in time to react.

Mitchell was doing the same thing and was in constant communication with Frank over the intercom. "To the left, left. That's it. We're down the middle. Easy now. Right turn coming up. That's it. You've got it."

The constant instructions coming over Frank's headset were a help to him. Even though most of the things Mitchell pointed out, Frank had already seen; but every once in a while, there was something Frank had missed. Mitchell's position on top of the track gave him a better view.

"Bridge coming up, Frank. Good, right down the middle."

Steve had done this before. Most of the time he had spent in Nam, he spent as the driver of One-One. But no matter how many runs he made he always got uptight. He knew firsthand the pressure Frank was feeling right now. He was impressed at how well Frank and Mitchell were doing, but he still found himself straining to see every turn and curve in the road.

Country on the other hand was having a ball. He was laughing and joking the whole time. "Hell, Steve," he said, "This is just like huntin' rabbits out of the back of my pickup truck back home. This is a real kick in the ass!"

"You're crazy as shit, man." Steve retorted. "I remember about five months ago we were doing this shit and One-Four ran off the road and rolled it. It killed their TC and put another guy in the hospital."

"Ah hell, man," Country said. "Sarge's got his shit together. He won't let that happen."

All of a sudden Mitchell felt the track leaning to the right and bouncing from running over rough ground. One-

One had gotten off the road. It was running over ruts and clumps of vegetation. Suddenly, they hit a small sand dune which caused the APC to become airborne a foot or more. It was all Mitchell and the others could do to hold on and stay on top.

Steve was holding on for dear life, his hands tightly gripping onto the right side fifty gun mount. The story of One-Four rolling over that he had just told Country came flashing back in his mind. Beads of sweat had broken out across his forehead and upper lip and his stomach was tying up in knots.

They say that a combat soldier in Vietnam goes through three stages during his tour. First is being new in country, being a cherry. This usually lasts for a month or two. A time of fear and uncertainty, not knowing what to expect or how to do things. During this stage a new comer is wide-eyed and very careful.

Then comes stage two. You move into it gradually, not knowing exactly when you got there. It lasts for eight or nine months and there are varying degrees of this stage. This is the time when you accept the fact that you are here and there's nothing you can do about it. You live life day by day and become more and more callous to the harsh realities of war, until at some point most soldiers find themselves simply just not giving a shit.

Stage three usually hits about six weeks before your time to go home. This is when you come down with short-timers disease. That lingering fear in the back of your mind of the awful irony of surviving the hardship of this place for a year and then getting killed just before going home.

In some ways it's like being a cherry all over again. You become extremely careful and almost paranoid.

Steve was infected with short-timers and this unplanned trip across the sand dunes was no laughing matter to him.

"Pull it back to the left!" Mitchell shouted to Frank over the intercom. "Don't jerk it, ease it back."

Frank started pulling the track back to the left and finally got it back under control in the center of the road.

"Okay, you got it. Hang in there, man." Mitchell said to Frank in a calmer tone.

Frank's neck and shoulders were stiff from the tension he was feeling. His jaws were tight from the grinding of his teeth. Sweat was running into one of his eyes, but he didn't dare take a hand off the steering levers to wipe it away as they roared on through the darkness.

Frank mumbled to himself, "This is another crazy idea thought up by some Mother-fuckin', white-ass, son-of-a-bitch."

"One-One, this is One-Six, over."

"This is One-One, over."

"This is One-Six. Slow down and bring us to a stop, over."

"One-One, roger."

Frank heard all the radio transmissions on his headset and began to slow to a full stop. The distance that First Platoon was assigned to cover was nine miles and they had reached that point.

"One-Six to all units. Take up defensive positions, out."

One-One being in the lead, stayed in the middle of the road facing ahead. The track behind One-One turned to the right and faced the right side of the road. The next track in line turned to the left and so on, alternating from right to left, until the last track in the column, and it turned around and faced back down the road in the direction from which they had just came. They would stay at this point for a while, sometimes as little as fifteen minutes and other times as long as an hour and a half. Then they would return back to base camp.

"One-One, this is One-Six, over."

"This is One-One, over."

"One-Six, nice job on the point, over."

"One-One, roger."

Frank climbed out of the driver's hole and looked up at Mitchell. "I almost fuckin' lost it back there," he said with a smile on his face.

Mitchell didn't answer just laughed more from relief than anything else.

"You scared the shit out of me!" Steve said.

"Ah, you're just uptight 'cause you're so fuckin' short." Country teased Steve.

"That's right! I am fuckin' short. Eleven days and counting and I don't want to get my fuckin' neck broke doing this shit!"

"Well, I have to admit my asshole was puckered a little bit," Mitchell said. "Being on point is just a little bit different."

"Ah, just a bunch of candy asses," Country said harassing the others.

"Shut up you fool!" Frank barked out. "You ain't got the sense to be scared."

"Oh, were you scared?" Mitchell asked teasingly.

"No more than you," Frank answered.

"All right, I'll give you that."

"Well at least the lieutenant thought I did a good job," Frank boasted.

"Yeah, right. The lieutenant didn't see us flying off the goddamn road, jumping sand dunes," Steve joined in.

"I had it under control the whole time."

"Sure you did Frank, sure you did," Mitchell said laughingly.

"Damn straight I did."

"So what was that little side trip all about?" Mitchell asked, leaning back with his hands clasped at the back of his neck.

"I just dids that to keep you dudes on your's toeses. Can't have yous getting too relaxed. Yous might doze off when yous should be keeping eye out for Charlie." Frank said using his ghetto dialect, which he turned on and off depending upon his mood.

"Yeah, and I didn't know they stacked shit six feet high." Steve said with a smile as if he had enjoyed the idea of saying it.

"That be six feet and one inch," Frank answered, "and it all be prime."

"Yeah, well all I know is that without me, One-One would be like an incomplete pie. All cherries and no crust." Steve boasted.

They spent the next hour talking and joking around with each other until the word came to move out. This time

One-Nine took the point and One-One was in the last
position for the return trip.

CHAPTER FOUR

Most of the time A Troop was split up by platoons to perform their assignments. But on this morning, First Platoon joined up with Second and Third Platoon and left the base camp for what was called Break Day. Every couple of weeks, A Troop would join together and leave the base camp, set up perimeter, and spend the day relaxing. Today they went five klicks south of the base and set up on the beach. Everyone looked forward to these Break Days. During this time, they would thoroughly clean and test fire all weapons, but most of the time they were free to relax.

Mitchell was sitting on top of his track reading a dog-eared paperback copy of The Graduate that had been passed around from track to track. He wasn't wearing a shirt for he had been in swimming an hour before and still wasn't fully dressed and with the hot, glaring afternoon sun beating down, it was more comfortable this way.

The rear lift gate of the APC was down leaving the back end open. Frank and Spec 4 Paul Bonds, one of the gunners on One-Two, were sitting on the lift playing chess. Frank had begun playing chess at the age of twelve, taught by his mother. They had spent numerous long evenings in their small apartment in Harlem playing the game, this had been her way of trying to keep him off the streets. Frank never knew his father and his mom did the best she could as a single parent, but eventually she did lose him to the streets of New York. But in those early years, he had developed a love for the game and had become a very skilled player. Paul was no slouch at the game himself and was the only one in the platoon that could give Frank enough competition to make it interesting.

Frank had Paul on the ropes and was rubbing it in. "I got you, man," he boasted. "Your king has had it. It's going to be checkmate real soon."

"It's not over yet," Paul replied, but he knew it was looking quite grim.

"Yeah, well you just keep trying man, but you ain't getting out of this." Frank said as he made his next move.

Steve was making Kool-Aid. To make their water supply safe for drinking, purification tablets were added, but this made the water taste alkaline. So generally, they made it into Kool-Aid to disguise the bitter taste. The last time anyone had seen Country, he was down at the water's edge with a bunch of other guys throwing a football around.

A call came over the radio. "One-Six to all units, mail call. All TC's come to One-Six and pick up the mail for your people."

"Hey Steve, would you come up and man the turret while I go and pick up the mail?" There was always at least one man on top manning a gun even in a relaxed time.

Mitchell grabbed his shirt and jumped to the ground, putting it on as he walked to One-Six. There were five letters for One-One track. One each for Mitchell, Frank, and Country. Steve had received the other two. As Mitchell returned to his track he passed Paul walking back to One-Two. He had conceded the chess match to Frank on the premise he had to go and see if he'd gotten any mail;

33

but in reality, it was hopeless for him and this was a good way out.

"Is the match already over?" Mitchell asked.

"No, I just got tired of listening to that asshole brag. Anyway, I got to check and see if I got any mail," Paul said with his customary smile on his face.

Back at the track, Mitchell gave Frank his letter and Steve his two. "Anyone seen Country?" Mitchell inquired.

"I guess he's still playing ball," Frank replied without taking his eyes off his letter.

"I'll give him this when he comes back." Mitchell stuck Country's letter into his pocket. He was anxious to read his own letter from Maggie. He walked around to the shaded side of the APC and sat down in the sand leaning his back against the track. He opened Maggie's letter and began to read.

> *Dear Bobby,*
>
> *I love you. I know you told me that it would take about a month before I would receive a letter from you, but everyday I can't wait to get home and check the mail. By the time you receive this letter maybe I'll receive one of yours.*
>
> *This past month has been busy for me. I went and spoke to Mr. Gray at the bank and he gave me my old job back at the same pay. I know, you told me he would; but I thought you were just saying that to boost my confidence. I told him I was pregnant, but he hired me anyway. He said it made him proud to help the family*

of "one of our boys in Vietnam." He started asking everyday had I heard from you. I told him that I would update him as soon as I had received your letter. I think he's just trying to be nice to me.

I got my first paycheck today and went out and spent most of it on maternity clothes. Mother says I don't show, but I can't button my jeans, not even lying on the bed, the way that always makes you laugh.

Tomorrow I'm going up to Flagstaff for the weekend to get out of this heat. So, I've been busy this evening helping Dad pack the camper.

I'm lying here in bed getting sleepy, wishing you were here beside me, holding me, and nibbling on my ear. I miss you so much and I love you more every day, even though you're not here. Maybe it's true, "Absence makes the heart grow fonder."

I'll close now and get some sleep, need to get my beauty sleep, and I've been getting a lot lately.

Love you always,
Maggie

He closed his eyes and smiled. He could see Maggie lying on the bed, squirming, trying to put on her old worn out jeans, and then his thoughts turned to the last day that they had spent together.

* * * * * * * * * * * *

"I don't think I'm showing yet, do you?" Maggie asked Bobby, turning around in front of him slowly showing off her figure. She was wearing a black swimsuit and by looking at her, Bobby couldn't tell that she was pregnant.

"No, you look sexy as always, and anyway, everyone knows pregnant girls are the most beautiful of all. They have a glow about them."

Maggie turned and sat in his lap smiling, "Oh, is your plan to keep me barefoot and pregnant?"

"Well, it's a tough job, but someone has to do it, and I'm the man for that job." Mitchell said and then declared victory in their game of dueling clichés as he pulled her closer to him and softly kissed her on the cheek.

"I'm glad we're spending this last day alone," Maggie whispered as she leaned her head on his shoulder.

Bobby had been home on leave for twenty days and they had spent the majority of the time visiting family and friends. They had decided to get a room at the Camelback Inn to spend their last night together.

Maggie raised her head and said, "With all this swimming I'm starved. What would you like for dinner?"

Bobby was hungry too, but the thought of having dinner at the Camelback Inn didn't really appeal to him. "You know what I really would like to have is a Whataburger. Anyway, it's going to be a year before I have one again."

"I could always mail you one," Maggie teased as she grabbed her towel.

"Nah, I'll just have two tonight to hold me over, " Bobby said as they walked hand in hand from the pool back to their room.

After getting dressed, they went down to Bobby's 1965 GTO. It was his pride and joy, and he had spent over two years getting it into cherry shape. But since he was drafted, he didn't have much time to drive it and Maggie had taken it over. She had a car of her own, a 1960 Ford Falcon, but now having a choice, the little Falcon got very little use. She loved to hot rod around in the GTO and that gave him something to worry about.

"I'll drive," Maggie said.

"No, I'll drive. You'll have plenty of time for hot rodding when I'm not here," Bobby said with a smile on his face.

"Oh, you always worry about me scratching the GTO," Maggie stuck her tongue out and followed it with a big smile.

"That's right, and I want you to take it easy and treat it with tender loving care while I'm gone."

Bobby drove across town to their favorite Whataburger at 43rd and Thomas with Maggie sitting close by his side.

"Let's eat in the car, so we can listen to the radio." Maggie suggested, knowing that was what they always did.

They had been sitting in the car for over an hour talking softly, listening to music, and watching the stars slowly appear in the night sky. The radio was playing Yesterday by the Beatles, Maggie's favorite song. She was leaning into Bobby's shoulder with his right arm gently holding her.

"It's going to feel strange, you not being here." Maggie's eyes filled up with tears.

"Not much different from this past year," He said trying to comfort her.

"Oh yes it will. Except for the time you were in boot camp, I followed you all over the south. But back here is home, and here we've been together almost all the time."

Maggie's voice crackled as a tear rolled down her cheek. They had met their sophomore year in high school and had been inseparable ever since.

Bobby leaned down and kissed the tear away. "Let's go back to the room," he said starting the car but never letting go of Maggie.

As Bobby closed the door to the hotel room, he turned Maggie around towards him and pulled her close. Lifting her chin until their eyes met, he saw the tears again clouding up in her pale blue eyes.

Maggie's lips quivered. "I'm scared, Bobby."

"Why Maggie May?" Bobby had been calling her this for several years, ever since the first time he had asked, "Maggie, may I kiss you?"

She bowed her head, "I don't want to say it."

"Are you afraid I won't come back?"

She looked up into his eyes and nodded not being able to speak, afraid if she answered it might come true.

"I told you that I'll be coming home. I have you and our baby to help me make it through. If you need to talk about it, I will, but....." Bobby didn't finish because Maggie raised up on her toes and kissed him tenderly.

He could taste her tears and that made him return the kiss more passionately. He was prepared to go to Vietnam, but didn't relish it. Maggie on the other hand, hadn't yet came to grips with it, maybe she never would. He wished there was something he could do, something he could say to make it easier for her, but there wasn't. So, he just held her close and loved her for as long as they had left.

This had been the best day Mitchell had spent in Nam. He had gotten a lot of rest and had enjoyed horsing around with the other guys. In fact, it was the first day since he had been here that he was able to relax. He was lying in the sand with his eyes closed just about to doze off when the peace and quiet of the moment was shattered by a radio call.

"One-Six to all units. Alert! Alert! Saddle up. We have to be rolling in two minutes. I say again, Alert!"

"Sarge! Sarge, we have to get ready to roll!" Steve shouted to Mitchell.

"I heard," Mitchell replied as he was climbing atop the APC. "Frank, get it started and get the lift gate up." Looking around he asked, "Where the hell is Country?"

"Here he comes," Steve was pointing in the direction of the ocean. Someone had gotten word to the twenty guys that were playing football and they had scattered in all directions, running full speed back to their respective tracks.

Country came running up to the back of the track, and while climbing on top he asked, "What the hell's going on?"

"We got to roll!"

"Yeah, but why? What the fuck is happenin'?" Country asked, his voice sounding apprehensive.

"Someone must have hit some shit somewhere and we're going to help," Steve speculated.

"Get your flak jackets on," Mitchell ordered to Steve and Country. "Make sure your weapons are ready." Mitchell looked down at Frank in the driver's hole and saw that he had already put on his flak jacket. Looking back over his shoulder again at Steve and Country, "Are you ready back there?"

"Ready!" Steve answered, giving Mitchell a thumbs up.

Over his headset Mitchell heard, "One-Nine, this is One-Six. On my word, you take the lead and go south down the beach. All other units fall in behind, over."

"This is One-Nine, roger."

Thirty seconds later, "One-Nine, this is One-Six. Move out!"

"This is One-Nine, roger."

One-Nine track broke out of the perimeter and headed south down the beach. One-One pulled in behind and the rest of First Platoon followed as ordered. First Platoon had the lead, followed by Second Platoon and then Third Platoon.

Each man of A Troop was carrying with him a feeling of trepidation. They knew they were going into a firefight, but they didn't know how bad of a fight it would be. But since the whole troop was being sent in response, it stood to reason that it must be bad. It was especially frightening for the new guys like Frank, Country, and Mitchell, who had never been in a firefight before.

The reality of war had just came crashing down on them and the next twenty-four hours would be a day they would never forget.

CHAPTER FIVE

Company B, Second Battalion of the First Air Cavalry, was conducting a search and destroy operation twenty-five klicks southeast of their base camp. The terrain was spotted with oases of dense vegetation, ranging in size from two hundred meters across to over fifteen hundred meters. These growths of jungle were separated by open sandy ground. Bravo Company was in the process of sweeping through these oases, one at a time, looking for any sign of enemy activity. They were searching for tunnels, bunkers, and caches of supplies that may have been hidden.

They had just crossed seven hundred meters of open sand, moving south toward one of the larger oases in the area. Spreading out along the north side of its perimeter, they began to sweep across. The first platoon had the east flank, third platoon the west, and second platoon would go up the middle. Using this formation, the grunts of Bravo Company could sweep an area six hundred meters wide as they moved through the jungle.

It was 1620 hours when Alfa squad of the third platoon made the first contact. One hundred and fifty meters in they came across a bunker complex. At the same moment they spotted it, they were fired upon by AK-47 and machine gun fire. One member of Alfa squad was killed instantly and two others were wounded. The remaining members of the squad took cover and returned fire.

A moment later, three hundred meters to the east, the second platoon came under attack. Within the next few minutes, two more contacts had been made. Captain Nash, the CO of Company B, soon realized that there must be a large bunker and tunnel system located in this oasis, because his unit was under fire from four different positions spread over five hundred meters. He ordered his troops to pull back to the northern perimeter, dig in, and set up a defensive position. He reported the contact to Second Battalion Headquarters.

Colonel Robert Moore was in command and immediately boarded his chopper to fly to the scene and evaluate the situation. He also ordered two UH-1B Huey gunships in for support.

What Company B had come in contact with was a force of over four hundred men, part of the NVA's (North Vietnamese Army) Thirty-second Regiment, First Division. They had slipped into this area two nights before and were preparing for an attack on Firebase Jane.

By 1645, Company B had pulled back and was in position on the north side of the oasis. The initial action had cost them two dead and five wounded. Colonel Moore was overhead along with the two Huey gunships. From his vantage point, he could see that the oasis was roughly circular and approximately sixteen hundred meters across. Company B had one-fourth of the outer perimeter covered. He ordered Company C of the Second Battalion airlifted in. They would be brought in by Hueys of the 186th Aviation Battalion, and he then ordered A Troop to also respond. A Troop's position on the beach, south of the base camp, placed them twenty klicks away from the battle.

Colonel Moore's plan was to have Company C to join up with Company B to cover the northern perimeter and to have A Troop cover the southern half. He knew that he had to get the entire perimeter sealed off before dark, or the NVA unit would slip out.

The NVA commander realized the same thing. He couldn't break and run in broad daylight with the Huey gunships overhead. For if they tried, they would be slaughtered trying to cross the open ground. So it was a race against time and the setting sun.

A Troop was pushing hard to get there as fast as possible. They first headed south along the beach for five klicks and then turned west, over the rolling sand dunes. The further inland they traveled, the more oases they encountered. They would have to weave their way around the jungle growths, staying in the open ground. It was a longer distance, but still the fastest way to go. They were rolling flat-out over the dunes like a bunch of overgrown sand buggies.

In the beginning, A Troop was navigating by map coordinates, but as they neared the objective, Colonel Moore made visual contact with them from overhead and then guided them in with radio instructions. It had been only thirty-five minutes from the time A Troop got the call, until they were rolling up to the south perimeter. As they approached, they could see the Huey's of the 186th Aviation Battalion bringing in Company C. There were twelve transport choppers carrying the grunts and four more gunships for support. Fine sandy soil was swirling around the choppers as they landed. The soil suspended in the air by the turbulent vortex of the helicopters, partially obscured their view.

"One-Nine, this is One-Six, over."

"One-Nine, over."

"This is One-Six. Look for smoke to your left. It will mark our left flank, over."

"This is One-Nine, I see lemon-lime, over."

"This is One-Six. That's a good ID. Take up that position, over."

"This is One-Nine, roger."

Colored smoke canisters were used to mark and identify positions of friendly units. The nicknames for the different colors were to confuse the enemy in case they were monitoring the American's radios. Green was known as lemon-lime, yellow as banana, purple as goofy grape, and red as Hawaiian Punch.

"One-One, this is One-Six, over."

"This is One-One, over."

"This is One-Six. Look for smoke to your right, over."

"This is One-One. I see goofy grape, over."

"This is One-Six. That's a good ID. Move to that position. You will be our right flank, over."

"This is One-One, roger."

Mitchell didn't need to give any instructions to Frank. He had heard the radio communications and knew what to do. He turned One-One and headed for the plume of purple smoke.

Lieutenant Neilley instructed all of the other tracks of the First Platoon as to what position they were to take up. One-One was to the far right, then he placed One-Two, then One-Seven, followed by One-Three, himself in One-Six, One-Eight, One-Four, One-Five, and One-Nine was at the left flank. This deployment put him in the middle, and his tanks positioned intermittently with his APCs. The One-Zero mortar track was approximately two hundred meters behind the rest of First Platoon, enabling it to use its 4.2 inch mortar tube for support anywhere along the perimeter.

Second and Third Platoon positioned themselves in a similar manner. Second Platoon linked up with First Platoon and Third Platoon linked up with the grunts of Company C.

"One-One, this is One-Six, over."

"This is One-One, over."

"This is One-Six. I want you to physically go over and make contact with the ground unit to your right. You need to know exactly where they are, over."

"This is One-One, willco."

Mitchell got up from the turret and grabbed his M-16. "Steve, I gotta go see where the grunts are. You take over 'til I get back."

"Okay, Sarge. Watch out going over there," Steve said as he took Mitchell's place in the turret.

Mitchell jumped to the ground and started running. Company B's first position was fifty meters to the right of One-One. There was a rise in the sand, running between their positions. On top of the track Mitchell could see over it to the grunts, but on the ground, the rise blocked his view. As he reached the top of the rise, Mitchell shouted out to get their attention.

"Hey, man. Over here. Hey!" He was on his knees waving his hands over his head.

One of the grunts waved back.

"I'm coming in," Mitchell shouted. The grunt signaled with his arm to come ahead.

"I'm TC of that APC over there," Mitchell said as he reached their hole.

"I'm Bravo squad leader, First Platoon," the grunt replied.

"We have to have a signal to use if we need to contact each other tonight," Mitchell advised.

"Right. How about Mississippi? We can use Mississippi for the password," the grunt suggested.

"Okay, with me," Mitchell agreed. "What did you guys run into in there?"

"Shit, man. There's tunnels and bunkers all over the fuckin' place. The gooks are everywhere." The grunt answered, pointing in the direction of the oasis.

"Did you guys get hurt?"

"Two guys wasted, four or five more were hit. That's the word I got."

"Jesus!" Mitchell shook his head, not wanting to believe it. "I gotta get back. You guys hang in there."

"Yeah man, peace," the grunt held up his hand, giving Mitchell the peace sign.

Returning to One-One, Mitchell told the others of the password he had agreed upon.

"Mississippi, I hate Mississippi," Country complained.

"Jesus Christ, Country. One password is as good as another," Mitchell snapped back.

"I know. I just hate Mississippi. It's the only place I ever got a speeding ticket and I wasn't even speeding."

Mitchell just shook his head, not able to make rhyme or reason out of Country's complaint. It's strange what one thinks of when fear has its grip on you.

Looking in the direction where the grunts were positioned, Frank asked, "What they got over there?"

"It's a three man hole. One has an M-60. It looks like they're dug in about every twenty-five meters."

"Did they say what happened?" Steve asked.

"He said they ran into a bunch of tunnels and bunkers. Says the place is crawling with gooks."

Frank turned back towards Mitchell, "Did they get anybody fucked up?"

"Ah, a couple. Four or five more got hit," Mitchell answered.

By this time, the sun was dropping below the horizon and night was falling fast. Colonel Moore's plan had succeeded and the entire perimeter was covered. Now the problem was going to be keeping the NVA sealed up until morning. They would be trying anything they could to break out. And in Nam the saying was "the night belonged to Charlie." They liked to do their fighting at night, whereas the American units preferred daylight to take advantage of their superior firepower.

Lieutenant Neilley's voice came over the radio, "One-Six to all units. Stay on your toes. Charlie could be trying to get out anywhere. If you see any movement to the front, it will be the enemy. So fire and then report their position to me. This is One-Six, out."

A Troop was set up in the positions that they would stay for the night. They had arrived too late to set out their normal defensive apparatus, such as trip flares and claymore mines. It was going to be a long night.

Frank had left the driver's hole and was back with Steve and Country in the gunner's area. He was armed with his M-16 and the M-79, 40 millimeter grenade launcher, it was known as the Thumper in Nam.

Steve passed up two extra boxes of fifty caliber ammunition to Mitchell, who was in the turret. The inside floor of the APC was layered with metal boxes of fifty caliber and M-60 ammunition, two boxes high. The One-One track had on board over 18,000 rounds of fifty caliber and 10,000 rounds of M-60 ammunition.

By now, the darkness of the night had covered them like a blanket. Their adrenaline was running high and their nerves were on edge. They weren't talking a lot, but when they did, it was just above a whisper. They were listening for any sounds of enemy movement. They heard firing some distance away. It sounded like it was coming from the north side of the oasis. Just a few burst of automatic weapons fire and then quiet.

"Perhaps the gooks are already probing the perimeter, or maybe just some of the grunts are getting nervous," Mitchell thought.

The mortar track, One-Zero, fired an illumination round. First, they heard the sound of the round being fired, and a few seconds later the explosion high above the oasis. Then they saw the night light up as the round, being supported by a small parachute, and floated slowly to the ground. All of the mortar tracks were now operating on A

49

Troop Command frequency, so Mitchell on One-One track could no longer hear the radio transmissions to and from One-Zero.

"It sure would be nice if they'd keep it lit up like this here all night," Country said wishfully.

"Yeah, but I don't think we can count on that," Steve answered.

Five or six minutes passed before the silence was broken again. Several bursts of automatic weapons fire followed by fifteen seconds of quiet and then more firing. Then another illumination round was fired. This time by one of the other mortar tracks. Mitchell couldn't be sure of which one. The far side of the oasis was lit up and soon the firing had stopped.

"Steve, you've been in firefights before, right?" Country asked.

"Nine or ten," he answered, his eyes never leaving the tree line.

"What's it like?"

Mitchell and Frank had both wanted to ask the same question, but macho bravado had prevented it. But now that Country had asked, they too anxiously waited to hear Steve's answer.

"What's it like?" Steve pondered. "It's hard to say. They're never the same," he paused and thought for a second. "One thing that is always the same is that you're scared shitless."

Colonel Moore decided to call for an artillery barrage on the NVA's position to keep them pinned down. The only fire base that was in range to provide support was Firebase Jane. It was located twelve klicks southeast of the battle. Battery A, First Battalion, Twenty-ninth Artillery was stationed there.

The Second Battalion's forward observer was Lieutenant Sawyer. His job was to coordinate between the ground units and the artillery battery to bring the artillery fire in on target. Battery A was made up of four 105 millimeter howitzers. Lieutenant Sawyer radioed Firebase Jane and gave them the map coordinates of the oasis. The artillery battery then made all of the calculations and aimed the 105s. But before firing live rounds, they would first fire marking rounds to check their aim, and if necessary, Lieutenant Sawyer could advise them if any adjustments needed to be made.

Mitchell and the others on One-One heard the first marking round coming in. It exploded high in the air fifty meters in front of One-One's position. The marking round reminded Mitchell of aerial fireworks on the Fourth of July.

"That's too damn close!" Steve complained.

"I think they're just trying to get zeroed in," Mitchell replied. "Surely, they'll bring it further inside the oasis," he added.

They heard the second round on its way. It exploded far on the north side. A minute later a third marking round came in. This time it exploded in the center of the oasis.

"That one was bracketed by the other two," Mitchell said.

"Yeah, it looks like they got it zeroed in," Steve agreed. "They should be sending the real shit any minute."

Lieutenant Sawyer informed Firebase Jane that their last marking round was on target, and they could fire for affect when ready.

Mitchell heard the loud roaring whistle of the round coming in. Then there was a flash of bright light that enveloped him as the explosion hit just to the left of One-One. The concussion from the blast stunned Mitchell. The first 105 high explosive round had come in short, hitting twenty-five meters to the left of One-One.

Mitchell was awake but in a state of limbo, somewhere between consciousness and a bad dream. The first thing he saw was his hands. He was staring at his hands, they were moving upward but in slow motion. Everything seemed to be in slow motion. His mind was blunted. He was having trouble thinking clearly. He turned to look back at the others. He couldn't see Frank. Country was still standing, holding on to the M-60. He looked disoriented. His mouth was wide open and a blank stare was on his face. He was stunned, not able to speak.

Steve had both hands covering his face. There was blood pouring out from under his hands and between his fingers. Mitchell climbed out of the turret and knelt down on one knee in front of Steve.

"Steve! Steve!" Mitchell shouted. He could barely hear his own voice because of the loud ringing in his ears.

Frank sluggishly stood up from the floor of the APC. The force of the blast had knocked him off his feet. He seemed confused and he had a wild look in his eyes.

Looking at Frank, still shouting, Mitchell asked, "Frank, are you all right?"

Slowly looking up and down at himself, Frank stuttered, "I....I... guess so."

Mitchell could barely hear him. His voice seemed muffled and echoing, as if he was speaking into a metal barrel.

"Steve's hit!" Mitchell turned back to Steve and cried out, "Steve! Steve!" But Steve didn't answer. "Take his hand!" Mitchell said to Frank.

Mitchell took hold of one of Steve's hands and Frank took the other. They deliberately pried them away from his face.

"Holy Shit!" Frank gasped, stunned by what he saw.

Steve's upper lip was mangled. Some parts of it they could see through, exposing his teeth and gums. He was spitting out blood and fragments of his shattered teeth. His nose was missing, totally gone, completely wiped off his face, all the way to the skull. Steve was bleeding severely and going into shock.

"Give me that towel!" Mitchell said grabbing for the towel that Frank had around his neck. He folded it and placed it over Steve's face.

"Hold this!" He said to Frank. Mitchell then stepped back up to the turret and radioed for help.

"One-Six, this is One-One, over."

"This is One-Six, over."

"This is One-One. We need a medic over here fast, over."

"This is One-Six, roger. We'll get the medic track rolling. Who's hit? Over."

"This is One-One. It's Steve, over."

"This is One-Six. How bad? Over."

"This is One-One. His face is all messed up. He's bleeding real bad. I don't know, over."

"This is One-Six. Just hold on. The medic's on their way, over."

"Ah, One-One, roger."

Mitchell came back to Steve, kneeling down beside him. Taking hold of the towel, he started applying pressure to his face. "Get up there and keep your eyes open. Monitor the radio," he ordered Frank, motioning to the turret.

The ringing in Mitchell's ears had let up some and his mind was clearing. "Steve, Steve can you hear me?" Mitchell said softly, but still Steve didn't answer. He could hear Steve moaning, half crying. He sounded like a small child whimpering.

Country spoke for the first time, "Here comes the medic track." He was getting over the initial shock of the blast, but still was confused about what had happened.

Mitchell looked up and saw it passing behind One-Two and moving towards them. About halfway between One-Two and One-One the medic track stopped. Mitchell hadn't noticed before, but there were two men kneeling over a body lying on the ground. Two of the medics jumped from the track and ran to attend the injured soldier, and then the medic track continued on its way.

Country opened the back hatch and helped Mitchell lift Steve through it onto the canvas stretcher the medics had waiting on the other side. Mitchell softly spoke, "Hang in there, Steve. You'll be all right. They'll take care of you now."

Steve unable to speak, reached up and grabbed Mitchell's arm, hesitatingly releasing it as the medics carried him away and placed him inside the track.

"I'll be right back," Mitchell said to Country. "I'm going to see who got hit." He climbed through the back hatch and headed for the place where the medics first stopped.

Paul Bonds was standing over the body lying on the ground. The two medics had given up, there was nothing they could do for the soldier.

"Who is it?" Mitchell asked.

"It's Sergeant Becker," Paul answered. "He never had a chance."

The artillery round had hit less than twenty feet from Becker. He was killed instantly. Sergeant Becker was TC of One-Seven and also the platoon sergeant for First Platoon. He had been at One-Two checking on their position and was on his way to One-One when the round hit.

Mitchell didn't look very close at the body, but from a glance he could see that it was badly mangled.

"This is some bad shit," Paul said, then looked over at One-One, "Who got hit on your track?"

"Steve."

"How bad?"

"He's alive, but his face is all messed up."

"I'm telling you Sarge, this is some bad shit."

"Yeah, I know. I gotta get back to my guys. Stay cool," Mitchell said then turned and ran back to his track.

As he climbed on top of One-One, Frank said, "It's our own shit, man!" His anger exploding with each word, "Our own fuckin' artillery!"

"Who got hit over there?" Country asked, pointing to where the body was lying.

"It's Sergeant Becker," Mitchell answered.

"How is he?" Country asked with a slight quiver in his voice.

"He didn't make it."

"You mean he's dead?"

"Yeah, he's dead."

Frank threw his hands up in disgust, his rage was still spilling out. "Shit, man. It's bad enough havin' the fuckin' gooks running around trying to kill us. We're getting blown away by our own guys. This is bullshit, man! Bullshit!"

"I know! I know!" Mitchell was frustrated and angry also. "We have to pull ourselves together now. That's over with, we need to concentrate on what we're doing," Mitchell said as he took Frank's place in the turret.

Frank took the right side fifty caliber without being told.

"What do ya think happened with the artillery, Sarge?" Country asked.

"I don't know. The marking round was on target, but all the live rounds came in short. Maybe there was something wrong with the ammo. I don't know." Mitchell guessed.

"Who the fuck knows?!" Frank added.

A Troop's commanding officer had gotten the artillery barrage stopped after four live rounds had been fired. The first round killed Sergeant Becker and wounded Steve, the three others luckily were even shorter and had fallen further behind the perimeter, doing no damage. But until the problem was solved back at Firebase Jane, there would be no artillery support. This was going to make keeping the NVA pinned inside the perimeter all night, even harder.

"Is Steve going to be okay?" Country asked.

"He's going to be all right," Mitchell answered.

"How bad was his face? I didn't get to see his face."

"He doesn't have a face anymore." Frank said, still showing the anger he was feeling.

"He'll be all right. Things always look worse at first than what they really are. They'll be able to fix him up." Mitchell was trying to calm Country's fears and perhaps his own.

Frank noticed that Country was really scared and that Mitchell was trying to calm him down, so he didn't say any more about Steve. Even though it was hard to keep his anger inside, he turned and glared out into the dark jungle.

They didn't talk for a time. It was unusually quiet, Mitchell thought. He didn't hear any sounds at all. The contrast from the chaos of just a few minutes before was amazing. It was very still, no breeze, the air was heavy. There was no sounds of the wind blowing through the leaves, or the nightly chirping of the insects. Mitchell and the others just sat there staring into the tree line, thinking about Steve and Sergeant Becker.

Mitchell heard the sound of a helicopter coming from the southwest. At first he could barely make it out, then it became louder as it approached, the rhythmic sound of the main rotor; chopping through the silence. He looked over his left shoulder and could see it setting down three hundred meters away. It was the Medevac coming to pick up Steve.

The one thing that combat troops in Vietnam could count on was that if they were hit, a medic would be there and be there fast. From the time Steve was hit, it was less than three minutes before the medics had picked him up and were treating him, and now he was being loaded onto a helicopter and flown to a field hospital. From the time he was hit, to arriving at the hospital and to the waiting doctors and nurses, it would be only twenty-five minutes. This kind of response would account for thousands of lives being saved.

Mitchell watched the Medevac lift off and then listened to the sound of it as it disappeared to the southwest. Then nothing, complete silence again. He could hear himself breathing. His lungs expanding and contracting with each breath. His heart beating still a little faster than normal.

For the next few hours, they would only hear sporadic firing from around the perimeter, mostly on the north side. At 0120 hours, firing broke out to the right of One-One's position. A few burst of automatic weapons fired at first, but it quickly turned into a major exchange. The grunts on the other side of the rise in the sand were engaged in an all-out firefight. The NVA weren't just probing, they were trying to break out.

Mitchell could see the tracer rounds as they flashed across in both directions. He could see the explosion of the 40mm grenades being launched from the M79s. The first four positions of Bravo squad, First Platoon were under attack.

"Keep your eyes open guys. They're trying to get out." Mitchell yelled to Frank and Country.

"Must be a whole fuckin' bunch of 'em." Frank said as he swung his fifty caliber in the direction of the rise.

The firing was very heavy and the night was lit up by constant streams of tracers coming from both directions. This was the biggest fight of the night so far. The mortar track, One-Zero, fired an illumination round, lighting up the perimeter. The intensity of the fight was letting up, but not completely.

Country had moved from his left side gun and was standing beside Frank watching the fight. "There! They're coming across right there!" Country yelled, pointing to the rise in the sand.

"Where?" Frank asked, not seeing anything.

"There!" Country yelled again. "Right there!"

Mitchell saw them. There were four NVA soldiers crossing the rise and running back towards the oasis. He pointed his fifty caliber in their direction and then pressing down with both of his thumbs on the butterfly trigger, he opened fire. Using the tracers as a guide, he walked the burning, hot lead into the running gooks. Two were hit and fell to the sand, never moving again. The other two disappeared into the vegetation.

"You got some of them!" Country yelled.

"Yeah, two! Sarge, you got two of 'em!" Frank said.

Mitchell was staring at the two bodies lying in the sand. He didn't take his eyes off them until the illumination round burned out and they were no longer visible. It had happened, Mitchell thought. That unanswered question, that lingering fear he had from the first day he was drafted. It had suddenly happened. He just killed two men and he had done it without forethought. He had seen the enemy and coldly and calmly took aim and killed them. He looked down at his hands that while firing were as steady as a rock, but now they were trembling. He was breathing faster and taking shallow breaths, his mouth dry. He didn't feel sadness or exhilaration, just nervousness.

The firing stopped, the NVA pushed back into the oasis, and the silence once again crept upon them.

CHAPTER SIX

The rising sun brought with it a feeling of relief to the crew of One-One. Daylight in Vietnam always made you feel more secure, more in control; and after the night they had been through, this morning it was even more so. There was a light haze over the area, made up from the smoke of all the firing and explosions from the firefight. The air was very humid and no breeze was felt. The temperature was climbing and in an hour or two it would be over one hundred degrees.

"Look at this!" Country sounded surprised as he leaned over the left side of the APC.

"What?" Mitchell asked.

"This!" He pointed at a gouge in the hull about an inch deep just below his gun mount. "A piece of shrapnel must of hit here. Damn, there's a bunch of 'em!"

Country jumped to the ground on the left side of the track. Mitchell and Frank moved to the left side and looked over. Country was counting all the damaged spots.

"Ten, eleven...fourteen! We were hit in fourteen places!"

Mitchell turned and his eyes met Frank's. They could tell they were both thinking the same thing. It was a miracle that only Steve had been hit.

"How do ya figure?" Frank asked, still staring at Mitchell.

"Luck. Just plain blind-ass luck," Mitchell answered, shaking his head.

"Take a look at this. Some of these are deep as hell. I wonder if a flak jacket would have stopped this shit," Frank questioned as he used his finger gauging the depth of the gouge.

"I don't think so. Sergeant Becker was wearing a flak jacket and it tore him to pieces," Mitchell answered grimly.

Their conversation was interrupted by a call coming over the radio.

"One-Six, to all units. All TCs report to my location. This is One-Six, out."

When all the TCs from First Platoon had gathered in back of One-Six track, Lieutenant Neilley began his daily briefing.

"In about thirty minutes, Delta Company of the Second Battalion is going to be airlifted in here. They'll be setting up a hundred and fifty meters behind our position. When they're in place, we'll pull back to where they're at. After that there will be an artillery barrage called in."

The mention of an artillery barrage made some of the TCs grumble. One-Nine's TC said sarcastically, "You think a hundred and fifty meters is far enough away to keep from getting our shit blown away, this time?"

"Yeah, we don't need any more shit like last night," one of the other TCs added.

Lieutenant Neilley cut them off, "What happened to Sergeant Becker was tragic, but we still have a job to do. Now listen up!" He continued on with his briefing, "The artillery barrage will be followed by an air strike. Now here's the part I know you all are going to like. After the air strike, A Troop along with Delta Company will sweep through the oasis and take out..."

Before he could finish, the grumbling started up again, "Oh shit, man. How come us?"

"Listen up!" Lieutenant Neilley barked loudly. "If I was in command, I would do the same thing. We have the firepower and can break through the jungle. Anyway, it's about time we start earning some of that money Uncle Sam's paying us," he said facetiously. "Now get back to your tracks and get your people ready!"

Mitchell turned to leave as did all the TCs. "Mitchell," Lieutenant Neilley called out.

He stopped and turned back to face the lieutenant.

"I got word a little while ago from the rear. Steve is going to be all right."

"That's good news, sir; real good news. Thanks for telling me."

Lieutenant Neilley glanced toward the tree line then back at Mitchell. "Look, it could get hairy in there today, so stay on your toes. Okay?"

"Yes sir, I will."

Lieutenant Neilley turned and walked away, his shoulders slightly slumped. The death of Sergeant Becker was weighing heavy on him. Since he'd been in command of First Platoon, Becker was the first man he had lost.

Upon returning to One-One, Mitchell found Frank and Country eating. They had broken out the C-rations and made some Kool-Aid.

Mitchell took his place in the turret and looked toward the oasis. He could see the bodies of the two NVA soldiers that he had killed the night before, starting to swell in the hot sun.

"You want something to eat, Sarge?" Country asked.

"Yeah, what do we got?"

"Hey, your favorite, Beans 'n Weenies," Country said, handing him a box of C's. "You want some Kool-Aid, too?"

"Sure, what kind did you make?"

"Grape. All we have is grape and orange, and Frank wanted grape."

Frank looked up grumbling, "We've had orange for the last three days and I'm sick of orange."

"Grape's fine with me." Mitchell paused for a moment and then continued, "Lieutenant Neilley says Steve's going to be all right."

"Why did it have to happen to Steve," Country said more than asking. "He only had a few days to go."

"It's just bad luck, Country. It could of happened to any of us. The whole side of the track was splattered by shrapnel." Frank's voice softened, remembering last night, the fear on Country's face. "I guess his luck just ran out."

Handing up a cup of Kool-Aid to Mitchell, Country asked, "Is that what you think, Sarge? Is it just luck?"

"I don't know. You could call it luck, some call it fate." Mitchell was speaking slowly and deliberately. "I just think that if it's intended to happen it will, no matter what you do." Mitchell looked down at the trigger of his fifty caliber machine gun. "I guess a year here is just like playing Russian roulette, 365 pulls and one day the chamber might be loaded." Even though he tried not to, his eyes found their way back to the bloated bodies lying in the sand.

The Hueys of the 186th Aviation Battalion were bringing in Delta Company. They landed two hundred meters behind A Troop, a Huey setting down approximately every seventy-five meters, a total of fourteen choppers in all. Their rotors were kicking up the sand, causing a small sand storm. The grunts would pour out of the Hueys as fast as they could and then it would lift off. The whole operation took four minutes.

"Frank, get it started up so we'll be ready to move," Mitchell ordered. Frank climbed down into the driver's hole and started the diesel engine.

A few moments later, a squelch came over the radio, "One-Six, to all units. Comm Check, over." All units were to respond in order, making sure that their communications were in good working condition.

"This is One-One. Loud and clear, over."

"This is One-Two. Loud and clear, over." And so on, until all of First Platoon's tracks had reported in.

"This is One-Six. Pull back to a position directly behind where you are now. Move back to where the ground units are located. This is One-Six, out."

Frank turned One-One around one hundred and eighty degrees and headed for the grunts position. All of A Troop was doing the same. They moved back approximately one hundred and seventy-five meters.

"This is good. Stop and turn it around." Mitchell ordered to Frank over the intercom. Frank stopped and spun the APC around to face the oasis once again. The grunts of Delta Company moved up and knelt in the sand between and behind the tracks.

One-One was in its new position for only five minutes when they heard the first marking round coming in. It exploded well inside the oasis, then a second and a third marking round, all were on target. Then the sky was quiet. Mitchell felt a shiver running up his spine, anticipating what was coming.

He heard the whistles of the first live rounds coming in. They exploded inside the oasis, six hundred meters in front of One-One. Nevertheless, Mitchell still flinched, fearful of another round coming in short. He saw the flash of the blast before he heard the sound. Then the flash gave way to a plume of dark smoke. There were two explosions almost simultaneously and then a few seconds later, two more. More rounds came roaring overhead to burst violently in the oasis, throwing vegetation and sand high in the air. The rounds came in volleys of four now, volley after volley, unrelenting. The barrage had been going on for five minutes, sixty rounds had fallen on the oasis. Mitchell found himself thinking about the gooks inside. Just the one round that came in short the night before caused so much damage and confusion, what must the NVA soldiers be going through. It was incomprehensible. These thoughts were upsetting to Mitchell and so he tried to think of something else...anything else.

He thought of Maggie and the letter he had received the day before. Reaching into his pocket, he pulled out her letter and found with it the letter for Country that he placed there and had forgotten. Turning to his left and leaning back, he called to Country.

"Hey!" Country stepped forward so he could hear Mitchell. "This letter is for you. I forgot to give it to you yesterday when all the shit started."

"Thanks," Country said, glancing at the envelope. "It's from my mom."

Mitchell turned back and began to reread Maggie's letter. Country leaned against the inside of the APC, his arm resting on his M-60, and started reading. Frank was still in the driver's hole. He was tired from being up all night and had a slight headache. He crossed his arms in front of him on top of the driver's hole and placed his head down, closing his eyes, hoping to rest them for a few minutes. The artillery barrage continued, volley after volley, showering destruction on the oasis. It must have been a strange sight for the grunts to look up at One-One and see in the midst of this pandemonium, one man asleep and two others casually reading letters.

The barrage continued for several more minutes. By the time it had ended, there had been at least one hundred and fifty high explosive rounds deposited on the oasis. The sound of silence caused Frank to raise his head and focus his attention forward.

"They really blew it to shit," Frank said, watching the plumes of smoke bellowing up. The barrage had covered virtually the entire area of the oasis, some fires were burning and occasionally the sound of secondary explosions could be heard.

"Yeah, it must be a living hell in there," Mitchell said as he put Maggie's letter back in his pocket. "But it's going to get worse when the air strike comes in."

"You got that right."

"Have you ever seen an air strike, Sarge?" Country joined in.

"No, not for real."

"Do you think there'll be many gooks left when we go in?"

"Yeah, I think so. The lieutenant said it could get hairy in there, so I think there'll be some."

A Cessna 0-2 Skymaster, forward air control aircraft, passed overhead from the south. The small prop plane was armed with marking rockets and flares. Its purpose was to mark the enemy's position for the jet fighter-bombers that were on their way. It passed over the oasis from the south to the north, and then made a long turn to the east, passing back over the oasis, east to west.

"They're shooting at it!" Frank shouted.

The Cessna had drawn fire from the ground on its last pass, several burst of AK-47 fire.

"I think they're making a big mistake," Mitchell remarked. "The dumb fucks are just giving away their positions."

The Cessna turned and came back over the oasis, firing marking rockets. The smoke came up from two different locations, approximately six hundred meters apart. It then turned to the south and began orbiting over the top of A Troop's position.

Forty-five seconds later, two F-4 Phantoms roared in from the west. They were flying low and fast. They crossed right over the oasis and then made a turn to the south and back to the west. They disappeared for a moment and then one of the F-4s came roaring back. It came in even lower this time. As it approached the smoke from one of the marking rockets, it dropped eight, five hundred pound bombs, in rapid succession. Then the Phantom climbed and banked to the south. The bombs impacted in a chain reaction over an area of four hundred meters. The explosions were earsplitting, rumbling like thunder. First you saw the fireballs of the blast, then large dark clouds of smoke and debris mushrooming into the air. The explosions were so powerful that Mitchell could feel the earth quiver. A few seconds later, the second Phantom came streaking over the oasis. It attacked the area marked by the second rocket with another load of eight, five hundred pound bombs. Everything in the area was blown sky high, with shattering thunderous explosions. As far back as One-One's position, a few pieces of shrapnel were kicking up the sand.

The two F-4s formed up together and screamed back for a second pass. This time they dropped pods of napalm. Napalm is composed of naphthenic and palmitic acid, forming a highly flammable, thickened gasoline mixture that sticks to any surface that it comes in contact with. Upon impact, the pods exploded into huge balls of fire. Because of the forward momentum from the jets, the fires started rolling like an enormous wave, engulfing everything in its path. It was a massive inferno, a wall of fire spreading over four hundred meters. Even from One-One's position, they could feel the blast of heat. It was like opening a hot oven door. If there ever was such a thing as hell on earth, this was it. Mitchell, Frank, and Country just stared, speechless, in awe of the destruction they were witnessing.

The F-4s having dropped their full loads, turned south heading back to their base. The Cessna also left the area.

"Holy shit!" Frank said, breaking the silence. "How could anything survive in that?"

"I don't know," Mitchell answered, shaking his head. "But you hav'ta figure there'll be plenty of them left. If they're down in those tunnels, somehow they'll survive."

"Could you feel that heat, Sarge?" Country asked. "I couldn't believe how much heat there was way back here."

"Yeah, it was incredible, now check you're sixty and the other fifty back there. Hand me up another box of ammo," Mitchell ordered, getting his mind on business. "Look Country, I want you to cover the left side when we go in. I'll cover the front and right. Okay?"

"Okay Sarge, I gotcha," Country answered, nodding his head.

"Frank, keep your eyes open. If you spot anything, sing out."

"I'll sing out with my M-16, blowing their ass away."

"That'll work."

The word came to move out. A Troop started rolling slowly towards the oasis, the grunts of Delta Company walking behind the tracks for cover. Some of the vegetation was burning, but no large fires. The napalm was like a huge flame-thrower, a very intense fire for a short time and then mostly smoldering afterwards. The way the sweep was to work was for the tanks and APCs of A Troop to break through the vegetation and be first to engage any of the NVA that still were able to fight. Delta Company would search and clean out the tunnels and bunkers on the ground.

The oasis wasn't covered completely by jungle. There were many clearings and ribbons of sand running through it. Along the edges of these interior clearings is where the tunnels and bunkers would be found.

One-One started into the oasis. First, it was tall elephant grass, then the vegetation thickened with trees and vines. Frank carefully ran One-One onto the trees, letting the weight of the APC break them down. The grunts followed behind using the path that the track had cleared. They were one hundred and fifty meters in when they came upon the first small fires, just some of the grass burning. To the left was a bomb crater approximately fifteen meters across, the trees and vines completely blown away. One-One continued on. Fifty meters further in, they came across the first clearing. It was twenty-five meters wide and ran fifty meters to the right and one hundred meters or more to the left. Mitchell could see that One-Two was breaking into the clearing off to their left. Then off the far side to his right, he saw two or three bodies.

"Hold it," Mitchell said to Frank over the intercom. "There's something over there. Over to the right."

Frank stopped the APC and scanned the clearing. Mitchell pointed his fifty caliber gun in the direction of the bodies. There wasn't any movement.

"Move up slowly."

Frank eased One-One forward until they were within fifty feet of the bodies. There was an impact crater from one of the 105mm rounds a few feet from where the bodies were lying.

"Look at this shit," Frank said observing the bodies.

"Is there two or three of them?" Mitchell asked. "I can't fuckin' tell."

"Beats the shit out of me," Frank answered.

The bodies were badly mutilated, ripped into jagged pieces, one body thrown on top of the other. It was impossible to tell which legs and arms went to which torso. The grunts moved up and searched the remains, finding only two AK-47s. They then searched for tunnels but found none.

After five minutes, it was decided to push on. One-One broke through the jungle on the other side of the clearing, still moving north. They traveled another two hundred and fifty meters before the vegetation started to thin as they neared another clearing. The jungle was pitted with 105mm impact craters and as they got to the edge of the clearing, Mitchell could see a larger crater caused by one of the five hundred pound bombs. There were small brush fires still burning. This area had been hit by the napalm, as well.

Frank eased One-One onto some small trees. The front of the APC was climbing inch by inch higher into the air until the weight broke the trees down, dropping the APC suddenly back to the ground. He pulled back hard on the steering levers bringing the APC to a quick stop, startled by the horrible sight that was now visible directly in front of him. Impaled on a broken tree trunk was a NVA soldier.

The jagged wood was sticking completely through the body. It had entered through the lower abdomen and was protruding out from the small of the back about a foot. Most of the small intestines, which were coiled in the center of the abdominal cavity, were now ripped out, hanging from the top of the jagged, burning stump and stringing back down inside the smoldering body. It was seared and charred, having a blacked and reddish color about it. All of the clothing had been burned away except for the boots. The facial features, the nose, ears, and lips had been smoothed away by the fire. Parts of the face were burnt down to the bones, but other fleshier areas around the cheeks and jaws were still partially remaining, scorched and blistered. The right cheekbone had been shattered, enlarging the eye socket, causing the eyeball to fall out of the skull. It was dangling an inch or so from the head, still connected by the central retinal artery and optic nerve. It was a gruesome and hideous sight. The crew of One-One stared at it, almost in shock.

Hearing a RPG (rocket propelled grenade) being fired from a bunker on the far side of the clearing jolted their attention. It streaked towards them. Mitchell could see it in its flight, but there was no time to react. The RPG traveled above the right front corner of the APC, missing it by a foot. Mitchell, sitting in the turret, was less than two feet away as it roared passed his face. He saw the white and orange explosion as it hit some trees thirty feet behind the track. Had it not been for the NVA soldier's poor aim, the crew of One-One could have well been casualties themselves.

Mitchell and Country immediately opened fire on the bunker. After firing half a box of fifty caliber rounds into the bunker, Mitchell reached for the M-79 grenade launcher and fired it. The grenade exploded on the outside of the bunker, causing little damage. He broke down the M-79, expelling the shell casing, reloading it, and taking aim again at the opening in the bunker. This time he had hit his mark, smoke and debris came bellowing out. A third round was fired and again entered the opening and exploded inside the bunker, killing all three of the NVA soldiers inside.

Some of the grunts had spotted another bunker, no firing had come from it, but they were still reluctant to approach it.

"Hey Sarge! Soften up that bunker to your right," one of the grunts hollered up to Mitchell.

Mitchell turned his fifty caliber machine gun and peppered the bunker with forty rounds. Then the grunts moved cautiously towards it. As the first grunt entered, he suddenly jumped back and fired a burst from his M-16. He slowly stepped back further, his M-16 trained on the bunker's entrance.

A NVA soldier came limping out with an M-16 wound in his chest and one of his knee caps completely blown away. With each step, his knee would bend backwards, as if hinged the opposite of a normal knee. He was smiling, his hands raised above his head crying, "Chieu Hoi!" (Chieu Hoi is Vietnamese for open arms; an amnesty program to encourage enemy soldiers to surrender.)

"How could he be walking with his leg like that?" Country asked.

"I don't know. He's got a bullet hole in his chest, his leg is blown to shit, and he's smiling," Mitchell answered in amazement.

"I wonder what kind of shit he was smoking last night." Watching in disbelief, Frank added, "Jesus, he should be dead."

A Troop and Delta Company spent the next four hours sweeping and clearing out the oasis. One-One encountered no further resistance that morning, but from time to time they could hear other units down the line engaged in firefights, and some of them sounded quite intense.

The losses to the NVA in this battle had put an end to the planned attack on Firebase Jane. The final count was as follows:

A Troop, Third Squadron, Fifth Armored Cavalry
    2 - Killed in action
    6 - Wounded in action
Second Battalion, First Air Cavalry
    9 - Killed in action
    17 - Wounded in action
NVA's Thirty-second Regiment, First Division
    119 - Killed in action
    84 - Wounded in action
    108 - POWs

It was estimated that between seventy-five and one hundred NVA soldiers had escaped during the night.

The battle had taken place on the evening of August 19th and the following day, August 20, 1968, which was coincidentally Sergeant Robert Mitchell's twenty-first birthday.

CHAPTER SEVEN

A Troop returned back to base camp just before dark. They pulled into the staging area inside the perimeter and were ordered down for the night. No guard duty, no radio watch, nothing but ten to twelve hours of sleep for everyone. The events of the nineteenth and twentieth had left them completely exhausted.

It was 0615 hours the morning of the twenty-first. Mitchell had joined the other TCs at One-Six for the daily briefing.

Lieutenant Neilley began, "Well, I must say, you men look a hell of a lot better this morning than you did when we came dragging in last night. I guess a good night's sleep can do wonders. I have good news for you. We have no assignment for today, but we will be going on the perimeter tonight. So, today we are going to get all of our equipment squared away. I want a complete maintenance check on all tracks. All weapons cleaned and maintained, including personal weapons. Any questions?"

Nobody had any.

"Okay, I'll be coming by each track this afternoon to take a look, so let's get it done and the rest of the day we can take it easy. One more thing, Sergeant Hill, you have five men in your crew, right?"

"Yes, sir."

"You will have to give one to Mitchell on One-One. They're down to three. This will be a permanent reassignment, so you pick the man."

"Yes, sir."

"Okay, that's it."

Sergeant Leroy Hill was the TC of One-Four. He was twenty-two years old and was on his second enlistment in the army, having joined four years earlier. He had decided if he could survive this year in Vietnam, he would stay in and make the army his career.

"Well Leroy, who are you going to let me have?" Mitchell asked as they walked away from the briefing together.

"I guess I'll give you Dave. He's my newest man."

"How new?"

"He's been with us for only six days."

"What's he like?"

"What's he like? What's the matter, you think I'm going to give you a dud or something?" Leroy was grinning.

"Yeah, I wouldn't put it passed you, trying to pull something like that," Mitchell ragged back.

"No, really he's all right, man. He's a surfer from California."

"A surfer? He's not a flake is he?"

"No man, he's okay. He was trained Eleven-Delta, so he can do some driving for you."

"I'll let him back up Frank. But, Frank's my driver, even if he bitches about it."

"Yeah, man. Well, don't let his bitching fool ya, 'cause I know the brother and he likes being your driver."

"If you say so. Hey, send Dave over right away, so he can get started with the rest of us on this clean-up."

"Sure thing, man."

PFC David Taylor was nineteen years old. He had lived in San Diego, California his whole life and his only interest had been hanging out on the beach, surfing. He was drafted right after he graduated from high school. His father had the money and connections to have prevented it, but didn't, hoping that the service might help his son grow up.

"Hey Dave. I hear, you get to be part of a good crew now," Country said in his usual friendly manner.

"Hey dude," Dave replied, stepping into the back of the track.

Frank looked over at Mitchell and asked, "Country already knows this guy?"

"Hell, Country knows everybody." Mitchell stepped down from the turret, offering Dave his hand. "I'm Bobby Mitchell."

"Dave Taylor."

"This is Frank." Frank nodded his head in acknowledgment. "And I see you already know Country. Leroy told me you're trained Eleven-Delta."

"Yeah, if you dudes need a good driver, I'm your man."

Mitchell glanced at Frank, whose expression made it clear that he was anxious to see how Mitchell was going to handle this.

"I'll have you back up Frank as driver and man my right-side fifty, okay?"

"No problem, Sarge. Anyone else Eleven-Delta on this track?"

"No man, we're real fuckin' soldiers." Frank growled.

Country busted out laughing. Dave looked confused. It would take him a few days to understand Frank's dry humor.

"Don't mind Frank. He doesn't like anybody. Okay, let's get started on this clean-up. Dave, you help Frank pull the maintenance on the APC. I want you guys to check the oil, transmission fluid, water, belts, you know the drill. Check the track and all the connecting pins. Country and I will clean up this pigpen while you're doing that," Mitchell said as he kicked an empty C-ration box out the back lift. The inside of the track had empty ammo and C-ration boxes thrown around and sand was everywhere.

Dave threw his bag in the netting along the wall and asked Frank, "Where do you want to start?"

"Let's start with the engine."

Frank and Dave began their engine checks. Mitchell and Country began cleaning the inside. After all the garbage had been thrown out, Country started sweeping out the APC. Mitchell was outside shaking the sand out of the poncho liners that they used for blankets.

Country had worked his way to the back and was sweeping down the lift gate. "Sarge, Dave said he would teach me how to surf."

"Surf?" Mitchell questioned. "I thought you told me you couldn't swim."

"Well, I can't, at least not very good."

"Don't you think it might be a good idea to learn how to swim before you take up surfing? Anyway, where the hell are you gonna find a surfboard around here?"

"Dave said he heard they have them down at China Beach."

"Yeah, I hear they have air-conditioning and tennis courts too, but a lot of good it does us here. The only way you are ever going to get to China Beach is on R&R, and there are a hell of a lot better places to go than China Beach."

Country stopped sweeping and asked, "Where can we go on R&R?"

"Hawaii, Bangkok, Sydney, but it's going to be a long time before any of us get R&R, another six or seven months."

"Where you going to go, Sarge?"

"I'm going to meet Maggie in Hawaii."

"Maybe I'll go to Hawaii too. You can surf there."

"Yeah, you can surf in Hawaii," Mitchell said laughingly, shaking his head. Country's credulous outlook on life never failed to bring a smile to Mitchell's face.

Frank came around the side of the track, taking the five gallon oil can from its bracket mounted on the back of the APC. "Hey, Dave actually likes doing this shit. Maybe we should let him do it all the time."

"Maybe we'll just let him help you."

"Sarge, you don't think I'm trying to get out of work, do you?"

"Oh no, Frank. I know you would never do a thing like that." Frank started laughing as he walked away.

The crew of One-One spent three hours cleaning and doing the maintenance on the APC and weapons. Later that afternoon, Mitchell and Frank took part in a poker game on One-Four track. Besides themselves, Leroy Hill, Paul Bonds, and Sergeant Michael O'Shea, the TC of One-Two, took part in the game.

They had been playing for about four hours when the word came that they would be moving to the perimeter in fifteen minutes. Frank was the big winner, he was ahead one hundred and fifty dollars. Mitchell was up maybe twenty dollars or so, all the others were losing. It was decided that they would have one last hand before breaking up the game.

"Who's deal?" Leroy asked.

"Mine," Frank answered, picking up the cards and shuffling the deck.

They were sitting in a circle with Leroy to Frank's left, followed by O'Shea, Paul, and Mitchell. "Ante up." Each man placed fifty cents into the pot.

"This is going to be Five Card Stud," Frank said as he began to deal. "Last hand, so let's make it a good one." He dealt the first card down to each player, then the next card was face up. An eight to Leroy, a jack to O'Shea, a six to Paul, a trey to Mitchell, and a five to himself. "Jack's high." Frank said, pointing to O'Shea.

O'Shea looked at his hole card. It also was a jack. Two dollars," he said, pitching the money into the pot.

Paul had an ace in the hole to go with his six, "I call."

Mitchell checked his hole card, it was a trey. "A pair of treys," Mitchell thought, "... that's worth two bucks."

"I'll see you," he said.

Frank didn't have anything, but he was the big winner. "What the hell," he said, throwing the money into the pot.

Leroy also called the bet.

Frank started dealing again. "Jack, nine, a big ace for Paul, king for Sarge, and shit for the dealer," he said, giving a running account of each card dealt. "That ace makes you big man."

Paul rechecked his ace in the hole, making sure it hadn't mysteriously changed in the last thirty seconds. "Three dollars," he said, not wanting to scare anyone into folding.

Mitchell called.

"Last hand and I can't play," Frank complained as he folded his hand.

Leroy called the bet, having three spades and three parts of a straight.

"I'll see you," O'Shea said, feeling good about his pair of jacks back to back.

"Okay, pot's right," Frank said as he dealt out the fourth card of the hand. "Deuce of spades, three spades for Leroy; pair of nines for One-Two's Tango Charlie; pair of sixes for Paul, and a ten for Sarge. Why are you still in? You ain't got shit!"

"I know what I'm doing," Mitchell answered.

"Pair of nines is high."

O'Shea checked his hole card. He was feeling pretty strong with his two pair, but was a little worried about Leroy, he had him figured right for four spades. "Five bucks," O'Shea said confidently.

"I'll see you," Paul said. He had O'Shea figured for two pair and his aces and sixes would beat that, but he also was worried about Leroy's spades.

Mitchell didn't have any business staying in with his pair of treys, but he was playing a hunch. He was a few dollars ahead, and it's always easier if you're putting someone else's money in the pot.

"I might as well go all the way," Leroy said as he pitched his five bucks in.

"Okay, last card coming. If you don't get it now, you ain't never gonna get it," Frank said as he began to deal. "Five of clubs, right color, wrong shape."

"Damn!" Leroy said as he saw his flush busted.

"Five of diamonds, no help for Sergeant O'Shea." Frank continued dealing, "Eight of clubs for my man Paul, and three of diamonds, that's a pair of treys for Sarge. That pair of nines is still big," Frank pointed to O'Shea.

"They were worth five last time, they're still worth five," O'Shea said as he placed five more dollars into the pot.

Paul still thought he had O'Shea beat, but was confused about Mitchell. "He must have a king in the hole," Paul thought, ".....he must have been playing kings."

"I'll call you," Paul said.

Mitchell had caught his third trey. He figured both Paul and O'Shea for two pair. Either of them could've had three of a kind larger than his, but he was feeling his hunch even stronger. "I'll call your five and raise you five."

Leroy had already picked up and folded his busted flush.

"Jesus Christ, man! What do got over there?" O'Shea said looking at Mitchell's cards.

"A pair of treys," Mitchell replied.

"I can see that. It's what I can't see that's got me worried."

"Ah, bullshit. He's just bluffing," Paul said.

"Maybe so," Mitchell said with a grin.

"I know so. You've been bluffing all day."

"Okay, I'll call your raise." O'Shea placed five more dollars in the pot.

It was Paul's turn to bet, but he was sitting there quietly, hesitating.

"Well, what are you going to do Paul? If he's bluffing, why aren't you in there?" O'Shea was now ribbing Paul.

"I call. I think I got 'cha all beat." Placing five dollars in the pot and then turning over his ace in the hole, revealing his aces and sixes.

"That beats my jacks and nines," O'Shea said.

"Well, let's see it Sarge," Paul said to Mitchell.

Mitchell with a straight face and no comment, turned over this third trey.

"Kiss my ass!" Paul said, throwing his hands in the air.

Frank was laughing, "He didn't kiss it, but he sure did kick it."

Mitchell, no longer able to keep a straight face, started laughing as he reached to pick up the pot.

During that afternoon, Dave and Country had walked down and sat on the beach, watching the unloading of cargo from a freighter that was anchored a quarter mile off shore. The area was bustling with activity. Large amphibious crafts would go out to the freighter and tie up alongside, pallets of supplies were being unloaded by cranes into them. They would then return to the beach, driving up out of the water and onto the sand until they reached the edge of the make-shift loading pad. It was constructed of sheets of corrugated steel connected together, forming an area the size of two football fields. The front gate of the amphibious crafts would drop onto the steel, making a ramp for the navy personnel on forklifts to off load the pallets.

To the right of the freighter, approximately three quarters of a mile offshore, they could see a large hospital ship, easily recognized by the large red cross painted on its hull.

"I wonder if that's where they took Steve." Country said, pointing to the hospital ship.

"Steve?" Dave asked.

"Yeah, he's the guy that got hurt on our track the other night."

"Oh, when the artillery round came in short and killed Sergeant Becker?"

"Yeah," Country answered.

"Maybe," Dave paused. "How bad was he hurt?"

"He got hit in the face by some shrapnel. I didn't see his face, but Frank told me that his nose was completely ripped off."

"Completely gone? Shit man, that must've hurt."

"Yeah, and he only had a week to go."

"Bummer."

They didn't talk for a moment, then Dave changed the subject. "This would be a pretty cool beach if it didn't have all this military shit around." He raised his hand pointing to the water's edge. "I could imagine some dudes down there waxing their boards and a bunch of beach bunnies wearing bikinis hangin' around."

"Bikinis, now that sounds good," Country laughed.

"Oh yeah!" Dave was nodding his head.

"Do you have a girl back home?" Country asked.

"Nay, nobody special. How 'bout you?"

"No," Country paused for a moment. "I was dating a girl when I got drafted, Donna Clark, but when I came home from AIT, I found out she had been screwing half the town while I was gone, so that ended that."

"Bummer, dude."

"It was no big deal, I didn't like her that much anyway."

That evening A Troop moved to the north perimeter to pull guard duty for the night. First Platoon's position started right on the beach and One-One was the closest to the water. The first bunker was only twenty-five meters from the ocean and One-One was set up just to the left of it. Mitchell was sitting in the turret and looking out over the beach. It was a beautiful night. The moon was shining on the water and the sky was full of stars. There was a light breeze blowing in from the South China Sea, making the temperature comfortable. It was quiet. Mitchell could hear the waves breaking on the beach. If it wasn't for the small Navy patrol boats cruising just offshore, this scene could have been any resort beach in the world. Mitchell was thinking just how beautiful this country could be.

Frank came up top of the APC and sat down beside the turret. "What you thinking about, Sarge?" He asked in a quiet voice.

Mitchell didn't answer right away. He was trying to think of something to say, not wanting to admit his true thoughts for fear that Frank might think of him as soft.

"Oh, I was just thinking about the poker game today."

"Yeah, that was a sweet thing you did to Paul with those three treys."

Mitchell chuckled and then asked, "How much did you win?"

"Oh, about a hundred and ten," Frank answered. "You did pretty good too, didn't you?"

"I won sixty-five bucks. Most of it was on that last hand."

"Yeah, that was a good pot."

They were quiet for a moment, then Frank said. "We did pretty good yesterday, too."

"I guess so," Mitchell answered, "for being scared shitless."

"Yeah, scared, but we kept our shit together. We didn't lose it."

"No, we didn't"

"Good thing not to lose it out here."

"It's a good thing not to lose it anywhere."

Frank grinned, "Amen to that."

They both sat quietly for a moment, listening to the breaking of the waves. Frank leaned back, resting his head on the gun shield. "It's kind of pretty here, isn't it, Sarge?"

Mitchell was surprised hearing that from Frank, it was a side of him he hadn't seen before. Mitchell answered as he was watching the moonlight reflecting off the water, "Yeah, it really is."

CHAPTER EIGHT

On October 7th, Lieutenant Colonel John Sheldon took over as commanding officer of Third Squadron. With the change in command came many other changes in the operations of the squadron and assignments given to it. One of the biggest changes was being reassigned to the 101st Airborne Division. On October 12th, the entire squadron packed up and moved from Joy Beach to its new home at Camp Evans. It was the first time that Mitchell had seen all of Third Squadron together. All of the armored vehicles of A, B, and C Troop, plus all the support tracks were in one huge convoy. They moved southwest from Joy Beach on Highway Nine to Quang Tri and then south on Highway One to Camp Evans. The trip was only twenty-six miles, but took three hours. The large convoy crept along, often stopping because of civilian traffic.

Upon arriving at Camp Evans, the squadron split up, each troop going to its assigned headquarters. All of the troops were in the same general area, the northeast quadrant of the base, but not in sight of each other.

A Troop's headquarters were more elaborate here than what they had before. The headquarters building was a permanent structure, twenty feet by sixty feet, as was the supply building. They were made of wood with glass windows and concrete floors. There also were barrack tents, one for the officers, one for NCOs, and two more for enlisted men; however, only the members of headquarters' platoon would get any use of them.

The parking and staging area for the tracks was a large open dirt field that laid between the headquarters buildings and a large helicopter pad of the 224th Aviation Battalion.

It was 1230 hours when A Troop pulled into its new home and were ordered down. In fact, they were told that they would be here for at least forty-eight hours, so they could take advantage of some of the things the base had to offer.

Camp Evans was a major base, much larger than Joy Beach. There was a brigade of the 101st Airborne Division, along with an Aviation Battalion, an Artillery Battalion, and a full field hospital with a Medivac helicopter company. There was an airstrip large enough to land C130s, a fuel depot and an ammunition supply area.

What the men of A Troop took advantage of was the PX. They stocked up on junk food like cookies, potato chips, and cans of Vienna sausages. Some bought Polaroid cameras and film to take pictures to send home. Others got battery-operated tape recorders to listen to music and record messages for loved ones. There was a lot of money spent that afternoon at the PX.

That evening, A Troop was treated to their first hot meal in over three months, and they poured into the mess hall almost to a man. For the soldiers stationed in the rear area, this meal was nothing special. In fact, it was one of the simpler menus of the week; beef stew served over rice with corn and applesauce on the side. But for the men of A Troop, it was a feast. The atmosphere around A Troop was festive, almost like Thanksgiving or Christmas dinner would have been back home. For Mitchell, the most special item of all was milk, a pint carton of cold, whole milk. He realized how much he had missed drinking it and savored every sip.

After dinner, they scattered in many directions, some going back to their staging area while others went off to discover what the base had to offer. Within a couple of hours, almost all of the men were back at their tracks.

They had discovered an interesting phenomenon, nobody spoke about it specifically, but all had noticed it. The soldiers stationed in the rear areas when off duty seemed to socialize in segregated groups. The whites primarily socialized with other whites, and the blacks with blacks. Much of the racial tension, bigotry, and prejudice that was so much a part of life back home in the States, also seemed to exist here. But it wasn't that way at all with A Troop. Maybe it was because they had to live so close together twenty-four hours a day, or maybe it was because they depended on each other for their lives. Whatever the reason, at least for now they were different and they didn't feel comfortable in that other world.

There was no guard duty or radio watch for A Troop that night. It was a party atmosphere and they were thoroughly enjoying their time off and each other's company. Music could be heard everywhere, all types; rock, motown, country and folk. Guys that had never listened to more than one type of music before, were now being exposed to and learning to appreciate the different styles. For now they were all brothers, brothers in arms.

Later that night, Mitchell and Frank found themselves alone, talking. The mood had become more sober, the conversation more reflective.

"This place is as up tight as the world." Frank said. "The brothers are all hanging out together, white dudes someplace else."

"You picked up on that too?" Mitchell asked.

"Fuckin' hard not to." Frank replied. "Brothers giving me bad ass eye cause I'm walking round with your white ass."

"I guess it's the times we live in." Mitchell said.

"That the way it is where you from out there in the fuckin' wild west?" Frank asked.

"Pretty much, I guess."

"You don't come across that way, seems to me."

"Yeah, well I found out a long time ago that assholes come in all colors."

"A fuckin' men to that."

Mitchell's gaze settled on the huge chopper pad of the 224th Aviation Battalion as he talked. "When Martin Luther King was killed, I was in NCO school at Fort Benning, Georgia. They stopped our training and loaded us up on buses, sent us to Atlanta. Must have been five or six hundred of us. Stuck us in warehouses by the ball park. Gave us M-16's with live ammo and fuckin' bayonets."

"Gonna' use you to beat down the riots if'n they got out of hand." Frank said.

"Either that or they were expecting the NVA to attack Fulton County Stadium."

"NVA attack not likely." Frank said.

Mitchell smiled. "No, not likely, but I remember it scared me almost as much as this place does. The thought of having to draw down on Americans at home in the states; shit, I was sick at my stomach the whole time we were there."

"Do ya think you could've done it, if'n the order came down?"

"Hell, I don't know. I just thank God it didn't come to it."

"A fuckin' men to that, too."

It was 0830 the following morning and Lieutenant Neilley was on his way to a meeting with his C.O., Captain William Tice, commanding officer of A Troop, a man that Lieutenant Neilley had great respect for. As he walked into A Troop's headquarters building, he was greeted by a clerk.

"Good morning, sir."

"Good morning," Neilley replied.

"Captain Tice is expecting you. Right this way." The clerk showed Neilley to an office in the back left corner. He first knocked on the door and then opened it, "Lieutenant Neilley is here, sir."

"Oh, good. Come on in Jeffrey," Captain Tice said with a smile on his face.

Lieutenant Neilley entered the office and the clerk closed the door behind him. Captain Tice was sitting behind a plain metal desk. There was a four drawer file cabinet in the corner and on the wall a large map of I Corps, covering from Hue to the south and the DMZ to the north. In the seven months Neilley had served under Captain Tice, this was the first time he had seen him behind a desk and for good reason. Tice lived in the field alongside the men of A Troop. The smile on his face told Neilley that Captain Tice wasn't taking this rear echelon shit too seriously.

"You look real comfortable behind that desk, sir." Neilley said jokingly.

"You like that do you? I've been thinking of taking this up permanently," Captain Tice said lightheartedly.

The joke was lost on the straight-faced First Lieutenant seated in one of the two wooden chairs in front of the desk.

"Jeffrey, I'd like you to meet Lieutenant John Wise. Lieutenant Wise, this is Lieutenant Jeffrey Neilley, my first platoon leader."

"Glad to meet you, Neilley," Lieutenant Wise said as he stood and shook Neilley's hand.

"Sit down gentlemen so we can get to business," Captain Tice said motioning to the chairs. "Lieutenant Wise is going to help us set up and train a new unit that we are going to form from part of First Platoon."

"What kind of unit?" Neilley questioned.

"Colonel Sheldon wants each troop of the squadron to have a scout section made up of four APCs. It will be used for finding the best routes for the troop to take when moving from one operating area to another. They'll scout and clear areas for night perimeter, before the rest of us move in. Things like that."

"I see," Neilley said glancing at Lieutenant Wise. He was thinking to himself, "Why do we need help in training for that?"

Captain Tice continued, "Also, there is to be a small group picked from the scout section. This group is to specialize in ground operations, reconnaissance patrols, and aggressive ambush activity, and that's where Lieutenant Wise comes in. Lieutenant Wise here is a member of the

94

Special Forces, the 192nd Ranger Battalion, he specializes in this kind of stuff." Captain Tice leaned back in his chair and nodded his head in Lieutenant Wise's direction.

Lieutenant Wise opened a personnel file he had in his hands. "In reviewing A Troop's personnel, Captain Tice and I have come up with a NCO that we think would be a good man to lead the scout section," he said in a matter of fact tone.

"Who are you considering?" Neilley asked.

"Sergeant Robert Mitchell," Wise answered.

Neilley wasn't surprised hearing Mitchell's name, in fact, he couldn't think of anybody better.

Lieutenant Wise continued, "In your September evaluation, Lieutenant Neilley you said of Sergeant Mitchell, ' he performs all duties assigned to him in a professional manner. He shows good leadership ability, he remains calm and in control under combat conditions." Lieutenant Wise looked up from the file at Neilley as if he wanted verification.

"That's correct," Neilley answered. "He's done a good job, especially in a firefight."

Wise looked back down at the file, "You go on to say, Sergeant Mitchell has shown a great ability in navigation, by map coordinates and terrain recognition."

"So..." Captain Tice interrupted looking at Neilley, "do you think he can find his way around?"

"You give him a map, a compass, and grid coordinates, and he will get there," Neilley answered confidently.

Captain Tice nodded his head in approval. He didn't know Mitchell well, but he did have confidence in

Lieutenant Neilley's judgment. He then pointed his hand at Lieutenant Wise, signaling him to continue.

"All his training has been in the infantry, his MOS is 11B40. After NCO School, he was an instructor at the Advanced Infantry School. He went through Airborne Jump School and Ranger training." Lieutenant Wise looked up from the file, "If he knows everything that it says in here, I won't have to teach him much," he said with an air of arrogance. He paused and slowly rubbed his chin, then looked directly at Lieutenant Neilley. "What can you tell me about his attitude? His aggressiveness? His....." Lieutenant Wise was searching for a word.

Neilley interrupted, "Do you mean is he gung ho?" He was beginning not to care for Wise's attitude. "Sergeant Mitchell does his job well, but I don't think he likes it."

"What do you mean he doesn't like it?"

"I mean he doesn't like the war. He doesn't like killing, not many of us do!" Neilley's tone was showing a little irritation.

"Well...," Wise looked back at the file, "I see here he has been credited with seven confirmed kills in the last two months. For someone who doesn't like killing, he seems to be quite proficient at it."

That statement angered Neilley. He had been in the field for seven months and had seen his share of death and killing, and didn't care for the almost obsession with body count that prevailed in Vietnam at this time. Captain Tice sensing the friction building between the two lieutenants, interrupted before Neilley could say anything.

"Okay gentlemen, I think we all agree Sergeant Mitchell is the man for the job. We'll form the unit and assign Mitchell to head it up. Lieutenant Wise, how do you plan to proceed with the training?"

Wise's eyes turned back to the Captain, whose tone of voice made it clear that the verbal jousting between the two young officers was to come to an end.

"Sir, I suggest you have Sergeant Mitchell select his team and then prepare them for an actual mission, an ambush. I will review his preparations and then go with them on the mission."

"What kind of time frame are you looking at here?" Tice asked.

"I have to coordinate the formation of scout units with B Troop and C Troop also, sir. I would estimate four or five days and I can be back for this."

"Let me know twenty-four hours ahead of time. Anything else you need, Lieutenant?"

"No sir." Lieutenant Wise answered in a very military tone.

"Very well, that will be all. You're excused, Lieutenant."

Lieutenant Wise stood up from his chair at attention and saluted. Captain Tice returned the salute, still seated behind his desk. Wise then walked to the door and left the room.

"That guy is just a little too cocky for me." Neilley said after the door had closed.

"Don't be too quick to judge, Jeffrey. He's new in country and just trying to make a good impression. He has a job to do just like the rest of us."

"Yes sir."

"I see some value in this scout plan." Captain Tice got up and moved to the map on the wall. "Our new area of operation is going to put us into a lot rougher terrain. It's not going to be as easy getting around as it was in the sand dunes. Having a route checked out ahead of time could be very helpful." Turning and looking back at Neilley, "Some ambush patrols also might help stop Charlie from lobbing mortar rounds at our night perimeter."

"I agree." Neilley said.

"Well, go give Sergeant Mitchell his new assignment." Neilley got up and headed for the door. "Oh Jeffrey, Mitchell's an E-5, isn't he?"

"Yes sir."

"Squadron says the scout section is to be led by a Staff Sergeant, so if he gets the assignment, he gets the stripe. I'll send the paperwork in today."

"Very well sir, I'll give him the word."

Maggie entered the bank's employee lounge and saw her friend and co-worker, Stephanie, already sitting in a chair with two cold cans of Coke on the table beside her.

"Maggie, I have a Coke already for you." Stephanie said, motioning her to sit down.

"Thanks, Stephanie. I could use one." Maggie said as she sat down and took a sip.

"No problem. You look a little tired and anyway, it was my turn to buy." Stephanie was five years older than Maggie and had become like a big sister to her. "Did you see the doctor yesterday?"

"Yes. He said the baby's doing fine and my due date is December 15th. I only wish Bobby could have been with me. I got to hear the baby's heartbeat."

Stephanie could see that faraway look Maggie got when she started thinking about Bobby. "Why don't we go out to dinner and catch a movie after work? You don't need to be sitting at home and worrying about Bobby all the time."

"I don't." Maggie knew she couldn't fool Stephanie, so she added with a smile, "At least not all the time." She took another sip of the Coke. "Okay, I'll go. A movie sounds fun and I'm always hungry," patting her swollen stomach. "But first, I need to stop at the store and pick up some items for my Halloween care package for Bobby. I want to mail it tomorrow."

"A Halloween care package?" Stephanie looked inquisitively.

"Yeah. I send Bobby a package about once a month, full of goodies like juices, cookies, nuts, candies, and things that are easy to cook, like soups and chili." Maggie's eyes were twinkling. "And anything else I think he would like or he asks me to send. The guys over there call them care packages. Bobby says a lot of guys receives them from their families."

"It sounds like you enjoy getting that together."

"I do." Maggie beamed with pride. "It's not a lot, but it makes me feel good and I know Bobby and the guys on his track really appreciate them."

"Well, my break's almost over," Stephanie said getting up from the chair. "I'll pick you up at your house around six o'clock and we can take my car."

"Great, that will give me enough time. Thanks for asking me."

"What are friends for." Stephanie said closing the door and leaving Maggie alone in the room.

Maggie started thinking of something special for this Halloween package. She decided to send Bobby and the guys on his track some Halloween candy and decorations. The thought of Bobby riding around Vietnam with a ghost in his track made her giggle to herself. Glancing up at the clock, she noticed her break was over, but she didn't feel tired anymore and was looking forward to this evening.

The rest of the afternoon went by fast and before Maggie knew, it was three o'clock. As she was leaving, she stopped by Mr. Gray's office. "Good night, Mr. Gray."

"Have a nice evening, Margaret." Mr. Gray answered. This had become a ritual with them. The only time they would talk longer was when Maggie would step into his office and tell him of a letter she had received from Bobby.

Walking out the front door, Maggie noticed a group of anti-war demonstrators across the street in front of the Navy Recruiting Office. She stopped and stared for a moment, trying to read a sign that caught her attention. She didn't like the idea of war, but she was proud of Bobby being a soldier and knew that serving his country was equally important to him.

Suddenly someone yelled out, "That woman there. Her husband is one of the baby killers!" The mass of protesters ran across the street toward Maggie, causing one of the cars driving by to stop, screeching its brakes. The long-haired boy who had yelled out, Maggie recognized as Pete Trout from high school. The crowd surrounded her immediately and Pete pointed a finger at Maggie's stomach, trying to intimidate her. "How would you like it if someone killed your baby?"

Another voice in the crowd angrily added, "What gives you the right to have a baby, when its father is a baby killer?"

Maggie's eyes were wide in terror, her lips trembling. She was afraid that this mob was going to hurt her and her baby.

The screeching of the tires had caused Mr. Gray to look out the window. He didn't see Maggie, but saw the group of protesters run across the street. He stepped closer to the window to make sure no one had been hit by a car. The protesters were surrounding someone. Mr. Gray left his office and ordered a guard to follow him outside. As he opened the bank's front door, he heard the crowd harassing someone. He then spotted Maggie crying and begging the mob to leave her alone. He turned to the guard and said, "Thomas, call the police."

"You, you hoodlums, leave her alone! Get away from here now!" He yelled as he pushed his way through the crowd.

A voice shouted back at him, "What's with you old man, you on her side? You must be a war monger, too."

"I'm warning you, get out of here! I've called the police." Mr. Gray said as he forced his way to Maggie's side.

In the distance sirens could be heard and the crowd started scattering. Some dropped their signs on the sidewalk.

Mr. Gray walked Maggie back to the bank with an arm over her shoulders. The guard, Thomas opened the door for them. "What did you tell the police?" Mr. Gray asked.

Thomas smiled, "I only said there was an emergency at the bank."

"Margaret, are you all right?" Mr. Gray focused his attention back on her.

"Yes, sir. They just scared me. I'm okay." Maggie was drying her tears with the handkerchief Mr. Gray had offered.

"Would you like to rest for a while?"

"No, I just want to go home."

"I'll have Thomas walk you to your car. Monday I'll assign you a parking space out back. You don't need to be hassled by those...." he paused, his voice showing disdain, "protesters."

Mr. Gray motioned to Thomas to come over to where they were standing. His voice had changed back to the soft, but firm voice that she was used to. "Thomas, would you please escort Margaret to her car." Looking back at Maggie, "When you come in Monday, park in my space out back. We'll arrange a permanent space for you then. Take care of yourself and I'll see you Monday." He turned and walked away towards his office.

"Ma'am, let me know when you're ready." Thomas spoke in a soft and gentle voice.

Maggie looked up with tears still in her eyes, "I'd like to go home now, Thomas." They walked in silence to her car. As she opened the door she said, "Thank you, Thomas."

"My pleasure, Ma'am. Drive careful."

Maggie could see in her rear view mirror Thomas standing there watching her drive away. She was shaking and by the time she got home, she was crying again. She ran into the house, glad that today was her mother's Bridge day and she didn't have to talk about what had happened. Letting her purse drop to the floor, she fell upon her bed crying.

Maggie woke up to the sound of the doorbell. The last thing she remembered was clutching her pillow, crying. The doorbell rang again. She looked at the clock. It was ten after six. She hurried to the door and opened it just as Stephanie was pressing the buzzer another time.

"I'm sorry, Stephanie. I had fallen asleep." Maggie was trying to smooth out her dress.

"Is everything okay?" Stephanie could see Maggie's eyes were puffy and red.

"Yes. No, not really. I mean everything is okay, it's just that I got scared at work today."

"What happened?"

"Come in and I'll tell you about it." Maggie opened the door wider and gestured for Stephanie to step inside. Closing the door behind them, Maggie looked down at her hand and let out a short chuckle.

"What's funny?" Stephanie asked as she sat down. She was confused and wished that she hadn't left work early and missed whatever had happened.

"I just noticed I still have Mr. Gray's handkerchief. I'll need to wash and press it so I can give it back to him on Monday." Maggie opened her hand, showing the tear stained handkerchief as she sat down.

Stephanie looked puzzled. "What the hell happened?"

"As I was leaving the bank, I noticed some anti-war demonstrators across the street. All of a sudden they started running towards me and yelling at me." The tears began to well up in her eyes. "One was a boy that Bobby and I went to school with. He said, 'How would you like it if someone killed your baby?" Maggie was holding her stomach. "Another person yelled, 'What gives you the right to have a baby, when its father is a baby killer?" With that, Maggie started sobbing, rocking back and forth on the couch, wrapping her arms over her stomach.

Stephanie came over and sat down beside her, putting her arms around Maggie, as a tear rolled down her cheek. "Maggie, no one is going to hurt you and your baby."

"I know, it's just..." Maggie let out a sniffle, "Bobby's not a baby killer. They had no right to say that. Pete knows Bobby. Why did he say that?"

"Who's Pete?"

"The boy that..." Maggie didn't finish. She began crying on Stephanie' shoulder.

"They're just a bunch of jerks. Of course, Bobby's not a baby killer. Those jerks just like to attack anyone or anything associated with the war. I'll just come by and pick you up for work and that way we'll leave together. I bet they won't bother the two of us."

Maggie raised her head and started drying her eyes. "Thanks, but I'll be all right. Mr. Gray is giving me a parking space out back." She then told Stephanie about Mr. Gray coming to her rescue.

"Hey, let's forget about those idiots," Stephanie said. "Why don't you wash your face and change your clothes. We can still catch the late movie after dinner."

"I am hungry, but I never did get my shopping done." Maggie replied.

"Well, let's get some dinner and we'll go shopping together and you can tell me more about Bobby and those care packages."

CHAPTER NINE

It had been nine days since Mitchell was put in charge of the scout section, which Captain Tice had designated as Tracks One-One, One-Two, One-Three, and One-Four. In that time, Mitchell had led three ambush patrols, the first one was with Lieutenant Wise and the other two on his own.

All seventeen men of the scout section volunteered to be part of the ground team. On the first three ambushes, he utilized and evaluated all seventeen men in different combinations and settled on the six that along with himself would make up the seven man team. He made his decision on the training and aptitude that each man had shown for ground activities and made sure to take no more than two men off of any one track. He also decided to have another NCO to be part of the team and be second in command. Mitchell selected Sergeant Brian Banks, the TC of One-Three, because he felt that Brian made good decisions under pressure and was respected by the other men. The other five men selected were Paul Bonds, off of One-Two, Frankie Sanchez from One-Three, Michael Davis and Keith Dixon off of One-Four, and of course, Frank, Mitchell's driver on One-One. Mitchell and Frank had developed a close friendship over the past two months. The two of them seemed to anticipate each other's moves, which made them a very effective team.

A Troop was operating in an area twelve klicks south of Camp Evans, along the Song Bo River, near the

village of Ap Thanh Tan. There had been a considerable
amount of enemy activity in this area over the past two
months, including night terrorist attacks on the village.
With this in mind, it was decided to set up an ambush near
the village in hope of intercepting the enemy that were
engaging in these attacks.

Earlier in the day while scouting for a good location
to have the troop set up its night perimeter, Mitchell came
across some small foot trails leading into the village from
the southwest. One trail in particular showed signs of
recent use and at one point had a sharp turn in the trail with
good cover along its side. It was perfect for an ambush and
Mitchell decided that this would be the place he would use.
It was located one thousand meters southwest of the
village. The map grid coordinates of the ambush site had to
be precise to enable the mortar tracks to provide fire
support to the team if something went wrong. The exact
map coordinates were HX408285.

The entire land area of Vietnam was covered by
topographic maps used by the military. Added to these
battle maps were man-made features such as roads, bridges,
and villages. The entire map was divided by grid lines
using the Universal Transverse Macerator Grid forming
squares, each representing an area of one thousand meters
by one thousand meters. These grid lines were numbered
along the longitude and latitude. To locate any given point
on the map, one would read the coordinates west to east
then south to north.

Mitchell, Captain Tice, and Sergeant Tom Kelly,
the TC of the mortar track One-Zero, were huddled
together reviewing a map of the area. "The ambush site is

going to be here at coordinates 408285..." Mitchell pointed at the map, "...and the staging area will be at coordinates 402278."

"Okay Kelly," Captain Tice directed, "I want you to calculate illumination on both sites and fire cover starting one hundred and fifty meters out from both sites."

"No problem, sir. We'll have them covered in all directions."

"Good. Is your team ready to go?"

"Just about." Mitchell answered. "I'm going to give them a final briefing and equipment check. We'll be moving out at 1900 hours."

"All right then, good luck and I'll see you in the morning."

"Thank you, sir."

Mitchell returned back to where One-One and One-Two were parked on the perimeter. The tracks were spaced twenty-five to thirty meters apart, forming a large circle with the command track, the three mortar tracks, and the medic track in the center of the perimeter. On nights that the ambush team went out, One-One and One-Two would park side by side and act as one unit. The same was true of One-Three and One-Four.

The members of the team were waiting for Mitchell's return. They were standing around Spec 4 Keith Dixon who was entertaining them by telling a joke.

"There were these two hippies who decided to go into the country on a walk to get closer to nature," Keith began. He didn't like hippies and often made them the butt of his jokes. "And so they were walking along when one of them saw some tracks on the ground. 'Look here man,' he said to the other hippie, 'these are some awesome deer tracks.' 'No,' the other hippie said, 'I think they're rabbit tracks.' 'No, I think you're wrong. I'm sure they're deer tracks.' 'No man, rabbit tracks.' The second hippie said, 'I'm sure of it.' And they were still arguing when the train hit them."

They all laughed except Sanchez. "Shit Taco, don't you get it?" Frank said teasingly. "They were standing on a fuckin' railroad track. It wasn't deer or rabbit tracks. It was a railroad track."

Now they were laughing at Sanchez. "Shit man, that's dumb." Sanchez said, a little embarrassed by not getting the joke.

"I wouldn't talk too much about dumb if I were you," Keith added.

Mitchell interrupted, "Listen up, we have to get ready." Gathering the men around him, he passed out the patrol's radio frequency. "Our call sign is going to be Rightfield and command is Homeplate. Mike, set the radio on the patrol frequency."

PFC Michael Davis was to be Mitchell's RTO (radio-telephone operator) and carry the PRC-25 radio. He also would be armed with an M-16 rifle. All the others were armed with an M-16 and carried eight magazines of ammunition, except for Keith. He carried an M-79 grenade launcher and a .45 caliber pistol. In addition to three extra pistol magazines, he packed thirty-two high explosive rounds and twelve canister rounds. The canister round was filled with hundreds of small pellets, effectively turning the M-79 into a very large shotgun. Mitchell elected not to include an M-60 machine gun. He believed the patrol had

109

ample fire power and didn't need to be burdened by the strain on mobility that a machine gun would impose. He decided to take along four claymore mines, enough to cover sixty meters of the trail, the area of the ambush killing zone. The killing zone is the area in which you hope to catch all the enemy personnel inside of at the same time. If all goes right, you should be able to kill everyone inside the zone within eight seconds. If not and it takes longer than eight seconds, the members of the ambush team become endangered of being casualties themselves. Mitchell packed one of the claymores and the other three were carried by Frank, Sanchez, and Brian. Each man except for Mike and Keith would take along two hand grenades. Mitchell was taking the only map and compass. He also carried a starlight telescope, a night detection devise. Brian packed three star cluster signaling flares. They only would be used if the patrol lost use of its radio and needed the troop to come to its rescue.

Each man carried a canteen of water, but no food would be taken and especially no cigarettes. They all were wearing 'boonie hats', full brimmed, round, floppy, soft hats, replacing the normal steel helmets. Mitchell felt that the lack of protection the helmets provided was outweighed by the decreased chance of noise. A tree branch hitting on the steel helmets caused a level of noise that was unacceptable. Being able to move through the jungle as quietly as possible was a must. Each man had around his neck a towel for suppressing coughs and sneezes. Mitchell checked each man to make sure he had nothing in his pockets that might make noise. He had them tape their dog tags together with electrical tape, so they wouldn't jingle.

Using a sketch, he showed each man where his position would be and explained what he was to do.

It was 1900 hours and the ambush team was ready. It would be daylight for about forty-five more minutes, enough time for the patrol to travel on foot to the staging area eighteen hundred meters away. Mitchell shot an azimuth with his compass and they struck out almost due east.

Although no contact had been made on the first three ambushes, Mitchell had stressed to his team to always expect someone to walk into their trap each time out. After dark in Vietnam, all civilian movement stopped. They stayed inside their huts and waited until sunrise, when once again it was safe to go out. Anybody moving through the jungle at night was the enemy.

Mitchell took the point and led the patrol. Mike followed with the radio, then Frank, Brian, Sanchez, Keith, and Paul bringing up the rear of the column. They were in single file eight meters apart. The staging area was an old bomb crater where they would set up, providing them with good cover. The plan was to stay at the staging area about an hour, until it had become completely dark. The team would then travel the last eight hundred meters and slip into the ambush site. Arriving at the bomb crater, they spread out taking up positions along the ridge of the crater's circular perimeter.

Mitchell moved over beside Mike, "Let me have the handset." Mike complied.

Mitchell then keyed the handset, "Homeplate, this is Rightfield, over." He waited ten seconds for a response, not getting one he keyed the handset again. "Homeplate, this is Rightfield, over."

"Rightfield, this is Homeplate, over."

"Homeplate, how do you read me? Over."

"Lima Charlie, Rightfield, over."

"Roger Homeplate. We are at our Sierra Alpha. Will contact you again when ready to move, over."

"Roger Rightfield, out."

Mitchell gave the handset back to Mike. It was 1935 hours and beginning to get dark. "Okay, keep your eyes open everybody. We'll be here for an hour or so." Mitchell instructed the team.

By 2015 hours, night had completely fallen and the men's eyes had adjusted to the darkness. The temperature had dropped to eighty degrees and a gentle breeze could be felt. Mitchell would give it a few more minutes and then they would move.

"Okay, everybody get ready to move," Mitchell said quietly.

He then once again took the radio handset from Mike. "Homeplate, this is Rightfield, over."

"This is Homeplate, over."

"This is Rightfield. We'll be moving from Sierra Alpha to target in two minutes, over."

"Roger Rightfield. You're moving in two minutes. Good hunting, over."

"This is Rightfield, roger, out."

At 2030 hours the patrol set out on the last eight hundred meters they had to cover to get to the ambush site. Mitchell using his compass once again shot an azimuth this time to the northeast. If his navigation skills were good and they were, it would take them directly to the designated site. The going was slower at night than it was during the daylight. They had to be as quiet as possible and stay ever aware of their surroundings, so not to fall victim to an ambush themselves. They needed to stay spread out but not so far that they would lose sight of the man in front of them. Mitchell stopped four times, rechecking directions with his compass. It took over half an hour to cover that last eight hundred meters.

It was 2115 hours when they came to the foot trail. Mitchell thought the sharp bend in the trail, the exact site for the ambush, was a little ways to the left. The patrol closed up and waited while Mitchell headed down the foot trail in search of the site. He was correct. He had gone less than fifty meters when he came to the sharp bend. "Not bad," he thought to himself. "I just missed it by a few meters."

Mitchell quickly returned back to his team, who were kneeling down in the tall grass and broad-leafed bushes alongside the trail. Each man had been shown on the sketch before leaving on the patrol, where his position would be; but Mitchell reviewed again with each man his position as he sent them, one by one down the trail.

"Frank, the sharp turn in the trail is about fifty meters this way." Mitchell pointed, speaking barely above a whisper. "You go around the turn and up the trail twenty meters."

"Right, Sarge."

"Okay, go." Mitchell said, tapping Frank on his shoulder. Frank was to be the left flank of the killing zone.

"Mike, you set up twenty-five feet this side of Frank."

"I got it," Mike answered in a whisper.

"Go!" Mitchell tapped him on top of his head.

"Keith, you're this side of the turn. I'll be between you and Mike." Keith nodded his head and started down the trail.

"Sanchez, you're next. Twenty-five feet this side of Keith. Then Brian, you go, same spacing. Paul you're our right flank. Okay guys, go!" Each man moved out to get into position. The foot trail varied in width, three to five feet, cutting through the semi-thick jungle of low trees, vines, brambles, and elephant grass. At the ambush site the ground on the south side of the trail sloped gently down. The difference in elevation between where Mitchell chose to place his team along the south side of the trail and the trail itself was only two to three feet, but it could make a big difference. If after the ambush had been triggered and some of their prey were able to return fire, it would likely be without a definite target in sight. Most of the time this type of fire is directional and aimed on a flat plane, which would cause the bullets to go slightly over their heads. Paying attention to these kinds of details is what gave the men of the scout section so much confidence in Mitchell's ability to lead.

Each man settled into his designated position, offering him good concealment and some degree of protection. They were fifteen to twenty feet from the trail. The claymore mines had been placed in the tall grass five to ten feet off the trail. It was 2120 hours and everything was set, nothing to do now but wait.

Mitchell signaled Mike to contact Homeplate to let them know that the patrol was in position. From this time on, no voice communications were used, a prearranged signal took its place. Mike keyed the handset and broke squelch twice, letting Homeplate know that all was well. Homeplate then acknowledged by doing the same. Then on the hour the same procedure would be used each hour until the mission was over.

Mitchell placed himself at the bend in the trail, giving him a good line of sight down the trail in both directions. Being in this position was absolutely essential if he was to control the ambush. Only if they were discovered, would any other member of the team open fire first. Otherwise, the decision when and if to trigger the ambush was Mitchell's alone.

The sky was partly cloudy with a three-quarter moon, providing just average visibility. Mitchell removed the protective cover caps from the eye piece and front lens of the starlight scope. It was similar in appearance to a regular telescopic rifle sight, but three times as large. Using it would give him a clear observation up to five hundred meters even on the darkest night. He pushed the power switch into the on position, activating the device. He raised the scope to his eye and peered through it, scanning the trail in both directions. It took some getting used to the eerie green images, but with a little practice, it provided the user with a view as luminous as day. The trail was clear, so he switched the scope off to conserve the batteries.

Mitchell became keenly aware of the silence that surrounded him. He could hear every breath he took and the slightest movement of his arms or legs seemed to be magnified out of proportion. It was just his nervousness getting to him and he knew it, but there was precious little he could do to change it.

Frank was lying in the prone position. His eyes scanning back and forth on the trail in front of him. He had been out with Mitchell twice before, but this time seemed different. It was nothing he could put his finger on, just a feeling. He too was nervous and it had caused his mouth to become dry. He leaned onto his side and reached for the canteen on his belt. Opening the canteen, he took two large sips of water. It had a bad taste because of the purification process but at least it was wet and that was what he needed. He didn't replace the canteen to his belt but instead placed it on the ground beside him, thinking he would need it again.

At 2200 hours Homeplate transmitted the prearranged signal. Mike had the handset close to his ear. The squelch made him jerk. He, like all the others, was on edge and the unexpected sound startled him. He reached for the handset and pressed the transmitter button twice, returning the signal.

It was human nature to be nervous when out on a mission like this one and that was good. It kept them on their toes, but after being in position for a few hours, complacency began to creep in and they would lose some of their focus. Because of that, Mitchell planned to remain in the ambush for a maximum of four hours. If no contact was made by then, the team would pull out and spend the rest of the night at the staging area. But tonight this was going to be a moot point, because at 2225 hours, Mitchell spotted a group of NVA soldiers and some VC supports moving up the trail from the east.

Their outlines were sharp and clear in the green tint of the starlight scope. He could even see the weapons in their hands. At the first site of them, Mitchell felt his stomach sink. The feeling much like you might have if you descended quickly in an elevator or made a sudden drop from the top of a roller coaster. But then all the training that was drilled into him at NCO and Ranger School kicked in and he began making decisions almost as if he was on auto-pilot.

He lowered the scope and turned his head to look at Keith some twenty-five feet to his right. All the members of the team had been trained to look at the man in position on either side of them several times each minute, in case hand signal communications were needed to be passed along. It was four or five seconds before Keith turned to look at Mitchell. Mitchell raised his right arm and formed his hand into a closed fist. This was the signal that he had seen something. He then opened up his index finger and pointed down the trail, telling Keith the direction. Keith then turned to pass the signal on down the line. Mitchell looked to his left and saw that Mike was already looking at him, so he repeated the same gesture. Using this technique, every man was silently alerted within thirty seconds.

Paul was positioned on the right flank and was the first man the unsuspecting enemy would pass. He heard them before he could see them. He could hear the faint sound of voices and some laughter but still couldn't see anything. Then out of the darkness, he saw the first fuzzy figures appear. They were casually walking along, totally unaware of the deadly trap awaiting them. In fact, they seemed unconcerned about any danger at all. Paul's first thoughts were, "Oh God, please don't let them see me. Please, please don't let them see me." He flipped the selector switch on his M-16 from safety to full automatic. The sound of the switch couldn't have been heard more than a foot away, but in Paul's mind it sounded like he had just banged two iron pipes together. "Please God, don't let them hear me," he thought.

Now the lead gook of the column was directly in front of Brian. His nervousness had caused the palms of his hands to become wet with sweat. His heart was beating so fast he thought it was going to explode inside his chest. He was barely fifteen feet away from armed enemy soldiers. This was a first and he was scared.

Mike reached to turn the power switch on the PRC-25 radio to the off position. He didn't want there to be any chance of a transmission, planned or otherwise, to come over the radio now. He and Frank were around the bend in the trail and still couldn't see the gooks. They were getting anxious, especially Frank.

"How many are there?" Frank thought. "Where the fuck are they? Oh shit, don't fuck up now." He was holding his M-16 by the pistol grip in his right hand and the claymore mine detonator in his left, waiting for what was to come.

Keith was a powerful, young man, an avid weight lifter before getting drafted and he had the physique to prove it. His biceps bulging out from the rolled up sleeves of his fatigues. He had a squeezing hold on the M-79 in his hand, causing the muscles of his arms to be flexed and taut.

He had lost an uncle to the war in 1967, a young man that was more like a big brother because of their relationship and the closeness of their ages. As he stared at the enemy soldiers passing in front of him, he thought of his dead uncle. "It's payback time motherfuckers, payback time!"

The lead soldier was now around the turn and only a few meters from Frank and the left flank of the killing zone. Mitchell followed their every move all the way. His mind was racing a hundred miles an hour. He counted eleven of them. The last man in the column was now inside the zone. Mitchell stared down the trail behind the last man. The trail was empty, nothing as far as he could see. The lead man was getting closer and closer to Frank's position. "They're all in the zone," Mitchell thought. "They're all in the zone. If I'm going to do it, it's gotta be now. It's gotta be now."

The claymore exploded in a ball of orange flame and boiling cloud of black smoke. Mitchell had detonated the mine without consciously knowing it, and in the next second, all the other claymores were detonated. The ambush had now been sprung. The blast of the first claymore instantly killed two of the NVA soldiers. One took the full brunt of the explosion, dismembering him and throwing his body parts into the vegetation on the other side of the trail. The second was hit in the head by a few shrapnel pellets, penetrating his brain. He was dead before he hit the ground.

Frank squeezed down so hard on his detonator that it broke the return spring, but the mine exploded. The blast ripped the legs off the point man of the column, killing him. When the black smoke cleared, Frank could see the number two man in line. He had been hit by shrapnel and had fallen to his knees and was struggling to get back to his feet. Frank took aim with his M-16 and fired off a burst. Three of the rounds hit their target, the chest of the young soldier. He crumpled to the ground dead.

At the instant the ambush was triggered, Mike had the third enemy soldier of the column lined up in his sights. He pulled back on and held the trigger of his M-16, firing a continuous burst until the magazine was empty, riddling the enemy soldier's body with a dozen rounds.

One of the VC that saw two of his buddies blown away in front of him turned to run. He had an AK-47 in his hands but wasn't firing. In the confusion of the hell he found himself in, instead of running away from the ambush, he turned and was running straight into it. Keith swung the muzzle of his M-79 into the direction of the oncoming gook. It was loaded with a canister round. Keith pulled the trigger. The blast caught the gook in his right thigh and hip, spinning him around ninety degrees, knocking him off his feet, causing the VC to fall face down in the grass. Keith quickly broke down his M-79, ejecting the spent round. He slammed another canister round into the weapon and closed it up. He looked up and saw his foe, who had landed just six feet in front of him, raising up onto his hands and one knee, dragging the injured leg behind him. He was reaching for the AK-47 that had fallen a few feet from him. Keith aimed the M-79 and fired. This time the blast hit the gook behind his left ear, exploding the back of his head into a bloody mass of skull fragments and pinkish gray brain tissue.

A split second before Sanchez detonated his claymore, one of the enemy soldiers had stopped and turned, looking straight at him. He didn't know if he had been spotted or not, but it didn't matter. After the explosion, the soldier disappeared and not having a specific target, Sanchez began to spray the trail with his M-16.

The last two soldiers at the rear of the column died when Brian exploded his claymore. The two in front of them were mowed down by M-16 fire from both Brian and Paul.

The ambush took only ten seconds. All eleven of the enemy were down and none of them had fired a shot. Those ten seconds had been a deluge of exploding claymore mines and automatic weapons fire, creating a gauntlet of deadly lead. For those in its path, it had been sudden, terrifying and lethal.

The firing stopped and Mitchell was scanning up and down the trail, looking for any movement, listening for any sound. "Anyone hit?" Mitchell shouted out. No one responded. The men found themselves discomposed. In this setting, the violence was very close and personal, something new for everyone involved, and it had left them all quite shaken.

"Paul!" Mitchell shouted.

"Yeah Sarge," Paul replied.

"Take up a position on the trail. Give us security on the right flank."

"Right!" Paul shouted back.

"Frank!"

"Yo!"

"You do the same on the left flank."

"Okay Sarge," Frank answered.

Mitchell was giving out orders instinctively from all the training that had been drilled into him. "Mike, call in and let them know everything is okay. Tell them we'll call back with a complete report in a few minutes."

Mike keyed the handset, "Homeplate, this is Rightfield, over." There was no response. "Homeplate, this is Rightfield, over!" Still there was no response. He keyed the handset for a third time with the same results and was just about to panic when he remembered that he had turned the radio off. Flipping the power switch back on, he completed his message to command.

In the meantime, Mitchell, along with Keith, Sanchez, and Brian, moved onto the trail to search the bodies and police the area. Mitchell instructed the others to be very careful, if any of the bodies moved at all, even a twitch, to shoot them before getting any closer. Keith started with the Vietcong that he had killed just a few feet in front of his position. He retrieved the AK-47 and three full magazines of ammunition off the dead body. He was going through the pockets looking for any papers and documents. The satisfaction that he thought he would feel didn't materialize. His uncle was still dead and nothing would change that. In fact, the only thing that had changed was this young Vietnamese soldier with half of his head blown away would never see his family again and perhaps, Keith himself had changed. "There is no payback." Keith thought.

Mitchell was on his knees, removing a web belt from one of the NVA when he heard Sanchez call out.

"This one's movin'!"

"Shoot him!" Mitchell shouted.

Sanchez looked at Mitchell, scared and hesitant.

"God damn it, Sanchez, shoot him!" Mitchell screamed as he was getting to his feet.

Sanchez looked back at the enemy soldier, who now was leaning on his side, reaching into a canvas bag on his belt. Before Sanchez could react, a burst of automatic weapon fire erupted. He saw the red tracer rounds flash across in front of him and bury into the body of the wounded enemy. Brian sewed a thread of lead into the gook's chest, whose facial expression changed from fear and panic, to pain and then death. He rolled over onto his back, an American M-26 fragmentation hand grenade dropped from his hand, luckily he had not had time to pull the pin.

"I'm sorry Sarge," Sanchez started apologizing as Mitchell approached him. "I don't know what I was thinking. I...I didn't see the gre..grenade."

"Neither did I," Mitchell answered. "I know it's hard, but in this situation you can't wait to see if there's any danger, you just can't take that chance."

"I know Sarge, I just....." Sanchez couldn't think of what to say. He was upset about making a mistake and seeing the grenade had almost put him in a panic. Fear gripped him to the point that his chest felt tight, he was short of breath.

"It's okay man. We're all just trying to get by. Just remember, all it's about is getting home. Just getting home. You can't give them a fuckin' chance cause they won't give you one. We have to do whatever it takes." Mitchell realized he was talking to himself as well as Sanchez. It was hard being hard, but he couldn't think of any other way. Putting a hand on Sanchez's shoulder, he emphasized, "Just getting home, man; that's what it's about!"

"Okay, Sarge," Sanchez's voice revealed he was still regretting his mistake.

"Don't worry about it. Let's get this mess cleaned up and get the hell out of here."

The men went back to work, searching and policing the ambush site. They dragged the bodies off the trail, placing them all together. They gathered the enemy's weapons and ammunition and carried it with them as they made their way back to the staging area.

It was 2315 hours when they reached the old bomb crater where they spent the remainder of the night. Nobody got much sleep, they were all too keyed up. They spent the time telling each other their individual experiences and silently reflecting on what had happened.

Shortly after sun up, Lieutenant Neilley and the First Platoon arrived at the staging area to pick them up. The whole platoon then returned to the ambush site to do another search. Now having the benefit of daylight, two more weapons were found and more documents were recovered from the bodies. The ambush had been an overwhelming success, a text book example of how an ambush should work. No doubt this was due in part to the preparation and planning that Mitchell put into the mission. But an even larger contributing factor was the complacency of the enemy. Their own casual and indifferent attitude surely lead to their deaths. A scenario that was played out over and over again on both sides throughout the war.

The final count of the action tallied eleven enemy dead; weapons recovered were:

        Seven - AK-47s

        Two   - 7.62mm SKS Carbines

        One   - Type 56 Chinese Assault Rifle

        One   - American .45 Pistol

        Three - American Hand Grenades

        Five   - Chinese Hand Grenades

                Over seven hundred rounds of ammunition and one U.S. Army canteen, three quarters filled with water. It was Frank's, he had forgotten it in all the confusion.

CHAPTER TEN

Mitchell was in the turret of One-One, the lead APC in A Troop's column rolling south on Highway One. He was sitting on a 2x6 board placed across the hatch hole and was leaning back on the hatch cover. His flak jacket hung over the metal cover providing some cushion. His right leg was propped up on the gun shield of the fifty caliber and he held the butterfly trigger with one hand. He was wearing sunglasses, partly to shade his eyes from the glaring afternoon sun, but mostly to protect them from the dust that was being kicked up by the oncoming traffic. Heavy military trucks loaded down with supplies were rumbling along the dry, dirt road. Thick clouds of dust from the passing vehicles swirled up and lingered in the roadway for lack of a breeze to blow them away. Mixed in with the military trucks were some civilian traffic, mostly Vespas scooters and three-wheeled lorries. Every once in a while an old beat up bus, overloaded with passengers, passed by.

Dave was driving and wearing the only pair of goggles that One-One had. Mitchell would let Dave experience driving in situations like this when there was very little chance of seeing any action.

Frank was manning the right side fifty caliber. He had a towel over his nose and mouth trying to stop the dust from clogging his nostrils and drying out his throat. He wore a floppy boonie hat, pulled down low, close to his dust-filled eyebrows. He was squinting, peering from behind the towel and brim of the hat, looking a little like a grungy Lawrence of Arabia. Frank was watching Country, who had fashioned a sign out of an empty C-ration case and was flashing it to the oncoming trucks. "USA OR BUST" was written in black camouflage stick on the cardboard. The Americans passing in the opposite direction would flash the peace sign and some would yell out encouragements like, "You got it man!" or "Right on!" Country would return the peace sign along with his big smile.

A Troop had been operating northwest of Camp Evans for the last two weeks. They had left the Song Bo River area shortly after the successful ambush that Mitchell and his team had pulled off near Ap Thanh Tan. But now they were ordered back. When A Troop moved out, the NVA returned. Intelligent reports along with recent enemy activity led Division Command to suspect an attack on the Song Bo Bridge was in the works. In fact, there had been two rocket and mortar attacks in the past five nights.

The compound guarding the bridge was manned by a unit of the ARVN (Army of Republic of Vietnam), a force of about one hundred men. If the NVA could take out the bridge, it would make it much harder to move supplies along Highway One. So A Troop was ordered to take over security of the bridge and relieve the ARVNs.

The compound's perimeter was roughly square shaped, each side three hundred and fifty meters long. It was made up of thirty sandbag bunkers with rolls of looped concertina wire running along the entire perimeter, approximately one hundred feet in front of the bunkers. The river ran through it from the west to the east and Highway One from north to south, placing the bridge in the center of the compound. The steel truss bridge was two hundred and fifty feet long and spanned the Song Bo at one of its narrowest points. The banks were steep and the water deep and swift.

The compound also housed a portable water purification plant, which provided all the drinking water for Camp Evans and many of the surrounding fire bases. It was operated by a unit of twenty Army Engineers.

First Platoon was assigned the southwest quadrant of the perimeter, and One-One took up the first position next to the river. It was 1600 hours when Dave shut off the engine and dropped the rear lift gate. He removed his CVC helmet and came climbing out of the driver's hole. When he removed the goggles, it left a pattern on his face that was covered by dust everywhere, except around the eyes and the bridge of his nose. Mitchell teased him about looking like a raccoon.

Frank got the five gallon water can out of the APC. He and Country began washing the dust off their faces and out of their hair. Mitchell and Dave jumped down from the top and joined them.

"First thing we need to do guys, is get the guns cleaned." Mitchell was toweling off his hair while he was talking. "Frank, either you or Dave clean the fifty caliber while the other pulls maintenance on the track."

"Which one do ya want, surfer?" Frank asked.

"I don't care."

"Okay, I'll clean the fifty." If given a choice, Frank would always choose not to do the maintenance.

"Country, you and Frank get going on your guns. I'll do mine when you're finished." Mitchell never had all three machine guns broke down for cleaning at the same time. They never knew when they might need some fire power, so this was the SOP that he used. While Frank and Country cleaned their machine guns, Mitchell cleaned his personal M-16 and the Thumper.

Inside each individual meal box of C-rations was a small accessory pack sealed in brown foil. It contained a plastic spoon, a packet of instant coffee, sugar, salt, chewing gum, and most important of all was a one-time use pack of toilet paper. Many of the items would be thrown away if not used immediately, but not the toilet paper. The crew of One-One had a special ammo box just for the T.P. Every time anyone opened a box of C's, they would save the toilet paper and place it in the box.

Frank was digging around inside the APC looking for something. After a minute or so, he called out to Country, who was on top, "Where's the fuckin' shit paper?"

"The last time I saw it, it was behind the driver's seat," Country answered.

"Well, it's not there now. Dave!" Frank continued, "Have you seen the T.P.?"

"No dude, I thought it was behind the driver's seat."

"I've looked, it's not there." Frank was now mumbling to himself. "How am I suppos'ta take a shit with no fuckin' toilet paper?"

"Oh hell Frank, just use your finger," Country joked, looking over at Mitchell with a grin on his face. Mitchell just raised an eyebrow, knowing it wasn't a good idea for Country to get into a ragging contest with Frank, but it never seemed to stop him.

"I'll use your T-shirt if I don't find it soon!"

Country jumped down inside the APC and joined in the search.

The canvas tool bag had fallen on top of the T.P. box and hidden it from view. Country looking under the tool bag, picked up the box and turned to Frank with it in his hand. "You'd shit in your pants if it wasn't for me," Country continued the teasing.

"Give me that, I gots'ta go bad." Frank grabbed the ammo box, opened it and took two packs of paper, then crawled out the back of the track and ran for the latrine.

Having a latrine was a luxury for A Troop. Most of the time they would just dig a little hole and squat over it. That wasn't the most relaxing way of relieving one's self.

After twenty minutes, Frank was returning to One-One at a much more leisurely pace than when he had left.

"How was it Frank?" Country asked.

"It was great man. You can just sit there comfortable and take all the time in the world. Just you and a couple of thousand flies to keep you company."

A squelch came over the radio, "One-One, this is One-Six, over."

Dave was inside the APC near the radio. Taking the handset, he handed it up to Mitchell who was standing up through the rear hatch. "This is One-One, over," Mitchell replied.

"One-One, I need you to meet me in five minutes. Six wants us to see him, over." Six was the call sign for A Troop's commanding officer, Captain Tice.

"Roger One-Six. I'll be there in five. This is One-One, out." Mitchell handed the mike back to Dave. "I want you guys to get the claymores and trip flares put out while I'm gone." Strapping on is .45, he continued giving instructions, "I want three claymores, one straight out front, one to the right covering the river bank, and one to the left. Mitchell pointed in the directions he wanted the mines placed. Frank's eyes followed his hand and immediately understood where Mitchell wanted the charges to be set. "Give me four trip flares, covering the river bank and tying in with One-Two's on the left. Frank you see to it while I'm gone."

"Right Sarge," Frank answered.

Mitchell then ducked down and crawled out the back of the APC and left to meet Lieutenant Neilley.

There was a large circular bunker in the northwest quadrant of the compound, directly across the river from the water purification plant. It was equipped with a portable generator and electric lights. Captain Tice had set up the command post in this bunker. Both his track and the medic track were parked outside. Mitchell met up with Lieutenant Neilley and the two of them walked across the bridge making their way to the command bunker. As they entered the bunker, they saw that Second and Third Platoon's leaders were already there standing around a small wooden table with Captain Tice.

"Gather 'round, gentlemen," Tice said as he motioned to Neilley and Mitchell. "We can go over tomorrow's operations."

There was a map of the area on the table and Captain Tice was using it as he spelled out the assignment for each platoon and the scout section. "Gentlemen, we will be working out of this compound for the next month or so. At least that's the plan the way it stands right now. For now our operating procedure will be, during the daylight hours, two platoons will leave the compound on various assignments, the other platoon will remain here for security. When the main force moves out in the morning, the remaining platoon will spread its units along the perimeter. Tomorrow that will be Third Platoon. First Platoon minus the scout section and Second Platoon will be going out with me. We'll be doing a search and destroy sweep north of Ap Thanh Tan." Captain Tice pointed to the map showing the location and direction of the sweep.

The sun had set and it was dark enough inside the bunker to require the use of the lights. Mitchell heard the generator running outside and the electric light swinging above the table would flicker from time to time.

"Mitchell, I want you to take your scouts and look for possible ambush sites here, along the north bank of the river and south of the Ap Thanh Tan road."

"How far out?" Mitchell asked.

"Six or seven klicks," Tice answered. "Then come back and check out the south bank for six or seven klicks." Captain Tice pointed out on the map the exact area he wanted covered. Mitchell nodded his head in the affirmative.

"We'll be moving out at 0700 tomorrow morning. Is everybody clear on their assignment?"

All four men answered yes and the briefing ended.

Lieutenant Neilley stayed, chatting with the other platoon leaders. Mitchell left alone to return to One-One.

It was almost completely dark as he walked across the bridge. There was no traffic on Highway One after sundown. It was quiet, except for the sounds of the portable generators used at the water purification plant and the one at the command bunker.

Mitchell could see some lights flickering from the twenty or so huts that were clustered two hundred meters south of the compound at the junction of Highway One and the Ap Lai Thanh road. He could smell the cooking odors coming from the different huts as the families fixed their evening meals. It was appetizing and he realized he was hungry but not looking forward to another meal of C-rations. When he got back to One-One, he found Frank on top in the turret and Country was busy writing a letter to his mom and dad.

"Where's Dave?" Mitchell asked.

"He's over at the latrine," Country answered looking up from his letter.

Mitchell grabbed some C-rations and climbed on top to where Frank was sitting. "Did you get the claymores and trip flares out?"

"Yeah, three claymores placed where you wanted them and four trip flares running from the river over to One-Two's."

Mitchell eyed the three wires coming from in front of the APC running into the turret and hooked into the three separate detonators. Frank saw him evaluating the layout and added as he pointed to each detonator, "Right, center, left. Instant death for any little gook with the balls to try it."

Mitchell didn't answer, just nodded his head.

"What kinda fun and games do they have for us tomorrow?" Frank asked with the distinct sound of cynicism in his voice.

"Scout section will be on its own tomorrow. We'll be checking out ambush sites."

"Ambush sites?" Frank questioned, wanting more information.

"Yeah, we'll be going out most nights for a while to the west, both sides of the river. They want us to get those little shits that's been dropping mortars on this place for the last week or so."

"How did we get into this shit?"

Mitchell shifted his eyes to look up at Frank. "Well, you volunteered for it, remember?"

"Yeah...., I just figured you needed somebody to take care of ya. But what about you? What's your excuse?"

Mitchell took a deep breath and then blew it out his mouth, fluttering his lips. "I....just outsmarted myself. Back in the world, I signed up for every special school I could get, thinking the longer I stayed in the States, the better. But now all that special shit is coming back to haunt me."

"Yeah," Frank chuckled, "Sergeant Mitchell, Airborne Ranger."

"Watch it." Mitchell laughed as he spoke, "Don't you know us Rangers are the baddest mothafuckers on earth. We eat regular G.I.s for breakfast."

"Wooooo........." Frank threw his hands up in front of him pretending to be scared and then the two of them broke out laughing.

The breeze had shifted and was now blowing from the southeast carrying with it all the smells of the village, just south of the perimeter. The spicy aroma of the cooking filled the air.

"Damn, that smells good!" Frank said taking a big sniff of the air.

"Yeah, I know. I noticed it a little while ago walking across the bridge."

"We oughta get over there tomorrow and see what they got. I hear they sell all kinds of shit."

"Yeah....we could do that," Mitchell answered. "We're going to be on our own. We can find time to check it out. Maybe we can get some ice. It'll be nice having something cold to drink for a change."

Mitchell had opened up the C-rations and was eating crackers with cheese spread and a can of fruit cocktail. He washed it down with warm Kool-Aid. Just another gourmet meal of G.I. jungle cuisine.

The routine for pulling guard was for each of the four crew members to sit a two hour watch. The shifts would start at 2200 hours and go until 0600. The most coveted shifts were first and last. If you were pulling the shifts in the middle, you had to break up your sleeping time. So to keep things fair, Mitchell had everyone rotate shifts.

Country was sitting in the turret, manning the fifty and the claymore detonators. That's where Mitchell insisted they be when on guard.

Mitchell was at the latrine taking advantage of what was for them a convenience they didn't often have at their disposal. Frank and Dave were asleep inside the APC.

It was 2320 hours. The sky was clear and filled with stars. Country had seen three shooting stars in the past hour. He kept track of them out of boredom and made the same wish on each one. He wished he could go home and see his Mom and Dad. He had shipped out for Vietnam three and a half months ago and that was the longest time he had ever been away from home. Writing the letter earlier that evening had got him thinking of home and he was daydreaming about it. It was November and the harvest was over, the hay bales would be stacked high ready to feed the livestock throughout the winter. He remembered the cool, clean, crisp November air and thought how nice it would be to breathe it, instead of the stale, humid air that surrounded him. He could see his mother in the kitchen, cooking and canning the fruits and vegetables. "Peach cobbler," Country whispered aloud to himself. "That's what I wish I had right now. Some piping hot, deep dish peach cobbler." It was his favorite and his mom made it often this time of year. She used the fresh peaches that they grew right there on their own place. Just thinking about it was making Country's mouth water. He leaned back with a smile on his face and his mind filled with images of fall back home on the farm.

The whistle of the first mortar round coming in wasn't fully noticed by Country, but the explosion that followed when it hit one hundred meters behind One-One's position put a sudden end to his daydream of home. It startled him to such a degree that he couldn't focus his

136

thoughts for a few seconds. The second round hit in the river, even closer than the first. Now he realized what was happening and was scrambling to find his steel pot and flak jacket.

The attack had caught Mitchell literally with his pants down. If it wasn't for the real danger he was in it would have been laughable. He had gone to the latrine to take a relaxing crap and right in the middle of it, all hell broke loose. He wasn't wearing his flak jacket or steel pot. The thin wooden shit house wasn't going to provide any protection if a round was to hit close. He stood and pulled up his pants, kicked open the door and ran flat out, trying to get back to the safety of his track. If he was going to die, it wasn't going to be with his pants down sitting on the shitter.

Just before he made it back to One-One, a third round hit, this time in the concertina wire between One-One's and One-Two's positions. Mitchell dove to the ground as deadly pieces of shrapnel peppered the ground around him. He then crawled under the APC and curled up into the fetal position, looking out from under the track. "That was damn close," he thought. He felt a sharp pain in his forehead above his left eye. Putting his hand to the area, he felt the warm blood running down his face. He hadn't been hit by the shrapnel, but instead had banged his head into the APC while scrambling for cover. Two more mortar rounds hit as he laid under the APC. He looked out from the back and could see the inside of the perimeter. He had heard the rounds explode, but they didn't hit any part of the perimeter that he could see. Suddenly there was a bright orange flash, the latrine had taken a direct hit. The explosion disintegrated the wooden structure, splintering it into a thousand pieces.

The attack ended after twelve rounds had fallen in or around the compound. The Troop's mortar tracks fired illumination rounds lighting up the entire area.

On top of One-One Frank raised his head looking around trying to gain a perspective on what had happened. "Where's Sarge?" Frank asked, realizing that Mitchell wasn't with them.

"He went to take a shit," Country answered as he turned back looking over his shoulder. His eyes and Frank's both focused on the pile of rubble that a moment before had been the latrine.

"Jesus, oh Jesus!" A sick feeling ran through Frank's body as he spoke. He jumped to the ground still looking at the destroyed latrine. He took a few steps and then started into a slow jog as he called out, "Sarge! Sarge!"

"Here, Frank."

Frank stopped, startled by hearing his name. "Sarge?" He questioned as he looked around, not knowing where the voice was coming from.

"Down here Frank," Mitchell said as he was crawling out from under the APC.

Frank was both surprised and relieved, seeing Mitchell, "What are you doing down there, Sarge?"

"Hiding man, what did you think?"

"We thought you were......" Frank didn't finish the statement, he just turned and pointed to the remains of the latrine.

"I was," Mitchell answered. "I ran like hell when the shit started and it was a damn good thing I did." He had gotten back on his feet. "Anybody hit?"

"Ah, no. We're all okay. How 'bout you?" Frank asked, looking at Mitchell's forehead.

"I just banged it, diving under the APC."

Frank then broke out in a laugh. "Can you believe this shit? The only thing those fuckin' gooks hit was the latrine. Why couldn't they hit something useless, like the bridge or something? No, they hav'ta blow up the goddamn shitter."

"Oh well," Mitchell answered. "At least I got to use it once."

CHAPTER ELEVEN

The scout section spent the morning checking out the area between the bank of the river and the AP Thanh Tan road. They had made their way back to the compound and crossed the bridge heading south. The area was bustling with activity. There were no less than nine vehicles, water trucks and jeeps pulling water trailers, lined up at the water purification plant to take on a load. Highway One had its normal daytime traffic rolling along in both directions. The four APCs of the scout section made their way through the compound to the junction of Highway One and the Ap Lai Thanh road. They pulled off the side of the road and stopped at the edge of the small village. From this point on there were huts and roadside stands lining the road on both sides. The daily commerce was busily taking place, the buying and selling of goods by Vietnamese civilians and American G.I.s.

Mitchell keyed the mike on his CVC helmet. "This is Scout One to all scout units. You can let some of your people go into the village, but at least two men stay on each track. Everyone must be back in forty-five minutes. Do you roger that? Over."

"This is Scout Two, roger."

"This is Scout Three, roger."

"Scout Four, roger."

"Okay, this is Scout One, out."

Frank climbed out of the driver's hole, anxious to go into the village and explore all it had to offer. Country was going with him. Mitchell and Dave would stay aboard the track.

"Frank, bring back some ice and pop if you can get it."

"Right, Sarge," Frank answered as he looked through his wallet checking his money. "Let's go Country." Frank and Country jumped to the ground, starting for the village.

"Forty-five minutes, guys!" Mitchell shouted to them as they left. "Be back here in forty-five minutes."

Frank waved his hand in acknowledgment without looking back.

The huts set back from the road approximately thirty feet and were nestled between the trees that provided the shade for the small stands in front of each family's hut. Most of the stands displayed their various goods on homemade tables, constructed from the wood of old mortar and artillery crates. Some of the vendors had large wooden spools discarded by the Army after the wire or cable that they had held was used up. These spools were three to four feet in height. Lying on their sides, they served very well as display tables. The majority of the merchandise was meant for the Americans, but not all.

The traditional gas stations didn't exist outside the larger cities. Their storage tanks would have been too good of a target out here. Instead, each morning trucks came up from Hue and provide the roadside vendors with ten to fifteen, one gallon cans of gasoline that they would sell. As Frank and Country walked by the first stands there were two civilians on their Vespas scooters buying a gallon can each.

There were thirty or forty small children running around. Some asking for candy or cigarettes and others hustling G.I.s to go to a particular stand, probably ran by their Mama-san. These children didn't know a time that Americans weren't around and most of them could speak pretty good English.

A small boy maybe eight or nine years old, came running up to Frank and Country, grabbing Frank by his hand. "What you look for man?" the small boy asked enthusiastically.

"What?" Frank asked with a big smile on his face.

"What you look for? What you need? I show you, man."

"Ice," Frank answered. "We want some ice."

"No sweat man, I show you," the boy said pulling on Frank's hand trying to get him to follow. "Come on man."

Frank and Country began walking, following the boy's lead. As they passed another stand, Country noticed it had ice for sell.

"Frank, we can get some ice right here," Country said, pointing to the stand they were passing.

"No man," the little boy shouted. "That number fuckin' ten ice. I get you number one ice. Come on man."

Frank was laughing now, thoroughly enjoying the little guy's persistence. But the Mama-san working the stand didn't seem to be amused. She chattered something in Vietnamese, shaking her fist at the boy, obviously angry about his attempt to steal a sell away from her. The boy just gave her the finger and kept pulling on Frank's hand. "Come on man!"

"Shit, she's really pissed-off," Country said in a laugh.

"No shit," Frank answered.

They moved on being pulled along by their aggressive little guide. "What your name man?"

"My name's Frank. What's yours?"

"My name Ringo," the boy proudly announced pointing to his little chest with his thumb.

"Bullshit," Frank answered. "What's your real name?"

"You call me Ringo," he insisted. "Don't fuck with me, Frank. I kick your ass."

Frank was now laughing so hard he couldn't talk. He probably couldn't pronounce his Vietnamese name anyways, and he liked the kid's attitude. "All right, anything you say, Ringo."

They passed by two more huts before arriving at Ringo's home. The hut was much like all the others with a crudely built wooden roadside stand and a large spool lying on its side being used for a display table, placed about ten feet in front of the hut. Behind the stand, up against the front wall of the hut was an old faded red Coca-Cola box cooler. There was no electricity to run it, but even if there was it had long ago lost that ability. But the box was insulated and that is where Mama-san kept her daily supply of ice. Each morning about 0900 a truck from Hue would come by and sell ice to Mama-san and others in the village, which in turn they would resell mostly to G.I.s at a substantial profit.

Mama-san although not yet forty, looked old and weathered, her skin wrinkled from years of working in the rice paddies. Her husband had been killed in 1965 by the V.C. for actively supporting the Americans and opposing the Communists. Her oldest son who would have been sixteen had he not been killed in 1967 when he was run over by a Deuce and a Half driven by an ARVN soldier right in front of this very hut. Ringo was the man of the family and the little guy worked hard at it. He had a younger sister, a baby-san only four years old.

He also had a half-sister, who Frank watched as she walked from the front doorway of the hut, carrying a large pot filled with water and a dozen ears of corn. She placed it on an open fire at the side of the hut beneath the shade of a large tree. She was taller than her Mama-san, in fact she was taller than most of her countrymen. Her breasts were larger than the average Vietnamese woman and her hips a little fuller. These were undoubtedly traits inherited from her European father, a tall, dark complexed Frenchman who had a brief but passionate affair with Mama-san, nineteen years ago. Being impure of race and a fatherless child had caused her to be shunned by most of her people. But it hadn't dimmed the brilliance of her beauty. Her coal black hair flowed down to the middle of her back. Full lips when separated by a shy smile revealed perfect gleaming white teeth. Her large dark eyes seemed to be filled with goodness. Her skin was smooth and clear. Frank was struck by her. He couldn't take his eyes off of her.

She saw him staring at her; she was too shy to look at him directly, but couldn't stop herself from glancing up at him over and over. Most of the time the G.I.s would be forward towards her, some even vulgar in their approach.

But Frank seemed to be just as hesitant and shy as she was and she liked that.

Frank wanted to say something to her but for the first time in his life he was at a loss for words. He had never had a problem approaching girls back home. He would just swagger up to them and say "Hey mama, you're sure lookin' fine," or some other line, but that didn't seem appropriate now. He just stood there staring like a love sick grade schooler.

"Frank....Frank!" Country had been negotiating with Mama-san on the price of the ice and pop. He had to step over and touch Frank on his arm to get his attention. Frank turned his head to look at Country.

"How many Cokes should we get?"

"I don't care," Frank answered. Coke was the furthest thing from his mind.

"I'll get us two each," Country said making the decision for himself. He saw the corn the girl was cooking, "God, some corn on the cob sure would be good. Go see if we can buy some," Country instructed Frank, and then walked back to close the deal with Mama-san for the pop and ice.

A big grin came across Frank's face, now he had the excuse he needed. He walked over to her, "Um hi," Frank said nervously.

She didn't answer, just shyly smiled and bowed her head slightly. Not sure of what to do, Frank bowed back after a slight hesitation.

"Um, can I buy some of your corn?" pointing to the pot cooking on the fire.

"Sorry, it not ready."

"Oh, that's okay. I'll wait," he smiled broadly.
"What's your name?"

"May Le." She looked up into Frank's eyes smiling,
but quickly lowered her head. Frank could see her still
smiling but too shy to look at him in the face.

"May Le. That's a pretty name. My name's Frank."

She again slightly bowed her head, acknowledging
his words.

Kneeling down, she placed two small pieces of
wood in the fire. She was aware of Frank still standing
there, staring at her, but for some reason, she didn't feel
threatened by him as she had so many times in the past by
other American soldiers.

Frank kneeled down beside her, handing her another
piece of wood. She reached to take the wood out of Frank's
hand, "Thank you.....Frank." This time she looked at him
and didn't turn away.

"You're welcome, May Le," Frank answered in a
soft, gentle voice, slowly releasing the wood.

Frank heard Country calling to him. He stood up
and turned around. Country was holding a large chunk of
ice in his hands with Ringo beside him carrying a small
basket filled with the bright red cans of Coca-Cola.

"I'm taking this ice back to the track before it
melts," Country said. "Ringo's going to carry the pop. Are
you going to get us some corn?"

"It's still cooking. I'll bring it as soon as it's done."

"Okay man, I'll see you in a little while. Come on
Ringo." Country turned and started walking quickly back
toward the track parked at the edge of the village. He
wanted to get the ice back before it melted in the hot

blazing sun. Ringo was running behind him trying to keep up with Country's long strides.

On their way back, they passed the stand where the Mama-san and Ringo had had words. Seeing the chunk of ice in Country's hands and the basket filled with pop, she glared angrily and then shouted something in Vietnamese. Ringo laughed and stepped towards her defiantly giving her the finger once more. The Mama-san ran forward wielding a broom, trying to hit Ringo. But he was too fast for the old woman and ran out of her reach, then stopped to taunt her again. Country watched the old woman with her broom and being dressed in loose black pajamas, he thought she looked just like a witch, all she needed was a tall black hat.

"Leave that old witch alone," Country said to Ringo.

"She number fuckin' ten," Ringo answered.

"Ah, well she might tear your little ass up with that broom."

"She can't catch Ringo," the little boy said confidently.

One-One had on board a small metal insulated box. It's original purpose was to transport hot food from the mess hall to the field, but it served as a pretty good cooler and would keep the ice for eight or nine hours. Country placed the ice and pop into the cooler. He then got two packs of Kools and gave them to Ringo for helping him. Cigarettes of all brands came in the C-ration supplement pack, but since no one smoked Kools, they were used for trading with the gooks.

"Stay away from that witch!" Country warned Ringo, as the boy took off looking for another customer.

"How long is Frank going to be?" Mitchell asked of Country.

"He's waiting for the corn to finish cooking, maybe ten or fifteen more minutes. He was talking to a girl."

"A girl?"

"Yeah, she was kinda pretty too. I don't know if he's more interested in the girl or the corn."

"I bet it's the girl," Mitchell added.

The corn was ready and Frank paid May Le a dollar for four large ears. She put them in a paper bag and handed them to him.

"Will you be here tomorrow?" Frank asked wanting very much to see her again.

"Yes, I be here....every day. I live here." May Le was being very deliberate, trying to speak her very best English.

"Good, I gotta go now, but I'll see you tomorrow, okay?" Frank was looking for a response, but May Le just smiled shyly.

"I'll see you tomorrow, here." Frank pointed to the spot where they were standing. "Tomorrow! Right here, okay!"

"Okay, Frank," May Le answered, her lips breaking into a full smile, followed by a little bit of a giggle.

"Okay then, I'll see you tomorrow." Frank was smiling broadly.

"Bye, May Le."

"Bye.....Frank," she answered.

Frank turned and began to jog down the side of the road. He had traveled only fifty feet or so when he looked back and waved. May Le was watching, still smiling and waved back.

CHAPTER TWELVE

The scout section spent the afternoon reconning the area south of the Song Bo River, west of Highway One and north of the Ap Lai Thanh road. The terrain was more rugged south of the river than on the north side. They had only traveled two klicks west of the bridge compound before they ran into a series of steep hills separated by deep narrow valleys. The vegetation becoming ever denser the further west they traveled.

The mortar attack the night before had originated from this vicinity. It was carried out by a group of twenty hard-core V.C. that operated in this area. Some had come up from Hue, the rest from nearby villages including Ap Thanh Tan and Ap Lai Thanh. Several had their wives and small children with them. They were well equipped by the NVA and had support from a few of their families in the nearby villages.

That evening Mitchell led his ambush team out of the compound to a position on top of Hill 876, three and a half klicks southwest of the bridge. It was one of many possible sites the V.C. could use to hit the compound. The team left at dusk and walked south a short distance to the edge of the small village, then took the Ap Lai Thanh road west. Leaving the road they made their way through a narrow valley and finally climbing to the top of Hill 876. There they set up what was more of a listening post than an ambush. If the V.C. came this way, they would be ready for them. But more realistically, the plan was that from this vantage point, if an attack occurred, the team would be able to pinpoint it and hopefully intercept the V.C.'s retreat. They were in position at 2115 hours.

At that same time, two young Vietnamese men slipped out of the tree line and into the back of the second hut south of the junction of Highway One and Ap Lai Thanh road. It was the old witch's hut, the old Mama-san that Ringo had a running feud with. One of the young men was the old woman's son and leader of the V.C. He put his arms around his Mama-san, hugging her briefly. She offered them food, a bowl of cooked rice and vegetables. Her son took the bowl with his left hand because his right hand was crippled. It had two fingers missing, the little finger and the ring finger. They had been chopped off with a machete by an ARVN major two years earlier during questioning about possible V.C. activity. At that time, neither he nor his Mama-san were part of the V.C., but that act of brutality pushed them over to the V.C.'s side. The old woman kept a very close eye on everything that happened along the highway and especially on the soldiers guarding the Song Bo Bridge. She watched Mitchell and the ambush team leave the compound that evening and told her son the direction they took.

The son of the old witch and his companion finished their food and then slipped out of the village to return to their hiding place. They made their way over a series of three hills on the south side of the Ap Lai Thanh road and two-thirds the way up the fourth hill where there was a large natural cave.

The entrance was well camouflaged by natural vegetation. Once inside, the cave opened up into a large

151

chamber, twenty-five feet wide and sixty to seventy feet long. It provided the V.C. group with a place to live and storage for food and weapon supply. They had a well-hidden observation post on top of the hill that was manned at all times. Two tunnels had been dug from the cave to the surface providing two separate escape routes other than the cave's entrance. They had put a lot of work into the cave and it provided the group with a very good location to operate out of. The leader of the V.C., knowing that Mitchell and his ambush team were out that night, chose not to launch an attack on the compound and instead they settled in for the night. He would check with his Mama-san each evening to see what kind of routine the Americans had before planning another mortar attack.

It was Mitchell's intention to stay out until just before dawn, but at 0115 hours it started to rain. Just a drizzle at first, but by 0200 hours it was coming down hard and showed no sign of stopping. Mitchell crawled over to Sergeant Brian Bank's position.

"Brian, I'm thinking of pulling us out."

"Sounds good to me Sarge. This rain is pretty damn bad." Brian looked up at the sky briefly and then lowered his head so the brim of his boonie hat would once more protect his eyes from the rain.

"We've been out for five hours and I don't think anything is going to happen now. Anyways, I can't see a goddamn thing."

"You don't have to sell me," Brian said. "I'm ready to go right now."

"Okay, but hold tight for a moment. I'm going to check with Homeplate." Mitchell moved over to Mike, who had the radio. "Let me have the handset."

Mike unhooked the handset from the web belt over his left chest. "What's up Sarge?" he asked as he handed it to Mitchell.

"I'm going to pull us out. There's no need to stay in this damn rain any longer." Mitchell took the handset and keyed the transmitter button. "Homeplate, this is Rightfield, over." He waited for ten seconds and then keyed it again. "Homeplate, this is Rightfield, over"

"Rightfield, this is Homeplate, over."

"Homeplate, this is Rightfield. We will be leaving Alpha Sierra to return to base. Will call again to get clearance to enter perimeter, over."

"Roger Rightfield. You are leaving Alpha Sierra and will call before entering perimeter, over."

"That's an affirmative, Homeplate. This is Rightfield, out."

Mitchell passed the word to the team to pick up their gear and gather around his position. "We're going back." Mitchell's announcement met with everyone's approval. "Brian, you take the point. Take us back through the valley to the road, then take the road to the village and hold there."

"Okay Sarge," Brian answered.

"Paul, you follow Brian, then Mike, me, Sanchez, Keith, and Frank, you get the rear. Now stay in sight of the man in front of you. Any questions?" No one spoke. "Okay, move out Brian."

Brian led the team down the hill and through the valley to the Ap Lai Thanh road and then to the junction of the road and Highway One.

Getting back inside the bridge compound's perimeter in the middle of the night could be a dangerous proposition, and the last thing Mitchell wanted was to get himself and his team shot up by their own guys. Mitchell took the handset from Mike and called in, "Homeplate, this is Rightfield, over."

"Rightfield, this is Homeplate, over."

"Homeplate, this Rightfield. We are on Highway One two hundred meters south of perimeter. Contact all units, advise of our position and our intentions of coming in, over."

"This is Homeplate. Will do Rightfield, over."

"Roger Homeplate. I will be switching to One-Six's frequency now. This is Rightfield, out."

The First Platoon was guarding the southern part of the compound where Highway One entered. Mitchell wanted to have direct communications with the tracks in the area of the perimeter where the team would be entering. "One-Six, this is Rightfield, over."

"This is One-Six, over."

"This is Rightfield. Has Six notified you of my intentions? Over."

"Roger Rightfield. Signal before you come in, over."

"This is Rightfield. Will signal in one minute, over."

"Roger, one minute. All units, this is One-Six. Rightfield will be coming in. Hold your fire. All units respond, over."

"This is One-One, roger."

"This is One-Two, roger."

All the remaining tracks of the First Platoon responded in order. After Mitchell heard the last of the First Platoon, One-Nine, acknowledge the message, he stepped to the middle of Highway One and using his flashlight, he signaled with four short flashes. He then called One-Six again.

"One-Six, this is Rightfield. Identify signal, over."

"This is One-Six, four. I say again, four. Over."

"This is Rightfield, roger. I'm on my way in."

The next night Mitchell and his team went out again. Once again the old witch saw them leave and passed the information on to her son, and just like the night before the V.C. chose not to attack. The third night Captain Tice elected not to send out the ambush team and shortly before midnight the mortar rounds began to fall on A Troop. The attack consisted of twelve rounds just like the first night but this time they weren't so lucky. Second Platoon's Two-Four track had taken a direct hit. Three of the four crew members were wounded and medevaced to the hospital. One of them, their driver, was in critical condition with a head wound.

The following night the ambush team went back out and again no contact was made and all was quiet back at the compound. It was 0615 hours when the team entered the bridge compound. All of the team members except for Mitchell returned to their tracks. Mitchell had been instructed to report directly to Captain Tice as soon as he returned, so he headed straight for the command bunker. As he entered he saw Lieutenant Neilley and Captain Tice looking over some intelligence reports from S-2. Both men looked up as Mitchell walked in.

"Sergeant Mitchell, you look a little tired." Captain Tice placed the report back in a folder as he spoke.

"Oh, I'm fine sir. Just need a little nap."

"What do you think is happening out there? Every night I send you out nothing happens. If I hold you in a night, all hell breaks loose. Do you think its coincidence?"

"Well, sir, I've never been that big on coincidences."

"Neither have I," Captain Tice said emphatically. His voice showed his irritation. He wasn't blaming Mitchell, he was just upset with the situation.

"Do you think they could be picking up on you out there?" Lieutenant Neilley asked.

"I don't think so sir. We've set up in three different sites. Once we leave the road I'd bet money nobody has us spotted."

"You take the Ap Lai Thanh road each time out, right?" Captain Tice asked.

"Yes sir, we leave the compound at the south side of the bridge, walk down to the road junction and take it for about two klicks. Then once it's good and dark, we move off into the hills."

"Maybe the V.C. has eyes in the village," Lieutenant Neilley suggested.

Captain Tice thought for a moment then nodded his head agreeing. "Maybe they just know you're out there someplace and so they lay off and wait for another night."

"Could be. We walk right by the village when it's still light. If someone was watching, they'd know we were going someplace."

"Okay gentlemen, this is what we'll do." Captain Tice unfolded a map and placed it on the table in front of the threesome. "We'll be doing a search and destroy sweep in this area today. This afternoon we'll use the Ap Lai Thanh road to return back on." Captain Tice pinpointed a spot on the map. "If we drop you and your team off here about three klicks west of the compound, you can lay low until dark and then move into position. The troop will return to the compound and if anybody is watching it will seem like business as usual."

Mitchell nodded his head.

"It looks good sir," Lieutenant Neilley added.

"Okay, then the troop will be moving out at 0800 hours. Try and get a nap, Sergeant."

"Yes sir, I will."

It was almost 1600 hours that afternoon when the ambush team was dropped off along the road. Mitchell ordered Sergeant Banks to go through an equipment check with the team while he went over map coordinates for the ambush site with Captain Tice. The team would be going back to Hill 876, of the three sites they had used Mitchell felt it was the best. Completing his brief meeting with Captain Tice, he returned to the team.

"You all set to go here, Brian?" Mitchell asked.

"All set," Brian answered, handing Mitchell the starlight scope that he always carried on these missions.

"Mike, make a radio check before the troop pulls out."

"I already did, Sarge. Homeplate is monitoring our frequency and the transmission was loud and clear."

As the troop started to roll, some of the soldiers hollered encouragement to Mitchell and his team. One of the guys from Second Platoon yelled out, "Get those mothafuckers, Sarge!" Earlier that day, they had received word that the driver of Two-Four had died from the wounds he had suffered in the last attack.

None of the ambush team knew the dead soldier personally, but he was part of A Troop, one of their own, and they felt an obligation to avenge his death. It was an unwritten code. Charlie had sneaked up and killed one of A Troop's own and the rest of the troop expected the scout section's ambush team to get even. Mitchell hadn't encouraged this kind of thinking, but nevertheless that was the way it was.

The last of A Troop's tracks had cleared the drop off point and were disappearing down the road, concealed by the dust the column was kicking up.

"Frank, I want you to take the point. Go up the valley five or six hundred meters and find us a place to hide until dark."

"Right Sarge," Frank answered, slinging a bandoleer of seven magazines of ammo over his shoulder.

"Sanchez, you're second, then me and Mike. Keith, you're next, Paul and Brian, you get the rear. Okay, let's move."

The floor of this little valley was narrow and abound with light to moderate vegetation growth, small trees ten to twenty feet high, under brush, and knee-high grass. The team had traveled up this valley just five nights earlier. The pace was steady, but slow enough to check for booby traps. Frank led the team over a quarter of a mile through the valley when he stopped and signaled for Mitchell to come to his position. Everyone got down either on one knee or in the prone position while Mitchell made his way to the front of the column.

"How about this?" Frank suggested, pointing to a spot just off to the left. It was a clump of five or six low growing trees. The upper limbs had grown together forming a canopy while the lower limbs drooped to the ground.

"Let's check it out," Mitchell said quietly and signaled for the rest of the team to stay in place. The two of them moved over to the clump of trees and crawled through the branches. Inside it opened up into a small clearing, fifteen feet across.

"This will do fine. Go signal the others to come in."

Frank climbed back through the low limbs and guided the rest of the team into the hiding place. Once everyone was inside, Mitchell split the team up into two groups. Frank, Sanchez, and himself made up one group; Brian, Mike, Paul, and Keith made up the other.

"We'll be here for about four hours. We'll take the first watch." Mitchell was referring to his group. "The rest of you try and get some sleep. We'll switch off in two hours."

Everyone found themselves a comfortable spot, took off some of their extra gear and settled in. Sanchez was in position to watch up the north end of the valley, while Mitchell and Frank were side by side watching the south end. Mitchell checked his watch, it was 1700 hours. "Almost three hours before dark," he thought. He would keep the team here until 2100 hours. He took out his map and began studying the terrain between Hill 876 and the bridge compound.

"Where do ya figure they're shooting from?" Frank asked, looking at the map over Mitchell's shoulder.

"I'd bet they'll be along here somewhere," he was pointing to Hill 876 and the ridge to the east. "They don't need to get any closer than that. If they come up 876, we'll be waiting for them and if they choose this next ridge, maybe we'll be able to spot them and cut them off."

"How many do ya think there'll be?"

"Not too many. Just enough to carry a mortar tube and some rounds. Maybe, three or four guys."

"Just three or four guys you think?" Frank was hoping Mitchell's guess was right.

"Well, three or four is enough to do the job. Why risk more?" Mitchell reasoned.

"I hope you're right, Sarge."

"Yeah, me too."

"You know this shit's crazy."

"What do ya mean?" Mitchell asked.

"Here we are, you and me, and we're hoping that there'll be three or four guys coming up this hill tonight so we can kill them."

"Actually," Mitchell smiled, "I'm hoping there won't be fifteen or twenty."

"You know what I mean. What's the point in this? What's the point of the whole fuckin' war?"

Mitchell was going to make a joke but looking at Frank's face he could tell he was serious. They had been together over three months and this was the first time they had talked about the legitimacy of the war.

"I don't know, Frank." Mitchell looked up from his map, "I guess if you're a politician back home, the war has one purpose. If you're a general sitting in Saigon, it's a different one. But the one thing I do know, if you're a lowly soldier like you and me, the only point is to get your ass home in one piece."

"Then why try and find these guys at all? Why risk a fight?"

"We could do that, but if someone doesn't get them, they're just going to keep on firing mortars at us. And next time instead of Two-Four getting hit, it may be One-One and one of us going home in a body bag."

"So you're saying, sometimes the best way to stay alive is by killing someone else?"

"Sometimes the only way to stay alive is by killing someone else." Mitchell didn't know if Frank bought his answer; hell, he didn't even know if he bought it himself. But it was the only one he could come up with and Frank really wanted an answer, so even a bad one was better than no answer at all.

"Yeah, I guess so," Frank said after a moment of thought. "It's just hard to make sense of it sometimes, you know what I mean, Sarge?"

"Yeah, I know what you mean, Frank. I'm not sure we'll ever make sense of it."

* * * * * * * * * * * *

It was 2140 hours when the ambush team arrived at the top of Hill 876. They set up in a five man line facing southeast, giving them a good view of the ridge to the east and the valley running to the south. Mitchell placed two men, Paul and Sanchez, fifteen meters behind the line facing west, covering their backside.

It was a cloudless sky and the moon was almost full. The visibility was very good and with the help of the starlight scope the V.C. could easily be seen if they came this way.

The ridge was six to seven hundred meters east of Hill 876 and one hundred and fifty to two hundred feet lower in elevation. The valley between them was much like the one the team had just traveled through. It was covered with light vegetation and knee-high grass. On pass the ridge were a couple of small rolling hills flattening out into a low plain that the Song Bo River ran through. From this vantage point high atop the hill, Mitchell could see the flickering lights of the village by the bridge compound some three klicks away.

Once again the team was setup in more of a listening post than an ambush. There wasn't a particular trail or spot that they expected the V.C. to walk by on. The hope was to see them long before they got into position to fire their mortars and to plan a response depending on where the V.C. were headed.

Mitchell used the starlight scope to scan the east side of the hill, then the valley and up the ridge. Then he moved back to Paul's and Sanchez's position and scanned the backside. He would repeat this same procedure every five minutes.

It was 2310 hours when he first spotted the V.C. They were coming up the valley floor from the south, five hundred meters to the right and four hundred feet below.

"I got something," Mitchell said just loud enough to be heard by Brian and Frank who were kneeling on each side of him. Both men focused their attention on Mitchell, but remained quiet.

"Yeah, it's definitely gooks." Mitchell paused for a few seconds. "Looks like four, no five, yeah five of 'em."

From the direction the scope was being aimed, Brian could tell he was focusing on the valley below. "How far?" he asked.

"Maybe five hundred meters, at the bottom of the valley," Mitchell answered, handing the starlight scope to Brian to take a look. He raised the scope to his eye and began searching in the direction Mitchell was pointing.

"I got 'em. They're still moving north."

"How many do you make?" Mitchell asked.

"Five, definitely five."

"Let me take a look," Frank whispered.

Brian handed the scope to Mitchell who in turn passed it over to Frank.

"Down at the bottom of the valley moving this way," Mitchell said to Frank, pointing once again. It only took Frank two or three seconds to find the gooks. He watched them for a half of a minute then lowered the scope and handed it back to Mitchell.

"What do we do now?" he asked.

"Just wait and see where they're going." Mitchell raised the starlight scope back to his eye. "Brian, go let Paul and Sanchez know we got something, but tell them to stay in position for now." He was still peering through the scope as he spoke, "And have Mike bring the radio over here."

Brian moved off to comply with Mitchell's instructions. A minute and a half later he and Mike returned, crawling up behind Mitchell.

"Are they still coming?" Brian asked.

"Yeah, still making their way up the valley." He watched the V.C. for three or four minutes. By now the gooks were two hundred and fifty meters closer than where they were first spotted. "They're turning," Mitchell said. "They're starting up the ridge."

"Looks like you were right, Sarge," Frank commented.

"Yeah, it looks like it." Mitchell lowered the starlight scope from his eye and handed it to Brian. "They're starting to climb up the ridge, down there at about two o'clock."

Brian raised the scope and using the imaginary face of a clock, he pointed it in the direction of two o'clock. He scanned the area for a couple of seconds.

"Do you got 'em?" Mitchell asked.

"Ah......, okay, I got 'em now. They're still climbing."

"Watch 'em. Mike let me have the handset." Taking the handset, Mitchell keyed the transmitter button. "Homeplate, this is Rightfield, over."

"Rightfield, this is Homeplate, over."

"Homeplate, I need to talk to Six, over."

"Roger Rightfield, wait one."

Sergeant Miller was the man on the other end of the radio. He was Captain Tice's R.T.O. and was manning the communication net in the command track. Captain Tice was asleep inside the command bunker and Miller went to wake him. Just the sound of Miller stepping through the doorway was enough to raise Captain Tice from his light sleep.

"What is it?" Tice asked.

"Rightfield's on the horn. It's Mitchell. He wants to talk with you sir."

"Tice moved quickly out of his bunker and into the back of his track. "Rightfield, this is Six, over."

"Six, this is Rightfield. We have five Victor Charlie moving onto the ridge to our Echo. Request a four-deuce barrage on ridge at grid coordinates 463282, over."

"Get my map," Captain Tice ordered Miller. "Roger Rightfield, wait one."

Sergeant Miller unfolded the area battle map for Tice to look at. He had the team's position on his map and he followed the ridge line east of Hill 876 with his finger and then crossed checked the coordinates that Mitchell had given him.

"This is Six. Say again grid coordinates for fire mission, over."

"This is Rightfield. Grid coordinates four-six-three-two-eight-two, over."

"This is Six. That's four-six-three-two-eight-two. Confirm, over."

"This is Rightfield. That's affirmative, over."

"This is Six. How soon? Over."

Mitchell checked the luminous dial of his watch. "This is Rightfield. I have 2318 hours now. Request for fire mission at 2330, over."

"This is Six. Will do at 2330 hours, over."

"Roger Six. I'll move my team back down the valley. If the four-duce don't get 'em, they should run back the same way they came. We'll try and cut 'em off, over."

"This is Six. Stay clear of fire mission, over."

"This is Rightfield, roger that, out."

Mitchell gathered the ambush team around him and explained what was going to happen. In twelve minutes the mortar tracks of A Troop were going to open fire on the ridge and that should be just about the time the gooks would be setting up to fire on the compound. Mitchell figured he had those twelve minutes as a head start to get to the south end of the valley.

Mitchell took the point and led the team along the crest of the hill heading south and down the east slope into the valley. His intention was to get to the mouth of the valley and set up an ambush in the area where he first spotted the V.C. His hope was that if the V.C. retreated, it would be back the same way they had come.

At the same time, the V.C. were making their way atop the ridge. They were led by Three Fingers, the old witch's son. He and his four comrades were in good spirits; the word of their success from the last attack had filtered its way from the compound to the village and through the old witch to Three Fingers. Of course, the degree of damage done had been exaggerated by the time the information had reached him. The word the V.C. got was at least three Americans had been killed and many more wounded, so they were quite full of themselves as they made it to the top of the ridge and began to set up their 82mm mortar. One of the V.C. carried the mortar tube itself, another the heavy round base plate. A third carried the tripod and six rounds of ammunition, and the fourth man had twelve more rounds on him. Three Fingers was the only one of the group with a rifle, a Russian-made AK-47.

They were in the middle of assembling the mortar when they saw the flashes of A Troop's 4.2 inch tubes being fired. It was 2330 hours and the first volley of the barrage was on its way. The V.C. didn't realize what was happening until the first three rounds came raining down on the ridge. Their happy-go-lucky attitude suddenly changed to one of terror as the rounds exploded all around them. They dove to the ground as the deadly shrapnel flew through the air. During the few seconds between the first volley and the second, Three Fingers ordered his men to break down the weapon and retreat. Each man retrieved the part of the weapon he was responsible for. The last piece to be picked up was the base plate and that man was last in line as they ran down the west side of the ridge. The next volley of rounds exploded on the ridge. A red-hot jagged piece of shrapnel hit the V.C. carrying the base plate in his right leg. It ripped away a large amount of flesh and muscle of his lower leg, shattering both the tibia and fibula. He crumbled to the ground screaming in pain as the other four dove for cover. Three Fingers ran back to help his fallen comrade and ordered the ammo bearer to pick up the base plate. With the injured V.C. being literally dragged along, they continued down to the valley floor. Three more volleys of 4.2 mortar rounds fell on the ridge, but by now the V.C. had made it to safety. Stopping for the first time long enough to examine the wounded man's leg, Three Fingers took the shoulder strap off his AK-47, using it with a small piece of wood made a tourniquet. He placed it above the right knee trying to stop the bleeding from the badly mangled lower leg.

Mitchell and the ambush team had made it to the mouth of the valley and set up in a straight line along the base of the west hillside, concealed in the brush and small trees. The east half of the valley floor was extra thick with underbrush in this spot and travel was much easier along the west side. If the V.C. took the easier path, they would pass right in front of the ambush. Mitchell was searching up the valley with the starlight scope. They had only been in position five minutes when he spotted the V.C. coming straight down the valley. He alerted the team that they would have only a few minutes to wait.

The V.C. were moving quickly. Three Fingers' only thought was to get his wounded comrade back to their cave.

Being caught by the mortar barrage had surprised him and left him a little confused. The thought that a deadly ambush may be waiting just ahead, never crossed his mind.

The V.C. carrying the tripod was the first in the column, followed by the one with the tube, and then the ammo bearer carrying the base plate. Three Fingers was lagging behind, struggling to carry the wounded man. Mitchell wanting to get all five V.C. in the killing zone, waited and waited, but it was not going to happen. The column was strung out too far. By the time Mitchell opened fire, the lead man had cleared the zone. He dropped the tripod and ran, disappearing into the night. The next two took the full brunt of the ambush. All seven men of the team opened up, riddling them both with M-16 fire in the first second.

Three Fingers was twenty-five meters behind and not in the initial killing zone. He dropped his wounded friend and opened fire in the direction of the ambush team. The green tracers coming from the AK-47 flashed all around Mitchell. None of the rounds hit closer than five feet of any team member, but they were under fire and that got their attention. Three Fingers continued firing as he ran for the thick brush on the east side of the valley. Mitchell, Frank, and Brian, all fired back but to no avail as he disappeared into the thick undergrowth.

Suddenly there was silence. Mitchell looked back and forth in front of him. Of the five enemy soldiers they had gotten only two. "Shit!" he said aloud. "Where'd they all go?" he added, his voice sounding apprehensive.

"I saw one run into the brush on the far side," Frank answered.

"What about the lead man?" Mitchell asked Paul, who was the last man in the ambush line.

"He was gone before we opened up," Paul said, his voice cracking from nervousness.

"Damn it!" Mitchell shouted. "Keith lob some H.E. into that brush on the far side."

Keith broke down his M-79, removed the canister round and replaced it with a 40mm high-explosive round. He aimed and fired. The round exploded one hundred meters away in the thick brush on the far side of the valley. He reloaded and fired again. Keith put a total of seven rounds into different parts of the thicket.

Mitchell motioned Keith to cease fire. He took the starlight scope and scanned in all directions for over a minute. He didn't like it, but they would have to move from cover and search the area, knowing some of the V.C. had escaped the ambush.

"Paul, you and Sanchez look around down there," Mitchell pointed to the south. "Brian, Keith, Mike, check out the two we got. Frank, you're with me."

Mitchell and Frank moved to the north end of the zone. They had gone about twenty meters when the wounded V.C. tried to move and gasped in pain. Frank reacted to the movement, opening up with three quick burst, a dozen rounds in all. The V.C. was hit twice, in the chest and head; now he was no longer in pain. Frank moved up to search the dead V.C. followed by Mitchell a few seconds later.

"That makes three," Frank said.

"Yeah, but there's still two more out here, someplace." Mitchell was pissed off that the ambush hadn't gone well, thus putting his team in danger.

Paul and Sanchez found the discarded tripod, but no sign of the man who was carrying it, so they returned to the main group.

Mitchell and Frank continued to search, slowly making their way to the east side of the valley. Three Fingers was hiding in the thick vegetation and at one point Mitchell had walked within fifteen feet of him. He had Mitchell lined up in the sights of his AK-47, but didn't pull the trigger. His own self-preservation was more important than killing Mitchell. Of course, Mitchell never knew, but he was feeling more and more uncomfortable with the situation.

He and Frank made their way back to the rest of the team. "Did you see anything?" Mitchell asked Paul.

"We found the tripod, but no gooks."

"Okay, that's it." Mitchell said. "Pick up the mortar tube and the rounds. Let's get the hell out of here!"

CHAPTER THIRTEEN

"When I throw the ball, you run out of the way. Don't let the ball hit you. Number ten if the ball hits you." Country had an old soccer ball that he got from the guys on One-Five. He was trying to explain to Ringo and seven other small kids how to play dodgeball. "Frank, come over here man."

Frank was leaning against the tree next to Ringo's family hut. Country and the children were in the open area between that hut and the one south of it.

"What?" Frank said, "You wan'na hit me with that?"

"Yeah! Come on Frank, it won't hurt. What'sa matter, you chicken?" Country teased.

Ringo jumped in on the teasing, "Come on Frank. What matter, you chicken Frank? You chicken!"

Frank pretending to be more hesitant than he really was slowly walked over to where Country and the kids were playing.

"Okay, stand right there. I'll throw it at ya and ya show 'em how to dodge it. Okay, ya ready?"

"I'm ready, shithead. Just throw the ball."

"Ooooh, its shithead is it? See how you like this." Country faked a couple of hard throws and had Frank jumping from side to side with each fake.

The kids were all smiling, enjoying the show the two G.I.s were putting on. Country finally let go with a real throw and Frank was a little slow to react. As he turned to run out of the way, the ball landed solidly on Frank's butt. Ringo and the others roared with laughter as Frank hammed it up for them.

"Now that's number ten," Country said. "Don't let the ball hit you."

"Okay," Frank said. "Now it's my turn. You get in the middle. Ringo you get on the other side. Me and you against Country."

Frank and Ringo took turns throwing at Country, as he ran back and forth between them, dodging their throws. After a half a dozen throws, Country let Ringo hit him, but not making it so obvious that the kids could tell.

"I hit you! I hit you!" Ringo shouted with glee. "You number ten! I hit you!"

They started the game again, this time with all the children in the middle and Frank and Country doing the throwing.

May Le came out of the hut carrying a basket filled with the family's clothes. She was taking them down to the river to do the wash. She stopped underneath the tree watching these two American soldiers with loaded M-16s strapped over their shoulders and a bandoleer of ammo across their chests, playing dodgeball with eight small Vietnamese children and enjoying it, just as if they were ten years old all over again.

She watched for two or three minutes before Frank saw her. Frank excused himself from the game and walked over to her, she was why he was here. She was the reason he had been spending every minute he could get away in the village.

"Hi!" Frank said smiling, his eyes flowing over her and then settling on her large dark eyes.

"Hi.......Frank," May Le answered, her gentle smile and beautiful eyes freezing Frank's stare.

"Let me carry that for you," he said as he took the basket from her arms.

"Thank you." They didn't speak for a few seconds, just looked into each other's eyes. Then May Le dropped her head and giggled a little. "Your friend nice."

"Who, Country? Oh, he's okay. But what about me, don't you think I'm nice?"

"Yes Frank, I think you nice. I think you number one nice," she said as she took hold of his hand.

"And I think you are number one beautiful," his voice sounded sincere, because he was sincere and she was beautiful.

Leading him by the hand, she started walking down the roadside heading to the south end of the village. "Am I beautiful like girls in USA?" she asked playfully.

"Oh, well I don't know. The girls in the good old USA are boo-coo beautiful," Frank teased back, after a few seconds he added, "But I think you're the most beautiful of all."

She smiled and her eyes beamed with happiness. It didn't matter if she believed his line or not, she loved hearing him say it.

At the south end of the village there was a well-traveled path leading east to the river some two hundred meters from the road. The path led to a spot on the river where it widened out and a sandbar had formed. This is where all the villagers did their laundry. There were two mama-sans washing their clothes when May Le and Frank arrived. The sandbar was over two hundred feet long and the mama-sans were at one end, so May Le and Frank moved down to the other end. Frank set the basket down as May Le removed her sandals and rolled up the legs of the black pajama pants she was wearing to above the knee. She dumped the clothes out of the basket onto the grassy bank. Taking one garment at a time, she waded out onto the sandbar and washed it using a bar of hand soap.

Frank sat on the river bank and watched as she meticulously first washed and then rinsed out each garment. He thought how easy it was back home with washers and dryers to do the laundry, automatic dishwashers, flushing toilets, and running water. Here was May Le standing knee deep in a running river, washing the family's clothes by hand, smiling and singing sweetly a Vietnamese folk song. He watched her every move. He noticed how the sunlight seemed to glisten off her long, black hair.

They didn't talk a lot, but after rinsing and wringing the water out of each piece of clothing, she would give it to Frank to put in the basket, making sure to gently touch his hand each time.

They were there for an hour, May Le washing the clothes and Frank watching. When they did talk it was about America and how different things were there. When all the wash was done, Frank picked up the basket carrying it in one arm and took May Le's hand in his, they started walking back up the path.

Halfway back May Le stopped and turned to face Frank. She took his right hand with both of her hands and held it gently, she looked up into his eyes. She didn't speak but instead she raised his hand placing it on her chest, close to her heart. She didn't know the English words to say, but she wanted Frank to know she cared for him, that she felt close to him, and he was in her heart. Frank felt all those things, but he also felt her firm round breasts. He felt them rise and fall with each breathe she took. It took all the willpower he could muster to not react to the luscious mounds his hand had found itself nestled on. After all, it had been over four months since he had had any contact with a woman and he was only human. Even with his best efforts, his self-control wasn't totally successful. But because of the loose fitting nature of his fatigues, it wasn't too noticeable.

She raised his hand to her face, kissing the palm tenderly. Frank slowly slid his hand over her cheek and to the back of her neck. Lowering his face to hers, he felt her soft warm lips on his, kissing her for the first time, tasting the sweet essence of her soul.

When their lips separated, she laid her head against his chest, pulling him close to her. He gently stroked her hair and then kissed the top of her head. The sound of the two mama-sans coming up the path made them separate suddenly. Feeling like two school kids not wanting to get caught necking, they stood sheepishly as the two old women approached. The two mama-sans bowed their heads as they passed by, Frank and May Le bowed in return. Once the mama-sans were a safe distance away, they broke out laughing and then continued back to the village holding hands.

* * * * * * * * * * * * *

The 101st Airborne 7th Battalion 404th Infantry was operating north of the Song Bo River, primarily between the village of Ap Thanh Tan and Firebase Jack. Although A Troop sometimes operated north of the river, it primarily worked south of the Song Bo, between the bridge compound and Firebase Strike. Along with its daily assignments, it also had the responsibility of acting as a reactionary force for the grunts of the 404th. If this situation occurred, the river was a natural barrier. The time it would take for A Troop to travel back to Highway One, cross the bridge, and then double-back to reinforce the 404th was unacceptable. The M-113 APCs did have amphibious capability. Therefore, it was decided that the APCs would forge the river and take the most direct route if needed, while the M48A-1 tanks would take the long way around.

On this day, the scout section assignment was to find at least three suitable crossing sites along the river between a spot four klicks west of the bridge and grid coordinates 350260. Mitchell on One-One led the scout section along the south bank of the river. He was looking for was a place where the river was wide and the current slow. The banks on both sides needed to be a gradual slope to the water. If the water was shallow enough for the tracks to cross without having to float, it would be great, but that was not very likely. They had traveled about five klicks when they came to an area that looked suitable for crossing.

"Hold it up here," Mitchell instructed Frank over the intercom.

Frank brought the track to a complete stop. Mitchell removed his CVC helmet and stood up in the turret looking out across the river. "This looks like a pretty good spot," Mitchell said to no one in particular.

"How deep do ya think it is, Sarge?" Country asked. His lack of swimming skills suddenly becoming a real consideration rather than just a minor concern when talking about surfing someday.

"I don't know. I don't think we can drive all the way across. I think this old bucket is going to hav'ta float."

"Do ya figure it's over my head?" Country asked, the concern showing on his face.

Mitchell looked back over his shoulder at Country, "Yeah, in spots. What's the matter?"

"Well, you know I don't swim too good."

"You don't hav'ta swim too good to make it to the bank."

"Well, actually I don't swim at all!" Country admitted.

Mitchell smiled then chuckled a little. "If we sink, I'm sure someone will help you get out."

"I hope so," Country said. "I'm not shitting you. I go down like a rock."

Dave spoke up, "If we sink, I'll help you back to shore. I've been swimming for as long as I could walk. Don't worry dude, I won't let you drown."

Mitchell sat back down in the turret and put his CVC helmet on, keying the intercom. "Frank, let's give it a try here. Lower the splash board."

The front of an APC is slanted toward the back. This configuration would allow the water to flow up and over the top of the APC when moving. To counteract that, the APCs were built with a board, three and a half feet by five feet, which folded down in front of the vehicle angling forward. The splash board would create a wake and prevent the water from coming over the top of the APC.

Frank lowered the splash board and locked it in place. Mitchell radioed the other three tracks of the scout section and told them to hold their position on this side of the river.

"Okay Frank, let's go for it, slow and easy." Mitchell ordered over the intercom.

Frank began to drive One-One ever so slowly into the river. The murky water made it impossible to see the bottom if the river was more than two feet deep. They had traveled only ten feet when the bottom was no longer visible. Creeping forward, One-One continued into the river. They were forty feet off the bank and the water level was four feet and getting deeper. The APC was still running on the bottom.

Mitchell thought that it was about time for this thing to start floating. He turned, looked over his shoulder and shouted to Dave, "During your Delta training, did you take one of these through the water?"

Dave stepped up by Mitchell and answered, "One time, it was just a little pond not a running river."

"Shouldn't we be floating by now?" Mitchell asked. He was getting a little concerned. The water was within eighteen inches of the top of the APC.

Dave looked at the water level. "Yeah, I think so."

"Oh shit!" Country said, his head turning first to look at the water level and then back at the river bank behind him.

Because of the extra weight from the 28,000 rounds of ammunition that One-One was carrying, it was going to take more water to float the APC. The only question was how much more, or if it would float at all being loaded this heavy. One-One continued moving further into the river and the water level continued to rise.

Frank keyed his intercom, "Shit Sarge, I don't know if we're going to float."

Mitchell was seriously beginning to wonder himself. "Keep easing her forward," he answered back to Frank over the intercom.

They were over a hundred feet off shore now and the water level was within ten inches of the top when Mitchell finally felt the APC bob up and down a little. He let out a sigh of relief, it was finally floating free.

"Yeah!" Dave shouted out once the APC was floating. Country jumped at Dave's sudden yell.

"Hey dude, its okay. We're on our way now," Dave said laughing out loud.

Country didn't answer. He just kept looking at the water.

The motion of the tracks churning in the water was the only means of propulsion for the APC in the amphibious mode. A top speed of about three miles per hour was all it could make. They traveled over another one hundred feet floating free before the tracks once again made contact with the bottom. Then they climbed their way out of the water onto the river's north bank.

Mitchell keyed his radio. "Scout Two, this is Scout One, over."

"This is Scout Two, over."

"Okay, Scout Two, come across, but take it slow. The water was less than a foot from our top, over."

One-Two made its way across and was followed by One-Three and then One-Four. They all made it across without an incident, but not without the same anxieties felt by One-One.

Once on the north bank, they spent a few minutes checking the inside of their APCs to see if the rear lift gate or the rear hatch had leaked during the crossing. There was some leakage in every track but not enough to worry about. One-Four had the most water inside, maybe a half-gallon, not enough to cause any real problem.

Mitchell marked the location of this crossing site on his map and then ordered the scout section to move out. With One-One in the lead, they made their way west along the north bank. Their progress was slow, Mitchell was taking his time to check for crossing sites. After an hour or so, they came upon another site that looked promising. Using terrain recognition and from reverse azimuths of known dominant terrain features, Mitchell plotted the location at grid coordinates 408253.

He keyed his intercom, "Frank, climb on out. I'm going to have Dave take this one."

Frank locked the brakes and then removed his CVC helmet and climbed out of the driver's hole.

Mitchell turned to look back at Dave, "Dave, get down in the hole. You're going to take it across this time. I want you to have some experience doing this shit, too."

"Right Sarge!" Dave sounded excited about getting the chance to drive through the river.

His enthusiasm made Country even more nervous. "Don't go fucking around acting like a hot dog," Country warned.

"Hey dude, no sweat. I can do this in my sleep," he bragged as he was climbing into the driver's hole.

Frank was standing next to the hole. Looking Dave straight in the face with a stern and serious expression he said, "I don't want to get my ass wet. So take it easy, got it?"

"Okay dude, that's righteous."

One-One pulled up to the north bank of the river. It was at least one hundred meters wide at this point. Mitchell had once again picked this place for the crossing, because of its width, the current was very slow, and the banks on both sides were a gentle slope down to the water.

"Okay, lower the splash board," Mitchell ordered over the intercom.

Dave leaned forward, unlocking the lever and pushed the board forward into place.

"Alright, ease her in just like before."

Dave slowly drove One-One into the river. This time the river's bottom descended much quicker than it had at the first site. They were only twenty-five feet from the bank when the tracks no longer touched the bottom. One-One was floating again, with the water level only about ten inches from its top. It was obvious that the river was deeper here than it was at the first crossing and Country wasn't liking it at all.

One-Two followed fifteen meters behind and One-Three entered the water twenty meters behind One-Two. The three APCs were in single file with One-One a little over half way across when it was fired upon from the north bank. A burst of AK-47, some of the rounds penetrating the wooden splash board and hitting the hull just below Dave's position. The bullets hitting so close startled him and he let up on the accelerator.

"No! No! Don't stop! Keep on going straight across!" Mitchell screamed into the intercom. He instinctively knew not to stop. Stopping or turning around to go back would only put them in more jeopardy than they were already in.

Mitchell opened fire with his fifty caliber. An RPG round came roaring from the north bank missing One-One to the left by a mere six feet.

"Go goddamnit, go!" Mitchell shouted.

Dave accelerated again. One-Two and One-Three were directly behind One-One and couldn't return fire. Country's nor Frank's side guns could fire straight ahead, only Mitchell was positioned to fight back. He continued to fire his fifty caliber into the vegetation where the attack was coming from. After firing forty to fifty rounds, Mitchell let up on the trigger, there was no more firing coming at them. The whole thing had taken less than thirty seconds, but it had seemed like forever out in the open.

One-One continued across the river to the south bank, followed by the other two APCs. Dave pulled One-One onto the bank and up to the edge of the vegetation. One-Two pulled up to the left and One-Three to the right.

They stopped to look for any movement, hearing or seeing nothing.

Mitchell keyed his radio, "Scour Four, this is Scout One. Come on across, over."

"This is Scout Four, roger."

Mitchell picked up the handset of his PRC-77, its frequency was set to A Troop's command. "Six, this is Scout One, over."

"Scout One, this is Six, over."

"This is Scout One. Received enemy fire while making river crossing, over."

"This is Six. What is your location? Over."

"This is Scout One. Grid coordinates 408253. Say again, 408253, over."

"This is Six. Are you still under fire? Over."

"This is Scout One, negative, over."

"This is Six. Hold your location. We're on our way. Do you have any casualties? Over."

"This is Scout One. Negative, no casualties, over."

"Roger Scout One. Can you estimate size of enemy force? Over."

"This is Scout One. Not sure, received automatic weapons fire and at least one Romeo Papa Golf round from south bank, over."

"Okay, Scout One, hold there. This is Six, out."

Mitchell jumped off the track armed only with his forty-five pistol. "Come on down, Frank."

Mitchell then shouted to Paul on One-Two. "Paul, help us take a look around."

The three of them started searching through the brush where the attack had come from. It took Paul only thirty seconds to find something. "Oh shit," he softly said to himself. He turned his back on it and called out, "Over here."

Mitchell and Frank ran over to Paul's position, he had an anguish look on his face, his left hand covering his mouth. There were three bodies lying behind him. A man was lying on his back with the top of his head blown away, his AK-47 just to his side. A woman lying face down, an AK-47 on the ground beneath her. Beside the woman was a small child, a little girl no more than two years old. She had been hit in the mid torso by two fifty caliber rounds almost completely tearing her tiny body in half. The others with the RPG launcher had gotten away.

Frank dropped his head staring at the sand, no longer able to look at the tiny body with its internal organs spilled out on the ground, but her delicate face still as beautiful as any porcelain doll.

Mitchell stared at the mangled body of the little girl, his eyes filling up with tears. His voice was cracking, "Why?! Why?!" Slowly lifting his hands and then hopelessly dropping them back to his side, shaking his head. "How could they do this?" He paused, looking at Frank and Paul. "How could anyone put a little baby in the middle of an ambush?" He suddenly became overwhelmed with emotions. Standing over the woman's body he started screaming at her at the top of his lungs, "What were you thinking? What the hell were you thinking, you fucking bitch?" Suddenly he fired two rounds from his forty-five into her lifeless body, as if somehow punishing her for placing the child in harm's way. The tears had flooded his eyes and were now running down his cheeks. He was feeling rage and hatred for the woman and extreme guilt for the killing of the baby girl. Looking up at the sky he screamed, "SHIT!"

Frank rushed over to Mitchell putting both his arms around him, pinning Mitchell's arms to his side, in an effort to comfort him and prevent him from raising the forty-five again. "It's not your fault man," Frank said. "It's not your fault. You were just doing what you had to do."

Mitchell didn't answer, he just dropped his head.

"It's okay man. It's okay," Frank said. Feeling the rage leaving Mitchell's body, he released the bear hug he had on him.

Mitchell still didn't speak to Frank but nodded his head yes. Mitchell had killed before, many times, and he had seen some hideous sights in the last four months but this, this was different. Seeing the baby girl ripped apart by bullets he had fired had hit him hard. Harder than anything in his young life. It didn't matter that the V.C. had opened fire on him or that he fired back in self-defense. It didn't matter that he never saw the child. All he could see now was the baby girl's beautiful little face staring up at him from the ground with her heart and lungs literally splattered all over. Mitchell lifted his empty hand to dry some of the tears from his eyes.

"Why don't you go back to the track, Sarge. Me and Paul will take care of this."

Mitchell still didn't speak. He looked up at Frank and nodded his head again, then slowly walked away.

CHAPTER FOURTEEN

Frank and May Le were standing under the large teak tree next to her hut talking quietly. Their relationship had grown to one of considerable fondness, warm and romantic. It was obvious by the way they looked at each other and in the sound of their voices when they spoke. Frank's rough, tough-guy persona completely disappeared when in her presence. May Le was sweet and respectful to everyone, but she simply beamed with happiness when she was around Frank.

Mitchell was at the display table in front of the hut examining one of a dozen leather watch bands that May Le had for sale. The weather and his own sweat had taken its toll on his. It was frayed and about to break. The band he was looking at was natural leather and light tan in color. It was two inches wide and had two straps and buckles.

Mitchell walked the twenty feet to where Frank and May Le were. "How much for this one?" He asked showing May Le the watch band.

She smiled and then bowed her head respectfully, "For you, no charge."

The going rate for the band was three dollars and Mitchell knew it. "No, no darlin', you got more use for this than I do." Mitchell said as he placed the five dollar MPC bill in her hand.

He turned his eyes to Frank, "I'll see you back at the track."

"Right Sarge, I'll be along in a little while."

Mitchell nodded his head, then walked away.

"Your honcho, he look sad," May Le said as she watched Mitchell walk away.

"Sarge?...Yeah, well he had some bad things happen a few days ago." Frank turned his head also watching Mitchell. "Funny how it always seems to happen that way."

"Funny?" May Le questioned.

"No, not that kind of funny. I mean it just seems like bad things only happen to good guys."

"Your honcho, he good guy?"

"Yeah....Yeah! He's a good guy."

May Le had been working the family's stand alone for the last two days. Her mama-san along with Ringo and her baby sister had traveled to the village of Ap Laong Mai. It was near the beach on the Street Without Joy. There May Le's grandmother laid on her death bed. The old grandmother was dying from just too many years of too much hard work. Her sixty-seven years of struggle to survive was almost over and May Le's mama-san would be there to say good-bye. May Le had respect for her grandmother as she did for all elders, but she had not been around her for ten years and wasn't really grieving her death. After all, she was dying from natural causes and these days in Vietnam that alone was something to be grateful for.

This also gave May Le and Frank the chance to be together, to spend the evening alone, perhaps the entire night. They had talked of little else that afternoon.

"I gotta go now," Frank touched her cheek gently as he spoke.

"You come back, yes?" May Le asked, her eyes wide and her face filled with hope.

"You bet I will, at sundown, just before dark."

"Before dark?"

"Yes, before dark. I'll be here."

"I make food for you, number one food."

"Good, I'll be boo-coo hungry," Frank said with a big smile and rubbing his stomach. "I gotta go now. I'll be back, okay."

"Okay Frank, good-bye."

The ambush team would be going out that night and Frank had talked Mitchell into letting him stay in the village and pick him back up in the morning. The team's mission for the night was to set up a listening post a couple of klicks west of the compound and Mitchell didn't expect that they would make any contact. Anyways, he was a sucker for love, so he agreed to Frank's plan.

It was 1900 hours and the ambush team had gathered at the back of One-One to be briefed on the mission and go through the customary equipment check. The team had to be told of Frank's plan and now he was undergoing some good-natured teasing by his envious buddies.

"Now Frank, tell me again about this special mission you're going on tonight. You say it's a close reconnaissance of the civilian population?" Paul teased.

"Yeah, a really close reconnaissance," Keith added.

"Don't do anything I wouldn't do," Sanchez put in his two cents worth.

"Fuck you guys!" Frank barked back. "You're all just jealous."

"You got that shit right," Keith admitted.

"Okay, knock it off," Mitchell broke up the bullshitting. "Let's get going. Brian, you take the lead. We'll go out through the village, drop off Frank, and then continue south on Highway One for about a half a klick."

The team made its way out of the compound and into the village. Mitchell stopped a few seconds with Frank in front of May Le's hut. "We'll be back about sunup to get you. Take it easy, buddy."

"Right Sarge. Hey, thanks man."

"Sure thing. See you at sunrise," Mitchell said slapping Frank on his shoulder and then jogging to catch up with the rest of the ambush team.

The doorway of the hut didn't have a hung door but instead there was a curtain that could be pulled across the opening. During the day it was always open and then closed at night for privacy. Frank walked up to the doorway, the curtain was already closed. He knocked on the wall next to the doorway. May Le opened the curtain and took Frank by his hand, leading him quickly inside the hut and closed the curtain behind him. Once safely inside, she tilted her head upward, leaned forward, and kissed him softly on his lips.

"I glad you come," she said.

"Yeah, so am I," Frank answered. Thinking to himself, "Nobody could be happier about this than me."

"Come, you sit here." She led him by his hand to a wooden table with four straight back wooden chairs around it. In the middle of the table was a candelabrum with five lit candles in it, providing most of the light for the room.

He laid his M-16 against one of the chairs and then removed the bandoleer of ammunition from his shoulder and hung it over the back of the chair. Before he sat down, he put his arms around May Le and pulled her gently to him, kissing her long and tenderly. He could smell the freshly cut flowers she had in her hair just above her right ear. The fragrance of the flowers and her recently washed hair filled Frank's senses. She smelled clean and fresh, and holding her made him feel clean. He hadn't felt that way in a long time.

"You sit. I get you something to drink."

Frank sat down at the table and May Le disappeared out the back doorway.

The hut was built mostly out of boards from discarded mortar boxes. The roof was made of bamboo and grass. There was no heating or plumbing systems, and no electricity. The floor was hard-packed dirt, swept clean. The cooking was done in a separate shed behind the hut. Along the back wall of the hut next to the doorway leading out to the cooking shed was a large cabinet. It had numerous drawers and shelves. There were ceramic dishes on some of the shelves; plates, bowls, cups, and glasses. On top of the cabinet was a ceramic washbowl and a pitcher filled with water. Along the north wall, Frank saw a dresser with a mirror and a small stool sitting in front of it. The dresser looked very old but in good condition. On top of the dresser was a candlestick with a lit candle and three small black and white photographs in metal frames. He guessed them to be pictures of Mama-san's family. On the front wall was the only window in the hut. It was just an opening, no glass or shutters. It too had a curtain that was pulled closed. Next to the window sat a Windsor chair. It, like the dresser, looked very old but in good condition. Along the south wall there were four woven grass mats and two large hinged-top baskets filled with bedding, pillows, blankets and handmade quilts. Even though the hut was of primitive construction and had dirt floors, it was uncommonly clean. Frank thought of his own home back in New York. He couldn't remember it ever being half this neat and clean.

May Le reappeared through the back doorway carrying a large glass filled with ice and citrus water. It was a drink made from lemons, limes, and oranges, slightly sweetened; somewhat like lemonade but more piquant.

She handed the glass to Frank, "You drink. It number one good."

He took a big gulp of the cold, tangy liquid. "This is good! Thank you."

"You like?"

"Yes, I like. It's number one good." He could see in her face the pride she took in pleasing him. He thought how she was even more beautiful tonight than the first time he saw her.

She was wearing her finest clothes. A long, silky white tunic reaching almost to her knees. It was close fitting across her breasts and tailored down to her waist with slits on each side from the waist down, allowing it to flow over her hips. Underneath she wore a pair of pants made of the same material. They too were tighter fitting than the normal black pajama type pants she wore every day. The outfit was spotlessly clean and it showed off her shapely figure in a way Frank had never seen before.

"You stay, I get you food now," May Le said, smiling sweetly, her eyes twinkling with happiness.

Frank took one of her hands in his and kissed it, then said, "Good, I'm boo-coo hungry. If I don't get some food soon, I may just hav'ta eat you."

She giggled out loud and hurried out the doorway to the cooking shed. She soon returned carrying two bowls. One was filled with steamed rice with vegetables and shrimp. The other had two large ears of corn on the cob. She didn't eat but instead sat at the table and watched him as he ate, refilling the glass with the citrus water each time it got even a third of the way empty. Frank ate all that she had brought him and a second bowl of rice and vegetables.

When Frank could no longer eat another bite, May Le removed the bowls from the table, leaving the pitcher of citrus water and two glasses. She walked over to the cabinet and took a deck of playing cards from one of the drawers. She tried to show Frank how to play a card game that he had never heard of before. He couldn't understand the rules, so he decided to teach her how to play gin rummy, but she didn't grasp the idea of the game neither. Next he tried blackjack but without success. Finally, they discovered that they both knew how to play solitaire and double solitaire. For the next hour and a half they played cards and sipped on the citrus water. They didn't talk much, May Le's English was limited and Frank could only say a few words in Vietnamese, none of which were appropriate for this situation. The lack of talking didn't stop them from communicating. They let their eyes and body language do their talking and neither had trouble understanding.

Frank was shuffling the deck preparing to deal out another game, when May Le stood up from the table.

"Where you going?" Frank asked.

"I not go away. You sit." She smiled lovingly and walked over to the grass mats. She unrolled one and placed it on the floor. Removing some bedding from one of the baskets, she first covered the mat with a heavy blanket and then placed a handmade quilt over the blanket. Next, she took two pillows from the other basket and put them at one end. Then she took a second quilt and neatly covered the first.

Frank sat at the table watching her meticulously making the bed. "This is a good sign," he thought, "especially if she just makes one bed."

Once she finished making the bed, she slowly crossed the room to where the dresser was. She sat down on the stool and looked at herself in the mirror. She reached up and removed the flowers from her hair. Taking a hairbrush from one of the dresser drawers, she began to brush her long black hair. Frank still sitting at the table, watched her for three or four minutes, brushing her hair and softly humming a sweet melody. Placing the hairbrush on the dresser, she stood up still facing the mirror, her back towards Frank. She slowly began to unbutton her tunic. Starting with the top button at the high collar and slowly working her way down until all the buttons had been undone. She placed the thumbs of both her hands into the waistband of her pants, slowly pulling them down and stepping out of them. She neatly folded her pants and put them on the stool. Frank quietly got up from the chair but remained standing by the table his eyes fixed on May Le, his body trembling with anticipation. She slipped the tunic first off of one shoulder and then the other, not letting it fall to the floor but instead folding it and putting it on the stool.

She stood for a few seconds looking at her naked body in the mirror, then slowly turned to face Frank. She had a loving look about her, as if to say, here I am for you, all of me, for you to see, for you to have.

Frank's eyes moved over her, from head to toe and everything in between. His stomach felt like a net filled with butterflies fluttering trying to get out. For some reason, he was more nervous than any time before. Even more so than the first time, when he was only fourteen.

May Le was the one to take the three steps that separated them. Standing before him, she began to unbutton his fatigue shirt starting at the top button. Frank helped by undoing the last two buttons. He removed it and laid it on the chair. She placed both of her hands on his bare chest and then slowly moved them up and around his neck.

He responded by putting his hands on her hips, and sliding them around her tiny waist. He pulled her close to him, her luscious breasts pressed against his chest. They kissed more passionately than ever before. He took his right arm from her waist and placed it behind her legs, lifting her off the floor and into his arms. She laid her head on his shoulder as he carried her across the room to the bed. Kneeling down on one knee he gently laid her down, kissing her tenderly. They made love for most of the night, finally falling asleep in each other's arms an hour before dawn.

* * * * * * * * * * * *

The next day was Thanksgiving. All of A Troop would be staying in the compound, no outside assignments. That afternoon at 1600 hours, there was to be a full Thanksgiving dinner delivered to the troop, brought down from Camp Evans. It would be the first hot meal for them in six weeks and everyone was looking forward to it. But that was going to be later, right now everybody's mind was on the big game. The challenge had been made by Lieutenant Jerry Ross, the Second Platoon's leader. He had earned his commission through the ROTC program while attending the University of Georgia. There he had been the starting right guard for the Bulldogs his senior year. He had made some disparaging comments about the quality of football that was played at West Point and Lieutenant Neilley wasn't going to take it lying down. So the challenge was made and accepted. A football game between First Platoon and Second Platoon. To the victors' four cases of beer and to the losers, total humiliation.

Captain Tice and his RTO, Sergeant Miller, were refereeing the game. It was being played on a roughly laid out field inside the compound. It was a little smaller than a regulation field, measuring about eighty yards long by forty-five yards wide. It was all dirt, some of which had been packed down hard by all the tracks driving over it. The game was to be played in two forty-five minute halves, no stopping of the clock. If Captain Tice thought a team was taking too much time between plays, he would penalize them ten yards and a loss of a down. It was eight men per team, full-contact, tackle football, but there was to be no blocking below the waist in hopes of lessening the chances of injuries. Even so, the game was taking almost as many casualties as the war itself. A gunner on One-Five had severely sprung his ankle and the TC of Two-Two had broken his left arm. Captain Tice hadn't figured out how to explain that to headquarters, but what the hell, he'd think of something.

The score was Second Platoon - 20, First Platoon - 14. About six minutes were left to play and Second Platoon had the ball, driving down to the fifteen yard line, about to score again. They had been running the ball more than passing, with Lieutenant Ross and two other big lineman, the running game was working well for them.

First Platoon was playing a three, three, two defensive set. The three linebackers, Lieutenant Neilley, Frank, and Keith were stacking it up on the line, trying to stop the running game. Mitchell and O'Shea were defensive backs, O'Shea played short and Mitchell covering deep.

When Second Platoon hiked the ball, it was a fake run over right guard. All three of First Platoon's linebackers poured into the right side of the line piling it up. The fake was a good one and O'Shea's first steps were towards the line. The Second Platoon's one wide receiver started straight up the field and passed O'Shea, whose first steps forward were too much to recover from. Second Platoon's receiver was streaking down his left sideline and had blown passed O'Shea. Mitchell broke to his right, running flat out trying to get to him. He saw their quarterback release the pass. It came off his hand a little wobbly. Mitchell's only hope was that the pass was short because if it was on target, he wouldn't get there in time and Second Platoon would score again. The pass was fluttering through the air like a wounded duck and Mitchell saw his chance. He broke behind the receiver, he had judged the ball perfectly and it fell into his arms. He had intercepted the pass on the two yard line, his momentum carried him out of bounds at the three.

"Yes!" Keith yelled. "Yes! All right Sarge!"

"Way to go Mitchell!" Lieutenant Neilley shouted out.

"No fuckin' way, he was out of bounds!" screamed one of Second Platoon's players, followed by more complaints from others.

Captain Tice's decision came quickly and decisively. "The interception was made in bounds, he ran out after the catch. First Platoon's ball at this spot."

First Platoon were clapping their hands and cheering the call.

"Five minutes to play," Captain Tice called out.

"Huddle up," Lieutenant Neilley shouted to his team. "We gotta get some breathing room. This will be a pitch to Frank around the right side. Keith, you be the lead blocker. On two."

On offense First Platoon was playing a four man line. Lieutenant Neilley was doing the quarterbacking, Frank and Keith were the running backs, and Mitchell was playing wide receiver. Frank lined up behind Neilley and to the left, Keith to his right. Mitchell was split out at the right end. When the ball was hiked, Mitchell took off up field pulling one defender with him. Keith and Frank turned and started around the right side of the line. Neilley pitched the ball to Frank and he followed Keith's lead block. They broke through the line and were about eight yards up field. Keith blocked off one defender but another hit Frank, stopping him but not knocking him down. He spun around trying to run again. By now Lieutenant Ross had raced down the line and hit Frank from the back, his 6'3", and 240 pounds burying Frank into the ground. Frank held on to the ball but came up with a mouthful of dirt and gasping for air. The hit had partially knocked the wind out of him. The good thing was that Lieutenant Ross had hit Frank so hard, it had knocked him another two and a half yards up field giving First Platoon a first down.

"How's that taste, man?" teased one of Second Platoon's players.

"I guess he couldn't wait 'til after the game for his Thanksgiving dinner," another added.

"Fuck you, assholes!" Mitchell yelled at them as he stopped to help Frank to his feet. "Nice run, man."

But Frank didn't answer, he couldn't, he just kept spitting out dirt.

"Four minutes to play," Captain Tice called out.

First Platoon was back in a huddle, Lieutenant Neilley diagramming a play. "This will be a quarterback option, run or pass around the right side. Mitchell, you go up field fifteen yards then break inside or out. If you're open I'll throw, if not I'll run it. Keith you have the lead block. Okay, on one!"

First Platoon broke the huddle and came up to the line. Lieutenant Neilley began calling out the signal, "Down, set, hut!"

The ball was snapped. Mitchell took off up field, running as fast as he could. About fifteen yards up he gave a head fake to the inside and then broke to the sideline. He was being covered by the driver of Two-Three track, a black kid from Chicago. He had good speed and didn't go for Mitchell's fake. He was all over Mitchell like stink on shit. Lieutenant Neilley had the ball in the throwing position but seeing that Mitchell was covered he pulled it down and ran. Keith laid a good block on Lieutenant Ross taking him out of the play. Neilley rolled up field for a twelve yard gain before being pulled down by two men.

The First Platoon was moving up the field but at this pace, they would run out of time before scoring. The time remaining was down to three minutes.

"Same play," Lieutenant Neilley said in the huddle. "Mitchell, find some way to shake your man. This time on two."

First Platoon broke the huddle lining up to run the play. "Down, set, hut, hut!"

At the snap of the ball, Mitchell drove off the line, this time taking it a full twenty yards up field before making his cut. He broke hard to the inside. The kid from Chicago must have been expecting another head fake, because he hesitated for a split second before going with Mitchell on the inside move. Mitchell had a step on his defender but he wouldn't have it for long. The kid from Chicago was faster than Mitchell and was making up the difference. Neilley had thrown the pass on Mitchell's break, leading him over the middle of the field. The pass was on line but high and Mitchell had to leap in the air to bring the ball down. The ball met Mitchell's hands at the same time his defender's shoulder met the small of Mitchell's back. He landed on the back of his neck and shoulders, dazing him momentarily. The ball was still firmly clenched in his arms, even though he didn't remember catching it. It was a twenty yard gain and First Platoon now had the ball in Second Platoon's half of the field.

"Nice catch, Sarge," Frank said. This time it was his turn to help Mitchell up.

Mitchell was a little slow getting back to the huddle. His legs were wobbly and his head filled with cobwebs.

"We gotta get something big. We're running out of time!" Lieutenant Neilley began to diagram a play in the dirt. "Frank, this is going to be a halfback pass. I'll pitch to you. You sweep wide to the right. Mitchell go deep down the right sideline. Frank, you watch him all the way and give a pump fake deep at Mitchell. I'll try to get loose after I pitch it. Then I'll break down the left sideline. If we catch 'em by surprise, I should be open. So throw it as far as you can. Okay, let's do it! On one!" First Platoon lined up.

"One minute, thirty seconds to play," Captain Tice called out.

"Down, set, hut!"

The ball was snapped. Lieutenant Neilley turned and pitched to Frank. He began a wide sweep to the right, Keith staying in front to block. Mitchell started up the right sideline pulling both of Second Platoon's defensive backs

201

with him. The flow of the play had everyone moving to the right, everyone except Lieutenant Neilley. He broke up the left sideline and was wide open. Frank saw him running free and so he reared back and threw the ball across and down field as far as he could. By the time Second Platoon realized what was happening, it was too late. Nobody was within fifteen yards of Lieutenant Neilley as he ran under Frank's pass, catching it and carrying it across the goal line.

"Touchdown, First Platoon!" Captain Tice declared, raising his arms above his head signaling the score.

There was less than a minute left in the game. The try for the extra point would be the last play. If First Platoon was successful they would win 21 to 20. If not the game would end in a tie; in which case, all bets would be off and First Platoon had worked too hard for that. Besides they weren't just playing for four cases of beer and bragging rights anymore. No, the wagers had escalated far beyond that. Over two thousand dollars had been bet on the game. Mitchell had sixty dollars riding on it and Frank another fifty dollars, themselves. So it all came down to one play. The ball was placed on the three yard line.

They huddled up around Lieutenant Neilley. "Okay guys, we gotta get this one in. We'll run a quarterback option to the right. Frank, I'll fake to you over the left guard and then roll out to the right. Mitchell, you do a little hesitation block and then break to the corner. If you get open I'll throw, if not, I'll run it. Let's get it guys, on two."

They broke the huddle and moved up to the line. Nobody on either side of the line was laughing or joking around now. Everything was riding on this last play including most of the money in the compound. There were over a hundred men watching the game including the engineers from the water purification plant.

Lieutenant Neilley was looking over the defense. First Platoon had run the ball inside both times before on the extra point and he was hoping they were thinking that was what he was going to try again. "Down, set, hut, hut!"

The ball was snapped. Neilley turned to his left taking one step. Frank came charging for the line. Neilley stuck the ball into Frank's stomach and then pulled it back as he flew by. Neilley then rolled to the right as Frank plowed into the line. On the snap, Mitchell had blocked into the line and then rolled off and broke for the corner of the end zone. Frank's fake was convincing, piling up most of Second Platoon's defenders. But one of the linebackers stayed home and was between Lieutenant Neilley and the end zone. Mitchell was open, so Neilley cocked his arm and let the pass go. The ball came off his hand right on target, a perfect spiral. Second Platoon's linebacker made a desperate jump into the air, slapping at the ball. The tips of his fingers touching the ball just enough to change its flight and turning the perfect spiral into a wobbling projectile that was surely to come up short of its intended target. Mitchell only had time to take one step back to the ball and then he dove, stretching his body out as far as possible. He was flying through the air, his body parallel to the ground, his hand reaching out desperately trying to catch the dying pass. The ball made contact with his hands just before he landed hard, chest first. Mitchell pulled the ball in and held on.

First Platoon - 21, Second Platoon - 20. Half of the crowd was cheering wildly, the other half groaning from the disappointment.

Keith was the first one to reach Mitchell. Picking him up and holding him in a bear hug, Keith kept screaming, "Great catch! Great catch!"

Then the rest of the team came piling on, knocking Mitchell and Keith down to the ground and jumping on top of them. From the way they were acting you would have thought they had just won the Super bowl.

The turkey, mashed potatoes, and gravy tasted especially good for First Platoon. The four cases of beer were washing down the big meal. That and all the cash they had picked up from the side bets were making all the scrapes and bruises seem worth it, at least for now. Tomorrow it may be another story.

It was about an hour before dark, Mitchell was on top of One-One sitting in the turret. Frank climbed up and sat down beside him, leaning his back against the fifty caliber gun shield. He had two cold beers in his hand. He gave one to Mitchell, then reached into his breast pocket and pulled out sixty dollars and handed it to Mitchell, his share of the side bet money.

"To the victors go the spoils," Mitchell said.

"Amen to that." Frank answered as he raised his beer to invite a toast. Mitchell raised his.

"Life's good." Frank said.

"It surely is my good man and we should live it with gusto, sing like no one's listening and dance like no one's watching."

Frank grinned, "You be inta some weird shit."

"Indubitably." Mitchell smiled back.

"I think I be moseying over to the village for a bit."

"Make sure you mosey on back before dark."

Frank's grin widened, "Indubitably," he said as he climbed off the APC and headed off to see May Le.

Along with the meal, mail was brought down from Camp Evans. Mitchell opened a letter from Maggie.

Dear Bobby,

I love you! And miss you still.

I'm enclosing a new picture of me. It's a good thing you're not here. I look like I swallowed a beach ball. The next time you see me I'll look better than when you left.

The doctor said the due date is still December 15th, so next Wednesday (the day before Thanksgiving) will be my last day at the bank.

Stephanie gave me a surprise baby shower today at work. I received five cute outfits, three blankets, two diaper bags, a stroller, lots of receiving blankets, and a three month diaper service. Mr. Gray gave us a $50.00 Savings Bond for our baby's college fund.

This probably bores you, but it's the only way I can share with you.

Stephanie lets me talk to her about the baby and you, but I think sometimes I bore her too. But she says I never do.

Oh, I almost forgot! (Not really!) Your car had a flat tire.

I called my Dad and he came by work and changed it for me. The next day he went with me to Firestone and I bought four new tires. Dad said he'd pay, but I wouldn't let him. I don't think he knew how much money I've saved. Everything you send home I put in the bank plus at least half of my checks. He said it sure is different from the old me, when I was always broke. I guess I'm just growing up. I better, we'll be parents in a few weeks.

I hope you're okay. The pictures you sent home, you look thinner. I hope you got my last care package with the cigars. You can pass them out when our baby is born.

I have so much I want to say but not in a letter. I'll just wait 'til I see you. I'll always love you!

Maggie

Mitchell folded the letter replacing it back in the envelope, keeping the picture out. He put the envelope into his fatigue shirt pocket. He smiled as he was looking at Maggie's picture, then rubbed his finger over her big stomach and kissed her picture.

"Just a couple of more months Maggie May, just a couple more months."

Mitchell slept well that night. It was the first night in the last five he hadn't woke up in a cold sweat from the same nightmare. The images of the little girl's mangled body and her beautiful face staring back at him. Instead this night, he dreamed of Maggie, sweet Maggie May. Just like always, when he needed her most, she was there.

CHAPTER FIFTEEN

Three Fingers was a bitter and angry young man. He blamed the Americans for everything that was wrong in his life. Even though it was ARVN soldiers that had tortured him and crippled his hand, he blamed the Americans. In his way of thinking, if the Americans weren't here, the NVA would have long ago overran the south and Hanoi and the communist would be in control of the entire country. To him, Ho Chi Minh was a god, and an American, any American was Satan. His bitterness went beyond just Americans; his own countrymen that didn't share his views had become his enemy, even some of his own family. He and eight others had gone into his uncle's village early one morning and at gun point gathered the villagers together. He warned them of helping the dirty G.I.'s and then to make the point he selected the old papa-san, his mother's only brother out of the crowd. Forcing him to his knees, he put the barrel of his AK-47 to the old man's temple. He announced to the villagers, anyone helping the Americans would die just like this old man was going to die. He pulled the trigger, blowing a hole through his uncle's head. The old man fell to the ground, the blood gushing out like a fountain.

His hatred had gone beyond anything rational. Over the last two years, he had become just plain mean and cruel. He liked the power that came from intimidating the villagers and worst of all he had learned to like killing.

Three Fingers and the last six remaining members of his V.C. group had spent the evening smoking American cigarettes and drinking strong rice wine. Since A Troop took over security of the Song Bo Bridge, eight of his group had been killed. Five by Mitchell and the ambush team, three others by the grunts of the 404th. The rest had ran off, no longer having the stomach for fighting or for Three Finger's totalitarian iron boot rule. What remained was no longer an organized military unit. It was now just a group of thugs led by a brutally cruel madman. Three Fingers still talked about the virtues of communism and the glory of Ho Chi Minh, but in reality he had become a common bandit.

The ambush team was settled in for the night. They had set up a listening post two and half klicks west of the compound; at one of the five locations Mitchell had used over the last month. It was a large deadfall of logs and branches on the east slope of a ridge overlooking the Song Bo River. The fallen trees provided them with good protection and the location allowed them to watch two different approaches to the bridge compound.

There hadn't been an attack on the compound for three weeks, not since the team encountered Three Fingers and his gang, killing three of them and capturing their mortar tube.

Frank was back with the team. The last two times out, Mitchell had let him stay with May Le, but her mamma-san, Ringo, and baby sister had returned, so Frank and May Le would now have to find a new place to be together.

Mitchell was leaning back against a large log, his M-16 across his lap. Frank was sitting to his right and Brian Banks to his left. The three were talking quietly.

"Brian," Mitchell asked, "do you spell your name with a I or a Y?"

"With an I. Only wimps spell Brian with a Y. So you decided to name the baby Brian."

"Maybe, if it's a boy."

"What if it's a girl?"

"If it's a girl, Maggie picks the name. That was the deal we had. If it's a boy, I pick the name, a girl she gets to name her."

"Has she decided on a girl's name?" Brian asked.

"Yeah, she's going to name her Christina. She'd like it if it's a boy to name him Robert Junior, but I won't do that. I think the kid should have a name of its own."

"Well, Christina is okay," Frank added. "But, Brian for a boy? Hell that's a wimpy name with a Y or I. You should name him something manly like Frank."

"Thanks for that unbiased opinion Frank, but I think I'm going with Brian."

"With an I!" Brian added.

May Le was jarred from a deep peaceful sleep, when she was jerked to her feet by the hair on her head. A hand slammed hard over her mouth, muffling her screams.

She was wide-eyed with terror, but in the darkness all she could see was shadows, several of them moving about in the hut. She began to struggle trying to escape the grip that held her. She was kicking wildly at anything that moved. The hand that had a grip on her hair, released it and placed the forearm across her throat, pressing hard, making it impossible to breathe.

The struggle she was putting up was enough to awake Ringo. He was lying on the grass mat next to the one May Le had been sleeping on. He raised his head, still half asleep, unable at first to focus clearly. Realizing that someone or something had a hold of his sister, he jumped to his feet, rushing to her defense. He ran head-on into the steel butt plate of an AK-47, hitting him solidly across his forehead and the bridge of his nose. The force of the blow split open his forehead and shattered the cartilage in his nose. The little boy fell to the dirt floor not making a sound, the blood gushing out of the two inch cut that had been opened up on his head. The last thing he saw before the rifle butt had knocked him unconscious was the hand over May Le's mouth. A disfigured hand, a hand with only three fingers.

Seeing Ringo brutally knocked down caused May Le to stop struggling for a couple of seconds. She realized she was next to the wall of the hut. Raising her feet off the floor and placing them on the wall, she pushed off as hard as she could. She and Three Fingers went stumbling backwards across the room, running into the table and chairs. They fell to the floor, freeing May Le from Three Fingers' grip. She only got halfway back to her feet before the butt of an AK-47 slammed in to the back of her head.

She fell face first on the floor, semi-conscience she tried to raise herself to her hands and knees. By then, Three Fingers had gotten back to his feet. Throwing a chair out of the way, he reared back his leg and kicked her in the right side of her head. She fell onto her side and then rolled over onto her back. She was still conscience but just barely. She couldn't focus her eyes and didn't have control of her arms or legs. Blood was running out of her right ear and the earlobe was almost torn off.

May Le's mamma-san had been struck four times in the face by another of Three Fingers' men. Still another had her baby sister held to the floor with a razor sharp machete at her throat, warning Mamma-san if she moved or made a sound the baby would die.

Three Fingers stuffed a rag into May Le's mouth, then taking a leather strap he tied it tightly around her head, holding the rag in place. Then with the help of one of his men, they placed a bamboo pole, four feet long, across her back, hooking her arms around it. Using rope, they tied her hands and cinched them tightly across in front of her body. May Le winced in pain.

Three Fingers walked over to Mamma-san and delivered a hard closed-fist blow to the side of her face, knocking her to the floor. He told her that May Le was going to be punished for her association with the Americans, and for Mamma-san to tell the rest of the villagers that they too would be punished if they continued to be friendly to the G.I.'s. He ordered two of his men to bind her hands and feet. They gagged her and left her laying on the floor.

Mamma-san watched in terror as Three Fingers walked back to May Le, fearful that he would kill her then and there, before her eyes.

He took a six foot length of rope and tied it around May Le's neck. Pulling upward on the rope, forcing her to her feet. Her legs were wobbly and she was dizzy from the blows to her head. Three Fingers pulled on the rope to lead her away. She only managed two steps before falling face first onto the hard dirt floor. He ordered her back to her feet, jerking on the rope and then kicking her in the ribs. Unable to use her arms or hands, she struggled to get back to her feet. The rope being jerked and pulled so hard it had already caused rope burns around her neck. There was a trickling of blood running from her nose and a larger flow running down her neck from her right ear as she was led out the back doorway and disappeared into the darkness.

Mamma-san was struggling to free herself. Her baby-san was crying and hopelessly tugging at the ropes, but unable to loosen the knots. She had squirmed and fought with the ropes for three or four minutes when she heard Ringo moaning as he began to regain consciousness. His head and nose was throbbing with pain. He was dizzy and confused. It took another full minute before he knew who or where he was. Seeing his mamma-san lying on the floor and his baby sister crying, tugging at the ropes, he crawled over to them. He managed to get her free, and Mamma-san's first concern was for Ringo. The blood from his nose and the cut on his forehead had covered his face and was running down onto his bare chest. She got him to his feet and sat him down in one of the chairs. Finding one of the candles on the floor, she lit it and placed it on the table. She went to the cabinet along the back wall, getting the washbowl and water pitcher she brought them back to the table. Using a cloth she began to wash the blood from his face. The cool water helped to clear Ringo's head. The pain was bad, but he would not allow himself to cry. His senses were coming back to him and he started to remember what had happened. He looked around the hut for May Le, not seeing her he shouted out her name. Mamma-san, still crying, hysterically told Ringo the V.C. had taken her, pointing to the back door.

Ringo bolted from the chair, running out the back doorway. His mamma-san was running behind him, pleading with him not to go. Paying no attention to her, his only thought was to find May Le and help her to escape from her captors. He crossed the small clearing behind the hut and disappeared into the tree line. He ran mindlessly for two or three minutes, before falling to the ground, tripped by vines. The fall caused his broken nose to be bumped by his own arm as he raised them instinctively to protect his face from the fall. The pain shot through his body like a bolt of lightning, stunning him for ten to fifteen seconds. While freeing himself from the tangled vines, it gave him a moment to think. He realized what he was doing wasn't very smart. Even if he did actually find them, what could he do, one little boy against a whole band of V.C. What he needed was help. "The G.I.'s!" he thought. He would tell the Americans, they would help him find his sister.

Now thinking clearly for the first time since running into the butt of that AK-47, he picked himself up and started to backtrack his way out of the jungle. It took

longer to find his way out than it did running mindlessly
into the jungle, but after five minutes of retracing his steps,
he was back in the clearing behind his hut. He ran past his
mamma-san, who was holding his baby sister, shouting to
her as he passed that he was going to the bridge and tell the
Americans what had happened. Ringo ran between the huts
on to Highway One, heading for the compound. Mamma-
san followed but fell far behind the fast running little boy.

One-Six Track was located on the perimeter at the
point where Highway One entered the compound. One of
their gunners was on watch, sitting in the turret. He saw
something moving in the road. He straightened up, placing
both of his hands on the fifty caliber machine gun, both of
his thumbs on the butterfly trigger. Focusing his eyes on
the moving figure, he swung the gun down and pointed it at
Ringo, who was about seventy-five meters from the
compound.

"Hold it!" The young soldier shouted out. "Hold it!
Stop!"

Ringo cried out. "G.I.! G.I.! Help me G.I."

"Stop right there. Stop!"

But Ringo continued to come closer. The young
gunner pushed down with his thumbs firing off a burst of
fifty caliber. Flames flashed from the barrel of the gun and
red tracer rounds streaked through the darkness. Ringo
froze as the rounds peppered the dirt road fifteen feet in
front of him.

"Stop right there, don't come any closer."

The shouting of the gunner woke Lieutenant
Neilley, the firing of the fifty caliber had caused him to

come frantically climbing onto the top of the APC. He heard Ringo cry out.

"Don't shoot G.I.! Don't shoot!"

"What the hell's going on?" Lieutenant Neilley asked.

"There's someone out there, sir; in the road. I think it's a kid."

Neilley reached for one of the hand held illumination flares that were kept in an empty ammo box beside the turret. He removed the top cover piece and placed it over the bottom end. The cover piece was used as the firing device. Holding the flare in his left hand and slamming the palm of his right hand into the bottom of the flare, he fired it. It shot into the air and three seconds later it exploded, lighting up the immediate area. They could now clearly see Ringo standing in the middle of the road, his hands raised above his head.

"Help me G.I.!" The little boy pleaded, "Help me. V.C. take my sister. Help me!"

"Stay there, kid." Neilley yelled.

He could see Ringo's mamma-san coming up the road. She was carrying her baby-san on her hip with one arm and desperately waving the other arm in the air. She had heard the firing and was fearful of finding Ringo gunned down in the road. Reaching him, she grabbed him, holding him close to her.

The other two members of One-Six's crew were now on top of the track. Neilley told his driver to get a weapon and come with him to see what was going on.

Neilley reached into the ammo box getting another flare, he handed it to the gunner in the turret. "Fire this one off as soon as that goes out." He said, pointing to the illumination flare slowly floating down from the sky.

Armed with his .45 pistol, Neilley jumped to the ground, followed by his driver, carrying an M-16. They cautiously started walking toward Ringo, looking down the road behind him and from side to side, to see if anyone else was about.

The blow to Ringo's head had caused him to suffer a concussion. All of the running he had done had left him weak and dizzy. The blood was again pouring out of the cut in his forehead. He slowly fell to his knees, on the verge of passing out. His mamma-san knelt down beside him, trying to hold both of her children, weeping.

Lieutenant Neilley and his driver had covered about half of the seventy-five meters when the flare overhead burned out. Almost instantly, he heard the second flare being fired. A few seconds later it lit up and he could see that the little boy had fallen to the ground. Quickening his pace, he was soon to where Ringo laid. He could see that the boy was hurt, his chest and face covered with blood. Mamma-san was too hysterical to make any sense, so Neilley decided to bring them into the compound. He picked Ringo up and held him in his arms, telling the mamma-san to follow as he turned and started walking back to the perimeter.

As he got back to his track, the gunner yelled down to him. "Sir, Six is on the horn. He wants to know what's happening."

"Here, take the boy." Neilley said to his driver. Slinging his M-16 over his shoulder, he took Ringo from Lieutenant Neilley's arms.

Neilley quickly climbed on top the APC taking the radio handset his gunner was holding. "Six, this is One-Six, over."

"This is Six. What do you got? Over."

"This is One-Six. Ah, I got an old woman, a boy, and a little girl. They came up the road saying something about V.C. The boy looks like he's hurt pretty bad and the old mamma-san looks like she's been slapped around too. Over."

"Any other activity? Over."

"That's a negative. Over."

"Okay, bring them to my location. We'll have the medics take a look at them. Maybe we can find out what's going on. This is Six, out."

* * * * * * * * * * * *

As he customarily did when out on a listening post assignment, Mitchell had divided the team into two groups for pulling watch. It was about thirty minutes before sun up and the group of Mitchell, Frank, and Mike were awake on the last watch rotation. Mitchell was restfully leaning against a fallen tree trunk, gazing down the slope of the ridge at the river below; when the quiet of the early morning was interrupted by the distant sound of machine gun fire. He leaned forward, focusing his attention in the direction of the bridge compound.

Frank who was sitting five feet to Mitchell's right, quietly asked. "Was that our guys?"

"It sounded like a fifty being fired down at the bridge." Mitchell answered, still staring in the direction of the compound. A fifty caliber machine gun makes a distinct sound and can be easily distinguished from other guns.

Then they say the first illumination flare light up.

"That's our guys for sure." Frank said.

"Yeah!" Mitchell said as he turned to Mike a few feet to his left. "Have you heard anything on the radio?"

"No Sarge. Not a word from Homeplate."

The three of them sat without speaking for another full minute. Then the second flare lit up. They watched and listened, but no more firing was heard.

"Should I wake up the others?" Frank asked.

"No, not yet. It doesn't look like anything serious. Someone probably got spooked by a dog, or a pig, or something." Mitchell speculated. "Mike, let me know if anything comes over the radio," he added.

The medics had managed to close the cut on Ringo's head and stop the bleeding. They had bandaged his head and taped up his broken nose. The three small cuts on Mamma-san's face had also been cleaned and attended to. While the medics were working on Ringo and his mamma-san, Captain Tice and Lieutenant Neilley had managed to get a fairly good detailed account of what had happened. They walked out of the command bunker and were standing by Captain Tice's track.

"It'll be sunup in about twenty minutes. We're not going to go anywhere until then." Captain Tice said to Neilley. "If we charge off in the dark we could run into anything and probably get someone killed."

"I agree sir. It could be just what they want." Neilley added. "You know, this looks like the same kind of thing that was going on over at Ap Thanh Tan last month. I hate this shit! We move in here and just when we start to develop a rapport with the villagers, start getting a little cooperation from them, something like this happens."

"Yeah, and there's damn little we can do to protect them from it. The best we can hope for is to find the ones that are doing it and make 'em pay." Captain Tice said with a determined tone in his voice.

"That's easier said than done."

"I know Jeffrey, but at least we can try. At first light I want you to take your first platoon and start a search. I'll contact Rightfield and have Mitchell take his team to the south of the Ap Lai Thanh road. They can work their way east, while you search to the west."

"Yes sir." Neilley answered. "We'll be ready to roll at first light." Neilley left and crossed the bridge, returning to his track.

"Miller." Captain Tice called to his R.T.O. "Get Rightfield on the horn."

The taking of May Le had not been by random chance. Her relationship with Frank had become common knowledge throughout the village. Three Fingers hated the

220

Americans and for her to love one was more than he could take and therefore he had singled her out. The idea of May Le having a romantic and sexual relationship with a G.I. had enraged him and for the past two days he had contemplated a way to get even.

The sun was just beginning to rise as Three Fingers and his gang arrived at their destination with their prisoner. She had been dragged along through the jungle for the last thirty minutes. Her arms being cinched so tight around the pole, it had caused the circulation of blood to be cut off until she had lost all feelings in them and now it was if they didn't even exist. She had fallen to the ground time after time only to be kicked and beaten relentlessly until she was able to struggle back to her feet. Numerous cuts and scratches covered her face and arms from the limbs of the trees and the razor sharp leaves of the rainforest thicket.

Finally being thrown down to the ground in a small clearing was at first a relief. But only for a moment, it then became apparent what was going to come next. May Le was sitting on the ground surrounded by Three Fingers and his six comrades. They untied her hands, removing the pole that her arms had been hooked around. Having no feeling in them, her arms fell limp to her side. She tried to raise them but they were lifeless, unable to move at all. Helpless to do anything to stop her captors, they commenced to tear off all her clothes. Now completely naked she was held down, a man holding onto each arm and leg, pulling until she was laying spread eagle on her back. They tied ropes to her wrists and ankles pulling them tight maintaining the spread eagle position, tying the ropes off to bamboo stakes they had driven into the ground. She was bound tight unable to move at all as the morning's first rays of sunlight shined into her eyes.

She looked up at her abductors standing around her laughing and deciding who would go second and who would be third. For it was understood that Three Fingers would be the first to violate, to torture, to rape this beautiful young girl. She closed her eyes, terrified and crying. A few seconds later she felt him on top of her. He forced himself inside of her violently, time after time, harder and harder. Not in any attempt to gain pleasure for himself, but only to hurt and humiliate her. She was horrified and sickened by what was happening. She couldn't move or fight back, she couldn't even scream because of the gag still tied over her mouth. Finally the violation had stopped. She opened her eyes, thinking that maybe it was over, but it was only just beginning.

May Le looked in horror as another one climbed on top of her. It happened again and again, until all seven had taken a turn. Mercifully, at some point her mind had become as numb as her body and she laid there in a daze, only semi-conscience.

It had been two and a half hours since Captain Tice had contacted Mitchell and ordered him and his team to search for the V.C. that had terrorized the village. Mitchell had been guiding the team in a slow systematic zigzag pattern, covering about one thousand meters wide as they moved east towards the village.

Brian was walking point and was the first to come up on the clearing. He immediately saw the body staked out. It was about seventy-five feet away, near the other side of the small clearing, but close enough that he could tell it was a female tied down spread-eagle. He stopped the patrol and every man dropped to the ground into a defensive position. Brian signaled for Mitchell to come up to the point.

"What do you got?" Mitchell asked as he crawled up beside Brian.

"Over there, on the other side." Brian pointed.

"What the hell!" Mitchell uttered in disbelief as he spotted the naked body. "Six said they had taken a hostage."

"Yeah, I think she's dead Sarge. How you wanna do this?"

Mitchell's eyes were scanning the tree line all around the clearing. This was the kind of thing that the V.C. might do to draw someone in and catch them in an ambush.

"Bring everyone up except for the last two men. Have them set up behind us about twenty meters for rear security."

"Right." Brian acknowledged as he moved off to carry out Mitchell's instructions.

He soon returned with Mike, Keith, and Frank. "Sanchez and Paul are set up for security." Brian reported.

"Okay, this is what we're going to do. Brian, I want you to make your way around the clearing to the left. I'll work my way around to the right. We'll make sure we're not walking into any shit. We'll meet up on the other side. The rest of you wait here. Okay Brian, take off and watch your step."

Brian and Mitchell started their search. It took them over four minutes to meet up on the other side of the clearing. Feeling safe that this wasn't bait for a trap, Mitchell entered the clearing walking up to where May Le laid. Brian followed close behind. They were stunned by what they saw. Her arms and legs were still tied to the four bamboo stakes. A fifth stake had been forced into her vagina, through the uterus, and out her lower back, driven into the ground beneath her. She laid there dead in a pool of her own blood. Hundreds of ants were swarming over her, crawling in and out of her mouth, ears, and nose. They were drawn by the blood and had amassed at every open cut on her body.

Mitchell closed his eyes. He felt sick to his stomach. His body was quivering, "Oh Lord!" He said, putting his hand over his mouth.

After a few seconds Brian spoke barely above a whisper. "My God. Sarge, do you know who this is?"

"Yeah," Mitchell opened his eyes looking across the clearing. "Yeah, I know."

The three men on the other side of the clearing could tell by Mitchell's and Brian's reaction that what they had found had stunned them. The way Mitchell stared in their direction hit Frank in his gut. Ever since the team had started the search and had been told that the V.C. had taken a female hostage, Frank was thinking of May Le, praying it wasn't her. But now the look on Mitchell's face, the sad, helpless look, confirmed his worst fears. Frank rose to his feet and began to walk across the clearing. Slowly at first and then faster with each step never taking his eyes off of Mitchell's face.

As he got nearer, Mitchell stepped out to grab him, not knowing what to say except, "I'm sorry Frank. I'm sorry."

Frank pushed on by, focusing only on May Le. "No, not her! Not her goddamn it!
Not her!" He cried out as he fell to his knees trying desperately to get the ants off of her.

After watching Frank for thirty seconds hopelessly battling the ants, Mitchell and Brian pulled him back up to his feet.

"We're too late man, there's nothing we can do for her." Mitchell said wrapping his arms around Frank. "I'm sorry man."

CHAPTER SIXTEEN

On this day First Platoon had stayed at the compound for security while Second and Third Platoon were out on a search and destroy mission ten klicks southeast of the bridge. It was late afternoon. Mitchell looked up towards the unbearably bright sky. There wasn't a cloud to be seen and not the slightest breath of a breeze to be felt. The glaring sun was burning down so hot that even an Arizona desert scorpion would have been searching for shade.

He was squirming back and forth, first lifting one cheek off the hard two by six board that covered the hatch hole and then the other. For the past two hours Mitchell had sat there and his butt was going numb. Finally he stood up, irritated by the sensation of a thousand tiny pins sticking in his ass.

"That's enough of this shit!" He decided and then looked back down through the open rear hatch at Country.

He was inside the track and was admiring the Playboy centerfold he had just taped to the wall. It was Miss April 1968. Seeing what Country was up to made Mitchell crack a bit of a smile.

"You know if you stare at those too long you can go blind," he teased.

"Yeah, well it might just be worth it if I could get my hands on them."

Mitchell took a big sip out of the can of Coke he had in his hand, emptying it of the last bit of cool soda.

One of the advantages of staying at the bridge during the day was being able to get ice. But for Mitchell that wasn't enough to make up for the boredom of the long hot day. He really would have preferred being out on the search and destroy.

"How about coming up here and taking watch for a while. I've been sitting so damn long my ass has gone to sleep."

"Sure thing," Country replied as he came climbing up out of the APC.

Mitchell raised his right hand, still holding the empty Coke can and pointed out in front of their position. "There's three or four pigs rooting around out there, about, ah hundred meters over by the river bank," he wanted to make Country aware so he wouldn't be startled by the pigs' movements.

"Okay, I'll look out for them." Country said, climbing into the turret and taking a seat.

Mitchell leaped from the top of One-One to the ground. He turned to face a two foot circular hole that had been dug for trash disposal. Using a basketball jump shot motion, he threw the empty Coke can into the hole some eight feet away. "Two points!" He softly said aloud, raising his arms over his head in triumph, then turned and walked the ten feet to the permanent perimeter bunker that One-One was parked beside.

The bunker was dug down into the ground about three feet with the top half of the walls being constructed out of sand bags, three layers thick. The roof was made of corrugated steel sheets with two layers of sand bags on top of that. Compared to being out in the burning sun, these bunkers were relatively cool and the men of A Troop would often take shelter there during the heat of the afternoon.

As Mitchell stepped down to the entryway of the bunker, he could hear music coming from a tape player inside. He recognized it as one of Country's tapes, but didn't know who was playing it. Ducking his head as he stepped through the low doorway, he stopped just inside to listen and to his surprise, Dave was singing along with Merle Haggard's "Sing Me Back Home." Dave looked up and saw Mitchell watching him, but this new audience didn't stop him. He continued singing through the chorus then stopped and looked at Mitchell with a sheepish grin.

"That's not your normal choice of music, is it Surfer?" Mitchell asked.

"Yeah, well I guess not. I don't know what it is. I try not to listen to this country shit but I can't seem to help myself."

Paul who was sitting in the other corner of the bunker laughed out loud and shook his head, then went back to reading the latest issue of Stars and Stripes. His chess board was set up in front of him on a make shift table, built out of old mortar boxes, but no one was playing. Mitchell stepped over to Paul and then sat down beside him.

"Couldn't get Frank into a match?" Mitchell questioned.

"Nah, I guess he's still not back to his old self. He told me maybe later and then left and went down by the river. Why don't you talk to him or something, Sarge? I sure hate seeing him down like this."

"I've tried," Mitchell answered. "Maybe I'll try again. You say he's down by the river?"

"Yeah, he left about twenty minutes ago."

Mitchell got up and slowly walked to the doorway, then stopped to listen to a little more of Merle now singing "Silver Wings."

He stepped out of the bunker and was softly singing along as he walked away.

Frank was sitting on the bank and throwing rocks into the fast moving current of the turbulent river. Mitchell sat down beside him. "What's happening?" He asked, trying to start a conversation.

"Same old shit," Frank answered, tossing another stone into the river.

"Yeah, I know man. In this place your either dying from boredom or ducking to keep from getting your ass shot off."

Frank didn't answer, just stared into the water. There was an uncomfortable silence for thirty seconds or so, then Mitchell decided to come straight to the point.

"Look Frank. It's been three days since we found her. Don't you think we ought to talk about this? You know, about what happened and how you feel about it."

"Talk!" Frank looked annoyed.

"Yeah, talk. Everyone needs to talk to someone, sometime."

"Talk," Frank said again and then paused for a second. "Okay, I'll talk. This thing with May Le is bothering me a lot. I mean, I really liked her. I really did."

"I know you did Frank," Mitchell answered sympathetically.

"You know the fucking bastards that did that to her, did it because of me, don't you?" Frank's anger and guilt came boiling out. "They tortured and killed her because she cared about me. Just fucking me, no other reason."

"Maybe...," Mitchell was going to try and answer, but Frank cut him off.

"Maybe?! There's no fucking maybe about it and you know it! You're not an idiot! You saw what they did to her!"

"Yeah, I saw. Okay they were sending a message, but it's not your fault. The way you two felt about each other, you don't plan that. Shit, it just happens. You can't blame yourself for this kinda shit, man. It wasn't your fault."

"Yeah Sarge, but I gotta do something."

"Like what?" Mitchell asked, knowing the question was just going to aggravate Frank, but he hoped to get it all out of him now that he was finally talking about it.

"Like what?! Like kill the motherfuckers, that's what!" Frank shouted back at Mitchell, slamming his fist into the ground.

"Okay, I'll go along with that. Let's kill the motherfuckers. Now the problem is, who are they and where the fuck can we find them?"

"You know it's the same bunch of Cong that's been fucking with us since we got here."

"Yeah, your probably right. But in the last month of looking for them, we only caught up to them one time, and we killed a couple of 'em, too. But shit Frank, this is their hunting grounds, their back yard. And anyways man, what are we suppose to do? Walk up to the C.O. and say,

'Sir we'd like to take a little time off from the war. You see there's these fucking gooks we'd like to kill for personal reasons.' I don't think so, Frank. The army frowns on that kind of thing, you know."

"Okay, Sarge. Okay, you made your point. But I'm telling you man, I gotta do something."

"Sarge!" Mitchell looked back over his shoulder to see who was calling him.

"Sarge, the lieutenant wants to see you." It was Dave, no longer walking closer, now that he had gotten Mitchell's attention. "He wants you over at the CP bunker."

"Okay, I'm on my way," Mitchell shouted back.

Dave acknowledged the answer by nodding his head, then turned walking back towards the tracks.

Mitchell rose to his feet, removed his booney hat and wiped the sweat from his brow. "Paul's over there in the bunker telling everyone how you're afraid to take him on."

"Yeah, sure. I've played that asshole twenty times and he ain't checkmated me yet."

"Hell, nobody in the whole troop has done that," Mitchell said. "But the question is, how close has Paul got to it?"

"Yeah, well I hav'ta admit the dude's pushing me." Frank said as he slowly stood up and stretched.

"So maybe, you're getting a little worried," Mitchell teased, hoping to lighten the mood.

"Fuck you!" Frank said. "Don't you got someplace yous' suppose to be? Hanging out with the brass planning strategy or something?"

231

"Aha, jealousy," Mitchell said, pointing his finger at Frank. "Beware of the green eyed devil."

Frank almost grinned, "Like I said before, fuck you."

Upon returning to One-One, Frank headed towards the bunker as Mitchell inquired from Country, "Did the lieutenant say what he wanted?"

"No, just for you to report to the command post right away."

Mitchell crawled into the APC through the rear gate to retrieve his M-16 then left to meet with Lieutenant Neilley.

The Huey was flying at fifteen hundred feet, six klicks south of Camp Evans. It had followed Highway One all the way since leaving Eagle. The chopper was lumbering through the air or at least that's how it seemed to PFC Anthony Paganini. He remembered something he had learned back in his ninth grade general science class. He recalled his teacher discussing the fact that a bumble bee by all rules of physics shouldn't be able to fly, but somehow it does. That was the feeling he had about this helicopter. The loud slapping of the main rotor, the constant jerking and bumping, gave Anthony the feeling that this chopper was struggling just like the bumble bee to overcome the forces of gravity.

This was his first time flying in a helicopter, one of many firsts he had experienced in the last few weeks. PFC Paganini was new in country and like all cherries he was anxious and overly analytical about everything. He stared out of the open-sided Huey, looking over the shoulder of the left side-door gunner. The gunner had been dozing off and on ever since they had flown over the old Imperial City of Hue and now was sound asleep. He was strapped in behind the M-60 machine gun that was hanging out of the open-sided helicopter. Paganini found himself studying the harness and straps that was holding the sleeping gunner and the single D-ring that was preventing him from falling to the ground below. A vision of the D-ring failing and the sleeping gunner falling from the chopper filled his mind. "Wouldn't that be a hell of a way to wake up from a nap," he thought. The nudging of an elbow in his ribs put an end to this bizarre daydream. One of the other replacements, which was being transported with Paganini, had spotted two F-4's flying west toward the inland hills and was pointing them out to him. Every few minutes seemed to expose Paganini to another new experience, another new image, and by now his mind was filled to capacity, leaving him, like most cherries, bewildered and apprehensive.

The Huey set down inside of Camp Evans on the large helicopter pad of the 224th Aviation Battalion. The replacements were directed to the east side of the landing pad where several jeeps were waiting.

As the eight replacements approached, one of the jeep's driver shouted out, "Everyone for the 406th Artillery come with me." Three of the new soldiers responded.

Paganini heard another driver call out, "A Troop, Third of the Fifth Cav."

"That's me." Paganini answered back.

"Well get your shit and get in." The driver said as he started up the jeep.

He placed his duffel bag in the back of the jeep alongside of two large mail bags and then climbed into the passenger seat.

"You're fucking late. That chopper was suppose to have been here a half hour ago. Let me see your orders, make sure you're in the right place."

Paganini handed the driver the manila envelope containing his orders. Thinking to himself, "What's with this asshole? I'm late. Like I got control over anything."

The driver read the front of the envelope, "PFC Paga.. ah... Pag...."

"Paganini!" Anthony said, helping him with the pronunciation.

"Whatever. A Troop, Third of the Fifth, you're the one." The driver replied handing him back his orders. Jamming the jeep into gear he tore off down the dirt road heading for the main gate.

The smart-ass driver was a headquarters company clerk and like most rear echelon personal, he wanted no part of Nam after dark. "I've gotta get your ass out to A Troop and get back here before the fucking sun goes down."

"Where are they?" Paganini asked.

"Song Bo River Bridge, about ten klicks south."

The trip to the bridge compound was a wild one, the driver passed everything they came upon, weaving his way through the everyday traffic on Highway One. He dumped Paganini out at the bridge compound command post along with the two bags of mail without saying a word and speeded back towards the safety of Camp Evans.

As Mitchell walked up to the command bunker he saw a new recruit in front of the command post. His new clean, crisp jungle fatigues made him stand out like a sore thumb. Standing next to Lieutenant Neilley, he seemed even smaller than his five foot five inch, one hundred and fifteen pound frame.

Paganini had always been self-conscience about his diminutive size and growing up on the Southside of Philly it became a matter of practicality. The smaller you were the tougher you had to be just to survive and Paganini was one tough little wop. He had become an amateur boxer and had gone as far as the semi-finals as a bantamweight in the Pennsylvania State Golden Gloves Tournament.

"You wanted to see me, sir?"

"Yes. Mitchell this is PFC Anthony Paganini," then using his hand to gesture to Mitchell, Neilley continued "This is Sergeant Robert Mitchell, TC of One-One."

Mitchell stepped forward extending his hand to the new recruit. Paganini shook it with a firm grip.

Lieutenant Neilley spoke again, "Paganini is the first of six new men we are getting in the next few days. Should bring us up to full strength. I'm assigning him to One-One."

"Yes, sir. It'll be good having a full crew for a change." Mitchell said.

Neilley turned to face Paganini, "It's good to have you as part of First Platoon. You'll be in good hands with Sergeant Mitchell."

Sensing that was the end of the Lieutenant's speech, Mitchell told the new man to pick up his gear and follow him. Doing so the two of them started to leave the command post when Mitchell stopped and turned.

"Sir, will I be taking the ambush team out tonight?"

"No, I talked to Six a little while ago, there's nothing on for tonight."

"Right." Mitchell acknowledged and then turned and with Paganini following, headed back to One-One.

They crossed the bridge without speaking and then Paganini said, "The Lieutenant says you're the best."

"He did, huh?"

"That's what he said."

"Well, maybe he says that about all his TC's." Mitchell said.

"It didn't sound that way to me." Paganini answered.

"Yeah, what did it sound like to you?"

"It sounded like he thinks you're good."

"Look man," Mitchell said. "Ass kissing don't count for much out here."

"I'm not ass kissing, just making a statement about something that might be important to me."

"How you figure?" Mitchell asked.

"How good you are might make a difference in me getting killed or not."

"True." Mitchell answered and then said, "Did he tell you that I'm also in charge of the scout section and by being assigned to One-One, you are now part of that scout section?"

"He mentioned it. Didn't go into any details."

"Well, that could make a difference in you getting killed or not."

"How so?" Paganini asked.

"Let's just say that every place this troop goes, we go first to check it out. Anytime the troop moves, we lead the way. We're on point, so to speak. It sometimes puts us in some pretty hairy spots without any help."

"Does it bother you?" Paganini asked.

"It's a job, someone has to do it."

"Did you volunteer for it?"

"No, it just kinda fell to me. First thing to learn is to never volunteer for anything."

"Did you try to get out of it?" Paganini asked.

"No." Mitchell answered not offering an explanation.

"I see." Paganini said.

"What the hell does that mean?" Mitchell asked.

"Nothing." Paganini answered with a smile.

Mitchell looked at him, "I can tell you're going to be a lot of fun."

They arrived at One-One and Mitchell introduced Paganini to Frank, Country, and Dave. By now the sun had fallen behind the western hills and the temperature was beginning to come down. Second and Third Platoon were entering the compound, returning from the day's mission without any incident.

"Frank, you and Country get the claymores and trip flares set out. Frank, I want you to take Paganini with you. Take your time and show him how it all works."

"Sure, Sarge." Frank said without much enthusiasm. "I'll give him the VIP tour."

He got four trip flares and the hammer from a wooden ammo box beside the turret.

"Come on Pagaweenie." Frank said, holding out two of the flares to the new man.

"It's Paganini! Pag-a-ni-ni!"

"Yeah, well whatever cherry. Maybe if you live long enough I'll learn to pronounce it to suit you."

Frank stepped off the top of the APC, his first step landing on the headlight guard and the second on the ground, then he continued on, not missing a stride. Paganini followed. His first step smooth and easy, but then he clumsily fell from the headlight guard to the ground. Frank looked back over his shoulder with a look of irritation on his face and then continued on his way, not saying a word. Paganini scrambled back to his feet, picking up the two trip flares and jogged to catch up with Frank.

Mitchell saw the little mishap and was watching Frank, the grungy old veteran, and Paganini, the crisp, clean cherry, walking away. Mitchell chuckled to himself. "The more things change, the more they stay the same."

Frank and Paganini had set out two of the four flares. Frank was taking the time to show Paganini how to conceal the stakes and the proper amount of tension to have on the tripwire. He explained the importance of having one tripwire overlap the next.

They were working on the third flare when Paganini asked, "I heard being part of this unit, I'm likely to see a lot of action?"

"Oh, you've heard that, did ya?" Frank answered.

"Yeah, I did. So is it true?"

"Oh sure," Frank said sarcastically. "As a matter of fact, we like to kill a dink a day around here, just to stay in practice."

"A dink?"

"Yeah, a dink, a slope, a gook." Frank's face was hard, his eyes cold. "They all mean the fucking same."

Paganini looked puzzled, he could hear the hatred in Frank's voice and wondered why.

Darkness came quickly and the crew of One-One were eating their evening meal of C-rations. Dave was on top in the turret and the rest sitting on the back lift gate. This was the first time Paganini had ever eaten C's and he was truly amazed at just how awful powdered eggs could taste. Discarding them after just three bites he was now working on some pound cake. He found it to be a little more to his liking.

"Where you from?" Country asked.

Paganini looked up from his pound cake, "Philly."

"Philadelphia?" Country said it in full.

"Yeah. We just call it Philly, ----the south side, actually." Paganini explained. "How about you, where's your home?"

"Pineville, North Carolina, the birthplace of President James Polk." Country said proudly.

"I guess that explains the name Country."

"Oh that," Country grinned. "My real name's Hollis, but Sarge don't like it much, so he started calling me Country. It kinda stuck."

"Hollis ---- I think maybe Sarge had the right idea." Paganini said.

"Yeah, he gave it to me the first day we got in Nam. We came over on the same plane. Ain't that right, Sarge?" Country said turning to Mitchell.

"That's right. Four and half months ago but it seems more like four years." Mitchell said more to himself than anyone else.

"Four and half months down sounds pretty good to a guy like me," Paganini said.

"Yeah," Mitchell shrugged his shoulders, "They say all things past --- so will this year." Mitchell stood up, turned and ducked down and crawled inside the APC. He retrieved his .45 caliber pistol in its military style holster and belt. He came back out on to the lift gate, placed the belt around his waist and buckled it.

"I'm going to check on the other scout TC's." Mitchell stepped off the lift gate and started to leave.

"Wait a second, Sarge." Country said and quickly crawled inside the track, returning with an issue of Playboy. "When you're down at One-Four give this to Keith. He's trading his August for my March."

Mitchell took the magazine from Country, "Any other errands you'd like me to run for you?"

"No, that's it. Thanks." Country smiled as he spoke, knowing that Mitchell was just kidding.

Mitchell tried to check with the TC's of One-Two, One-Three, and One-Four at least once a day. He was the next rung on the ladder of command for them and he took his responsibilities seriously. He spent the next hour talking first to Sergeant O'Shea, then to Brian Banks, and Leroy Hill. He made the Playboy swap with Keith and made his way back to One-One. Frank had taken over watch on top. Dave and Country were watching Paganini sharpening a knife.

"Hey, Sarge." Country said, his voice filled with excitement. "Get a look at this. It's some mean looking toad stabber."

"That it is." Mitchell said, staring at the knife.

Paganini was working it with an oil-stone, making slow smooth strokes along the twenty inch single-edged blade. Patiently working on the edge that already seemed to be razor sharp. It was a Civil War vintage Bowie side knife with a heavy straight-backed blade and wooden handle. It had a steel D hand guard and weighed two and half pounds. This was a serious knife. It could be used for both cutting and thrust, meant to be a tool and a weapon. Paganini placed the oil-stone on his knee and then tested the edge by sliding the blade over his forearm. It shaved the hair off as clean as a baby's butt. He then went back to work with the oil-stone, using slow rhythmic strokes down the long blade.

"Are you sharpening that thing or making love to it?" Mitchell asked.

"Ah, Sophia needs a lot of loving care."

"Sophia?" Mitchell questioned.

"Meet Sophia." Paganini said, handing the big Bowie knife to Mitchell to examine.

At first the weight surprised him, two and half pounds is a lot for a knife, but then he put his hand on the handle and through the D-guard in its proper position the knife felt balanced and agile.

"She's a real beauty all right," Mitchell said.

"You bet she is. She's the real thing. A Bowie from the Civil War, over a hundred years old now."

"Over a hundred, huh. It must be worth a pretty penny if it's that old." Mitchell reasoned.

"Probably, but I'll never sell her. My grandfather gave it to my dad and he gave her to me. No, Sophia's like part of the Paganini family, I'd never sell her."

Mitchell handed the knife back to Paganini, "That's a hell of a knife."

CHAPTER SEVENTEEN

Ringo hadn't slept at night since May Le had been taken and killed. He would sleep a little during the day, but not at all between dusk and dawn. This was the fourth straight night that he had stayed awake, standing vigil, guarding what was left of his family.

He could still remember vividly the day the VC killed his father. He was only six when it had happened, but it was still clear in his memory. They came into the hut late at night and dragged his Papa-san out into the street. Making Ringo, his Mama-san, and May Le watch as they tortured him by cutting off his hands, one at a time, and then finally ending his suffering by a bullet to the head. Then there was his older brother, who was ran down and killed, now May Le.

This was a lot for a nine year old boy to have to carry around inside. He couldn't sleep partly because of fear, but most of all, he was determined not to let anything happen to his Mama-san or his baby sister.

He was squatting next to the wall of the cooking shed behind the hut. He usually stayed there for fifteen or twenty minutes before walking around the hut, checking the sides and front, then back to the cooking shed. There was a light rain falling and the overhang of the cooking shed roof was only partly protecting Ringo. He would reach up occasionally to wipe the rain from his face, as he stared out across the open space between the back of the village and the tree line. He had an old butcher knife clinched tight in his right hand. It wasn't much of a knife, but it was the closes thing to a weapon Ringo had.

He had only been there ten minutes this time when he saw two figures come out of the tree line. His heart started beating faster as he watched them quickly move across the open ground, ducking into the third hut down from Ringo's. It was the old witch's hut.

"What's all this?" Ringo thought. "Who was that and why were they sneaking into the village in the middle of the night? Why that hut?"

He stood and slowly started to move toward the old witch's hut, creeping along quietly. He was about fifty feet away when he saw a light come on. Its dim glow shimmering through the curtain that was pulled closed across the back doorway. He got down on his knees and crawled the rest of the way to the door. Laying flat on his stomach, he looked into the hut through the three inch gap between the bottom of the curtain and the floor. He could see three pairs of legs, but couldn't see anything of the people from the waist up. He heard the old witch speak.

"You must be careful, my son," she said. "The people of the village are very angry. The killing of the girl has only brought them closer to the Americans."

A chill ran through Ringo's little body when he realized what he was hearing. Ringo reasoned that these must be the ones that had killed May Le. He was very afraid, but he had to see the faces of those that had murdered his sister. Raising his left hand, he slowly pulled back the bottom of the curtain an inch or so away from the wall; just enough to see into the hut. Two young men were standing facing the old woman by a table on which a single lit candle set.

One of the men was speaking loudly and angrily waving his hands about. "If killing the girl did not convince them, I shall kill more and more of them, until they do as I wish."

Ringo's attention was drawn to the man's hands. Spotting Three Fingers' crippled hand, he trembled all over. This was the hand he had seen across May Le's face before he was knocked out. He let go of the curtain and pulled back from the doorway.

"What can I do now?" Ringo thought. These were the men that had killed his sister, but what could he do. They were two grown men each with a gun and he was a nine year old little boy with a rusty old butcher knife. He continued to listen to the voices coming from inside. Three Fingers wanted some gasoline, two cans, but the old woman had none and said they would have to come back in two nights for it. Ringo listened until he could tell the men were about to leave and then he crawled back to the next hut, hiding behind a stack of old wooden mortar boxes that belonged to the old witch's next door neighbor.

Less than a minute later, the two men stepped out of the back doorway, slowly looking all around before they quickly crossed the open ground and disappeared into the tree line at the same spot where they had come out from.

His fear abated some and Ringo ran back to his own hut, sitting down against the wall of the cooking shed. The rain had stopped and the sky was beginning to clear. He sat there watching the stars as they appeared through the breaks in the clouds and began to think of what he should do next.

That morning, the scout section left the compound early, just as the sun began to climb over the eastern horizon. Mitchell's mission for the day was to travel northeast to the village of Ap Trang La and then on to the Pha Tam Giang inlet. Looking for the best travel route and to acquaint himself with the high ground. The rest of First Platoon and Third Platoon were with Captain Tice, guarding an ammunition convoy going to Firebase Jack. Second Platoon would be staying at the bridge.

By midafternoon, the scout section had returned to the compound and taken up their normal positions on the perimeter. Frank shut off One-One's engine and lowered the rear lift gate, then climbed out of the driver's hole. Mitchell remained in the turret, studying his map and making notes for the briefing he would be giving to Captain Tice later that evening.

"I'm going over to the village and see if there's any ice left to buy," Frank said.

"I'll go with him," Country said.

"How about me?" Paganini asked. "Would it be okay if I went along?"

"Dave," Mitchell asked. "Do you want to go?"

"Nah, I'll just hang out here."

"Okay Paganini, but stay with Frank or Country." Mitchell answered.

"Right Sarge," Paganini replied. He was excited about looking over a Vietnamese village for the first time.

Country had gone down inside the APC as Paganini jumped off the left side of the track to the ground. Frank was still standing on top.

"Are you ready to go, Paga-weenie?" Frank said.

"Yeah!" Paganini answered, not complaining about the misuse of his name this time.

"No you're not! Get your sixteen, man! Yous don't go no fuckin' place without it!" Frank said almost in a scolding tone of voice.

Mitchell looked up at Frank with a little smile, then returned his eyes back to his map not saying anything. Country came out of the back of the APC carrying his M-16 in one hand and Paganini's in the other.

"I got it," he said, handing the weapon to the cherry.

"You want me to bring you anything?" Frank asked Mitchell.

"Can't think of nothing," Mitchell answered. "You guys be back in a hour or so."

"Will do," Frank said and then jumped to the ground and the three of them walked away.

Frank went directly to Ringo's Mama-san to buy the ice. Anytime the men on One-One needed something, they would go to her first to do business. But she had already sold all her ice that day. Frank, Country, and Paganini were about to leave when Ringo came running out of the hut.

"Frank!" The little boy shouted. "Frank, I need talk to you." He grabbed Frank by his hand, pulling on him. "Come Frank, now! I need talk."

"What is it, Ringo?" Frank asked.

"Not here! Come, not here!" Ringo didn't want his Mama-san to know about the men he had seen the night before.

Frank turned to Country, "You guys go see if there's any ice to buy. I'll see what the fuck the kid wants. Meet me back here."

"Okay," Country said. "Come on, Paganini."

Frank then followed Ringo around the side of the hut to the cooking shed.

"The men kill my sister, I see last night." Ringo sounded excited and sad at the same time.

"What? You saw what?"

"The VC, ones killed May Le. I see last night."

"Where? Where did you see them?"

"They came that hut," Ringo was pointing towards the old witch's hut. "Witch's hut, last night." Pulling Frank by the hand he said, "I show you."

Hearing the news from the little boy sent a wave of emotions through Frank, feelings of hatred for May Le's killers and a compelling need to avenge her death. An eye for an eye was what was on his mind.

"Are they there now?" Frank asked, unslinging his M-16 and bringing it to the ready.

"No, they go away last night. Not stay."

"Which hut?" Show me." Frank said.

Ringo led the way in a slow run to the back of the old witch's hut. Frank looked through the open back doorway, the hut was empty. The old woman was out front working her stand.

"They go last night back this way." Ringo then led Frank across the open ground to the tree line. They stopped just inside the trees.

"How many came to the hut?" Frank asked.

"Two," Ringo answered. "One is old witch's son. One with fingers gone."

"What?" Frank asked.

"He have two fingers gone." Ringo demonstrated with his open hand, folding down his little and ring fingers as if they were missing. "He has three fingers. I see hand when take May Le," his eyes had filled up with tears. "He say come back two nights for gas. You kill them, Frank. I help you. You kill them."

"Yeah, maybe. Maybe I will. What did you say about coming back for gas? When? When are they coming back?" Frank asked.

"Two night." Ringo answered.

"Tonight? They'll be back tonight."

"No, no this night. Next night, two night." Ringo said holding up two fingers to help Frank understand.

"In two nights," Frank held up two of his fingers.

"Yes," Ringo said, nodding his head.

"Okay." Frank said, thinking to himself. "They came from this trail? Right here..." Frank pointed to the spot where they were standing. "...and left the same way?"

"Yes," Ringo answered. "They go this way." By now the tears were rolling down his cheeks and Ringo began brushing them away. "We kill them, right Frank? We kill them?"

"You bet kid, we'll kill the fuckin' bastards."

Frank and Ringo walked back to the front of Ringo's hut. Country and Paganini were there waiting. Paganini was holding a chunk of ice about the size of a loaf of bread. It was beginning to melt, the cold water covered his hands and an occasional drop fell to the ground. Country was paying Ringo's mama-san for the half case of Coke he had under his arm.

"Let's go!" Frank said, quickly walking past Country and Paganini, heading back to the bridge compound.

It took a half a minute for them to catch up to Frank, "What did the kid want?" Country asked.

"The motherfuckers that killed May Le, he saw them last night."

"Here?" Country asked.

"Yeah," Frank answered. You could hear the determination in his voice.

"Jesus!" Country said a little stunned by the news.

"What?" Paganini asked. "He saw who? Who's May Le?"

Ignoring Paganini, Frank continued his quick pace, anxious to talk to Mitchell. Country didn't answer either, deep in his own thoughts, knowing all hell was going to break loose.

Upon arriving at One-One, Frank told Mitchell every detail of what Ringo had said, while Country and Dave listened and filled in the history for Paganini.

"I'm going to kill those motherfuckers, Sarge. I'm gonna wait for 'em tomorrow night and blow their shit away."

"Hold it Frank, just a minute. You can't just go off and kill anybody you want. What the fuck are you thinking?" Mitchell said, trying to be realistic about it.

"I'm thinking the bastards that killed May Le are going to be right over there, tomorrow night," Frank pointed to the small village south of the bridge. "...and I'm going to kill 'em. That's what the fuck I'm thinking!"

"How Frank?" Mitchell said. "You can't go off and just kill people like that. There's rules, laws; you're in the US Army. You can't just run around doing that kind of shit."

"Why not?" If I can kill gooks for the US Army, then why can't I kill a couple for myself. What's the fuckin' difference, killin' is killin'."

"Leavenworth, that's the difference. Spending the rest of your life in Leavenworth. That is if you don't get killed yourself," Mitchell answered.

"I don't care about that shit, and anyway Sarge, what about what you said yesterday?"

"What?" Mitchell asked.

"Yesterday, over at the river, you said you'd go along with me about killing 'em. You said okay, but we didn't know who they were or where they were. Well, now we know. So, did you mean it? Will you help me or were you just blowing smoke up my ass?"

Mitchell looked into Frank's face, into his eyes. They seemed to peer right through Mitchell. Frank was stone serious. Mitchell felt his gut churning. Was his words coming back to haunt him? He did say it, but at the time he never thought this would happen. He didn't say anything, just stared at Frank's eyes.

Frank spoke again, this time in a lower and softer voice, "Listen to me, Bobby." This was the first time he had ever called Mitchell by his first name. "I'm going to do this. I need you to help me, but with or without you, I'm going to do it."

The two men looked at each other without speaking. Ten or fifteen seconds passed, then Frank added, "I mean it, Sarge. I really mean it."

"I know you do," Mitchell answered. Again silence for another ten seconds, "Oh, what the hell. I'll help you."

Frank smiled. Mitchell couldn't believe what he had just said. But his gut had quit churning and in a funny way he felt good about it.

"But, if I help you, we're going to do it my way. We're not going to just blow them away. All that would do is get us both in Leavenworth."

"Anything you say, Sarge. You got something in mind?" Frank asked.

"No, I'll hav'ta think on it."

"All right!" Country said, followed by Dave giving him a high five.

Mitchell's look turned stern as he said, "You guys aren't going to have nothing to do with this. Nothing, I mean it. I'm not going to let anybody else get involved in this. Frank has to do what he has to do and I'm going to help. But the rest of you are out of it. Got it?"

"Okay, Sarge." Country said. Dave nodded his head yes.

"You guys just keep your mouths shut. You understand, Paganini?" Mitchell said.

"I understand. I won't say anything." Paganini answered.

Mitchell had committed to helping Frank and he intended to keep his word. Now he had to figure out how.

The troop had returned from Firebase Jack and Mitchell had given Captain Tice his report on the terrain between the bridge and Pha Tam Giang. First Platoon would be staying at the compound the next day and that would give Mitchell and Frank a chance to prepare. "But prepare for what?" Mitchell thought. He needed a plan, a way to slip out of the perimeter, do the deed, and get back in, without anyone knowing or hearing anything.

He was sitting in the turret of One-One, watching Frank and Paganini putting out the claymores and trip flares. Mitchell knew getting in and out would be a straight forward proposition. Intentionally, leave a gap in the trip flare coverage in front of One-One, probably next to the river bank. Stay low for three or four hundred meters, then turn south, cross the Ap Lai Thanh road and come up in back of the village, then sneak back in the same way.

The actual killing of the VC could be done just like any other ambush. Find a spot on the trail, probably just inside the tree line. It would have to be done quietly, no guns, no shooting. Any gunfire coming from around the village now, would bring a response from Captain Tice. In fact, he would probably send the Scout Section's ground team in to investigate. That thought made Mitchell shudder.

"I must be fuckin' crazy," he whispered to himself.

Getting back to his thought process he reasoned it has to be quiet. Knives, Sophia...yes, Paganini's twenty inch Bowie knife would be perfect. Mitchell thought back on his hand to hand and silent weapons training in Ranger School. There he had done a lot of work with knives and there was another weapon that had intrigued him at the time. It was called a silent noose. It was simple, but very deadly and completely quiet. It was made from a length of fine but very strong wire, like a piano wire, connected between two hand grips. The simple motion of crossing one wrist over the other would automatically form the wire into a noose. You would attack the victim from the back, throwing the noose over their head and across their neck, forcefully pulling your hands apart, tightening the noose. The result is strangulation and depending on the force used, the cutting of the throat. Once applied there was no escape. Death was certain and completely quiet.

"Country, hand me up my guitar," Mitchell asked, his mind fast at work, designing the weapon.

Country handed up the inexpensive box guitar that Mitchell had bought at Camp Evan's PX. He hadn't cared for the inexpensive strings that were on the instrument when he bought it, so he had written and asked Maggie to send him a good set of Black Diamond strings from home. She did and that was what the guitar had now. He studied the strings, pondering which one would be best for the job. Both the small E and the B strings were a finer gauge of wire, making them better for cutting into the neck, but Mitchell was concerned about the string breaking. The G was the third smallest of the six strings. He believed that it would have more than enough strength and still be fine enough to cut into the flesh. Loosening the G tuning key until the string could be removed and disconnecting it from the bridge, he had the wire for his noose. Next he needed something to use for hand holds. The empty brass casing from a fifty caliber shell would work perfectly. It was just the right size to fit into the palm of the hand and provide a good grip. By now, Frank and Paganini were back at the track and along with Country and Dave were watching Mitchell, as he created this simple but deadly instrument. Using a sharp punch from the tool kit, he punched a small hole into the walls of the fifty caliber casing. He feed the guitar string through the holes and secured them. Just that easy, it was done. Mitchell held the weapon in his hands; it seemed almost elegant, but in a sinister way.

Mitchell laid out his plan to Frank. If Three Fingers came back alone, Mitchell would take him from behind using the silent noose and Frank would finish him off with Paganini's Bowie knife to the chest. If two of them came like they had the night before; Frank would take one man, attacking from behind, putting a hand across the mouth and killing him with the knife in his back. Mitchell would take the other using the noose. If more than two men came, then all bets were off. They would have to wait and come up with another plan. Frank agreed.

The next day Mitchell and Frank went into the village to Ringo's hut. They crossed the open ground from behind the hut to the tree line, making sure not to be seen by the old witch. Finally to the foot trail that Three Fingers had been using. Mitchell found a good place on the trail a short distance inside the tree line. The nature of the cover made it advantageous to attack the men when they returned into the jungle. So that is what Mitchell decided to do, let them go by into the village and take them out as they were leaving. Of course, the little boy was right there with them, watching and listening to everything the two soldiers said.

Back at the bridge compound, they spent much of the afternoon practicing the physical moves needed to overpower a man from behind. Because of Paganini's size being closes to the size of an average Vietnamese man, he was used as the target. They parked One-One so that only a four foot space was left between it and the permanent perimeter bunker. It served two very good purposes, one was to practice making the necessary moves in a small space like the trail would be. The other was to conceal their activity from anyone other than the crew of One-One. It wouldn't do to have someone see Mitchell and Frank practicing this kind of killing and all of a sudden finding two Vietnamese that had been killed the very same way.

It had seem like a game that afternoon, but now the sun was hanging low, just above the western hills. The reality of what they were planning to do that night was beginning to hit home. Mitchell and Frank set out the claymores and trip flares, leaving a thirty foot gap in the tripwires to the front of One-One, along the south bank of the river. Country, Dave, and Paganini were shown where the gap was. This was the corridor that Mitchell and Frank would crawl through, to slip in and out of the perimeter.

They waited until it was completely dark and then another hour. Mitchell and Frank were sitting on the ground with their backs against the bunker wall. Country was sitting across from them, leaning against the APC. Dave was on top in the turret and Paganini was sitting on top with his legs hanging over the side above Country's head. Mitchell and Frank had marked their faces and forearms with black and green camouflage stick. They both would be taking their M-16s, though they hoped not to fire them. Frank had Paganini's Bowie knife in its scabbard around his waist. Mitchell had his .45 on his hip and the wire noose slung around his neck with one hand grip tucked in his right breast pocket and the other in the left. No one had said much for the last ten minutes.

Mitchell broke the silence, "I don't suppose you've changed your mind?"

"Nope," Frank answered.

Mitchell took a deep breath and let it out, "I guess it's time, then."

"Yep."

Mitchell turned his eyes to Country, "I want you to stay awake until we're back. I don't care if it's all night."

"I will," Country answered. "Don't worry Sarge, I won't let you get shot coming back."

Mitchell looked back at Frank, "You ready?"

"Let's go," Frank said.

The two men moved off from the bunker, crawling low on their stomachs. They slithered like a couple of snakes through the low grass pass the gap in the tripwire and along the south bank. The vegetation was kept down for the first one hundred and fifty meters out from the perimeter for security reasons. This was the most dangerous area for them to be spotted. They moved slowly, flat on their bellies. The vegetation gradually began to get thicker and higher. At about three hundred meters it was safe to get to their feet. It had taken them twenty-five minutes to crawl that first three hundred meters. They turned south and were soon at the Ap Lai Thanh road. They crossed it and moved into the jungle behind the village. Mitchell led the way through the thick undergrowth. Reaching the foot trail, he turned east and followed it with Frank just a step behind. They had gone one hundred meters down the trail when Mitchell slowed up, knowing he was close to the spot he had picked for the ambush that morning. He was looking side to side, trying to pick out the spot in the dark. Suddenly, he saw movement from the right side of the trail, eight feet in front of him. A shocking chill shot through him as he swung his M-16 down, leveling on the target, flipping the safety switch to full automatic, all in one swift movement. He was just a split second away from instinctively pulling the trigger, when Ringo stepped out onto the trail.

"Jesus, fuckin' Christ!" Mitchell said, a little louder than he meant to. The little boy's eyes and mouth opened wide, he looked like a scared deer caught in the headlights.

"What the hell are you doing here?" Mitchell said, this time his voice more in control, just above a whisper. Ringo didn't answer.

Frank stepped around Mitchell and knelt down on one knee, "Ringo, what are you doing here?"

"I help. I help you and Honcho kill VC," the little boy said, still shaken by the knowledge that Mitchell had come so close to killing him.

Mitchell looked up to the sky and then closed his eyes for a second, still shaking inside.

"You shouldn't be here," Frank whispered to Ringo. "This is no place for you."

"No, I stay. I help," Ringo insisted. "VC kill my May Le, I help kill them. I stay."

Mitchell stepped up placing his hand on Frank's shoulder, "We don't have time to fucking argue. They could be coming down the trail any minute. Keep the kid with you, but keep him still and quiet. You take the right side here," Mitchell then pointed to the left side of the trail, six feet further down, "....I'll be over there." He stepped past Frank and moved into his position.

Frank took Ringo and got into his place. Frank was on his knees, sitting on the back of his ankles. The little boy squatted behind Frank, snuggling against him, leaning the side of his face on Frank's back with his left hand holding on to Frank's waist, and in his right hand the rusty old knife.

An hour passed without seeing or hearing a thing and then another ten minutes. Frank and Mitchell heard the sound at the same moment, it was Three-Fingers and one of his comrades coming down the trail. They weren't making any particular effort to be quiet. Mitchell and Frank had heard them for a good ten seconds before they came into sight. Mitchell studied them as they walked by, they were in single file about four feet apart. The only weapon Mitchell saw on the first man was an AK-47 assault rifle. The second man was carrying what looked like a SKS carbine and a two foot machete stuck in his belt on his left side. Mitchell waited thirty seconds after they had gone out of sight, then stepped out onto the trail. Frank whispered to Ringo to stay hidden, then stepped out next to Mitchell.

"Stay here," Mitchell whispered next to Frank's ear. "I'm going to make sure they go into the village."

Mitchell moved off, down the trail. He came to the edge of the tree line and watched the two VCs as they crossed the last fifty feet of open ground and ducked into the old witch's hut. Mitchell returned to the ambush site. Frank stepped back out onto the trail.

"They're in the old woman's hut," Mitchell said.

"How do you want to do it?" Frank asked.

"They'll probably be in single file, just like they were before," Mitchell said. "They'll come by me first, so I'll wait for both to go by and then I'll take the last man. As soon as you see me make my move; you take the first man, he should be just passed you. I'll wait until he's passed you to make my move. That's the way I got it figured."

"Sounds good to me," Frank said.

"That is unless you want to call it off," Mitchell said.

"No, no I don't want that, and anyways if we don't do it, that crazy kid will probably try it by himself."

"I gotta be fucking crazy," Mitchell said, shaking his head. "Well, let's get into place, before I think about it too long."

The two men moved back into their hiding places and waited. Frank moved Ringo to a spot about three feet behind him and whispered to the little boy to stay there. He then got back in position, leaning his M-16 against the base of a tree. He took Paganini's Bowie knife out of its scabbard and griped it in his right hand and got ready to administer his form of an eye for an eye justice.

Mitchell laid his M-16 on the ground beside him. He took the wire noose from around his neck, griping the fifty caliber shell casings tightly in the palms of his hand making a fist, the wire coming out from between his ring and middle fingers. Every minute or so he would practice crossing his left wrist over his right, making a loop and visualizing the moves he would use to kill the VC.

Twenty minutes had passed when Mitchell heard the VC coming back down the trail. It seemed like a much shorter time, maybe that was because Mitchell wasn't looking forward to this. But like it or not, they were coming and he readied himself. He stared at the first man as he approached. It was the one with the AK-47. He was carrying a one gallon can of gasoline in his right hand and had the AK slung over his left shoulder.

"Shit!" Mitchell thought. If the second man had his rifle slung over his shoulder, it was going to make it hard to get the noose over his head. Mitchell's eyes darted away from the lead man to the second, he was carrying a can of gasoline in his left hand and holding his SKS carbine in his right, down by his side. A feeling of relief flowed through Mitchell's body and all of a sudden he was surprisingly calm. He stared without blinking as the second man walked in front of him. The two VCs were separated by about six feet and the lead man was just now passing in front of Frank. He readied himself to spring out as soon as Mitchell moved. Ringo was watching wide-eyed, his little heart beating like a drum. When the second man was one step past Mitchell, he leaped to his feet onto the trail behind the VC. Throwing the noose over the gook's neck, he jerked his hands apart and back, throwing his elbows wide. The VC's forward movement stopped instantly and was pulled back towards Mitchell, the wire noose cutting into his neck, crushing his larynx and sealing closed his trachea.

261

He dropped the can of gasoline and his SKS carbine, his hands reaching instinctively for his neck. It did no good, the wire was already buried into the flesh.

Frank lunged from his hiding place the instant he saw Mitchell attack, but his right foot slipped on his first step, slowing him down. The lead VC hearing his comrade drop the can of gasoline and his weapon, stopped and turned to see what had happened. Frank had regained his footing and was just one full step away from Three-Fingers when he had completed his turn. They were face to face, and before Three-Fingers could react, Frank took the one step and using an upward thrusting motion, he drove the big Bowie knife into him. It entered his body in the V under his ribs where the sternum ends. The blade traveled upward and slightly to the left. It nicked a kidney, tore through the diaphragm, cut the heart, and ended up in Three-Fingers' left lung. He made a loud gasping sound, his mouth opened wide. Then some more sounds, like a cross between a cough and gurgling. Frank grabbed a handful of Three-Fingers' hair as he felt his weight leaning forward. He pulled hard back and down on the knife, removing it from the VC's body. Three-Fingers dropped to his knees, Frank held on his hair preventing him from falling further. The coughing, gurgling sound continued to come from his mouth. Frank looked down at him for a few seconds, listening to the strange sound. He raised the big Bowie knife high above his head and brought it down with a vicious force into the left side of Three-Fingers' neck. The sharp edge of the heavy blade cut deep, severing the carotid artery and shattering a cervical vertebra. The force of the blow had almost decapitated him. The gurgling sounds stopped. Frank stepped back releasing hold of the hair, the body fell face first to the ground.

Mitchell continued to pull hard on the hand grips, tightening the noose around the VC's neck. The gook dropped to his knees and Mitchell put a knee between the VC's shoulder blades, pulling even harder with this new found leverage. Blood was running out of the neck from all sides, the full three hundred sixty degrees. The VC's hands dropped from his neck and fell limp to his sides. His eyeballs rolled up in his head, Mitchell continued the pressure.

Frank looked at Three-Fingers laying face down for a few seconds, then turned and looked at Mitchell and his victim. He walked over and stood in front of them.

"Pick him up," Frank said.

Mitchell looked perplexed.

"Pick him up," Frank said again.

Using his arms and upper body strength, Mitchell raised the VC to about ninety percent of his full height. The body felt like dead weight. Frank thrust the knife into the second VC's gut, then raising his foot onto the VC's chest for leverage, he pulled it back out.

"I think he's done," Frank said coldly.

Mitchell let him fall to the ground and unwrapped the wire noose from his neck.

Mitchell looked past Frank and saw Ringo standing over Three-Fingers. The little boy kicked him four or five times in the head and then spat on the lifeless body.

Looking back at Frank, Mitchell said, "Get their weapons. I don't want to leave anything out here some other Cong might use against us." He then knelt down pulling the machete out of the dead man's belt.

Frank walked back to Three-Fingers, picking up the AK-47 and searching him for more ammunition. Mitchell had retrieved the SKS carbine and stepped off the trail to get his own M-16. When he stepped back into the trail, Frank had his M-16 in one hand and the AK-47 slung over his shoulder.

"What about the gas?" Frank asked.

"I don't want to leave it," Mitchell answered. "....but, I don't want to take it back with us. Ringo, you take the two cans of gas with you, take them home."

"Okay Honcho, I take," Ringo said, then ran and picked up the two cans. He turned to Frank, "We kill them, Frank. We did number one job, right Frank?"

"Yeah, we killed em, kid. Number one good job."

Mitchell stepped over to where Frank and Ringo were standing, knelling down on one knee, "Listen Ringo, you can't tell anyone about this. No one. It would be real bad for Frank and me if you tell. Number fuckin' ten bad. Do you understand?"

"I understand. I not tell. I never tell. I never do bad for Frank and Honcho, never!"

"Good, that's real good Ringo." Mitchell said. "Now you go home."

Ringo looked at Frank, "Thank you, Frank."

"Don't mention it kid, it was my pleasure. Now get the hell out of here and keep your mouth shut. Go!"

The little boy smiled up at Frank and then turned and ran down the trail towards the village, the swinging of his arms exaggerated by the cans of gasoline.

Mitchell and Frank took one last quick look around and then started up the trail in the opposite direction. They backtracked the same route that they had come and in thirty-five minutes had crawled through the trip flares and were within forty feet of One-One.

Mitchell cupped his hands around his mouth in order to direct his voice, "Country, ...Country." Mitchell called out.

"Yeah Sarge, I hear you," Country answered.

"We're coming in," Mitchell said.

They crawled another ten meters before getting to their feet. Country was at the front corner of the bunker to meet them.

"Did anyone call for us or come by?" Mitchell asked.

"No," Country answered. "Nobody came. The only radio calls were just com checks."

"Good," Mitchell said, the relief showed on his face. He had been so uptight that something would go wrong, that the muscles in his neck had bunched up in knots. They moved around to the back lift ramp of One-One.

"What happened?" Country asked, his eyes shifting between Frank and Mitchell. "Did you do it? Did they show up?"

Frank took the knife from his waist and handed it back to Paganini. "Thanks man, for letting me use her. I'll clean her up, if you like."

Paganini pulled the knife out of its scabbard. It answered the question, the twenty inch blade was covered with the brownish-red stain of the VCs' blood.

"I guess you got 'em," Paganini said.

"Yeah, two of 'em. They're both fuckin' history," Frank replied.

"Righteous!" Dave said, staring at the bloody blade.

Mitchell was rolling his neck, trying to loosen up the muscles, relieved that apparently they had gotten away with it. Frank began to tell Country, Dave, and Paganini the details. Mitchell sat quietly, thinking. They had gotten away with it. He had helped his friend kill two men. Even though they had been the enemy, they weren't killed because of that, because of the war. Frank and Mitchell had killed them because of what they did to May Le, for revenge.

"What does that make it?" Mitchell thought. "It wasn't war, it wasn't self-defense. Revenge.....Murder!" Mitchell didn't like that thought, but he kept hearing it in his mind. "Murder!" If they were tried by an impartial jury of their peers, they probably would be found innocent; but inside he knew they were guilty as hell.

Paganini was cleaning the blood from Sophia. Mitchell's neck muscles were beginning to loosen up, even though his mind was still playing guilt or innocent games.

All of a sudden, the silence was broken, a call crackled over the radio, "One-One, this is Six, over."

The sound almost paralyzed Mitchell. Frank jerked his head around, staring at him. "How could he know? How could he?" Mitchell asked, a churning, sick feeling suddenly filled his stomach.

"No way! Not this soon!" Frank said.

"No one came by. No one called, I swear!" Country said.

"One-One, this is Six, over."

"Answer it," Mitchell said to Country.

"This is One-One, over." Country said into the handset.

"This is Six. Get your Tango Charlie on the horn, over."

Country handed the handset out towards Mitchell, his hand was trembling as he reached for it. He put it to his mouth and ear then pressed down on the transmission key.

"This is One-One Tango Charlie, over."

"This is Six. Congratulation, it's a boy! Seven pounds, nine ounces, both mother and baby are doing fine."

CHAPTER EIGHTEEN

It was December 24, Christmas Eve, when A Troop was relieved from security of the Song Bo Bridge complex. Two companies of the 404th Infantry took over at 0900 hours and A Troop rolled north on Highway One. They moved passed their home base at Camp Evans without even stopping and continued north on pass the Highway Nine intersection. They finally left Highway One just six klicks south of Dong Ha, turning east, crossing the railroad tracks, and then traveling three more klicks. Here is where they set up a night defensive perimeter in the middle of a large open area.

For Frank leaving the Song Bo represented somewhat of a closure, an end to a very painful time. In the last seven weeks he had met May Le and had fallen in love for the first time in his life. He had experienced the complete gamut of feelings that falling in love had to offer. From the wonderment of his first time seeing her, to the young boy shyness of getting to know her, the childlike fun they shared, and through the consummation of their love. Finally ending with her premature and brutal death. He had avenged her death and now there was nothing left to do, but go on.

For Mitchell the last nine days had been a new beginning, a happy one. He was a father now. The birth of his son, Brian, had enabled Mitchell to put the guilt feelings out of his head and he had spent the last week being the proud father.

It was a few minutes past noon when A Troop had set up their perimeter. At 1230 hours Lieutenant Colonel John Sheldon, commanding officer of Third Squadron, landed his helicopter in the middle of A Troop's perimeter. At 1300 hours, Mitchell got a call to report along with Lieutenant Neilley to the command post for a briefing with Captain Tice and Colonel Sheldon.

Mitchell left One-One, walking down the line until he got to One-Six, where he joined with Lieutenant Neilley and the two of them continued to Captain Tice's command track in the center of the perimeter. Colonel Sheldon's helicopter had set down about one hundred feet from the command track and Mitchell could see the Colonel and Captain Tice standing together as they approached. A third man was with them, a young lieutenant that Mitchell didn't recognize.

Captain Tice was the first to speak, "Colonel, you know Lieutenant Neilley, my first platoon leader."

"Yes, indeed. How have you been Lieutenant?"

"As good as one can be in these circumstances." Neilley answered.

"How true," Colonel Sheldon replied. "Captain Tice's reports speak very highly of you, Lieutenant."

"Thank you, sir," Neilley said.

"This is Sergeant Robert Mitchell, A Troop's scout section leader," Captain Tice said.

"I've heard a lot of good things about you also, Sergeant."

"Thank you, sir," Mitchell answered.

"I understand you've just recently became a new father."

"Yes sir, nine days ago."

"Boy or girl?" Sheldon asked.

"Boy, sir."

"That's good, every man should have a son. Congratulations, Mitchell."

"Thank you, sir."

"Yes, well I think I should be the one thanking you Sergeant. Your work with the scout section and especially your ambush team has made my decision to form the scout units look pretty good."

"I've had a lot of good people helping me, sir." Mitchell answered.

"Indeed. That brings me to what I called you in for. I have a little mission for you and your team. Let's take a look at that map Tom. Oh gentlemen, this is Lieutenant Tom Webster, he's my intelligence officer."

Webster nodded his head to Neilley and Mitchell as he unfolded the area map.

Colonel Sheldon started giving the briefing himself, while Captain Tice, Lieutenant Neilley, and Mitchell listened intently. "Gentlemen, we're located right here and that tree line to the east is just over a thousand meters. Inside the jungle, maybe six to seven hundred meters, there is a well-established supply trail." A Troop's perimeter was circled on the map with a black grease pencil and the trail marked with a black line. "A reliable informant has confirmed that once or twice a week, between 2300 and 0100 hours, a group of VC has been moving supplies and weapons down this trail and the next shipment is going to be tonight."

"Why tonight?" Tice asked.

"It's Christmas Eve. They think that we'll be celebrating and they don't want to miss a chance on running a shipment down when we're not paying much attention." Colonel Sheldon answered.

"Makes sense," Tice said.

"How many?" Mitchell asked.

"Five to eight men."

"Ever anymore?"

"The information we have says five to eight, no more, Sergeant."

"Any reason to expect anything different for tonight?" Lieutenant Neilley asked.

"None," Sheldon answered. "So Sergeant, if you get your ambush team set up along here," the Colonel was pointing at the trail on the map, "tonight between 2300 and 0100 hours, it will be the VC's time to die."

"To everything there is a season," Mitchell said.

Colonel Sheldon looked up at Mitchell, "Ecclesiastes Three, one through eight, I believe. Do you read the bible, Sergeant?"

"No sir, but I do listen to the Byrds. Turn, Turn, Turn, 1966." Mitchell answered with a straight face.

Colonel Sheldon glanced over at Captain Tice, who just raised his eyebrows and looked back down at the map. Lieutenant Neilley covered his mouth with his hand, faking a cough to hide the chuckle he couldn't hold back.

Sheldon spoke again, "Sergeant, I want you to take a patrol this afternoon and look over the trail, pick out an exact ambush site for tonight."

"Yes sir. I can get my team together and be on the way in half an hour."

"Lieutenant Webster will be going with you. I want him to be on the mission tonight." Sheldon said.

Mitchell looked up quickly first at Colonel Sheldon, then at Lieutenant Webster, then back at Sheldon. "Will I be in command or will the Lieutenant?" Mitchell asked, his face didn't hide his concern.

"Don't get bent out of shape, Sergeant. Lieutenant Webster will just be going along as an observer. You will be in operational command." Colonel Sheldon answered in an authoritative voice.

"I apologize sir. It's just that my team and I are a very close unit and to be successful, we have to know what to expect of every man in any situation."

"I appreciate that, Sergeant." Sheldon said.

"And so do I," Lieutenant Webster added. "Whatever you tell me to do, I'll do."

Mitchell nodded his head in acknowledgment.

"Is there anything else, sir?" He asked of Colonel Sheldon.

"No Sergeant. I think that will do it."

Mitchell looked at his watch, it was 1325 hours. He looked up at Lieutenant Webster and said, "The patrol will be leaving from my track, One-One, at 1400. I'd suggest you bring your M-16 and seven extra mags."

"Will do, Sergeant." Lieutenant Webster answered.

"If you will excuse me, sir, I need to get my team ready."

"By all means, Sergeant," Sheldon said.

Mitchell turned and left to return to One-One. Once Mitchell was out of ear shot, Colonel Sheldon said to the remaining officers, "Sergeant Mitchell's not shy about stating his position, is he?"

"No sir," Captain Tice answered. "He tends pretty much to say whatever is on his mind."

"I can see that," Colonel Sheldon said and then laughed, "Turn, Turn, Turn, 1966."

At 1400 hours, the ambush team and Lieutenant Webster departed the perimeter heading east. They quickly covered the thousand meters and were soon at the edge of the tree line. Mitchell held up the patrol and gathered his team around him.

"Okay, this is the order. Frank you take the point, then Sanchez, Keith and me. Mike, you and the lieutenant follow after me, then Brian and Paul. Frank just take us east until you hit the trail, it should be six or seven hundred meters in. Everyone keep your eyes open for booby-traps. There's no rush, take your time. Any questions?" There wasn't any. "Okay, move out."

Frank started into the jungle and each man followed in line. About forty-five minutes and six hundred meters later, Frank came across the foot trail. He stopped and signaled back for Mitchell to come up. Mitchell made his way up to Frank and knelt down beside him on the edge of the trail.

"This looks like it," Frank said.

"Yeah, I think so," Mitchell agreed. "Bring everyone up."

"Right." Frank answered and moved off to pass the word to the rest of the team.

Two minutes later the team was gathered around Mitchell. "Here's what we're going to do. Brian, I want you to take Keith, Paul, and Sanchez, follow the trail south, four to five hundred meters. You know what we're looking for, good cover and a manageable killing zone. I'll take Frank, Mike, and the lieutenant with me and check the trail to the north. We'll meet back here."

"Right Sarge. Keith, Paul, Taco, let's go." Brian said and the four men moved out south on the trail.

Mitchell and the remaining members of the team headed north. For the next twenty minutes Mitchell searched the trail for a good ambush site, not finding anything satisfactory he decided to turn back and see if Brian had any better luck. Brian and his half of the team were waiting at the rendezvous spot when Mitchell returned.

"Did you have any luck?" Mitchell asked.

"Yeah, I think so. There's a spot about two hundred and fifty meters down that looks real good."

"Let's go and take a look," Mitchell said. "You lead the way."

Brian led the team to a spot on the trail where it narrowed to barely three feet wide. The east side was up against a steep berm, six or seven feet high. The west side was almost level and in two places trees had fallen, giving the ambush team excellent cover.

"What do you think?" Brian asked.

"Good, real good. We'll use it." Mitchell replied.

"How are we going to set up?" Lieutenant Webster asked.

Not answering, Mitchell took a small notebook and pencil out of his left breast pocket and began to sketch out the ambush site and everyone's position. He would pace off distances between the positions and get down in each spot and check the line of fire. Ten minutes later he had a detailed drawing showing every man's position and the placements of the claymores. He showed each man the drawing and had them get in their position, so they could visualize the overall site. After fifteen minutes of familiarizing themselves with the site, Mitchell led the team back out and stopped at the edge of the tree line. He selected a place right on the tree line to use for a staging area, taking his compass he shot an azimuth back to the troop's perimeter. He noted the degrees in his notebook and then led the team back to A Troop.

It was 1720 hours when they got back, Mitchell told his team to report back to One-One at 2030 hours for equipment check and final briefing, the team would move out at 2100 hours. Mitchell met with Captain Tice and went over the exact location of the staging area and ambush site. He coordinated with the TC's of all three motor tracks, in case fire support was needed. He arranged for the patrols radio frequency and confirmed they would be using their normal call signs.

At 2030 hours, all the members of the ambush team had showed up at One-One, but not Lieutenant Webster. Mitchell waited ten minutes more, still no sign of Webster. Mitchell wasn't pleased, he stepped over to Mike and took the radio handset.

"Homeplate, this is Rightfield, over."

"This is Homeplate, over."

"This is Rightfield. Is my observer there? Over."

"This is Homeplate, he's on his way, over."

Keith was talking with Frank and Paul as they were finishing putting camouflage on their faces. "Why are we taking this prick with us anyways?"

"Orders, I guess." Paul answered.

"Yeah, well orders or no orders, if he don't show up soon, Sarge may leave his ass behind," Frank said.

"Yeah, he looks like he's getting a little pissed off," Keith added.

A minute later, Lieutenant Webster walked up to the back of One-One.

"You're late, Lieutenant," Mitchell said.

"I had a little trouble finding a boonie hat to wear like you asked for."

"I see you got one," Mitchell said as he began to check the lieutenant over. Webster was holding an M-16 and had a bandoleer of seven more magazines of ammo across his chest. He had a canteen of water on his belt. Mitchell took it out and shook it.

Mitchell answered bluntly the question on the lieutenant's face, "A partly filled canteen makes noise." It was full and Mitchell replaced it on the belt.

"What do you have in your pockets?"

The lieutenant patted his fatigue pants' pockets. They were empty. He reached for his left breast pocket and pulled out a book of matches and a half pack of Winstons.

Mitchell took them from his hand, "Those stay here," he said as he pitched them onto the back lift gate of One-One. "Anything else?"

"No, I don't think so," Webster answered.

"Let me see your dog tags."

Webster got them out from under his fatigue shirt. They were hanging loose on the chain. Brian stepped up with a roll of electrical tape at the ready. Mitchell took it and taped the two dog tags together. Lieutenant Webster was feeling a little inadequate by now.

He said, "I've never done this before, Sergeant."

"No shit," Mitchell replied and then said, "Brian, get the Lieutenant's face and arms covered."

"Right." Brian answered and began applying camouflage stick to the lieutenant's face.

Mitchell finished his briefing and checked his watch. It was almost 2100 hours, once again he took the handset from Mike and radioed.

"Homeplate, this is Rightfield, over."

"This is Homeplate, over."

"This is Rightfield. Will be departing perimeter in one minute on route for Sierra Alpha, over."

"This is Homeplate, roger. Moving out in one minute. Good hunting, over."

"This is Rightfield, roger. Out."

Mitchell took out his compass and shot an azimuth that would lead him to the staging area. He led the team out of the perimeter across the open sandy ground east toward the tree line. Fifteen minutes later they were at the staging area. They would stay there for only a short time, just long enough for Mitchell to go over the marching order one more time and shoot another azimuth that he would use to lead the team to the ambush site. It had been completely dark for the last thirty minutes and the teams' eyes were already adjusted to the night. At 2120 hours Mitchell led the team into the jungle.

They made their way through the dark thick growth stopping on three occasions for Mitchell to check directions with his compass. An hour and ten minutes into the jungle, they arrived at the ambush site, coming onto the trail right in the middle of what was going to be the killing zone.

Mitchell knelt down on the edge of the trail and gathered his team around him. "You all know your positions, move out and get in place. Brian, you and Frank get your claymores set out." Pointing directly at Lieutenant Webster, Mitchell said, "Lieutenant, you'll be staying with me." Mitchell hadn't assigned Lieutenant Webster a firing position, not wanting to risk him panicking and screwing up the ambush.

The trail ran almost perfectly north to south. The team was set up in a line along the west side of it. Brian was the left flank and Frank the right. Mitchell, as usual, was in the middle and would make the decision if and when to open fire. He had the third claymore and began setting it out, placing it six feet off the trail and stringing the firing wire back to his position. He connected it to the detonator while Lieutenant Webster followed and watched his every move.

Once he had finished he whispered next to Lieutenant Webster's ear, "Okay Lieutenant, you move back to where I showed you. Stay there and don't move don't do anything, just stay quiet."

"Right Sergeant." Webster answered and crawled about eight feet behind Mitchell.

Mitchell checked the illuminance dial of his watch, it was 2240 hours. He took the protective covers off the starlight scope and turned it on, scanning the trail in both directions. Seeing no movement he turned the scope off and settled in, watching and waiting.

Lieutenant Webster had thought this was going to be a new and exciting adventure, but now began to realize it was going to be a night filled with fear and danger. He had never been out in the boonies before, much less on an ambush. An hour passed and Webster's nervousness was increasing. His mouth had become dry, so he reached for his canteen. His palms were so sweaty he had to dry them on his pants before getting a grip on the cap to open it. He took a drink then returned the canteen to his web belt. Focusing his eyes back on Mitchell, he laid there perfectly still with anxiety building up inside him.

It was almost midnight when Mitchell heard movement behind him. He jerked his head around looking over his right shoulder. It was Lieutenant Webster crawling towards him.

Reaching Mitchell's position, Webster asked, "Have you seen anything?"

"No!" Mitchell answered abruptly.

"Do you think they'll come?"

"How the fuck would I know. Either they'll come or they won't. Now get back to your position and stay there, and don't make any more fucking noise."

Mitchell glared at Webster as he crawled back to his spot. "I don't need this kind of shit." Mitchell thought. "That asshole's gonna screw around and get somebody hurt."

Forty-five more minutes had passed when Mitchell spotted movement through the starlight scope. They were coming from the north, just as Colonel Sheldon had said.

A chill shot through his body as the adrenaline began to flow. He raised his arm and hand, signaling to Mike, who in turn pass the signal on. Then he signaled Keith on his right and he too passed it on. Once again looking through the scope, Mitchell followed the VC's movement as they made their way down the trail coming ever closer to the killing zone.

In less than a minute, the first VC was passing in front of Mitchell's position. He had a large backpack on his back and was carrying a Russian assault rifle in his hands. The next two men in line were carrying an oversized bundle slung under two poles which they supported on their shoulders. The fourth man had a large sack over one shoulder and a carbine of some type in his hand. He was followed by two more VC using the same pole and sling method, supporting a large wooden crate. Thirty more seconds passed and Mitchell estimated that the lead man must be getting close to Frank's position. The two carrying the wooden crate were almost in front of Mitchell.

He was thinking, "It's just about time to pop 'em." He felt the muscles in his neck and shoulders tightening up. It wasn't easy for him to make the decision to kill these people, but he had done it before and he'd do it again.

"Now," He thought. "Do it now."

He started to squeeze his right hand closed, the hand that held the claymore detonator. Suddenly, a small child stepped out from behind the two VC carrying the wooden crate. A little boy no more than five or six years old. Mitchell's hand froze. The boy was marching, a wooden stick was high on his shoulder imitating a soldier carrying a rifle. He was lifting his knees high with each step, his free arm swinging at his side in perfect time.

The vision of the baby girl with the porcelain doll face flashed in Mitchell's head. The vision of her laying on the ground with that beautiful face and her insides blown out. He felt panic, nauseous, a cold sweat covering his body.

"I can't do this," He thought. "Not again. Not to a kid. I won't!"

Mitchell watched as the little boy marched past him. A minute later the VC had disappeared into the darkness never realizing how close they had been to death's door. Every member of the team had seen the little boy and knew why Mitchell hadn't open fire. Everyone except Lieutenant Webster.

The last two minutes, Webster had been more frightened than any time in his whole life. Seeing the enemy in front of him no more than twenty feet away had paralyzed him. Suddenly he couldn't breathe, his eyes staring wide open, unable to blink. The vision of the enemy soldiers were blurred, not registering clearly in his brain. He couldn't have told how many soldiers there were or what they were doing, all he knew was the enemy was right in front of him.

Mitchell laid silent on his stomach, the claymore detonator still clenched in his right hand. He looked down at it, then slowly laid it on the ground. Raising his hand to his forehead, rubbing it in hopes of fighting off the headache he felt coming on. He had let an enemy supply patrol walk right through his killing zone. An armed enemy unit, carrying supplies and arms to their comrades. Arms to kill Americans.

"There's going to be hell to pay for this." Mitchell thought. "How am I going to explain it. Fuck 'em! I'm in charge. It was my call. If they don't like it, what can they do to me? Not a fucking thing. Even if they court-martial me, it would be better than this. Jail, hell jail would be better than this. Fuck 'em!"

Mitchell laid there five more minutes contemplating his situation. Finally he signaled for his team to come to his position.

"We're pulling back to the staging area." Mitchell ordered, looking straight into Lieutenant Webster's face. He expected to hear something from him, questioning why the enemy patrol was allowed to go free, but Webster didn't say a word. He was still shaken from the experience. Mitchell didn't realize how frightened Webster was.

"I'll take the point. Everyone else will have the same position he had coming in." Mitchell said. "Any questions?" No one spoke. "Okay, move out."

Mitchell led the team out of the jungle. They set up a defensive position at the staging area and settled in for the rest of the night.

At dawn the ambush team returned to A Troop's perimeter. Lieutenant Webster proceeded to the command post in the center of the perimeter. The ambush team dispersed to their respective tracks. Mitchell knew it was only a matter of time before he would be debriefed about the mission.

Colonel Sheldon, Captain Tice, and Lieutenant Neilley had presumed that the team had made no contact, but that assumption was about to change. Webster had had five hours to get over his fear and think about the mission. He was feeling guilty about his performance. That and the way Mitchell had treated him with something less than the respect he felt he deserved, lead him to give a somewhat self-serving account of the events of the night before.

A call came over the radio, "One-One, this is Six, over."

Mitchell answered, "This is One-One, over."

"This is Six. Get your team together and report to the C.P. for debriefing. This is Six, out."

Mitchell put out the word for the ambush team to report to One-One. Three minutes later, they all were standing behind Mitchell's track.

"We're ordered to the C.P. for debriefing." Mitchell told them.

"How do you want to handle this?" Brian asked.

"I'll handle it." Mitchell said. "If any of you are asked a question, you just tell it like it was. No bullshit. Understood!"

"Sure Sarge, if that's the way you want it." Brian answered.

"That's the way I want it!" Mitchell's voice was adamant. He then started walking towards the command post with his team joining in around him.

Colonel Sheldon, Captain Tice, Lieutenant Neilley, and Lieutenant Webster were standing together just a few feet from the Colonel's helicopter. Mitchell and the team walked up to them.

"Sergeant Mitchell and team reporting as ordered, Sir." Mitchell said in a clear, confident voice.

"What happened out there last night?" Colonel Sheldon asked. "Lieutenant Webster says you made contact but you let the VC walk right on by. Is that right, Sergeant?"

"Yes Sir, we made contact, but I chose not to engage." Mitchell answered with a strong emphasize on 'I'.

"Why didn't you engage?"

"In my judgment, the situation was not good. It was my call." Mitchell was sounding a little defensive now. "I chose not to engage, Sir."

"I know that, Sergeant Mitchell. You said the situation wasn't right. What I don't know is what wasn't right." Colonel Sheldon was pressuring for an answer.

"I didn't feel good about it, it just wasn't right. I don't know what more you want, Sir."

Colonel Sheldon's voice became very stern, almost threatening. "Look Mitchell! I don't want you pissing on my leg and then trying to tell me that it's raining. I want to know what the hell happened out there last night and I want to know right now!"

Mitchell looked into Colonel Sheldon's face, he could tell the Colonel was serious. He glanced over at Tice and Neilley, they had a confused look about them. Both felt something was wrong, this was not like Mitchell. He wasn't the evasive type, and they knew he wasn't a coward.

"I'm waiting Sergeant!" Colonel Sheldon barked.

Mitchell looked at Lieutenant Webster. The smirk on his face showed how pleased he was with himself.

"Fuck it!" Mitchell thought. Then he spoke, "I didn't fire because of the little boy."

"What little boy?" Colonel Sheldon questioned.

"There was a boy, only five or six years old with the VC, sir. I couldn't engage without killing the boy. So I let them go by."

"I didn't see any little boy. There was no boy out there." Lieutenant Webster said, challenging Mitchell's truthfulness.

"What about it, Sergeant?" Sheldon asked.

"With all due respect Sir, I don't believe the Lieutenant could see his dick if he was holding it in his hand, Sir." Mitchell answered.

"I saw the kid." Frank spoke up from behind.

"We all saw the boy." Brian added.

Mitchell raised his hand as to tell the others to shut up. "The boy was there. It was my call. I let them go." Mitchell said.

Captain Tice interrupted, "Colonel Sheldon, if Mitchell said there was a boy there, you can believe the boy was there. Can I have a word with you, Sir?"

The Colonel looked inquisitively at Tice.

"I think it might help your understanding of the situation, Sir."

"All right Captain, if you think it might help."

Tice and Sheldon stepped a few feet away and spoke in low voices, which the others couldn't hear. Captain Tice told Sheldon about the incident involving the baby girl. Then they came back and stood in front of Mitchell.

Colonel Sheldon spoke. "You know that the weapons you let go by will be used against American

285

troops, don't you? Maybe killing some of your own people. Have you thought about that?"

"I've thought about it, Sir." Mitchell answered.

"That's something you're going to have to live with Sergeant."

"I know that Sir. I think I can live with it. What I'm sure of is I couldn't live with killing that little boy."

Colonel Sheldon was silent for a few seconds. "Well Mitchell, I don't believe I could neither. You and your men are dismissed."

"Yes, Sir." Mitchell answered, then he and the others turned and walked away.

"But Sir," Webster started to complain, but was cut off by Colonel Sheldon.

"Shut up Lieutenant. Get in the chopper." Turning to Tice and Neilley, "Captain Tice, Lieutenant Neilley, last night's mission never happened. Clear?"

"Yes, Sir." Tice answered.

"Very clear, Sir." Neilley added.

"Good, I've got to get back to headquarters. You gentlemen have your assignment for today, carry on."

CHAPTER NINETEEN

The decision to build Fire Base Alfa was made on October 21, 1968. On paper it seemed like a good idea. The NVA had established a supply trail in the valley west of Mai Loc, running from the DMZ south to the Song Thach Ha River. Hill 613 towered over the valley a mere mile and a half south of the DMZ. On a clear day using nothing more than a pair of good binoculars one could see the North Vietnamese flag flying over its base camp, less than six miles away.

Fire Base Alfa was constructed in eighteen days and on November 8th an artillery battery with four 105mm howitzer and an infantry company of the Third Marine regiment moved in to set up shop. For the next five weeks the Marines and their One O' Five's played havoc on the NVA's activities in the valley. The once busy supply stream was reduced to a trickle.

The NVA's high command decided this was unacceptable. So on the night of December 19th a force of over eight hundred heavily armed NVA regulars attacked Fire Base Alfa. The Marines fought valiantly, but before they could be reinforced, the base was overran and all one hundred and fifty-seven Marines died.

On January 15th, Alfa was reoccupied. This time the task fell to the 101st Air Borne Division. They moved in an artillery battery consisting of six self-propelled 155mm howitzers, two Infantry companies and A Troop, Third Squadron, Fifth Armored Cavalry. Four hundred and ninety-seven men in all. That was three times the manpower the Marines had had, and thanks to the Armored Cavalry, it was equal to six times the fire power.

The top of Hill 613 had been leveled off and the perimeter of Fire Base Alfa was shaped like an oval, roughly five hundred meters long and three hundred meters wide. There were forty-seven permanent bunkers, each one manned by five grunts of the 101st. Twelve of the bunkers had an M-60 machine gun and twelve others M-79 grenade launchers. In front of the bunkers were triple rolls of concertina wire. Each of the bunkers controlled four claymore anti-personnel mines. Thirty of the bunkers had a fifth detonator connected to a fifty-five gallon drum filled with a napalm-like gasoline mixture. These drums were partially buried in the ground at an angle. At the lower back end was a two pound shaped C-4 charge, when detonated would ignite the napalm and blow it forward creating a wall of fire. A Troop was deployed along the entire perimeter, their tanks and APC's taking up position between every other bunker. Fire Base Alfa was no longer the easy target that it was on the night of December 19th.

It was 2200 hours, January 16th, A Troop's first night at Fire Base Alfa. Paganini had just settled in the turret to pull first watch. Frank, Country, and Dave were inside the APC sleeping. Mitchell had made his bed for the night on top of One-One behind the rear hatch. He hadn't gone to sleep yet, his mind was on home, Maggie, and his new son. He had gotten word that afternoon that his leave had been approved and was scheduled to start February 5th. He had written Maggie a letter telling her the good news. "Just twenty days and I'll see her," he thought.

Without warning the one hundred fifty-five millimeter howitzers opened fire. It sounded like a very close lightning strike. The concussion shook the ground and flames leaped out fifteen to twenty feet from the long barrels of the big guns. One-One's position on the perimeter was in front and slightly to the left of the howitzers, only one hundred and fifty meters away.

Mitchell sat up startled by the blast.

"Goddamnit!" Paganini shouted as he jerked around looking back at the One Fifty-five's. "That scared the shit out of me!"

Frank, Country, and Dave came scrambling to their feet, standing up through the rear hatch.

"What the fuck's going on?" Frank asked.

"Fire mission." Mitchell answered.

"Well, they oughta give us some fucking warning. Yell fire in the hole or something. Shit, I almost had a fuckin' heart attack."

Two more of the big guns fired almost simultaneously, the fire shooting out, lighting up the night for a brief moment. Then ten seconds later, two more. The artillery battery was engaged in a harassing fire mission on the supply trail west of the base. There was no isolated target. The idea was just to drop rounds onto the trail randomly, in hopes of disrupting any enemy activity.

"It's going to be hell trying to sleep with this shit going on," Country said.

"Well, I guess we'll have to get used to it," Mitchell replied.

"Ya. It'll be like getting use to sleeping inside a fuckin' base drum." Frank answered as he ducked back down in the track and laid down.

Frank and Country were just exercising their rights as soldiers to complain. For a combat soldier in the field, sleep was a relative term. They never really slept, not a deep sound, restful sleep. It was more like dozing very lightly, with the slightest unusual noise arousing their attention. It didn't take the roar of the big guns to bring them back to full consciousness. The breaking of a branch or the unexpected movement of another was enough.

Two more times that night the big guns opened up. At 0130 hours and again at 0250. Each time without warning. It became a routine over the next few nights. The guns would fire sometimes three, sometimes four missions, but always at random times.

The morning of January 29th, First Platoon left Fire Base Alfa to rendezvous with a large supply convoy on Highway Nine, halfway between Khe Sanh and Highway One. At that point the convoy would split up. The majority of it would continue on to resupply firebases Carroll, Vandergrief, and Barge. The remainder would join up with First Platoon to be escorted north to Fire Base Alfa. These convoys were ran twice a week and for the men of First Platoon it was a nice change of pace from the boredom of life at Alfa.

First platoon arrived at the rendezvous point at 1020 hours. The convoy had not yet arrived so they set up a defensive position and waited. At 1130 hours the large column came into sight. It was strung out almost a mile, totaling over sixty vehicles. The portion of the convoy destined for Fire Base Alfa broke off from the main column, eleven vehicles in all. Five two and a half ton trucks loaded with rounds for the one-hundred fifty-five millimeter howitzers. Two more carrying C-rations and supplies, towing water trailers. There were two stake and platform trucks loaded down with prefabricated building supplies and a latrine on each. One flat bed tracker-trailer rig carrying a bulldozer and one fuel truck.

Lieutenant Neilley placed his tracks in pairs, One-One and One-Nine at the head of the column and One-Five with One-Seven at the rear. One-Two with One-Three and One-Four paired with One-Six were sandwiched within the column. At 1215 hours the convoy was organized and ready to roll.

"One-One, this is One-Six, move out. Keep up a good steady pace, fifteen to twenty miles per hour, over."

"This is One-One, roger."

Frank released the brakes of One-One and slowly accelerated with the convoy following behind.

These convoys had become a routine, every Monday and Thursday, roughly the same time of day. That was a mistake. Keeping any kind of a routine in Vietnam was just asking for trouble.

The night before a force of one hundred and forty men, part of the NVA's Fifth Division 217th Regiment moved into ambush positions along the narrow winding road halfway between Fire Base Alfa and Mai Loc. On the west side of the road, grass high enough to hide a standing man covered the ground. It quickly changed into thick jungle as the hill rose in elevation. The east side was a steep drop for twenty to twenty-five meters and then a dense expansion of jungle.

The NVA's commander placed his main force on the high ground along the west side of the road. Spreading out over a distance of five hundred meters, camouflaged and ready to fire their automatic weapons and RPG's point blank at the convoy. He had placed a fifty-seven millimeter recoilless rifle at the north end of the killing zone. At the south end of the ambush was a fifty-one caliber heavy machine gun and another one placed midway, dominating the road for the entire length of the killing zone. Further west up the hill, some two hundred meters away he had placed a team with an eighty-two millimeter mortar. It was to be used to rain down rounds on the road during the attack and then cover the NVA's retreat.

The morning of the 29th, the NVA had purposely let First Platoon roll through their ambush, knowing full well they would be returning with a fat, slow moving convoy. Five trucks loaded heavy with high explosive one hundred fifty-five millimeter rounds and a fuel truck would make easy targets.

The convoy had traveled six miles at a relatively slow pace. Lieutenant Neilley had instructed Mitchell to take it slow in hopes of keeping large gaps from appearing in the column. Mitchell had been relaxed on the first leg of the trip, knowing that if anything was going to happen, it would be on the return portion. They were now less than a mile from the ambush site.

Country was manning the left side M-60 and Dave the right side fifty caliber. Paganini was sitting between them. Country had learned to read Mitchell's body language and used it as a barometer to gauge whether or not to be concerned in a given situation. Mitchell's normal relaxed posture of leaning back on the hatch cover with one leg propped up on the gun shield had been replaced with him sitting up straight, both hands on his fifty caliber, his thumbs resting on the weapon's trigger. He was beginning to get uneasy. His head was consistently turning first looking down the road then to the sides, his eyes searching the hills. He hadn't seen or heard anything, it was just a feeling, a sixth sense. Mitchell didn't understand where the feeling came from, but he had learned to respect it.

Country leaned over to Paganini, "Get the Thumper ready. We might be needing it."

He reached his arm across Paganini and tapped Dave on his leg. Dave turned to look. Country didn't say a word, just pointed at Mitchell in the turret. Dave looked at Mitchell and then back at Country. He nodded his head in acknowledgment and then turned back and checked his fifty.

"What is it?" Paganini asked.

Country pointed to Mitchell. "If Sarge is nervous, it's time for all of us to be nervous."

"How can you tell?"

"I've been with him for a long time, I can just tell." Country said and then turned his head to scan the hillside.

Paganini picked up the M-79 that was resting in his lap. He broke it open and checked the forty millimeter high explosive round inside. He closed the weapon and held it in his hands.

Mitchell and his crew had no way of knowing that at that very moment they were entering the killing zone of the NVA's ambush. The convoy was rolling along at eighteen miles per hour and was spread out for almost a half of a mile. The NVA commander was waiting for the main body to fill his killing zone. Less than a minute later the NVA opened fire. Automatic weapons, heavy machine guns, and RPG's rounds poured down on the convoy.

Lieutenant Neilley immediately ordered the column to run through the ambush. This was standard counter-ambush procedure. Frank accelerated hard, quickly increasing One-One's speed to forty miles per hour. Mitchell, Country, and Dave sprayed the hillside with gun fire. At that same instant, One-Nine took a RPG hit midway in its turret. The explosion wounded its gunner, but didn't hinder the tank's mobility and it too sped up. The first two trucks of the column stayed with One-One and One-Nine, but the third, a fuel truck loaded with three thousand gallons of gasoline and diesel fuel took a direct hit from the fifty-seven millimeter recoilless rifle. It exploded instantly into a huge ball of flames, killing both the driver and his shotgun rider. This brought the remainder of the convoy to a complete stop. Lieutenant Neilley ordered all units to move, but the truck next in line behind the doomed fuel truck sat in the middle of the road, abandoned. Its driver and shotgun rider had bailed out and were hiding down in the tall grass on the east side of the road. By now mortar rounds began falling on the column. The recoilless rifle team was selecting stationary targets and picking them off one by one. A five ton truck loaded with building supplies took a direct hit, killing the driver. Then a fifty-seven millimeter round bore into One-Four's engine compartment, killing its driver. The track commander, Leroy Hill, and his two gunners, Mike Davis and Keith Dixon continued to fight.

By now One-One, One-Nine, and the first two trucks had passed safely through the killing zone and were a quarter of a mile beyond. Realizing that they were no longer under fire Mitchell ordered Frank to come to a full stop. He looked back over his shoulder. The first thing he noticed was that they were separated from the main body of the convoy. He then saw One-Nine's TC gesturing to his CVC headset, indicating he had no radio communications.

Mitchell keyed his intercom, "Turn it around, Frank. Take us back to One-Nine."

Frank pulled the left steering lever all the way back locking up the left track. He gunned the engine, spinning One-One around one hundred and eighty degrees, and pulled up beside One-Nine.

The TC of One-Nine shouted to Mitchell, "We took a hit, my gunner's hurt, but not too bad. It took out my radio. I don't know what's happening."

"We're clear," Mitchell answered, "but the rest of the convoy got held up."

At that moment, Mitchell heard Leroy Hill's radio call.

"One-Six, this is One-Four. We're hit! Our Engine's out, we can't move. The fire is spreading fast, we're abandoning our track, over."

"One-Six, roger. Take cover, someone will pick you up."

The crew of One-Four was part of Mitchell's scout section, they were his responsibility, but more than that they were his friends. He felt compelled to save them.

Mitchell shouted to One-Nine's TC, "You stay here! I'm going back!"

"You're what?"

"I'm going back! Turn your gun around and lay down as much fire as you can on that hill."

"All right," the tank commander answered.

Mitchell turned to face Country, Dave, and Paganini, "Get ready! We're going back in." He then keyed his intercom, "Frank take us back to the main column."

"What?" Frank yelled into his intercom, jerking his head around looking up at Mitchell.

"Move it, Frank. They need us back there. I want us rolling as fast as you can, just keep us on the road. Don't give them an easy target."

Mitchell called out over the radio, "This is One-One, we're on our way back. We'll pick up One-Four, over."

"This is One-Six, roger One-One."

Meanwhile, Hill had ordered his men off the burning APC. They had taken cover down the steep bank off the east side of the road.

One-Nine turned its turret around and began firing its ninety millimeter gun into the hillside where the NVA was positioned. A few seconds later, a lucky break that probably saved the convoy from total destruction happened. The third round that One-Nine fired at random from a full half of a mile away hit within fifteen feet of the NVA's fifty-seven millimeter recoilless rifle's position. Killing the three man crew and destroying the gun.

Just seconds later One-One re-entered the fight. They roared past the burning fuel truck right into the heart of the ambush, their guns spraying the hillside.

This was Paganini's first fire fight. He was scared but everything had happened so fast he hadn't had time to think. He was just reacting. Firing forty millimeter rounds from the M-79 as rapidly as he could.

Suddenly, Dave's head exploded. His steel helmet flew straight up into the air three to four feet. A five inch hole in the back of his head opened up as the .51 caliber slug exited. A round from the NVA's heavy machine gun had hit Dave in the face. The force of the blow drove Dave backwards into Paganini, knocking Paganini to the floor of the APC with Dave on top of him. Blood was gushing from Dave's head, saturating Paganini. He scrambled to free himself from Dave's lifeless body. Seeing his blood soaked fatigues, Paganini frantically checked himself for injuries. Realizing he had not been hit he rose to his knees. Dave was laying face down, the gaping hole in the back of his head in full view. Blood was no longer coming from this wound, instead it was now running out of the entrance hole above Dave's left eye and forming a puddle under his face. Paganini could see inside Dave's skull. He stared at the bloody pinkish-gray sponge-like tissue inside and stringing out over the jagged edges of the hole. Country was standing over them staring down at his friend.

Paganini looked up, "He's dead."

"No!" Country cried in disbelief. "No!"

He knelt down and rolled Dave's body over exposing what was left of his face. It was covered in thick blood. Country put his head to Dave's chest wanting to hear a heartbeat. Seconds later, he raised up and stared blankly at Paganini.

"He's dead." Paganini said again. "I can see his brains. He's dead, man."

Paganini stood up and took over Dave's fifty caliber. Country remained inside the APC, holding his dead friend's hand. His happy go lucky attitude and naive boyish personality draining away as the blood drained from Dave's body.

The moment the NVA had triggered the ambush, Lieutenant Neilley had radioed Fire Base Alpha, giving them the convoy's position. The gunners of the one-fifty-five's plotted the fire mission on the hillside and the barrage was now on its way. The high explosive shells from the big guns were laying waste to the NVA's position.

In the meantime, the convoy had started moving again, minus five trucks and One-Four which had all been destroyed. One-One roared passed the on-coming vehicles and headed for One-Four. Mitchell could see it burning in the road ahead, flames leaping ten feet high and a large plume of black smoke billowing above it.

The NVA had placed a blocking force behind the killing zone. Its purpose was to engage any vehicles that might turn around and try to escape. None had and now that blocking force was moving up the road towards the burning APC. Leroy, Mike, and Keith had spotted them and opened fire. The three crew members were outnumbered five to one and praying for help.

Fifteen seconds later, One-One pulled passed the burning track and stopped in the middle of the road firing all three of its machine guns at the oncoming gooks.

Between them and One-Four's crew, they killed six of the NVA before the rest turned back and disappeared into the jungle.

The ongoing artillery barrage had for all practical purposes put an end to the ambush. The NVA commander satisfied with the damage they had inflicted, ordered his force to retreat.

Within ten minutes it was all over, the convoy was no longer under fire. The artillery rounds were now falling further up the hill in an area they estimated to be the NVA's retreat route.

For the first time since they had reentered the fight, Mitchell turned around and looked back, "You all right back there?"

He saw Paganini manning Dave's fifty caliber and Country at the M-60, but Dave was not to be seen. They just looked back at him saying nothing.

"Where's Dave?" Mitchell asked. Still there was no answer. "Where the hell is Dave?" Mitchell yelled climbing up out of his turret.

"He's dead, Sarge." Paganini said gravely.

"What?"

"He's dead. He got hit in the head, there's not much left." Paganini said glancing at Dave's body.

Mitchell was now out of the turret looking down through the rear hatch. He could see Dave laying inside the APC. "Oh God," he said softly, a lump forming in his throat. He jumped down and knelt beside Dave whose face was covered with blood, the three-quarter inch hole above his left eye plainly visible. Mitchell placed two fingers on Dave's neck to check for a pulse. There wasn't one. Dave's eyes were still open, staring up at him. He pulled the eyelids closed and slowly stood up. Looking at Country he could see the tears had streaked his dusty face.

"Shiiit!" Mitchell screamed, "I swear I can't take much more of this fuckin' shit!"

First Platoon hadn't lost a man for over two months and now in just one day they had lost two and a third wounded. Back that evening on the perimeter at Fire Base Alpha, they were all quiet, feeling sad for their lose. But none felt worse than Mitchell. One-One had cleared the ambush and he had made the decision to go back. A decision that cost Dave his life.

Mitchell was sitting in front of the turret, leaning back on the fifty caliber gun shield, staring down the hillside. Leroy came and sat next to him.

"I know you feel real bad about Dave, man." Leroy began. "You thinkin' maybe it's your fault. It's not man. I know you guys were clear and you said "go back". You thinkin' if you don't go back Dave don't get killed. But you don't know that would happen. If you don't go back, maybe me, Mike, and Keith; maybe we all be dead now. I don't know....you don't know. Only God, he knows that kinda stuff. I liked Surfer, too. He was my man before he yours. But I gots'ta tell ya, I'm glad you came back."

CHAPTER TWENTY

It had been one hundred and ninety-three days since Mitchell had seen Maggie. One hundred and ninety-three days without feeling her touch, without kissing her warm, soft, sweet lips. One hundred and ninety-three days without smelling that clean, fresh smell that was uniquely hers, without looking into her loving, pale blue eyes. One hundred and ninety-three days, it had seemed like a lifetime.

The morning of February 5th, Mitchell climbed aboard a chopper bound for Camp Evans. There he took a C-130 to the R&R Center at Da Nang. The processing and waiting for his flight took over four hours. It gave him time to look around the air base. To his surprise, he saw air-conditioned quarters for the officers, snack bars, and even a swimming pool. "These rear echelon types have it pretty goddamn nice," he thought. Mitchell had spent the last six months in the boonies sleeping on his APC, eating C-rations, and fighting everything from the VC and NVA to snakes and malaria. "Yeah, pretty fuckin' nice," he said to himself. He stopped in a PX and picked up the latest issue of Stars and Stripes and was walking out the door when the clerk stopped him.

"That's ten cents, Sergeant."

Mitchell paused for a few seconds, smiled and then paid the clerk. The men of A Troop had always gotten theirs free with every mail delivery and it felt like a small victory knowing he had been getting something free that the guys in the rear had to pay for.

Two hours before the flight was to depart, Mitchell and the other one hundred and eighty soldiers scheduled for the flight were called to a large isolated room. There they were checked through customs and had their MPC (funny money) changed to real American greenbacks. Finally it was time to board. Every seat on the Northwest 707 was packed full. The flight to Hawaii would take twelve hours. Thanks to crossing the International dateline, by Hawaii's time, they arrived hours before they had departed Vietnam. The plane landed at Honolulu International Airport and taxied to the edge of the tarmac, never getting near the terminal. Mitchell and the others were loaded onto buses for transport to Fort DeRussey. The trip took twenty minutes.

Butterflies filled Mitchell's stomach in anticipation of seeing Maggie. The day he had been dreaming about for six months had finally arrived. The soldiers poured out of the buses and surged toward the long line of waiting wives. Mitchell was on the second bus to unload and spotted Maggie right away. In his eyes, her radiant beauty shining through all the others. She was wearing a white sundress with little yellow flowers. Even though she had given birth to their son less than two months before, she had regained her sexy figure and looked every bit as beautiful as the day he had last seen her. Mitchell ran to her and gathered her up into his arms.

Tears filled her pale blue eyes and were running down her cheeks. "God, it's good to see you." She said as she kissed him, then kissed him again and for a third time before Mitchell could speak.

Finally he said, "I've really missed you, Maggie May."

"I've been here all day, waiting and waiting." Her smile beaming, giggling between every word. "About thirty minutes ago they told us, you had landed and was on the way. I thought those darn buses would never get here." Her arms were around Mitchell's neck and she pulled him to her and kissed him again.

"You look beautiful," Mitchell said. "I've missed you so damn much."

"Oh God," Maggie said giggling at the same time, pulling his face to hers and kissing him two more times. "I couldn't bring the baby, he has an ear infection and the doctor said he shouldn't fly."

"Is he okay?" Mitchell asked.

"Oh, he's fine. It's just the pressure inside the plane would hurt his ears too much. But I got lots and lots of pictures."

Then a loudspeaker announcement instructed everyone to move inside to a briefing room. There they were welcomed to Hawaii and given two cards and a bottle of malaria pills. One card had Mitchell's return flight information on it. He was to report back at the airport no later than 0900 on the twelfth of February. The second card said that the bearer was on R&R from Vietnam and has been exposed to malaria, smallpox, typhus, yellow fever, and the plague.

Maggie and Mitchell read the card together. "Jesus, I may not be safe to be around," Mitchell joked.

"Well, that's a chance I'll have to take," Maggie answered.

Earlier that day Maggie had arranged for them to stay at the Holiday Isle Hotel, room 1109. After a short taxi ride from Fort DeRussey they walked through the hotel lobby and into the elevator.

"What floor?" Mitchell asked.

"Eleven." Maggie answered.

He pushed the button for the eleventh floor and the elevator door closed. For the first time they were alone. The elevator started up. Mitchell put his arms around Maggie and kissed her, this time with passion and she returned the kiss with equal passion. It was a long, deep, wet kiss filled with sexual desire. His right hand moved from her waist to her breast and then back around her waist pulling her tight against him. Their lips never parted until the elevator door opened onto the eleventh floor.

The room was nice and spacious with two full-size beds. In one corner was a table with four chairs. A color television was on top of the dresser and a small refrigerator at one end. Leading into the bathroom was a large dressing room with a double vanity. The bathroom had a tub and a separate shower. The balcony was small but there was room for the two patio chairs and table. The hotel was two blocks off the beach, but they could still see the ocean from their room. Maggie and Mitchell spent the next twenty-four hours there, leaving only briefly to buy junk food to bring back to the room. They spent this time getting reacquainted, talking and making love, then talking and making love some more.

About two in the afternoon on the second day they ventured out from their room. The Holiday Isle Hotel was located at the corners of Lewers Street and Kalakaua Avenue. They walked down Kalakaua for about three blocks, past the Royal Hawaiian Hotel and onto Waikiki Beach. It was packed with people which Mitchell sized up and quickly grouped into three categories. There were the locals, not many but enough to be noticeable. Then there were the regular tourists, many of them from other countries. The remainder were the military on R&R from Vietnam. They stood out like a ketchup stain on a white shirt. They spent two hours sitting in the sand watching people, picking out the G.I.'s from the tourist and talking about home and their baby. Three times they got up to go to the water's edge letting the surf wash onto their feet, but never going in.

By late afternoon they found themselves in a small restaurant on Kapahulu Avenue near the Honolulu Zoo. The place wasn't very busy, that's why Mitchell picked it. He wasn't comfortable in crowds. They were sitting in a corner booth eating cheeseburgers and fries.

"It's not a Whataburger, but it's not too bad." Mitchell said taking another big bite.

"When you finish that one, I'm going to order you another. You're getting too skinny. Don't you ever eat?" Maggie said only half teasing.

"C-rations aren't the most appetizing things in the world, sweetie." Mitchell answered.

"Well, what about all that stuff I've sent you in those care packages? I know, you share that with the other guys, don't you?"

"We share all the goodies we get from home. I guess it's just not enough to keep meat on us." Maggie smiled and watched as Mitchell took another bite.

"Tell me about your guys."

"I don't know what there is to tell."

"You know, how are they doing?"

"They're in Vietnam, Maggie. I guess they're doing the best they can under those circumstances."

"No, I mean how are they doing? Frank and Country, tell me about them. What are they really like? Your letters don't tell me much about them."

"There's not that much to tell. They're just guys like me, stuck in a place they don't want to be."

"Do you like them? Are you close friends with them?"

"You can't help but be close. We live together. We depend on each other." Mitchell's voice sounded more solemn, so Maggie decided to take the conversation in a more cheerful direction.

"How about Dave? Has he shown Country how to surf yet?" Mitchell looked away, the expression hardened on his face. "What?" Maggie asked, concerned by Mitchell's sudden mood change. "What's wrong, Bobby? What happened?" Mitchell didn't answer, he just continued looking away. "Bobby, please look at me. Tell me what's wrong."

He finally looked back at her. She could see tears in his eyes. But he still didn't speak.

"What is it Bobby? Please, tell me."

"Dave's dead. He bought it about a week ago."

"Oh, no." Maggie said, reaching across the table touching Bobby's hands. "I'm sorry. I'm so sorry."

"Well that kinda shit happens," he said trying to sound unaffected, but his face told another story.

"How did it happen?" Maggie asked, gently rubbing his forearms.

Mitchell looked at her for a few seconds, at the tears now filling her eyes, feeling the softness of her touch. "I don't think you need to know about those kinds of things....I don't think you want to know."

Another couple sat down at the booth next to theirs. Mitchell felt self-conscience. "Let's go," he said and stood up, taking Maggie by her hand and walking out.

PFC Eddie Goodman was from St. Joseph, Missouri. He had dropped out of high school in the eleventh grade and went to work in a radiator shop. It was hard, dirty work but he enjoyed it and he was good at mechanical things. He had dated Sharon for two years and right after her high school graduation they got married without the blessing of her parents. Sharon's family were middle-class and considered Eddie to be white trash. The two of them moved into a small one bedroom duplex in the poorer side of town. To help make ends meet, Sharon took a job at the lunch counter at Woolworth. Their relationship started going downhill almost from the beginning. Then Eddie was drafted into the Army and sent to Vietnam. In Vietnam, Eddie was a rifleman assigned to an infantry company in the Mekong Delta. He had spent the last seven months humping through the rice paddies and jungles south of Saigon. His unit had seen its share of action, suffered its share of death. All the while, Sharon's letters became less frequent and less supportive. Shortly after Eddie left for Vietnam, Sharon started taking classes at Missouri Western State College, at her mother's encouragement.

The pressure of war had taken its toll on Eddie. That and his deteriorating marriage was weighing heavy on his mind. He hoped this R&R would improve things in his life. The Goodmans had arrived in Honolulu one day after Mitchell and Maggie. They too were staying at the Holiday Isle Hotel.

After leaving the small restaurant, Maggie and Mitchell walked back to the hotel. They had gotten off the elevator and were walking down the hall to their room when Eddie and Sharon came out of room 1107. They smiled and said hello as they passed and then Mitchell unlocked the door to their room, stepped aside for Maggie and then followed her inside.

"Looks like we have neighbors next door now." Maggie said. "They must have gotten in today. I don't remember seeing them yesterday."

"I think we stayed too busy to see anybody yesterday." Mitchell teased.

Maggie giggled but didn't disagree. "You know everyone we've seen on this floor has been military." Maggie noted.

Mitchell thought about it for a few seconds. "They're probably segregating us from the other tourists. You know most people think anybody who has served in Vietnam comes back a little crazy."

"No they don't."

"Bullshit Maggie, you're naive."

"I don't think you're crazy."

"Oh, but I am. I'm crazy about you." Mitchell said grabbing Maggie in his arms. They fell onto the bed, wrestling, giggling, and kissing. This of course led to the inevitable.

Afterwards Maggie fell asleep. Mitchell laid there watching her, looking at her pretty face. She looked young and innocent. He smiled, she represented everything that was good to Mitchell. Then he thought about the bad, the war. "What if I don't make it back? What would become of her? Would she know how much I really love her? Would she miss me the way I've missed her? I'm not going to die." He thought defiantly. "The war wouldn't dare kill me. I've got too much to live for. She's too good to lose. And my son, there's no way I'm going to die without seeing my son." Mitchell quietly got up and walked to the table, picking up the pictures of his son. Smiling he whispered, "I'll be seeing you soon, little guy."

The next morning, Maggie and Mitchell were out early for a planned day of seeing the sights. Their first stop was the International Market Place. It was a large open-air market with more than a hundred shops, restaurants, and traditional thatched tiki kiosks that sold everything from souvenirs and trinkets to clothes and fine jewelry. They had browsed through the shops for over an hour when they came upon a jewelry stand. Maggie saw a pair of earrings that she fell in love with, they were pink coral set in fourteen carat gold. After some expected haggling over the price, Mitchell bought them. She put them on immediately and then kissed Mitchell on the cheek.

"Thank you, Bobby. They're beautiful."

"Is that all the thanks I get? A little kiss on the cheek"

Maggie smiled a mischievous smile. "I'll give you a proper thank you tonight." She whispered.

"Oh, okay." Mitchell said. "Do you see anything else you might want? You know, so maybe I can get more thank yous."

"You'll get as much thank yous as you can handle."

"Well, I can handle a lot." Mitchell bragged.

The protests against the war in Vietnam were taking place all across the country, including Hawaii. Mitchell had seen the long-hairs around wearing their beads and tie-dyed shirts, but for the most part he and Maggie had avoided them. This morning they were out in force at the International Market Place. They easily identified Mitchell as a soldier and twice had tried to hand him a flier, calling the military "baby killers" amongst other things. He would just walk on by, never acknowledging them. He already knew what the fliers said and anyways he was here to be with Maggie, not debate the rights and wrongs of the war. Then for the third time, one of the protesters tried to hand a leaflet to Mitchell. Just like before, Mitchell didn't acknowledge him. This time the long-hair with a shaggy beard grabbed Mitchell's arm, stopping him.

"Hey man, you need to read this. That is if you can read."

Mitchell looked at the man with a cold, hard, angry look. Slowly looking down at the man's hand holding his arm and then back at the hippie's face, locking on to his eyes. "If I were you, I'd take that hand off me." Mitchell's voice was cold and blunt.

"Sure, man." The protester said pulling his hands away. "You can walk away, you can run away, but you can't hide from what you're doing, from what you are."

"And what is that?" Mitchell asked.

"You're nothing more than a terrorist, a murderer."

"You don't know what the hell you're talking about." Mitchell said.

"Let's go, Bobby. Don't mind him. Please Bobby, let's go." Maggie said pulling on Mitchell's arm. Mitchell shook his head in disgust at the long-hair and then giving in to Maggie's pleas started to walk away.

"Go ahead, run away. Try to hide." The protester taunted. "But everyone knows you're nothing more than an immoral, murdering baby-killer."

Mitchell's blood boiled in his veins. An angry, mean, hatred look took over his face. He jerked away from Maggie and grabbed the hippie, shaking him, tearing his shirt and ripping the string of beads from his neck. "Listen, man!" Mitchell shouted. "You stay away from me and my wife. And if you call me baby killer one more fuckin' time, I'm going to rip your fuckin' head off and shit down your neck. You hear me, asshole?" Mitchell shook him again. "I asked you a fuckin' question. Do you hear me?"

"Yeah, I hear, I hear."

"Good." Mitchell said and shoved the man away, knocking him to the ground. He then took Maggie's hand and slowly walked away.

311

"I hate those people." Maggie said, remembering her own experience in front of the bank. "Why do they say those things? They must know it's not true."

"I don't know Maggie." Mitchell was still angry and hurt by what had happened. "Sometimes I think the whole damn world is upside down."

The altercation had put a damper on their plans. They returned to their room, it was the only place Mitchell felt comfortable. Mitchell walked out onto the balcony, leaning on the rail, looking toward the ocean. He was troubled by what had happened. He thought he had embarrassed Maggie, or even worse, scared her.

Maggie followed him out onto the balcony, asking, "Bobby, would you like a Coke?"

"No."

Maggie sensed he wasn't admiring the view. "Well, do you want to talk?"

Mitchell didn't answer right away. "Maybe I should tell her why it angered me so," he thought. "Then maybe she'd understand. If anyone would understand, Maggie would."

"I'm sorry I lost it with that guy."

"You don't have to be sorry, Bobby. I can't stand the things they do either, but you shouldn't let them get to you. Don't give them the satisfaction."

"I know, Maggie. But he pushed all the right buttons. He didn't know they were, but they were."

"What buttons? What do you mean?"

"Some of the things he said," Mitchell stopped for a few seconds. "Some of them hit pretty close to home. I want to tell you some things that has happened to me. I need to tell you."

"You can tell me anything Bobby, anything."

"Let's go inside." Mitchell said, wanting complete privacy.

Mitchell began, "A few months ago, I was leading the scout section across a river. The water was deep, the track had to float, so we were barely moving. Halfway across we got opened up on from the other side. AK rounds, RPG's, we were sitting ducks. My gun was the only one in position to fire back, so I did. I poured a hundred rounds of fifty caliber back at them. I never saw them, I just fired back to where the firing was coming from. A minute later we had made it across. The firing had stopped and we looked around to see what we could find. We found three bodies, all dead. One was...." Mitchell stopped, a lump was swelling up in his throat. "One was a little girl. She was no more than two years old, laying there next to her mother, both dead." Mitchell stopped for a few seconds, rubbing his eyes that were tearing up. "I never saw them, I just shot back. The AK-47 the mother had been using was still in her hand. But the little girl.....I killed that little girl. I didn't know she was there, but I killed her."

Maggie put one arm around Mitchell and used her other hand to wipe the tears from his cheek.

"So, I guess that's why I can't stand to hear that term, baby-killer."

"You didn't kill that little girl. Her mother killed her by doing what she did, not you Bobby."

"I know. That's what Frank said. That's what I keep saying to myself, but it still hurts."

Maggie kissed him tenderly, "It wasn't your fault. You can't keep blaming yourself. You're not a baby killer, you're not a murderer. You're just a soldier."

Mitchell shook his head, "Murderer, that's another story."

"What's another story?" Maggie asked.

"What the hell." Mitchell said. "If I'm confessing one sin to you, I may as well confess them all."

"You haven't sinned. I don't believe that." Maggie said.

"You remember me writing to you about May Le, the Vietnamese girl Frank got involved with?"

"Yes. You sent me a picture of her and Frank together. She's very pretty."

"Well, Frank got more than involved. He fell in love with her and she loved him. The VC knows everything that goes on. They have spies in every village. One night they came and took May Le. They took her to make an example of her for caring about an American. They tortured her and then they killed her. They killed her in a way that made it clear it was because of Frank."

"How? How did they kill her?" Maggie asked. The stories she was hearing were disturbing, but for the first time she was getting a feel for some of the horrific things Mitchell had endured.

"You don't need to know that." Mitchell said.

"Yes I do. You need to tell someone and ...I love you. You've been through a lot and I want to know everything. So tell me, how did they kill her?"

Mitchell paused for a few seconds, not knowing how to describe it. "They stuck a sharpened bamboo spike into her...you know...down there ...in her pussy. Then they drove it all the way through her body into the ground."

"Oh my god." Maggie gasped, closing her eyes as if that would block out the vision she was imagining.

"We found her that way. Frank saw her that way. It really tore him up. Anyways, a few days later, Ringo, May Le's little brother, found out who had done it and that they would be coming back to the village. Well, he told Frank and Frank decided he was going to wait for them and kill them. Nothing was going to change his mind. He wanted me to help him. I knew I couldn't stop him, he was going to do it with or without me. I didn't want him to get hurt or in trouble, so I came up with a plan and helped him do it. Two of them showed up. We killed them both. So you see, we didn't kill them because of the war. We did it to get even for what they did to May Le. Maybe some people would call that murder. I know the thought has crossed my mind more than once."

"They were the enemy. They would have killed you if they got the chance." Maggie insisted.

"Yeah, maybe. We're pretty sure they were part of the ones that mortared us a while back. They killed one of our guys. A guy in Second Platoon."

"See there." Maggie said. "They were the enemy and anyways, they deserved it for what they did to May Le. I want you to get those thoughts out of your head. You hear me, Bobby?"

"Okay, I'll try sweetie." Mitchell was feeling a little relieved after getting it off his chest. "You know, I think I'll take that Coke now."

Maggie poured the Coke into two glasses, handing one to Mitchell. "Are you getting hungry? I know I am."

"Yeah, I am. But I really don't want to go out."

"That's okay. There's that Jack-in-the-Box down the street. I'll go and get us something and bring it back."

"I'd like that, if you don't mind."

"I don't mind. I'll be back as quick as I can." Maggie said as she picked up her purse. "Anything special you want?"

"You know what I like. And knowing you, you'll get more than enough."

Maggie laughed and gave Mitchell a kiss on the cheek then left. Mitchell was glad that she could still laugh and her smile made him feel a little better.

* * * * * * * * *

Eddie was working on his third beer within the last hour when Sharon got back to the room. She had been out shopping for some civilian clothes for him to wear during their stay on R&R. He opened the bag and first pulled out a pair of striped bell-bottom pants. Eddie looked at them in disbelief, not saying a word he laid them on the bed. He glanced inside the bag again and removed a bright colored tie-dyed T-shirt. He stared at it for a moment. "What the hell is this shit?" Eddie asked.

"It's a shirt!" Sharon snapped back.

Eddie opened a second, smaller bag taking out a pair of brown sandals. "I asked you to get me some civvies to wear, not this goddamn hippie shit!"

"What's wrong with them? It's what everyone's wearing."

"Not me!" Eddied responded. "I'm not wearing this shit!" Throwing the sandals across the room. "Jesus Christ Sharon, why didn't you get me some love beads and a goddamn long hair wig to complete the look?"

"Well, it would be a lot better than the way you look now."

"What's wrong with the way I look?"

"What's wrong? My god Eddie, you may as well have U.S. Army stamped on your forehead."

"So, I look like I'm in the Army, so what! What's wrong with that?" Eddie questioned.

"You really don't know, do you Eddie? You're fucking pathetic." Sharon shrieked and stormed out the room.

Mitchell was on the balcony and had heard Eddie and Sharon fighting. He couldn't make out the words that had been said, but from the tone of the voices he knew they were arguing.

Eddie came out onto the balcony of his room. He had an open beer in one hand and a carton with three more cans in the other. He noticed Mitchell. "How goes it?" Eddie asked, hoisting his beer filled hand.

"Oh, okay. You?" Mitchell answered.

"Can't complain, no one will listen." Eddie said, forcing a laugh. "Say, you military?"

"Yeah." Mitchell said, nodding his head.

317

"Me too, R&R from Nam. You?"

"Same, same." Mitchell answered.

"My name's Eddie Goodman."

"Bobby Mitchell. It's nice to meet you, Eddie."

"Yeah, you too. Say you want a beer?" Eddie inquired holding up the partial six pack.

"No thanks."

"You sure? I've got plenty."

"No, but thanks anyway, maybe some other time, Eddie." About that time, Mitchell heard Maggie returning from Jack-in-the-Box. "Say, my wife's back." Mitchell said. "Maybe we can talk some other time."

"Sure thing, see ya."

Mitchell went back inside.

"Who were you talking to?" Maggie asked.

"Eddie Goodman, the guy next door."

"What about?"

"Nothing, he offered me a beer."

"Maybe we can get together with him and his wife some time." Maggie said.

"Maybe. It sounded like they were fighting earlier."

"Fighting, what about?"

"I don't know, just sounded like they were."

"I don't see how anyone could waste any of this precious time fighting." Maggie declared.

Mitchell chowed down on the cheeseburger, fries, and hot apple turnover Maggie had brought him, relishing every bite. One of the things he was enjoying about R&R was the food. He also found himself taking two and sometimes three showers a day. The luxury of having a steamy, hot shower anytime he wanted was an absolute pleasure. It was something he had always taken for granted before Vietnam, but he never would again. That and the simple things like flushing toilets, refrigerators, and air conditioning, he would never look at the same way. All those things were great but the thing he enjoyed most, the thing he needed most was Maggie. He had told her about the experiences that had troubled him so. He had told her of some of the shocking, horrid things he had seen and she had understood. She had taken away some of the anxiety, some of the pain. She had made it all, almost bearable.

Late that afternoon, just before sundown, they went down to the beach. They walked out onto a long concrete pier and looked back at Waikiki beach. They watched as the hotels' lights began to illuminate the shoreline. They gazed at Diamond Head towering in the distance. Gray clouds were gathering in the sky above the splendid mountain, offering a stunning contrast to the brilliant blue sky. Mitchell's arm was across Maggie's shoulders and she had her arm around his waist. They looked to the west and witnessed one of the most beautiful sunsets they had ever seen. The clouds now appeared almost black with slices of gleaming gold shining through them. The sun was just beginning to sink below the horizon, shimmering yellow and gold onto the dark, shadowy water. They stood there and watched in this quiet, peaceful place.

Later they sat on the beach for hours, talking, revealing their fears and apprehensions. They also vowed their love for each other and talked of the future. It was well past midnight before they returned to their hotel.

The next morning they were off to try sightseeing again. This time they rented a car, a new '69 Camaro. The car rental company provided them with a map of Oahu, marking all of the popular spots to see. They learned right away that normal compass directions were not used here. In their place, the Hawaiians used the terms, makai, meaning toward the sea, and mauka, toward the mountains. Diamond Head meant toward Diamond Head and Ewa was just the opposite, away from Diamond Head. So armed with their new found navigational skills, Maggie and Mitchell were on their way.

"First stop, Diamond Head." Mitchell said.

"I don't think we can miss it, just look up and drive in that direction." Maggie affirmed.

Fifteen minutes later they were at the base of the volcanic crater. After parking the car, they took the hiking trail and climbed to the top. It was worth the effort, the views of the ocean and Waikiki was spectacular.

Next they stopped at Halona Blowhole. Its natural rock formation spouted a rainbow of water as the waves crashed into the cliff side. They drove on to the North Shore, famous for its huge waves. They stopped for a while watching some very brave surfers. Mitchell thought of Dave, but quietly put it out of his mind. He was determined not to let bad memories spoil his time with Maggie. A stop at the Dole Pineapple Pavilion was next on their agenda. Finally that afternoon they ended up at Pearl Harbor. They took the ferry boat out to the Arizona Memorial.

This was the first public place where Mitchell had felt comfortable. He understood this place, he felt a bond, a kinship with the men who had served here and who had died here. The war in Vietnam was tearing America apart.

Patriotism seem to be almost none existent, but not here. Here he could see it in the eyes of the other visitors, he could feel it coming from the structure itself. That was fine with Mitchell, because he believed that patriotism is the foundation on which freedom stands and we should never take freedom for granite. Our freedoms are not carved in stone, only the names of the men who have died to protect them. There were 1102 names carved in stone at this memorial for the men who went down with this once proud battleship. They will forever remain entombed in the rusted, twisted hulk below.

Mitchell couldn't understand why America honored these men who gave their lives for their country and then despised him and his fellow soldiers serving in Vietnam so much. They were doing the same thing, serving their country when called on to do so.

He stared down into the water at the sunken battleship. Watching the drops of oil slowly leaking up from its fuel tanks. The oil had been leaking for twenty-eight years and would probably leak for another twenty-eight years. He tried to understand, to find an answer but he couldn't. He looked at Maggie by his side, holding his hand.

"The whole damn world is upside down," he said. He didn't say more, he didn't have to and she knew what he meant.

It was early evening, February 11th, this would be the last night Mitchell and Maggie would have before Mitchell's return to Nam. They had spent the day shopping for gifts that Maggie would take back for family and friends. They had returned to their room to change clothes

321

and freshen up before going out for dinner. Maggie was in the bathroom putting the final touches on her makeup, although Mitchell didn't understand why. He felt she was beautiful with or without makeup. He had opened the sliding glass door and gone out onto the balcony.

"Hey there, Bobby Mitchell. How they hell are you?" Eddie shouted to him from the adjacent balcony. His words slashed through the quiet tranquil night. They were loud and slurred. His posture was sluggish and unsteady. That and the bottle of Wild Turkey, two-thirds empty in his hand, lead Mitchell to conclude he was drunk. He was sitting on the balcony railing, his feet in the seat of one of the patio chairs. "How about a drink, Bobby Mitchell. Just one boonie rat to another, just one soldier to another. You know, some fuckin' people around here don't like soldiers. Did you know that, Bobby Mitchell?"

"Yeah, I know that Eddie." Mitchell answered.

"Yeah, I know that too, but fuck 'em! I say, just fuck 'em! Don't mean a fuckin' thing." Eddie continued, waving his arm about as he spoke, coming perilously close to losing his balance.

"Where's your wife?" Mitchell asked.

"Where's my wife? My wife, she's probably got her legs in the air for some fucking long hair back home by now."

"What?" Mitchell asked, shocked by what Eddie had said. "You mean she's gone back stateside?"

"Fuck her!" Eddie said, not paying any attention to Mitchell. "Don't mean a fuckin' thing! She can fuck the whole state of Missouri for all I care."

322

Maggie walked out on to the balcony, she had heard Eddie's drunken raving all the way inside the room.
"What's going on?" She asked, but before Mitchell could answer Eddie stammered.

"Hey there, Bobby Mitchell's wife. How about a drink. You want to have a drink with me? We can drink to good wives like you, Bobby Mitchell's wife."

Maggie looked at Mitchell who turned his face away from Eddie's view and then he spoke quietly, "He said his wife is gone, back stateside. I guess he's drunk out of his mind."

"Or we could drink to something else, if you want. I don't care. What you wanna drink to? We could drink to the war. That's the thing, to the war and all my fuckin' buddies back there."

"Maybe we shouldn't drink anymore tonight." Mitchell said. "Maybe you have had enough for tonight."

"Yeah, we can drink to my buddies, my dead buddies, or the ones with their arms or legs blown off. Yeah, Bobby Mitchell and Bobby Mitchell's wife, let's drink to them. We can be just like them."

"Eddie!" Mitchell shouted. "Eddie, listen to me. Where's your wife?"

Eddie didn't answer, he took another big swig of the Wild Turkey.

"When did she leave?"

"Yesterday, she left yesterday. She told me I was pathetic, pathetic she said. She told me her friends at school thinks she shouldn't have anything to do with me, because I'm immoral for killing the innocent people of Vietnam. She told me if I didn't get killed before, not to come home to her. She won't be there. She told me she's getting a divorce. She don't want to ever see me again. Well, fuck her! I say, don't mean a fuckin' thing. Right, Bobby Mitchell? Don't mean a fuckin' thing."

"That's right, Eddie." Mitchell replied. "Say Eddie, I'll come over there and have that drink. You go inside your room and I'll come over. Okay, Eddie?"

Eddie acted as if he didn't hear a word Mitchell was saying. "I don't need her. I don't need no fuckin' body."

"Listen to me Eddie. Come on, go inside your room and unlock the door so I can have a drink with you."

Eddie started sobbing, "I don't have no body. I got no place to go. I can't go back to the boonies. Oh God, I can't do it anymore." He was crying openly now. "I'm so scared. I can't go back, I can't go home. I guess I'll just stay here. I'll just stay here forever."

"Eddieee......" Mitchell screamed in horror as Eddie calmly leaned back, intentionally plunging himself from the eleventh floor balcony to the sidewalk below. Three seconds later, Eddie's war ended.

Maggie stared wide-eyed in shock from what she had just seen. Her body started trembling, "Oh, my God!" She cried.

Mitchell turned and stepped between her and the balcony railing, instinctively trying to protect her from the view.

"Oh, my God!" She cried again.

"Don't look, Maggie," Mitchell softly said, wrapping one arm around her shoulders and his other hand on the back of her head pulling her face into his chest. "Don't look ....Shhhh."

"My God Bobby, he killed himself."

"I know Maggie, I know." Maggie tried to raise her head. "No, no, don't look. Come on, come on, let's go inside." Mitchell said as he guided her back into the room.

"Why did he do it Bobby, why?"

Mitchell held her tighter, his feelings changing from shock of seeing Eddie jump to anger, for Maggie having witnessed it. "It's the goddamn war. It's not satisfied just to kill people in those goddamn jungles and rice patties. No, it has to reach all the way over here to kill. Fuckin' goddamn war."

Maggie and Mitchell spent the next four hours with the authorities. First the Honolulu police and after that the Army. The Lt. Colonel that headed up the Army's investigation told Mitchell that Eddie was the fourth soldier on R&R from Vietnam to commit suicide this month and it was only the 11th of February.

Mitchell's only response was, "The whole damn world is upside down."

Sometime after midnight, Maggie and Mitchell found themselves sitting on an almost deserted Waikiki Beach. They were watching the ocean waves gently lapping up on the sand a short distance from their feet. The sky was sparkling with stars and the moonlight was reflecting off the dark waters. Mitchell was holding Maggie in his arms, she was still shaken from Eddie's suicide.

"I've been thinking about what you said." Maggie said softly, her head laying against Mitchell's chest.

"What's that?" Mitchell asked.

"What you said about the war, not just killing over there, but killing here, too."

"Don't think about that, Maggie."

"But, I do think about it and I think it's the truth. The war did kill Eddie."

"I don't want to talk about it!"

Maggie pulled away from Mitchell's chest, looking him directly in the eyes. "Well, I do. I can't pretend it didn't happen. Bobby, in less than nine hours you have to go back. Go back to a place that is so horrible that Eddie killed himself rather than go back to. How am supposed to feel about that? How am I supposed to deal with it? Tell me Bobby, how?"

"I don't know what to tell you, Maggie. I wish I could say something or do something that would make it easier for you, but I just don't know. I have to go back, I got no choice."

"Yes you do, you can leave with me tomorrow."

"What?" Mitchell was surprised by what she had said.

"We can just get on the plane and go back to Phoenix together."

"You mean desert? The army would be after my ass in less than a week."

"We could hide someplace. We could go to Canada. I've heard that a lot of people are going up there to get away from the war."

"Oh sure Maggie, running and hiding, that would be a great life for you and for our son. No Maggie!" Mitchell said sharply, "You know I'd do almost anything in the world for you, but not that. I won't do that. It's not me, I just can't. Someday, Brian will be old enough to wonder and ask. What would I say? Your Dad ran away to hide because he was afraid to go back to the war. No Maggie, I won't do that."

"I just want you alive," Maggie said, tears pouring down her cheeks. "What good will you be as a father if you're dead?"

"Maggie....Maggie can't you see, I have to be able to look you and our son, and myself in the face and not be ashamed. If I can't do that, then what's the point in living?"

Maggie just looked at him crying, she knew it was his pride talking and she didn't give a damn about pride, but he did. So, she didn't say anything, she just cried.

The next morning Maggie watched him walk away to the plane that would take him back to the war. This time she didn't cry, she just stood there looking profoundly sad, wounded, almost as if a part of her had died. She was afraid the war was going to take him from her. If not by a bullet from an enemy soldier's gun, then by breaking his spirit, crushing his very soul. He was strong willed and independent, he always had been. But, she didn't know how long he could hold up under the weight he was trying to carry inside. She looked up at the morning sky and whispered, "Please God, let him come home to me."

CHAPTER TWENTY-ONE

Two days after Mitchell left for Hawaii an R&R
slot for Bangkok opened up. Frank was next on the list for
Bangkok and he jumped at the chance to go nine days
early. He traveled from Camp Evans to Da Nang and from
there a five hundred mile flight to Bangkok, Thailand.
Arriving there in the early afternoon, he was taken to one of
a dozen small hotels contracted by the U.S. Military located
in Bangkok's busy red light district. He was given a room
for the next seven nights.

Bangkok, the capital and largest city in Thailand
with a population of over four million, is rich in culture and
offers an almost boundless supply of things to see and do.
Its museums and libraries were filled with works of art.
Throughout the city there were hundreds of examples of
beautiful architecture and magnificent temples. But these
things were almost always wasted on the U.S. soldiers
coming for R&R. Unlike Hawaii, where married men went
to see their wives or other family members, Bangkok was
the place that most single men chose. They didn't come for
the culture or to admire the architecture, they came for the
girls. Sex was the business benefiting from their visits.

Frank settled into his room and changed into the
only civilian clothes he had. A pair of dark gray slacks and
a black polo shirt. He was an impressive looking guy, his
muscled arms filling up his sleeves and his chiseled chest
and abdomen showing through his shirt. He left his room
and walked down the two flights of stairs and through the

lobby into the street. It was bustling with traffic; cars, buses, motor scooters, and bicycles. Hundreds of pedestrians were walking up and down the street. He made his way through the crowd a half a block before entering one of the many small bars operating primarily to serve the American soldier. He took a table next to the wall and sat down. Leaning his chair back against the wall, he propped his feet up on the table. His face was neutral, his lips neither smiling nor frowning. His eyes were dark and bottomless, not giving a hint of any emotions.

A waitress came over to the table, "What you have G.I.?"

"Bud," Frank answered. "Cold!"

"Always cold here, G.I." the waitress said as she moved away to get the beer. She soon returned with a bottle of Budweiser and a glass. Frank pushed the glass aside and took a drink from the bottle. It was cold. There were flakes of soft ice crystals clinging to the sides of the bottle.

Ten or twelve other G.I.'s were in the bar, drinking and talking to the bar girls. In the background, Diana Ross and the Supremes were belting out 'Love Child' over a cheap stereo system. Frank noticed a bar girl watching him. She was sitting with two other girls talking with a group of G.I.'s at the bar. From time to time, she would smile and say something to the group, but her attention was directed towards Frank. He made eye contact with her and held her stare for a good minute. She smiled at him but his expression never changed. She got up from her stool and started across the room. Frank watched her and realized he was comparing her to May Le. She was small, barely five feet tall. She had a Coke bottle figure, but all of the proportions were smaller. Her black hair cut short above her shoulders. She was nothing like May Le.

She stepped up to Frank's table, "You buy me a drink, G.I.?"

Frank looked at her for a few seconds, "Sure baby, I'll buy you a drink."

She sat down and the waitress was immediately there to take the order. They had the routine down pat. "The girls can only drink wine. Is that okay?" The bar girl asked with a well-practiced smile and little girl's voice.

"Sure, why not," Frank answered. "Wine for the lady."

The waitress hurried away.

"My name is Joy."

"Ya, I bet." Name and job description, Frank thought.

"What your name, G.I.?"

"If your name is Joy, mine must be misery." She looked confused, not knowing the meaning of the word or never heard it used as anyone's name. "Frank," Frank finally said. "My name is Frank."

Joy smiled broadly, "I very happy to meet you, Frank."

The waitress returned with a tulip-shaped glass filled with wine. Frank noticed a few small bubbles of carbonation. "Fifty baht." The waitress said.

The baht is the basic unit of currency for Thailand. Approximately twenty baht equaled one U.S. dollar.

"Must be good stuff." Frank commented as he paid. Joy sipped her wine and Frank drank his beer. She smiled pleasantly and he stared blankly.

"You like me, Frank? You think me pretty?"

He didn't answer for a few seconds and when he did his voice was flat and emotionless. "Sure baby, I think you're pretty."

"You like me be your good time girl?"

"Good time girl?" Frank questioned.

"I can be very good, good time girl," Joy whispered.

"Yeah, I bet you can. How much it gonna cost me for you to be my good time girl?"

"Five hundred baht." Joy said.

"Five hundred baht." Frank repeated the price.

"Twenty-five dollar American," she sighed.

"Twenty-five American." Frank repeated.

"All night," she smiled. "I be very, very good, good time girl."

Frank looked at her for a few seconds, "Sure baby, why not. You can be my good time girl."

Frank finished his beer with one long gulp, Joy left her wine unfinished on the table. They walked over to the bar where Frank bought a bottle of Jack Daniels and a six pack of Budweiser. The bartender placed the liquor in a paper bag and with the bag under one arm and Joy wrapped up in the other, Frank walked out.

Joy was nineteen years old and had been a bar girl since she was fifteen. With the money she earned, she supported her entire family; mama-san, papa-san, four younger brothers, and two younger sisters. There was no other job she could get that would pay her anything close to

the money she made as a bar girl. She didn't think of
herself as a whore. She looked at it as providing a
legitimate service, fulfilling an essential need.

Frank's room was on the third floor of the hotel. It
was small, dominated by a full size bed in the middle of the
room. Along one wall was a dresser with a built-in
refrigerator at one end. There was a small round top table
with two chairs. The bathroom was small with a sink, toilet
and bathtub. One wall had accordion folding wooden
louver doors going out onto a small balcony that
overlooked the street. The room had a radio, but no
television. A ceiling fan hung over the bed turning slowly,
moving the humid air around the room. There was no other
form of air conditioning.

Frank placed the Jack Daniels on the table and the
beer in the fridge.

Joy put her arms around Frank's neck and raised
herself onto her tiptoes. She kissed him tenderly on the
mouth. Frank didn't pull away from the kiss, but his
response was cool at best.

"What you like Joy do for you?" She asked. She
had been doing this a long time and had encountered a
gauntlet of moods.

"Fix me a drink, would you baby?"

She opened the Jack Daniels and poured two inches
into a glass and then added a splash of water. Frank had
opened the folding doors and gone out onto the balcony and
was looking down onto the street. She followed him out
and handed him the drink. Frank leaned on the railing,
drinking his whiskey, staring at nothing in particular as she
gently rubbed up and down his back. When he looked at

Joy he wanted to see May Le, but he didn't. He felt uneasy, a little guilty about being there. He finished his drink and Joy made him another. The liquor felt warm as it drifted down his throat. What he wanted he couldn't have, what he could have, he didn't really want.

The next two hours passed in much the same way. Frank drank and Joy patiently tended his every need. She never pushed herself onto him or dwelt on sex. Eventually time, closeness of proximity, and Jack Daniels prevailed, and just as the sun was setting they made love.

The next morning, Joy left the room early and when she returned she brought fresh cantaloupe, honeydew, bread and cheese. Frank ate the melons, bread and cheese washing it down with Budweiser.

"You want I stay with you, Frank?" Joy asked. She made it sound sweet and innocent, not at all like the business proposition it was. "I can stay whole time you here, if you like."

Frank smiled at her for the first time since they'd met. "How much if you stay the whole time?"

"Hundred dollar American." Joy answered.

"Oh, so I get a discount for a long term contract?"

"I charge you less because I like you."

"Sure you do baby. But, what the hell, hundred dollars sounds like a good deal."

The next four days was spent much the same way. Frank and Joy would stay in the room or in one of the nearby bars. Frank would drink until he was drunk and then they would have sex. Joy was a pro and the physical sex was good. In fact, she had Frank doing it in positions he not only had never done before, but he had never thought of. But the sex was just sex and soon became meaningless. Frank was drinking too much and falling deeper into depression. The booze wasn't drowning out the pain, the sex wasn't making up for the loneliness.

It was early morning of his fifth day in Bangkok, Frank was laying in bed staring at the ceiling fan above him. He watched it slowly turn and was wondering what the hell he was doing. His head hurt from the hangover. His temples felt like someone was whacking them with a fire ax. The morning's first rays of light were penetrating the balcony's louver door and spilling shadows over the room. Joy was asleep beside him. He looked at her, studying the shadow patterns the louver door made on her naked back and bottom. No matter how hard she tried, she couldn't make him stop thinking of May Le. He turned his eyes away from her and back to the ceiling fan. He watched as it turned round and round. It had been turning since he got here, always moving but never getting anywhere. That wasn't the most profound thought ever pondered by mankind, but it was enough to bring Frank to a decision.

"Joy," he said softly. She didn't stir. "Joy," he said again, this time much louder.

She rolled over to face him. "What you need baby?" She said in a sleepy voice.

"When you go home this morning you don't need to come back. I'm leaving today."

She slid out of bed and got dressed. Frank only looked at her occasionally as she gathered up her personal belongings. Then she came back to the bed, leaned over and kissed Frank on his cheek. The kiss seemed different, real and sincere. "You be happy and safe Frank." Her voice and face both seemed a little sad.

"I think it's going to be some time before I am either of those," Frank answered.

She smiled, it wasn't a smile that showed happiness or pleasure and it simply said she understood. Joy turned and walked away.

Frank laid there for a few more minutes before getting up and taking a long, hot shower. He dressed in his fatigues, jungle boots, and boonie hat; packed his bag and headed down stairs to the lobby. He went straight to the military liaison desk where an Air Force E-5 was on duty.

"Can I leave before my scheduled departure date?" Frank asked.

"What?" The E-5 said.

"Can I go back today instead of on my departure date?"

The E-5 looked at Frank as if he was from Mars or something.

Frank lifted his arms, his palms up. "Well, can I?"

"I'm sorry brother, it's just that in the six months I been here doing this, you're the first dude who has ever asked to go back early."

"Well, can I or not?"

"I don't know why not. Let me check on today's flights." He picked up a clipboard with the day's flight manifest on it. "We have a flight at 1400 and another at 1930. They both have open seats."

"Good, I'll take the 1400," Frank said.

335

Mitchell's return flight from Honolulu landed in Cam Ranh Bay at 1600 hours local time. His transportation north to Camp Evans would not be leaving until 0800 the next morning. He found his way to an enlisted men's club and was sitting alone at a corner table, drinking beer and eating french fries. R&R had been a mixed bag of emotions. He loved the time with Maggie, but some of the other events, especially Eddie's suicide had left him troubled. He was staring down at his fries, mindlessly arranging them on the half empty plate.

"What's up Sarge?"

Mitchell looked up to see Frank smiling ear to ear. "Frank, what the hell are you doing here?"

"Same as you, waiting for a ride." Frank pulled out a chair and sat down across the table and reached over to take a french fry from Mitchell's plate. "After you left a slot opened up for Bangkok, so I took it."

"When you going out?" Mitchell asked.

"Done been. Got back an hour and half ago."

"Didn't you get the full seven days?"

"Yeah, but the drinkin' and screwin' got old fast. I got bored. Came back a couple days early."

Mitchell looked a little surprised. "Shit you say."

A Vietnamese woman that worked at the club came by carrying a tray of glasses and empty beer cans that she had cleared from another table.

Frank called to her, "Mama-san, I'll have a beer and bring another for the Sarge."

She acknowledged the order with a nod of her head.

"So how's Maggie?" Frank asked.

Mitchell smiled. "Maggie's great, just great."

"Yeah, I bet," Frank said smiling. "She too fuckin' good for you. You knows that, don't ya?"

"You won't get no argument from me on that," Mitchell said.

"And little Frank, how he doing?"

"It's Brian. The baby's name is Brian."

"Yeah, I know with a fuckin' "I". So how's the kid?"

"Maggie couldn't bring him. Ear infection, doctor said the plane ride would hurt his ears or something."

The Mama-san came back and placed two beers down. Frank paid her and she hurried away.

"That's too bad," Frank said, then took a long drink of his beer.

"I got pictures!" Mitchell said proudly, pulling out an envelope from his breast pocket. He handed the pictures to Frank.

He studied them one at a time, "Little Frank's really cute and his mama is just down right pretty."

"Give me those," Mitchell snatched the pictures back. Frank grinned and took another long drink.

"So, you did every girl in Bangkok in less than a week and had to come back early?" Mitchell teased.

Frank shrugged, "Yeah....well I don't know. It just wasn't making it for me." He plucked a couple more fries off of Mitchell's plate. The seriousness showed in Frank's eyes. It may not have been apparent to most people but Mitchell could see it. There wasn't much about Frank that he didn't see, that he didn't understand.

337

"Yeah, well R&R isn't always all it's cracked up to be," Mitchell said.

"It must have been good for you. I mean being with Maggie, being back in the world and all that." Frank said.

"You're half right. Being with Maggie was the best, I mean without that I don't know how long I could keep going. But there's shit going on back in the world that I just can't fuckin' understand. Man, I seen some shit you wouldn't believe!"

"What kinda shit?" Frank asked.

"There was this dude, a grunt on R&R just like me, staying in the room next to Maggie and me. I mean his wife came to meet him in Hawaii just to dump his ass. Tells him not to come home. Said he's immoral for being over here."

"That's cold," Frank said.

"That's not the half of it," Mitchell continued his story. "He's out on his balcony and me and Maggie are on ours and he's telling us all about it. He's drunk on his ass and I'm starting to get worried and all of a sudden he pulls a fuckin' Tinker Bell right off the balcony. Eleven fuckin' floors down."

Frank's eyes opened wider, "Jesus....he dead?"

"Hell yes he's dead. I mean eleven fuckin' floors. He splattered his brains all over the fuckin' sidewalk."

"Shit! Maggie see that shit?"

"Oh yeah, it was a fuckin' nightmare."

The mama-san came back by and asked, "More beer for you?"

"No, make it a rum and coke." Frank answered.

338

"And for you?" The mama-san asked, looking at Mitchell.

"Make that two."

"That kinda shit not good for Maggie to be seeing," Frank stated.

"Yeah, it didn't do much for me either." Mitchell looked down at the table, shaking his head. "Maggie freaked. I mean, afterwards we were on the beach talking and she said I should just go home with her. I mean, fuckin' AWOL. Run off and hide in Canada."

Frank looked at Mitchell for a few seconds then said, "Maybe she's right, be better than this place."

"Shit Frank, you know better than that. If I did that, I'd be on the run the rest of my life." Mitchell shook his head again. "No, in five months I'm out of this shit hole, out of the army." He paused for a short time, shaking his head. "No, I gotta see it through."

The mama-san returned with the two rum and cokes. Frank and Mitchell sat silent for a minute or two and drank. Frank signaled Mama-san for two more. They talked and drank for another hour and a half consuming six more rum and cokes each. Mitchell was feeling light-headed, the liquor was warm in his stomach and his face was hot and flushed. Frank was in much the same condition.

"The whole fuckin' world is upside down. I mean, protesters are everywhere. This one fuckin' hippie freak was yelling at me, calling me murderer, baby killer. Shit, I was going to rip his fuckin' lungs out, but Maggie begged me to let it go."

"Yous' shoulda' killed the mothafucker," Frank insisted. "Those mothafuckers don't know what the fuck they doin'."

"Yeah, I shoulda', but you know, didn't wanta upset Maggie."

"Maggie shouldn't be seeing that shit!" Frank added.

Another half hour passed and two more rum and cokes made their way into Frank's and Mitchell's systems.

"Every time I was doing that little good time girl, all I could think of was May Le. All I could see....." Frank stopped without finishing the sentence.

Mitchell could see the mist that filled his eyes. "You loved her big time, didn't you?"

"Yeah," Frank said with a little break in his voice. "Yeah, sometimes I hurts so bad inside, man I don't know....I hurts so bad."

"She's gone, Frank. I wished she wasn't but she is. It's gotta hurt for a while, but it'll get better. Time Frank, you gotta give it time."

Thirty minutes and two more rum and cokes later, Mitchell and Frank were standing in the middle of the room. Each had an arm around the other, singing 'The Ballad of the Green Berets'."

CHAPTER TWENTY-TWO

It has been seven weeks since Firebase Alpha was reoccupied. Just like the Marines before, the big guns now stationed there controlled the valley and for all practical purposes had put a stop to the NVA's supply route. Over the past month, the NVA command had been working on a plan to attack and once again eliminate the firebase.

On the first day of March, more than eighteen hundred men of the NVA's, 217th regiment, the same unit that had successfully ambushed the supply convoy, crossed the DMZ and set up a staging area nine klicks northwest of Alpha. The next day, they sent out six patrols scouting the firebase from all sides, evaluating its defenses. Armed with this information, the NVA commanders formulated a final plan of attack.

At 2100 hours on March 4th, the NVA moved into position. Their plan was to attack the firebase simultaneously from three sides, the north, east, and south. The only road to Alpha was from the west. Eight hundred meters downhill from the firebase, they had set up an ambush along the road, with the idea to have the ability to hit any soldiers retreating from the base or any reinforcement that may try to come to the rescue.

At 0200 hours the morning of the 5th, the attack commenced. The sound of trip flares popping off and then a burning, bright, white light came from the east perimeter. In a few seconds, some of Second Platoon opened up with machine gun fire.

Frank was on watch in the turret, Mitchell asleep on top along the left side of the APC. Country and Paganini were asleep inside. The gun fire brought all three to their feet.

"What's up?" Mitchell asked.

"I saw some flares go off, there..." before Frank could finish his sentence two more trip flares popped off simultaneously in front of One-One's position. "Shit!" Frank jerked his head around.

"Man your guns!" Mitchell shouted.

Country got on his M-60 and Paganini the right side fifty caliber. Frank climbed out of the TC's turret and Mitchell took his place. Frank slid into the driver's hole and armed himself with his M-16. A few seconds passed then more flares popped off to One-One's right and then to the left. Mitchell made out five or six shadowy figures moving towards the wire. He opened fire with his fifty and so did the grunts in the bunkers on both sides of One-One.

Within a minute of the first flare going off, the north and east side of the perimeter were under a full scale attack. Now enemy mortar rounds began to fall on Firebase Alpha, dozens of 82mm high explosive rounds rained down on the base. From the northeast, 75mm recoilless rifle fire began to pound at the bunkers along the north and east perimeters. All three of A Troop's mortar tracks fired illumination rounds, lighting up the entire area. Mitchell could see scores of NVA soldiers rushing the outer wire. The earsplitting noise of exploding mortar rounds, cannon fire, and countless machine guns seemed to slowly fade away into silence as Mitchell's concentration focused.

The smoke from the battle mixed with the flickering light of the illumination flares draped Firebase Alpha in an eerie fog. Mitchell now found himself in what could best be described as a ghostly dream of endless enemy soldiers desperately trying to bridge the wire of the outer perimeter. The gooks kept coming, Mitchell kept shooting.

Each metal ammo box contained a hundred round belt of fifty caliber. Mitchell didn't remember calling for more ammo but he must have or Country and Paganini just resupplied him without being asked, because there were nineteen empty ammo boxes scattered around the turret. The four foot long heavy machine gun barrel was beginning to glow red. Mitchell had fired almost two thousand rounds in less than fifteen minutes. He had never seen anything like this kind of an attack. Nobody at Alpha that night had seen anything like this. The NVA came in waves of humanity, storming the perimeter. At times they seemed to be two to three men deep, throwing themselves on to the concertina wire, desperately trying to form a human bridge for their comrades. Over one hundred claymores had been exploded and still the enemy kept coming. Tens of thousands of rounds had been fired and still the enemy kept coming.

The defenders along the north perimeter were holding off the attack, but the southeast perimeter was beginning to give way. The order came to the grunts of the 101st to blow the fifty-five gallon drums of napalm-like foo gas. Almost simultaneously, the thirty charges were detonated. For Mitchell what happened next was the most chthonian event of the war. The drums of foo gas exploded upward and outward into cone-shaped plumes merging with each other, forming a circle that coincided with the concertina wire of the outer perimeter. The flames boiled orange, red and yellow, thirty feet high. Within seconds this hellish ring of fire surrounded Firebase Alpha. The oxygen needed to feed the massive inferno was being sucked from the air. It created a noticeable draft blowing back into the huge wall of fire. Mitchell could feel the intense heat. He felt encircled, as if he was in the eye of a hurricane, but this was not a hurricane of wind and rain, it was one of fire. A few seconds later, he became aware of the lack of oxygen. He took a deep breath, but there was nothing there to fill his lungs. The harder he tried to breathe, the deeper he inhaled, the more panic he felt. This vacuum continued for only fifteen to twenty seconds, but for Mitchell and everyone else at Alpha it seemed a lot longer. Up until now, the science of combustion was just something he had learned about in school, but being in the vacuum caused by this astonishing fire was no longer a piece of incidental knowledge; it was real and it was terrifying.

The full fury of the fire lasted for only a minute, in that time almost all shooting had stopped. The initial blast was so luminous that it assimilated all vision. Then the huge boiling wall of fire began to die down and its arrant devastation was revealed. Hundreds of NVA soldiers had been caught in or near the wire at the time of the blast. They were now burning. Some hung up in the wire, some outside the wire, and others still on their feet running directionlessly. Their screams, loud and piercing drowned out all other sounds, even those of the raging fire.

Mitchell couldn't envisage what was before his eyes. The human mind has the ability to protect itself, when reality becomes too much to bare, it triggers a safety net, a filter between reality and perception. This happened to Mitchell. It now seemed hallucinational, nightmarish, like a subconscious vision of hell itself. A macabre scene of men burning, an abode of condemned souls.

Mitchell began to smell the stench of scores of burning corpses. The nauseating odor created by the burning of human flesh is unforgettable. He had experienced it before, but nothing as overwhelming as this. The sickening taste of vomit climbed up his throat. He swallowed it back. This unbelievable inferno had stopped the NVA's attack. The enemy had lost hundreds of men in the last few minutes. If there was to be a second attack, it would take them time to regroup.

In the very first minute of the attack, Firebase Alpha's commanding officer had called for air support. Mitchell heard it coming from the south. It was in the form of six AH-1 Cobra gunships. They split formation, three circling the east perimeter, three going west. Like its serpent namesake, the Cobra was designed to fight down among the trees and bushes where it could strike hard and fast. The Cobra operated with a two-man crew. The pilot, who is in the rear cockpit, sitting high up so he can get a good all-around view over the head of the gunner in the front seat. The gunner has a commanding view of the battlefield and has night vision sights to help him fire the weapons. The weaponry on a Cobra is substantial. In its nose there is a six barrel mini-gun which fires at a rate of up to one hundred rounds per second. On its stub pylons, it carries two more externally mounted 7.62mm M60 CA1 machine guns with a fire rate of four thousand rounds per minute, plus two rocket pods with seven 2.75 inch rockets in each pod.

The six Cobras were releasing their full destructive fury on the enemy. They gave very close ground support, firing their guns and rockets very near and sometimes inside the wire. They made numerous sweeps around the perimeter and when all their ordinance had been expended, they disappeared as suddenly as they had come. There was a strange, eerie calm.

Only minutes later, Mitchell heard the screaming of two thousand pound projectiles overhead, cutting through the air. They exploded six to eight hundred meters down the north and east slopes of the hill. The blasts were massive, the earth shook violently with each hit. They were coming from the U.S.S. New Jersey. It was firing its huge sixteen inch guns from a position twenty-three miles away, just off the coast. The rounds would come in volley of threes. The battleship had nine of the sixteen inch guns mounted on three turrets of three guns each. About every forty-five seconds a volley screamed in, bringing destruction and death to the enemy. The pounding continued for almost an hour. When it ended the NVA force was all but destroyed. It had been a slaughter. Of the eighteen hundred men that attacked Alpha, less than seven hundred escaped.

The rising sun brought with it the realization of the scale of death and the utter destruction that occurred. The remains of hundreds of NVA soldiers laid in the wire and scattered on the hillside. The landscape surrounding Hill

613, which the day before was a thick lush jungle, now looked like the surface of the moon. Mitchell had never seen carnage like this before and hoped he would never see it again.

This time the NVA failed to overrun Firebase Alpha. The Americans had held, but paid a price for Hill 613. Twenty-four of them had died that night, five were members of A Troop.

CHAPTER TWENTY-THREE

Country was thinking about a white cross. A simple wooden cross, the kind you see along a roadside or highway, the ones that are placed there to memorialize the spot where someone had been killed in a car wreck. They sometimes might have flowers or a ribbon tied to them. In fact, he was thinking of a particular roadside cross that was on Highway 51 between Pineville and Mathews, near his home in North Carolina. He remembered that it always had flowers tied to it. He would drive by almost every day, that is almost every day before he was drafted. The cross was placed there in June 1966 by the father of Tommy Blair. Country had known Tommy. They had gone to the same high school, but then everyone in Pineville went to the same high school. Tommy wasn't really a friend, more like an acquaintance. Country would see him around school, he remembered having a few classes together, but they didn't hang out. But every time he drove by that cross, he would think of Tommy and how one day he was alive and the next he was gone, killed in a car wreck at that very spot on Highway 51.

What had brought this all to mind was that One-One was rolling down the narrow, winding road leading away from Firebase Alfa. They were just about at the spot where Dave had died. Country was thinking that it would be nice if he could place a cross here to memorialize Dave, but he knew he couldn't.

Strangely, Paganini was also thinking of Dave. His remembrance likewise triggered by passing this spot. But his thoughts were not of a cross or memorial, he was vividly remembering the moment that Dave was hit. Seeing in his mind's eye, Dave's head exploding, being knocked to the floor of the APC with Dave's dead body on top of him. He had a clear vision of the gaping hole in the back of Dave's head, the bloody, spongy brain tissue spilling out. Paganini shuttered, closed his eyes, trying to think of something else.

Mitchell too was aware that they were passing through the ambush site that was so costly a month before. He was concentrating on the hillside, searching for any sign of danger. The muscles in his neck and shoulders bunched tight, his jaw biting his teeth together. Mitchell always felt the obligation for the safety of his crew. It had become a binding moral duty. Dave had died here, perhaps because of a decision he had made. He didn't like the way it made him feel.

Frank was thinking primarily about his driving, keeping One-One in the middle of the road, navigating the many turns. But now and then his mind would wander, mostly about a big New York pizza, double pepperoni.

"One-One, this is One-Six, over."

"This is One-One, over."

"This is One-Six. Slow it down a little, the column is starting to string out, over."

"This is One-One, willco."

Frank reduced his speed without Mitchell saying a word. One-One was in its usual position, the lead track, on point as A Troop rolled away from Boot Hill. That was the nickname they had given to Firebase Alpha, Hill 613; Boot Hill, because too many men had died there.

It was March 11th and A Troop had been ordered back to its home base, Camp Evans. This would be the first time they had been there in five months.

Mitchell led the troop east to Mai Loc, then south past Firebases Carroll and Barge; until they intersected with Highway 9, following it east to Quang Tri. From there they took Highway One south to Camp Evans. The trip was forty-two miles, and took A Troop just over three hours to complete. It was 1440 hours when they rolled through the main gate of Evans. They pulled into the parking area next to the large helicopter pad of the 224th Aviation Battalion.

Captain Tice had arranged for a special meal to be served at 1700 hours, so the men had two hours to kill. Some headed for the PX, others for the showers. Mitchell chose a shower.

A Troop's showers were located in the company area between the supply building and the enlisted men's barrack tents. The showers were simple wooden stalls about five feet high, with the bottom eighteen inches open so that your legs, from the knee down, could be seen. PSP steel sheeting had been laid down, forming a floor. There were six stalls in all. The water came from an open tank elevated ten feet high. It's only source of heat was the sun and the water came out from the shower heads, barely lukewarm. Still this was the first shower Mitchell had seen in almost a month. He stood with his face turned up, letting the water spray into it, flooding through his hair, running over his chest and back. He stayed in this position for a minute or so, enjoying the way the clean water felt running over his body. He reached for the bottle of shampoo, poured some into the palm of his hand and rubbed it into his hair, vigorously working it into a full lather. Picking up a new bar of Ivory soap, he lathered up the rest of his body. It felt good cleaning out every pore. "Ninety-nine and forty-four one-hundredths percent pure," he thought.

When Mitchell returned to One-One, Frank was there taking pictures with his newly purchased Polaroid camera. The one he bought the last time they were here had only lasted for a couple of months. It had started malfunctioning, probably because of lack of care and all the dirt, sand, and water it was exposed to. One day in January at Boot Hill, it jammed up and out of frustration Frank threw it to the ground, kicked it twice, and then shot it six times with his M-16, putting it out of its misery.

The new camera was functioning well and Frank happily took pictures of everyone. He had Mitchell pose for two individual shots and then handed the camera to Leroy.

"Leroy, my man," Frank said, "Take some pictures of One-One crew." Frank stood by Mitchell and motioned for Country and Paganini to join them.

Leroy looked through the view finder, framing the shot. "Shit," he said. "All of yous' together are so ugly it might break this brand new camera."

"Fuck you and your commentary, just take the goddamn picture!" Frank barked back.

He pushed the shutter button. The camera clicked, purred, and out rolled the undeveloped picture. Leroy carefully took it by one corner and handed it to Mike, who was standing beside him.

"You guys need to pose better," Mike advised. "You look like a bunch of convicts on death row."

"What are you, some kinda professional?" Frank said.

"Yeah, do something different."

Paganini placed his left forearm on Country's right shoulder. Country did the same to Frank and Frank to Mitchell. They now looked like a picket fence, their bodies being the pickets and their arms the stringer.

"That's more like it," Leroy said. "Hold that." He clicked the shutter, the camera purred and another picture popped out.

It was almost 1700 hours, when the men of A Troop started making their way to the Third Squadron's mess hall. It was located about a quarter of a mile from A Troop's parking area, closer to the middle of the large base. Once there, they strolled through the serving line, loading their trays full of baked ham, scalloped potatoes, corn on the cob, and freshly baked bread. A hot meal was a rarity for these guys, but one this abundant they hadn't ever seen. There was cold soda, ice tea, and milk to drink. After passing through the serving line, they took a seat at one of the long picnic style tables.

Once everyone was seated, Captain Tice addressed them. "Eat up men, there's plenty more, so help yourselves to seconds or thirds if you like. But, I suggest you save room for dessert. There is cake and ice cream. So enjoy men, you've earned it."

They had earned it and they did enjoy. For these men who spent ninety-nine days out of every hundred in the boonies, simple things became great pleasures.

After dinner, most of First Platoon gathered in one of the barrack tents. Each platoon had a tent assigned to them, although they were rarely there to use them. Some men from Second and Third Platoon would drop by to visit, but the crowd was mostly made up of First Platoon. There was a fifty-five gallon drum, cut in half, filled with ice, beer, and soda. The contents appeared to be made up of equal parts of Budweiser and Coors and less amounts of Coke and 7-UP. The beer and soda were free, courtesy of Captain Tice. A supply clerk was there with bottles of hard liquor, selling it for fifty cents a shot.

They had congregated into four or five groups inside the tent. Music was being played in at least two different areas. Upbeat conversation filled the air. The crew of One-One, along with Leroy, Paul, and Keith were together. They had arranged three cots into a horseshoe shape, sitting two or three men to a cot.

Mitchell and Frank, both had a can of Coke in their hands, Mitchell's was virgin and Frank's had been sweetened with a shot of Barcardi Rum. Leroy had a 7-UP laced with Seagram Seven. Keith, Paul, and Paganini were all drinking Coors; Country had a plain Coke.

"Listen you guys." Keith said.

"Oh shit!" Leroy said, rolling his eyes.

"No! No, listen. What do you do, if you want to drive a hippie crazy?"

"Okay, I'll bite." Paul said. "What do ya do?"

"You put them in a round room and tell them to go stand in the fuckin' corner."

"Shit, Keith. Your jokes are getting dumber every time I hear one." Frank complained.

"Yeah, well you guys are lucky," Leroy said. "I gotsa listen to 'em all day long."

"Wait a minute, I got another one."

"Oh Jesus, no!" Frank teased, looking at Leroy.

"That's my boy." Leroy grinned.

"No, it's a good one, trust me." Keith insisted.

"Go on, tell it." Country encouraged, he enjoyed Keith's jokes.

Keith told the joke and then another one, each worse than the one before. The group talked, joked, and laughed for a couple of hours. They debated if the Jets really were better than the Colts, or did they just get lucky. If Joe Namath would ever be the quarterback that Johnny Unitas was. Eventually, the conversation turned to cars.

"When I get home, I'm getting me a brand new Mustang." Keith said. "A big V-8 with a four speed. I'll take it cruzin', run circles around all those Camaros, Firebirds, and G.T.O.'s." He emphasized G.T.O.'s, knowing how Mitchell felt about his.

"Shit! I ain't seen a Mustang yet, my G.T.O. couldn't blow the doors off of."

Keith grinned, "What about you, Country? What kind of wheels you got, or do y'all still ride horses back on the farm?"

"I got wheels," Country said sheepishly.

"What you got!" Keith pried.

"Tell him, Country." Paganini teased at Country's expense. "Tell him what you got."

"I got a pickup truck."

"Pickup truck? What kind?" Keith asked.

"It's a '53 GMC, runs like a top." Country said proudly.

"'53 GMC pickup, oh boy, I bet you can really get the girls with that." Keith laughed.

"Hey, I did all right. I had this old mattress I'd throw in the back and me and Donna Clarke, we'd go to the drive-in and it was pretty good."

"Is that the same Donna you were going steady with, but when you came home from boot camp, you found out she'd been screwin' half the town?" Frank asked.

"Well, yeah....I didn't say Donna was good. I said my old pickup was good."

About that time, Brian came over to the group. "You guys ain't ever goin' guess where we're heading to."

"You heard something?" Leroy asked.

Brian nodded his head.

"What'd you hear?"

"A Shau Valley," Brian answered.

"A Shau, where you hear that?" Mitchell asked.

"I got it from a company clerk I know, a guy named Terry. He said he saw it on Top Sergeant's desk yesterday."

"Shit!" Leroy said.

"What's with the A Shau Valley?" Paganini asked.

"Charley owns the A Shau," Mitchell answered grimly.

It was silent for a moment, then Frank, who had had about six or eight rum and Cokes, said, "Goin' be some changes."

Mitchell looked at Frank, "Oh, like what?"

"Like we goin' own it." Frank answered.

"When you say we, do you mean just you and me, or can we get a little help from the rest of the crew, and say maybe Leroy or maybe all of A Troop; or maybe the combined forces of the U.S. military?"

"I figure Troop be enough."

Mitchell smiled, "I like your confidence, it scares the hell out of me, but I like it."

"Is it really that bad in the A Shau?" Paganini was showing some real concern on his face.

"There's no place worse than the A Shau," Brian said, smiling a nervous smile, then turned and started singing as he walked away, "As I walked out onto the Streets of Laredo…"

"Don't worry, Paga-weinee" Frank said. "Me and Sarge be there to take care of ya. Here take a drink of this. Make you feel better."

Paganini took a big gulp of Frank's drink, he closed his eyes and shivered a little. "Damn!" He said.

"Double?" Mitchell asked.

Frank grinned, "This'n a triple."

Mitchell smiled, "That'll take the film off your teeth."

CHAPTER TWENTY-FOUR

Brian's information was correct. It was 0900 hours, March 13th and A Troop was rolling south on Highway One. Its destination was the A Shau Valley. The valley was approximately twenty-five miles southwest of the old Imperial City of Hue. It ran parallel to and very near the Vietnam and Laos border. It was a big part of the famous or maybe more appropriately, infamous Ho Chi Minh Trail. It was estimated that as much as eighty percent of all men, equipment, and food to supply the NVA and Viet Cong came into the country through the Ho Chi Minh Trail. The valley was an NVA stronghold, as many as fifteen thousand enemy soldiers were believed to be operating in the A Shau. The North had made a major investment of men and weapons to keep the trail open and the supplies flowing. Likewise, the Americans were now making a major effort to stop it. Some of the bloodiest fighting of the war was taking place there.

The men of A Troop were all aware of this. Each of them, in their own way, was feeling apprehension, a foreboding uneasiness. They were heading for the hottest, hot spot of the war and after coming from Boot Hill, it was hard to imagine anything worse; but there was and it made them anxious and fearful about their future.

One-One was leading the troop. Mitchell could see the Song Bo Bridge coming up. All of the members of One-One's crew were recalling memories of the time they had spent there. But for Frank, this place held the deepest feelings. His eyes were tearing a little as he steered One-One across the big steel bridge.

Country leaned over to Paganini and said, "I wish we could stop for a few minutes, you know, maybe look around at the old place, maybe see Ringo."

"Paganini nodded his head, "Yeah, I wish we could."

One-One crossed the bridge and traveled the two hundred meters to the edge of the small village. To a man, they were staring at the dozen or so children along the roadside, hoping to see Ringo, but to no avail. They passed the Old Witch's hut, Three Finger's Mama-san. She was there outside her hut tending her stand. She glared at the Americans as they passed, her eyes filled with malice. A few hundred feet further down the road they came to the hut where Ringo and May Le had lived, but it was no longer standing. It had burnt to the ground. Frank focused on the rubble, the old Coca Cola box cooler was still there, its faded red paint was now burnt, blistered, and covered by black soot. He could see the charred remains of the furniture that he had come to know; the big cabinet that was along the back wall, the old Windsor chair, and the dresser were he watched May Le brush her hair. The dresser that she undressed in front of the night they first made love. Frank's stomach knotted up, he was confused, afraid for Ringo. "What had happened here?"

They were all thinking it, what happened, where was Ringo? In less than a minute they had passed through the village, the burned down hut no longer in sight. Maybe, Ringo and his family were in some other village having to leave here because of the fire; or maybe, something bad had befell Ringo. These days in Vietnam, the odds tended to favor the latter. Bad things seemed to far outnumber the good. They didn't know, they couldn't stop to ask, they would never know.

By early afternoon, the Troop had made its way through the city of Hue and was five miles short of Eagle when they left Highway One, heading west. Twenty minutes later they were at the Song Ta Trach River near the village of Lang Ming Mang. The army engineers had constructed a pontoon bridge across the three hundred foot span of river.

One-One was first to cross the bridge. They had been ensured that the bridge could easily handle the weight of the APC's, in fact it was designed to handle even the big M-48A1 tanks that were part of A Troop. Still this was the first time One-One had crossed a pontoon bridge and the anxiety midst the crew was running high. Frank eased One-One onto the floating bridge. The river's currents were steady but not particularly strong. The water was deep, the bottom was nowhere to be seen. As the APC passed over each pontoon, the bridge would undulate rhythmically, up and down, moving in a wave-like motion. They drove slowly to keep the oscillation to a minimum. The bridge seemed to sway side to side, as well as up and down, in a four-way sinuous ripple. Halfway across, Mitchell looked over his shoulder at Country, knowing of his lack of swimming skills and innate fear of water, he wanted to see how he was doing. Country was smiling wide-eyed, but the faint look of fear showed on his face.

"No sweat," Mitchell said.

"Right!" Country answered.

In a minute and a half, it was over. The relief showed on Country's face, as One-One left the snake-like bridge for steady ground. Crossing the river was a slow process, only one track at a time was driving over the bridge. It took almost an hour for the entire troop to cross.

At 1545 hours they were still moving west on a narrow road, halfway between Firebases Birmingham and Bastogne. Actually, calling it a road was being kind. It really wasn't much more than two ruts scarred in the ground and the vegetation pushed down by some heavily tracked vehicles cutting their way through. To the north there was a relatively flat clearing in the bottom of the small valley they were crossing.

Mitchell had gotten the word to move into the clearing and form a circle, large enough for the whole troop. One-One had done this many times. Mitchell and Frank were good at judging the ark needed to make a troop size perimeter with the proper spacing for the forty APC's and tanks. One-One left the road for a short distance and when Mitchell was satisfied with the terrain he told Frank to begin his turn. He led the troop in a long, wide right turn and three minutes later the circle was closed and the perimeter formed.

The first order of business was to sweep the inside of the perimeter, to make sure it was clear of booby traps and tunnels. It was clean. A Troop was in a new AO and extra precautions would be taken. One-One doubled up on its trip flares, putting out six instead of the normal three. A fourth claymore was also added to their night defenses. The other tracks did much the same thing. The order came down that they would be on high alert. That meant two men were to be awake on watch at all times. As the night closed in from the east it brought with it a wall of dark menacing looking clouds. Rain was the last thing anyone wanted to see.

It was 2120 hours and all four members of One-One were awake and on top of the APC. The shifts for standing watch wasn't going to start until 2200. The clouds were still thick overhead, but the rain had held off so far. Mitchell was in the turret, Country by his left side M-60 and Paganini on the right side. Frank was sitting beside the turret, behind the driver's hole. Mitchell was scanning the hillside to the west with the starlight scope when he saw it, a dim red glow he caught out of his peripheral vision. He focused the scope in and held it steady. He saw it again, this time clearly, a red glow, first bright, then dimming.

"Hello!" Mitchell said out loud.

Frank turned and looked Mitchell's way, "You see something?"

"You ain't gonna believe this guys," Mitchell said.

"What is it?" Country asked, as he and Paganini moved up closer.

"You ain't gonna believe it. I got somebody up on the hill smoking a cigarette."

"No shit?" Frank said.

"No shit. I told you, you wouldn't believe it."

"Where?" Frank asked, turning around and facing the hill.

Mitchell handed him the starlight and pointed, "Up there at about ten o'clock, maybe a thousand meters."

Frank scanned the area for about ten seconds. "Son of a bitch, that cigarette stands out like Rudolph's nose every time he takes a drag." Frank handed the scope back to Mitchell. "You gonna try and take him out?"

"Won't that give away our position?" Country said, not thinking it all the way through.

Mitchell and Frank both looked at him a little pathetically. "I think they know we're here." Mitchell said. "It's pretty hard to hide an armored cavalry troop."

"I wasn't thinking," Country said sheepishly.

"The fifty would reach up there, but I probably couldn't hit him before he ran." Mitchell was thinking out loud. "But, it would be nice to send them a message. Might make them think twice about messing with us."

"What you gonna do?" Paganini asked.

"I got an idea." Mitchell said. "I'm going over to One-Eight."

"Oh yeah!" Frank said, his mind was working along the same line as Mitchell's. "I'm going with you."

One-Eight was one of the three tanks in First Platoon. Its position on the perimeter was to the left of One-One, two tracks over. Mitchell and Frank jumped off the back of the APC and headed for One-Eight, taking the starlight scope with them.

The TC of One-Eight was an E-5 named Billy Dill. Billy was from Okmulgee, Oklahoma and a gung-ho tanker. In the Armored Cavalry there was a bit of friendly rivalry between the APC guys and the tankers. But Mitchell had to admit that Billy and his crew knew their stuff.

Mitchell and Frank walked up from behind the tank. Sergeant Dill was standing on top, beside the tank's turret. "Hey, Wild Bill," Mitchell called up.

"Hey Mitchell, to what do I owe this honor?"

"We's just thought we'd go slummin' tonight," Frank said.

"Yeah, well fuck you and the horse you rode in on." Billy teased back.

"Billy, I got something I want you to shoot for me." Mitchell said as he and Frank were climbing up the back of One-Eight.

"What?" Billy asked.

Mitchell handed him the starlight and pointed, "Right out there about one thousand meters, half way up the hill, there's a gook in a tree smoking a cigarette."

Billy looked through the scope and found the gook. "Yeah, there sure as hell is."

"Can you shoot him for me?"

"So, you want me to use my main gun to take out one gook up a tree?"

"That's the idea." Mitchell answered.

"That would be kinda' like using a sledgehammer to kill a piss ant." Billy said.

"It's always good to have the right tool for the job," Mitchell smiled. "Can you do it?"

"Oh, hell yes!" Billy said. "No problem."

"Well, let's do it!"

"Lock and load guys!" Billy ordered, his crew jumped into action. The loader and gunner both slid through the hatch and into the turret. The loader removed one of the huge cannon rounds from the ammo vault and loaded the tank's ninety millimeter main gun. The gunner turned on the night sighting device and Billy manipulated the turret. The main gun moved a little to the left and down slightly. "Target identified!" Billy said.

"Identified, one, one, five, zero meters," the gunner said.

"Fire!" Billy ordered.

The gunner squeezed his trigger. The big gun roared, a three foot flame blast from its mussel. The concussion made the fifty ton tank jump up and back slightly. The sound of the explosion cut through the quiet night like a raging thunder. Less than a second later the ninety millimeter high explosive round hit the hillside.

Mitchell looked through his starlight scope.

"Did they get him?" Frank asked.

"Dead on," Billy said.

"Yep, the cigarette's gone, the gook's gone, the tree's gone." Mitchell said, lowering the scope.

Frank and Billy were both grinning.

"The Surgeon General was right," Mitchell smiled. "Cigarette smoking is dangerous to your health."

Later that night as Mitchell was on watch, he began thinking about what he done to the gook smoking the cigarette. He was feeling a little guilty; not the killing so much, but the joking about it. He didn't know if it was conditioning from the military training or from all he had been through, but killing almost seemed to be an acceptable thing. It was okay in our society that some people could kill others; it was called war. Most of the guys in Vietnam were nineteen or twenty years old. Over here they had a license to kill, but back home they couldn't even legally buy a beer. "How fucked up is that?" Mitchell thought. All that was coming from this line of self-questioning was more questions, none of which he could come up with a satisfactory answer for.

"The hell with it," Mitchell whispered aloud. "The whole damn world is upside down."

The next morning A Troop waited at the night defensive position. B Troop was on its way to rendezvous with them. The two troops would be entering the A Shau together. At 1030 hours B Troop appeared rumbling up the narrow road from the east. As they passed, the Squadron's command and communication track and the Medic track that had been traveling with A Troop, pulled out of the center of the parameter and fell in behind B Troop. One-One was given the word to lead A Troop and fell in behind the medic track.

There was now eighty armored vehicles in one long column moving slowly west up the winding road. They snaked their way around Hill 750 that Fire Base Bastogne sat atop of. The terrain was getting rougher. Its features more mountainous; the overall elevation steadily rising. In places the road was cut into the hillsides. One side of the road, the land would climb steeply; the other side a sudden drop. The vegetation was thick; the trees and bush sometimes hanging over the narrow road.

The column traveled nine miles over the next hour and a half and were crossing through the head of a small valley. To the left, the tree line was fifty to sixty meters away from the road; to the right the little valley opened up for three or four hundred meters.

Out of the corner of his eye, Mitchell saw the smoke coming from the trees. A thin wisp of smoke, a faint contrail caused by the burning of propellant. Then he heard the sound. It was a sound he'd heard before, a hissing, a sibilant roar of exhaust gases. He had learned to fear the sound, it meant danger and sometimes death. He watched as seemingly in slow motion the RPG slammed into the turret of the Squadron's Medic track. Doc Miller was in the turret. It seemed funny to Mitchell that all medics were called Doc. There were thousands of them in Vietnam and as far as he knew they all were called Doc. If two of them were together they would be distinguished by using a last name; Doc Smith or Doc Jones, but never a first name, just Doc.

The RPG penetrated the turret, the blast burning a hole through the half inch steel, the molting fragments ripping into Doc Miller. The concussion of the explosion blew Doc into the air. It had impacted on the left side of the turret, sending Doc up and to the right.

"Of all the potential targets, why the medic track?" Mitchell thought. It was unarmed, no weapons of any kind. It was clearly marked; there was a three foot high red cross painted on both sides.

Doc Miller came down landing mid-torso on the top right edge of the APC. His body then did a half flip and fell to the ground. They had to have known it was a medic track, a non-combat vehicle, and still they chose it to fire on.

Witnessing this caused something to click in Mitchell's mind. If it was just this or if this was the last straw heaped on top of Boot Hill, Eddie's suicide, the protesters, the whole damn war, who knew, but something clicked and all of the sudden rage overtook reason. Mitchell stood up, grabbed his M-16, jumped to the ground and charged the tree line. He didn't say a word, he didn't think of the consequences, he didn't even consciously know what he was doing. He had no plan, he had no idea what he was charging into. His Colt military model 1911 .45 caliber pistol was strapped on his hip with a fully loaded clip. He took his M-16, it too loaded with a full magazine. He didn't think to take the bandoleer of seven more mags for his M-16 or put on his flak jacket; his actions were without any forethought, just reaction to what he saw. All he knew was he had to kill the ones who had done it. Click. All reason, all consideration of danger, all calculated planning disappeared. Click.

Frank was startled by the explosion and seeing Doc Miller blown off of the medic track. Out of the corner of his eye, he saw a blur that was Mitchell. He jerked his head around, looking at the turret. His eyes hadn't deceived him, Mitchell wasn't there. He looked back at Mitchell charging the tree line, and then he looked at Country.

"What the hell's going on?"

Country didn't answer.

"What's he doing?"

"I don't know," Country said. "He just took off."

"Jesus!" Frank climbed out of the driver's hole. He had his M-16 in one hand and a bandoleer of ammo in the other. "Get on the radio. Tell them we have a man in the trees, one of us. Don't shoot." Frank jumped to the ground and started for the trees.

"Where you going?" Country shouted.

"Tell them not to shoot, tell them." Frank yelled back.

The woods that Mitchell charged into were thick and hard going from the start. The forest floor was a tangle of enmeshing vines, snagging roots, and fallen trees. He wasn't taking the time to consider the easiest route or scrutinize the ground for the best footing. He was just busting through the woods without regard to his safety. He would become entangled, fall, free himself, get up, and race forward. He ran into branches, some would give way to the force of his forward momentum, others stopping him cold. At one point he tripped on some exposed roots at the edge of a ravine, tumbling head first down the eight foot deep gulch, and coming to rest on a small creek. He was reacting on impulse, born out of rage, nothing was going to deter him. Using roots and hanging vines, he climbed up the steep bank and out the other side, and continued on this maniac quest. After ten minutes of this mindless charge, he stumbled over a fallen log and was face down in the undergrowth. Click. He pulled his head up and looked around. He had no idea where he was and no memory of how he got there. At some unconscious level, he started to realize what he had done. Fear shot through him like an electrical shock. He was frozen with terror, then he began to shake, his breathing becoming fast and shallow. He was soaking wet, exhausted from his battle with the embrangled woods, his heart pounding, and panic was about to consume him.

"Take it easy Bobby," Mitchell said to himself. "Calm down, think. Think." He consciously slowed his breathing, taking deep breaths through his nose and exhaling through his mouth. "Think Bobby. You're in a bad spot here. Don't panic. Think. Think."

He had stopped shaking and was listening, laying very still. The sunlight filtered through the canopy of overlapping branches. He looked out before him at the jumble of trees and thick undergrowth. Only moving his eyes, he searched the area to his front, then his left and right. He rolled over and raised himself into a sitting position, scanning the woods behind him. He looked forward again, a drop of sweat from his forehead ran into his eyes, he wiped it away with the back of his hand, listening, concentrating on every sound. He heard them. The sound of their footsteps compacting the fallen leaves and twigs, their bodies pushing through the branches. They were in front and to the right. How far, Mitchell could only guess. Two or three hundred feet he thought, totally obscured by the dense forest.

"OK Bobby," Mitchell thought. "What do you do now? They're out there and are apparently still moving away. Either they don't know I'm here or they are satisfied with the one hit and don't want any more contact. I can turn around and go back to the troop. They are going to be jumpy. Oh, no, coming out of that tree line could be suicide. I better let them come for me, but how are they going to find me? I could signal, fire off some rounds. No, that would give away my position to the gooks. Shit! What the hell was I thinking? I wasn't thinking. Dumb! Dumb! Dumb!"

He listened again, the sounds of the NVA soldiers was getting weaker, still moving away. "Follow them,"

Mitchell thought. "Get behind and follow. If an opportunity comes I can take them out."

He got to his feet and began to move in the direction of the sounds. But this time he was moving carefully, quietly, easing through the trees and the underbrush like a lion stalking its prey. He would move for thirty to forty-five seconds and then pause, standing still, listening, redirecting his path, adjusting to the sound. He carefully pushed aside branches, crawled over moss-covered logs, and skirted around large rocks that were becoming more plentiful as he traveled. He began to go downhill. He couldn't see the change, but he could feel the lessening of effort needed to walk. Now he heard a different sound; it was barely distinguishable. As he got closer he realized it was water, the roaring, splashing sound of fast moving water. It was now drowning out the quiet sounds of the woods and those of the NVA he was following. Mitchell continued in the direction of the water. It got louder and louder. Three minutes later he saw it, a waterfall right in front of him. The first tier spilling over the edge of a sheer rock cliff, dropping maybe fifteen feet into a pool. Bubbling, splashing, foaming, the spray forming a mist. It then churned over a field of large rocks and then fell again, this time a lesser distance, maybe six to eight feet and then flowed to the east. There was too much water to call this a stream or creek. This was a river, fast moving, cutting a deep trench out of the earth. Mitchell moved to the bank of the river and saw a large flat rock to his left, fifty feet away. It would make a good vantage point, so he walked to it and once there he low-crawled on his stomach out onto the rock. Forty meters downstream he saw them. Three NVA soldiers waist deep in the water, half way between the river's banks. One was carrying an AK-47 assault rifle, the second had a RPG 7 launcher, and the third had a canvas sling over his shoulder with pockets in it, holding five more rounds for the RPG. Mitchell looked passed them to the far bank of the river. He saw no sign of any more NVA. Then he looked down stream, again no sign, and finally back toward the waterfall. No NVA there, just a small rainbow that had formed above the mist. He flipped the safety lever on his M-16 to full automatic. He was laying in the prone position, he pulled the butt of the M-16 into his shoulder. His right hand gripping the pistol grip, his right index finger resting on the trigger, his left hand underneath and steadying the barrel. He laid his cheek alongside of the stock and lined the rear sight on the front and the front sight on the back of the NVA carrying the AK-47. He was out of the water climbing up the rocky bank. Mitchell would kill him first, for he was the greatest threat.

Mitchell took in some air and exhaled, he did it again and then held it, concentrating, focusing on his target. He squeezed the trigger, firing a short burst of three rounds. They penetrated the NVA's back, almost in a straight line up his spine, the last bullet squarely between his shoulder blades. Mitchell instantly shifted his aim to the second soldier, again lining his rear sight onto the front and the front sight in the middle of the enemy's chest. A squeeze of his right index finger and three more rounds all within a five inch spread ripping into the NVA's chest. The third gook had lost his footing trying to run and was laying face down half in the water and half on the slippery rocks of the river bank. Mitchell adjusting his aim and squeezing the trigger again, this time with a little less control. A five round burst spit out the barrel of the M-16. Only two hitting the mark; one high up in his right shoulder and the other in the neck just at the base of the skull. All of this had taken place in less than five seconds. Mitchell laid there for half a minute staring at the three bodies on the far side of the river. They didn't move; they were dead.

It had been easy for Frank to follow Mitchell, his trip through the woods had been about as stealthy as a herd of elephants. His trail of disturbed ground, broken branches and especially Mitchell's tumble down the gulch through the creek and up the other bank were signs a blind man could have followed. But when Mitchell became a calculated stalker he also became almost impossible to track. All Frank heard now was the quiet sounds of the woods. He continued in the same general direction until he heard the sound of distant running water. He moved cautiously but steadily toward the water.

Frank froze motionless when he heard the first burst of fire. Pop, pop, pop. The shots so fast, their sounds ran together like a cracking hum. Then within a very few seconds two more bursts, their cracking sounds echoing through the trees. He stood still, listening. He breathed carefully, shallow through his nose. He tried to ignore the sound of his own heartbeat, concentrating, straining to hear. The woods were still, they had returned to their natural quiet.

Frank was pretty sure that the weapon he had heard was an M-16, probably Mitchell's. He was certain that it wasn't an AK and that it wasn't a two way engagement. Only one weapon was being fired. All those things would bode well for Mitchell, but Frank's concerns were still formidable.

He moved in the direction that the firing had come from. In four minutes he was out of the dense woods and looking at the fast flowing river. His eyes scanned the far side of the river and almost instantly spotted the three bodies on the rocky bank. After deciding they were no longer a threat, his eyes moved up stream. He saw Mitchell sitting cross-legged on top of the big flat rock overlooking the river. A feeling of relief rushed through Frank's body, a smile formed on his lips.

Mitchell had spotted Frank as soon as he had come out of the woods. He quietly watched as Frank made his way towards him. Frank walked out on the rock and sat down.

"You all right?" Frank asked without any sign of emotion.

"Fine," Mitchell answered in an equally unemotional tone.

Frank nodded his head, not looking at Mitchell but instead admiring the waterfall. "Nice waterfall," he said.

"Yeah, nice rainbow there above it," Mitchell acknowledged.

Frank nodded and was silent for half a minute. "What the fuck were you doing, running off like that? You's think you's John fuckin' Wayne or somethin'?" Frank's tone had changed greatly.

Mitchell smiled. "John Wayne's not stupid enough to do what I did."

"You're goddamn right he's not. Jesus man, Maggie's gonna be real pissed off if I let something happen to you."

"Maggie's going to be pissed at you?"

"That's right. My fuckin' responsibility."

Mitchell shook his head, smiling.

They didn't talk for a minute, then Frank said, "What we gonna do now?"

"I think we'll just sit here for a while."

It was about fifteen minutes later when One-Eight broke out of the woods onto the bank of the river followed by One-Six and One-One. Mitchell and Frank left their rock and walked down to meet them.

Billy Dill was atop the turret of his tank and shouted down. "You're nuts Mitchell. You too Frank, nuts!"

They didn't respond. They were heading to where Lieutenant Neilley was on the rocky bank, looking at the three bodies on the other side. He ordered them over with a hand motion.

"Was that all of them?" Neilley asked, pointing his chin at the three on the other bank.

"Yes, sir," Mitchell replied.

Neilley nodded. "Could have just as easily been thirty."

"I realize that now, sir."

"Well, why don't you tell me what the hell you were thinking, running off like that?"

Frank spoke up, "That's what I said."

Neilley aimed his dagger eyes at Frank. "Who are you to talk? I see you're here too." Neilley turned his attention to Mitchell. "Well, Sergeant?"

"There's no explaining the inexplicable, sir," Mitchell answered.

"You bet your ass there isn't." He shook his head with a half cynical laugh. "The Colonel's gonna love this. There's some media types traveling with him today. They're going to eat this up. They'll probably give you a medal. But you hear this, if you keep pulling stunts like this, you won't live long enough to wear it."

"Yes, sir," Mitchell answered. "I don't think I'll be pulling any more stunts like this."

"I sure hope not. Now, get over there and collect those weapons and look them over for paper."

Mitchell handed his M-16 to Frank, un-holstered his .45 and carried it in his right hand as he walked out into the cold, swift current of the river. It was hard to maintain his footing. The water was chest deep and flowing at a considerable rate. Mitchell faced upstream, leaning some of his body weight forward to offset the water pressure pushing against him. He would move by taking short side steps.

The first body he came to was the one that had been the ammo bearer. He was at the very edge of the water, his legs still in the river, his upper body on the bank. Mitchell removed the canvas sling with the five RPG rounds laying them in the rocks. He searched the body and found a leather pouch with a half a dozen papers and cards. Mitchell placed it in his left pant pocket. He moved up to the second body, retrieving the RPG-7 launcher and placing it with the sling. This NVA was laying on his back, the only one of the three that was. Mitchell tried not to look at his face. He had killed over a dozen men that he knew of and had searched many of them, going through their pockets, patting down their bodies. It was something that had to be done. But he always tried not to look at their faces. Seeing their faces personalized them; that was something he didn't want to do. Killing a nameless, faceless enemy was one thing, but seeing their faces gave them humanity, dignity and engraved their images into his memory. That was just too hard to take. He went through the gook's pockets finding nothing, but felt something under the shirt. Mitchell put his hand inside the NVA's shirt and found a plastic bag containing a map. This could be an important find. The plastic had protected it from most of the blood but there were three bullet holes in it. Putting the map inside his pocket, he moved on to the third man, who was less than five feet away. First Mitchell picked up the AK-47 and laid it with the launcher and sling. He was removing a web belt that had an ammo pouch containing three thirty round magazines for the AK. A belching, groaning sound came from the dead corpse behind Mitchell. It was expelling stomach gases, something that corpses have been known to do for hours after death. It startled Mitchell, he was already very anxious and this scared the hell out of him. Instinctually, he swung his right arm and hand around, pointing to the sound. He pulled the trigger of the big .45 automatic, its mussel was less than two inches from the NVA's face. The lead slug entered the right eye, ripping through the skull. The dead man's head was lying on solid rock and the only place for the debris to go was right back at Mitchell. His chest and face was splattered with blood, tissue, bone, and rock fragments. He stood motionless for a few seconds and then realized what had happened. He felt the mess all over his face, blood was in his eyes. He wiped them with the palm of his left hand and then looked at it. His stomach churned and then cramped. He felt vomit racing up his throat. He tried to swallow it back, but it was too strong. He heaved the beans and franks he had eaten earlier all over the dead body.

CHAPTER TWENTY-FIVE

As dawn broke it revealed a mist clinging to the valley floor. The fine droplets of water suspended in the air, clouding the surface, forming a concealing veil over the land. In an hour the hot sun would burn it away, but for now it draped the floor of the A Shau and only added to the uneasy anticipation of the future.

"Today's map reference coordinates are as follows, 460200 code name Car, 140410 code name State, and 370140 code name Color." Captain Tice was briefing his platoon leaders Lieutenants Neilley, Ross, Parker, and scout section leader Staff Sergeant Mitchell.

The NVA operating in the A Shau Valley were well equipped and could monitor American radio transmissions. So to be able to broadcast locations in the clear, a code system was used. Each day random map coordinates were assigned a code name. You wouldn't use the actual code name but instead you would use a word that pertained to the code word. If you were using map reference Car, you would say Ford, Buick, or any other model of car. Using map reference Color, a location might be broadcast as from Red, up six, left four. To find that coordinate you would start at map reference Color and go up six klicks and left four klicks.

Mitchell carefully noted the coordinates and their code names in his note book. Before leaving on the day's mission he would mark the locations on his map overlay.

His assignment was to lead the scout section on a recon of the area eleven klicks northwest of Firebase Destiny.

At 0730 hours One-One pulled out of A Troop's perimeter, followed by One-Two, One-Three, and Leroy Hill proudly on top of his brand new One-Four. The One-Four crew had been riding on other tracks since the old One-Four was destroyed. They picked up the new APC at Camp Evans on the way to the A Shau. It's red and yellow lettering was bright, it's gun-metal gray body still clean and void of the scratches, scrapes, and craters that covered the other tracks. It seemed strangely out of place.

They traveled slowly, covering only three to four klicks in an hour. Mitchell was making detail notes about the terrain, what route was best to take, what obstacles to avoid. It was almost noon when they got to the general area that would be the Troop's next NDP. The four APCs set up in a cross formation, each track facing out in one of the four compass directions. Mitchell ordered his ground team to search the area on foot for two hundred meters in all directions. They looked for tunnels, bunkers, and booby traps. The landscape was generally flat with small rises and mounds. It was covered with broad blade grass, ranging from a foot high to over a man's head. The taller grasses grew in clumps looking somewhat like green hay stacks. It took the seven man ground team an hour and a half to sweep the area.

At 1330 hours Mitchell was back on One-One satisfied that the location was clear. He picked up the hand mike of his command radio. "Rattlesnake Six. This is Scout One, over."

"Scout One, Rattlesnake Six, over."

"This is Scout One. Have located and cleared the November Delta Papa, over."

"Roger, Scout One. Give me a coordinate, over."

"Willco, Rattlesnake. Coordinate follows, from Arizona, down four, right five. Over."

"This is Rattlesnake Six. Confirm. From Arizona, down four, right five. Over."

"This is Scout One. That is an affirmative, over."

"Okay, Scout One, sit tight. We should be there by 1730 hours. This is Rattlesnake Six, out."

The sixteen men of the scout section settled in for what they expected to be a tranquil afternoon. The Troop wouldn't be there for another four hours. The four APC's were parked in the middle of a large meadow, running from the southeast to the northwest. You couldn't hide a cavalry troop so they did the opposite. They tried to set up their perimeters in the most open terrain possible. This spot was ideal. The meadow ran for over a mile to the north and south. To the west was a low ridge line six hundred meters away. To the east a series of knolls, all small and the closest at least four hundred meters in distance. Their NDP was very much in plain sight and no enemy could get to them without exposing themselves.

Paul came over from One-Two and was sitting on the back ramp of One-One playing chess with Frank. Paganini was in the turret on watch and Country sat alongside keeping him company. Mitchell was inside the APC studying his map and making notes concerning the terrain.

There was a blackjack game going on at One-Four, the players were Leroy, Mike, Keith, and Frankie Sanchez from One-Three. It was low stakes, just nickels and dimes.

The sun a little passed its apex, was shining bright and warm. The sky was dark blue and almost empty of clouds. It was a high sky. It seemed to extend upward forever, the kind of sky if you looked and pondered made you feel small.

After a half an hour Mitchell set aside his map and laid back, resting his head on a folded poncho liner. He called up to Paganini. "I'm going to catch some Z's. You stay alert up there."

"We'll keep our eyes open," Country answered for both of them.

After five minutes Mitchell slipped into an intermittent light sleep. Restful but never unaware. Subconsciously he still followed Frank's and Paul's chess match, still heard the small talk between Country and Paganini. It was only a half sleep, dozing. It was what he had trained himself to do.

One-One was equipped with two radios. One was the standard PRC-25 that all tracks had. It was kept on the First Platoon's frequency or when the scout section was out on its own, it would be on a frequency for their use. The second radio was a more powerful PRC-77 and was always tuned into Captain Tice's command radio net. It was the command radio that brought Mitchell back to full consciousness.

"Scout One, this is Rattlesnake Six. Over."

Mitchell sat up and reached for the hand mike of the PRC-77. Frank and Paul's attention left their game as they looked at Mitchell and listened.

Mitchell keyed the transmitter button. "This is Scout One, over."

"Scout One, this is Rattlesnake Six. I need you to move your units with all due speed to map reference Mississippi, down seven, right two. Do you copy? Over."

Mitchell reached for his map and instantly calculated the coordinates where Captain Tice had ordered him to go. It was four and a half klicks southwest of their present position. It was also right on the Vietnam-Laos border. This had happened before. While operating at the DMZ, A Troop had gone right up to the line while in pursuit of the retreating enemy only having to stop and let them go. Rules of engagement, restrictions placed on the Americans that played right into the hands of the NVA. They could hit and then retreat back across the border with impunity. It had frustrated Mitchell each time it happened and he saw it happening again.

"This is Scout One. I copy. Move with all due speed to Mississippi, down seven, right two. Over."

"This is Rattlesnake Six, that's affirmative. Units of Bravo Troop have engaged and are in pursuit. Your job is to cut them off and turn them back into Bravo. Over."

"This is Scout One, willco. Over."

"Rattlesnake Six, out."

Mitchell looked at Frank, "Crank it up, get ready to roll!"

Frank crawled through the APC and into the driver's compartment. Paul headed back to One-Two at a full run.

Mitchell grabbed the hand mike of the PRC-25, "This is Scout One to all scout units, saddle up, get ready to roll fast. Report when ready, out."

The blackjack game on One-Four ended in mid-hand. Sanchez bolted back to One-Three. The engines of the four APC's were rumbling to life, their rear ramps lifting to close, men were donning steel pots and flak jackets.

"One-Two, ready to roll."

"Roger, One-Two."

"One-Four ready."

"Roger, One-Four."

"One-Three, ready to go."

"Roger." Mitchell keyed his intercom, "Move out Frank, head southwest, start for that ridge."

Frank released the brakes and accelerated, the other three tracks fell in line.

Mitchell calculated a direction of 225 degrees using his compass he shot an azimuth and then lined One-One up. "A little to the left," he said to Frank over the intercom. Frank adjusted their path. "A little more." Frank adjusted again. "That's it. Find a landmark on this line and push it."

Frank picked out a group of trees on the ridge line straight in front of him, he honed in on them. He was driving fast and making as few course adjustments as possible. The ride was like trying to stay on a bucking horse.

Mitchell keyed the PRC-25, "This is Scout One to all scout units, Bravo Troop has got some gooks on the run. We're moving to cut them off. Be ready for a fight. Scout One, out."

At the top of the ridge, Mitchell reshot an azimuth, Frank picked out another landmark and the scout section pushed fast for grid coordinates 213430, Mississippi, down seven, right two.

In eight minutes they were lined up along the top of a hill overlooking a series of small ridges and valleys. Mitchell was scanning the area with his binoculars, Brian Banks on One-Three was doing the same.

"Scout One to Scout Three, do you see anything? Over."

"This is Scout Three, that's a negative."

Mitchell then keyed his PRC-77, "Rattlesnake Six, this is Scout One, over."

"Scout One, this is Rattlesnake six, over."

"This is Scout One, we're at Mississippi, down seven, right two, no contact. I say again, no contact, over."

"This is Rattlesnake Six, roger, no contact. Hold position, wait for further instructions, Rattlesnake Six, out."

In less than five minutes the new instructions came. "Scout One, this is Rattlesnake Six, over."

"Rattlesnake Six, this is Scout One, over."

"Okay Scout One, Bravo says they have turned more to the south, move your units to map reference Red, up twelve, left eleven, over."

Mitchell checked the coordinate on his map and marked the position. It was clearly inside Laos, a good three miles across the border. "This is Scout One, say again coordinate, over."

"Scout One, this is Rattlesnake Six, I say again, Red, up twelve, left eleven, over."

"Roger Rattlesnake, I copy. Red, up twelve, left eleven, give me confirmation, over."

"This is Rattlesnake Six, that's an affirmative. Move at once, over."

"This is Scout One moving to new coordinate, out."

Captain Tice knew that Mitchell understood where he was going and now Mitchell knew that Tice was aware of where he was sending him.

Mitchell keyed the PRC-25, "This is Scout One to all scout units, we're moving south to map reference Red, up twelve, left eleven, out." He then spoke to Frank over the intercom, "Move out south, I'll line you up as we go."

The scout section rolled off the hill due south and straight into Laos. They had traveled less than a mile when Brian called Mitchell.

"Scout One, this is Scout Three, over."

"Go ahead Scout Three."

"This is Scout Three. Do you know where this is going to take us?"

"This is Scout One, we're walking out into the streets of Laredo. Over."

"This is Scout Three, so I guess we should beat the drum slowly and play the fife lowly."

"Roger that, for I'm a young cowboy and I know I've done wrong."

"This is Scout Three, I guess we've all done wrong."

"This is Scout Four. What the hell are you dudes talking about?"

"This is Scout Three, we're heading into never, never land."

"This is Scout Four, no shit! Are we really going in?"

"This is Scout One, we are in!"

"This is Scout Four, rock 'n roll!"

Of the sixteen men in the scout section, none were Cherries. They all had been in Nam for at least two months and most a lot longer, but neither were any of them short-timers. Of the three stages a combat soldier goes through in Vietnam, they were all in some degree of stage two. To a man, they had accepted their fate. They were there until their D.E.R.O. (Date Estimate Return from Overseas) or until they were wounded or killed. They had become callous to the killing and the dying, living day to day, they routinely took more chances. They lived on the edge and in some way found excitement, a natural high out of it all. Now for the first time, for whatever reason, they were being turned loose. They were being allowed to cross that invisible line that their enemy had always hidden behind. Excitement ran high.

Red, up twelve, left eleven, turned out to be a long ridge overlooking a deep gully that had been cut into the earth by running water after years of downpours. From this vantage point, the scouts could cover the gully for about two hundred and fifty meters. They had only been in position for three minutes, when Mike on One-Four spotted movement.

"There, down there, to the left!"

Leroy hadn't seen them, neither had Keith. "Pop 'em!" Leroy shouted.

Mike opened up with his M-60. There were six NVA's out of the tree line in the bottom of the gully. Mike dropped two of them, the other four turned and was running back for the tree line. Leroy using Mike's tracer rounds as a guide, spotted the remaining four and opened up with his fifty caliber. Keith now saw them, but they were at the wrong angle for him to fire. Leroy and Mike mowed down two more before the rest escaped into the trees. One-Four was on the left end of the line the scout section had formed on top the ridge. They were the only ones to see the enemy.

"Scout One to Scout Four, what you got, Leroy?"

"This is Scout Four, there was a handful of 'em, showed up at the bottom, far left, over."

"How many, Leroy? Over."

"Six or seven I think. We got most of 'em, a couple made it back to the woods, over."

"This is Scout One, roger. Anyone else see anything? Over."

"This is Scout Two, negative."

"Scout Three, negative."

Mitchell waited for a full minute, no sighting. "This is Scout One to all units, open up on the bottom of the gully and the tree line, pepper every bush, every tree. This is an all out recon by fire, hit it!"

All twelve machine guns on the four APC's opened fire. Frank and the driver of One-Three were both lobbing M-79 grenade rounds as fast as they could. In the next two minutes, they poured 4,000 rounds of fifty caliber and M-

60 plus over thirty M-79 grenade rounds into the bushes and trees at the bottom of the gully.

"Cease fire! Cease fire!" Mitchell radioed to all the units. The shooting stopped and every man scanned the gully looking for any movement, there was none.

Mitchell keyed his command radio, "Rattlesnake Six, this is Scout One, over."

"Scout One, Rattlesnake Six, go ahead."

"This is Scout One. We're at map reference Red, up twelve, left eleven. Made contact, over."

"This is Rattlesnake Six, roger Scout One. You've made contact. Give me a sit-rep (situation report), over."

"This is Scout One, we fired on the enemy and took no return fire. I can confirm a body count of four. The enemy has turned and was last seen moving back north, size of force unknown. Have engaged in a recon by fire, no further sightings. Is Bravo on its way? Over."

The radio was silent for a full thirty seconds, no response forthcoming. "This is Scout One, do you copy Rattlesnake? Over."

"This is Rattlesnake Six, I copy your sit rep. Bravo is holding at map reference Red, up fifteen, left ten, over."

Mitchell knew without checking his map that Bravo Troop wasn't crossing the border. Realization hit. Mitchell and his men were alone, three and a half miles over the border and B Troop wasn't coming. The excitement disappeared and was replaced with common sense concern. Captain Tice had had the nerve to break the rules, but for whatever reason B Troop's C.O. didn't. It left Mitchell and his men at the broken end of the bottle. He decided that discretion was the better part of valor.

"Rattlesnake Six, this Scout One. In light of Bravo holding, I request permission to pull back, over."

"Roger Scout One, I think that is a good idea, over."

"Rattlesnake Six, this is Scout One pulling back to Mississippi, down seven, right two, over."

"Scout One, this is Rattlesnake Six, negative, return to NDP, over."

"This is Scout One, roger, returning to NDP. Scout One, out."

CHAPTER TWENTY-SIX

At 0700 hours, April 17th, the bay doors opened on a bomb hardened aircraft shelter. The location was Kadena Air Force Base, Okinawa. The plane being rolled out was a Lockheed SR-71, Blackbird. Its mission was a reconnaissance over flight of the Haiphong Harbor, North Vietnam and then the Ho Chi Minh Trail. It was one of two Blackbirds at Kadena, part of the Ninth Strategic Reconnaissance Wing.

The SR-71 was the most amazing plane ever built. It could fly higher and faster than any aircraft in the world. Its normal operating speed was over two thousand miles per hour. It flew at heights of up to 100,000 feet, the very edge of the earth's atmosphere. This unique reconnaissance ship came from Lockheed's top-secret "Skunk Works", the developers of other high-performance aircraft, such as the U-2. The SR-71 Blackbird was America's closest held secret. It was flown by the Air Force, but its missions were ran by the CIA.

The ground team had helped the two man crew into their pressure suits, identical to those worn by astronauts. They were now climbing up ladders to two separate cockpits. The pilot up front and the reconnaissance systems officer 'RSO' in the rear. They strapped the two men in and then dropped down to the concrete tarmac and removed the ladders. The line chief gave the aircraft a last visual check, looking for any abnormality. A layman would have thought there was some serious problems, because fuel was leaking out of the six tanks in the fuselage and wings. This was by design. The Blackbird's component parts fit very loosely to allow for expansion at the high temperatures it would experience at normal operating speeds. The tanks would seal as the temperature increased. The chief gave the thumbs up to the pilot and received a farewell salute in return. The SR-71 taxied to the runway, its belly packed full of panoramic, long-range and infrared cameras, electronic intelligence sensors and side-looking radars. Its two huge Pratt and Whitney J58 turbo ramjets roared as the plane shot down the runway and rose into the air.

The Blackbird took off with a light fuel load, climbed sub sonically to rendezvous with a KC-135Q tanker about ten minutes away. After filling up, it dove briefly and accelerated to supersonic. Then it climbed to 92,000 feet and a speed of Mach 3 where it cruised to the target. At 0820 hours the SR-71 had completed its reconnaissance of the Haiphong Harbor and had turned south and was starting its photo run of the Ho Chi Minh Trail.

Something went terribly wrong. Without warning, the high-flying reconnaissance ship lost communications with its base at Kadena. A massive mechanical failure brought the Blackbird down. The unthinkable had happened. One of America's most secret spy planes was down and worst of all, it was down somewhere inside the borders of Laos.

Within minutes the news was flashed halfway around the world to CIA Headquarters in Langley, Virginia. A six man crisis team was quickly convened, including the Southeast Asia Bureau Chief and the Assistant Director of Covert Operations.

Laos was passively being used by the North Vietnamese Army as a supply route and a basing area. The NVA had a free hand and controlled much of the area along the Vietnam-Laos border. The Soviet Union was North Vietnam's ally and supplied the war effort. The CIA's biggest fear was that the SR-71 and its top secret technology of its airframe, engines, long-range cameras, and electronic sensors would fall into the hands of the NVA and then be passed on to the Soviets.

Within thirty minutes, orders were sent to bases in Thailand. Over twenty aircraft were dispatched to locate the wreckage. Two Air Force technicians from Kadena, a reconnaissance systems expert and a engine and airframe expert, were on their way to Da Nang.

Danny Larson was the CIA's top field officer in I Corp. He worked out of Eagle. At 0930 hours he received a cryptographic radio message. It was short and to the point. *You are to recruit the best demolition expert available. Requisition fifty pounds of C-4 plastic explosives, detcord, electronic timed detonators and any other devices required by said expert. You are to pick up two Air Force personnel, who are in route from Kadena Air Force Base, estimated time of arrival 1400 hours. Your assignment is to take the Air Force personnel, the demolition expert and their equipment to locate a downed reconnaissance plane. Additional information will be forthcoming. End of message*

Larson got on his ground line phone to the 101st Division headquarters. He worked his way up the chain of command until he was speaking with Brigadier General James Clarke, Deputy Division Commander. General Clarke had the clout to immediately reassign Specialist E-5 Jerry Black of the 23rd Engineers to Larson. Black was the best plastics man in I Corp. Larson contacted Black, gave him the list of equipment and explosive needed, and instructed him to ready himself for an infield mission.

At 1210 hours, a F4 Phantom flown out of Thailand located the wreckage of the doomed Blackbird. It was at map coordinate 334362, eleven miles inside the border of Laos.

Back at Langley, the crisis team was informed that the wreckage had been located and they were now debating how to get Larson and the experts to it. The first thought was to fly them in by chopper, but that idea was quickly dismissed because of the terrain. There was no suitable LZ near enough. That fact and the fact that there were Soviet made mobile radar deployed along the border, meant it would have to be a ground operation. It would need to be mobile, be able to move fast and carry the equipment necessary to do the job. Once they got to the site, it would take some time to do the work, two to three hours. So the force would need significant firepower to protect itself and still small enough to hopefully not be detected. The consensus was that a small force made up of M113A1 Assault Vehicles, the type employed by the Armored Cavalry, would be the best method of insertion.

It was 1420 hours, A Troop had spent the morning on a search and destroy. For the last twenty minutes they had been stationary, holding at grid coordinate 170490. The men on One-One were taking advantage of this time to get something to eat. They were chowing down on some C's and washing it down with Kool-Aid.

"One-One, this is Rattlesnake Six, over."

Hearing a call coming from Captain Tice surprised Mitchell. Normally, the only time it would happen was when the Scout Section was out operating as a separate unit. Today they were part of First Platoon and under Lt. Neilley's control.

"This is One-One, go ahead Rattlesnake Six, over."

"This is Rattlesnake Six. I have to see you at my location, ASAP, over."

"Roger Rattlesnake, I'm on my way. One-One out."

"What kinda trouble you in now?" Frank asked Mitchell.

"I have no idea. I can't think of anything I've done, at least not lately." Mitchell stood up, grabbed his M-16, and jumped to the ground. "Hold down the fort, guys," he said and headed off towards Captain Tice's track.

As he approached the APC, he saw Tice and Neilley standing alone, fifty feet away from the track. The two men stopped talking and looked at Mitchell as he walked up.

"Mitchell," Tice said as a greeting.

"Sir," Mitchell responded.

"Mitchell, I got an order about five minutes ago from Colonel Shelton, personally. I'll tell you up front, I

394

don't know what it's all about, so I'll just give it to you like I got it."

Mitchell switched his eyes to Lt. Neilley, who looked concerned or irritated, maybe both. Mitchell looked back to Tice.

"You are ordered to take your Scout Section to grid coordinate 205415. Once there, you are to clear a LZ and wait for a chopper. On board will be a group of personnel, led by a civilian named Larson."

"A civilian, sir?" Mitchell questioned.

"Right, a civilian, Larson, he'll be in charge of the mission."

"And what is the mission?"

Captain Tice raised his eyebrows and then rubbed his chin before answering. "I don't know, Mitchell. I was ordered to send the Scout Section, ASAP, and not to discuss it with anyone. I told Lt. Neilley anyway, because it involves some of his people."

Mitchell nodded his head, "Can I see your map, sir?"

Tice handed him the map he was holding. The coordinate 205415 was marked with a black grease pencil. It was just over a klick from the Laos border. Captain Tice watched Mitchell study the map.

"About an hour ago, I got an inquiry about any trips across the border, unofficial of course, and then this," Tice said.

"You don't see many civilians out in the boonies," Neilley said suspiciously.

"CIA, you think?" Mitchell asked.

"Only a guess," Neilley answered.

"I'm in the dark, Mitchell. I don't know anything more than what I've told you," Tice said. "They weren't asking for volunteers, it was an order."

"I understand, sir."

"You better get going."

"Yes, sir."

"Good luck, Mitchell," Tice said, holding out his hand. Mitchell shook it.

"Thank you, sir."

"Be careful," Neilley said.

"Always," Mitchell answered, then turned and headed back to One-One.

"This stinks to high heaven," Neilley said. "If something goes wrong, we won't be able to help them. We won't even know where the hell they are."

"I know, Jeffrey," Tice said. "Whatever is going on, the decisions are being made way above our pay grade."

It was 1445 hours when the C-130 from Da Nang landed at Eagle. Larson was there to meet it, so was Black. "I'm Danny Larson, this is Spec 5 Black," Larson said as the two Air Force personnel came off the plane.

"Tech Sergeant Nash," one said.

"Master Sergeant Goldman," said the other.

The two Air Force experts with the help of some ground crew off loaded their equipment and loaded it into a waiting truck. All four men hopped in the back and rode a short distance to the waiting Huey. Their equipment was loaded into the helicopter along with what Larson and Black had stowed. The four men boarded, the Huey lifted off, turned west and soon disappeared.

"Crank it up, Frank. We're rolling!" Mitchell said while he was climbing up top.

"Where we going?"

"To clear a LZ at coordinate 205415, I'll get the rest there," Mitchell answered.

"Why am I thinking this is not good?" Frank said.

Mitchell didn't answer, he keyed his radio, "One-One to Scout units, get ready to roll, ASAP! One-One, out."

The Scout Section pulled away from the troop and headed southwest. It was 1530 hours when they arrived at coordinate 205415, a long flat top ridge overlooking a small valley that was the border between Vietnam and Laos. They set up in a cross formation, the APCs a hundred meters apart. Mitchell and his ground team quickly cleared the inside of the perimeter.

At 1550 hours, Mitchell saw the helicopter coming from the east. He watched as it came closer, one lone Huey. The distinct sound of its rotor chopping through the air got louder and louder, the only sound in an otherwise quiet afternoon. A minute later it was hovering over the center of the Scout Section's formation, slowly descending and finally making contact with the grassy ridge. Two helicopter crewmen helped Larson, Black, and the two Air Force personnel unload their equipment. The Huey was on the ground for less than two minutes. It lifted off, straight up twenty-five feet, banked to the right and then headed east, climbing as it flew out over the A Shau.

Mitchell jumped off of One-One and walked to the four men standing in the middle of his formation. Larson and Black were side by side, the two Air Force guys a few feet behind. Larson was wearing fatigues, jungle boots, and a boonie hat. His shirt had no markings on it, no insignias, no name tag. He was a medium sized man, 5'9", 160 pounds, light brown hair, red faced, his complexion wasn't suited for heavy sun exposure. He was armed with a .45 caliber pistol, carried in a shoulder holster under his left arm pit. Mitchell noticed all of these things and that Larson was older. The average boonie rat was nineteen or twenty, the average field officer was in their early to middle twenties. Larson was forty-one and looked every bit of it.

Black was wearing standard army fatigues. His name was over one shirt pocket, U.S. ARMY over the other. Specialist Five insignias on both sleeves. He held an M-16 in his right hand. Goldman and Nash had on Air Force fatigues complete with all insignias. Their uniforms were starched and pressed. Back at their base in Okinawa, serving in their technical jobs it was required, but here they looked ridiculously out of place. They carried no weapons of any kind.

"Are you in charge of these APCs?" Larson asked as soon as Mitchell was in front of him.

"They're my Scout Section."

"And your name?"

"Mitchell."

"I'm Larson, this is Spec 5 Black, Tech Sergeant Nash, and Master Sergeant Goldman."

Mitchell nodded and said, "And you are?"

"I told you, I'm Larson!"

"No, I mean, he's Spec 5 Black, he's Tech Sergeant Nash, he's Master Sergeant Goldman, I'm Staff Sergeant Mitchell. What are you?"

Larson looked hard at Mitchell, narrowing his eyes, "I'm not in the military, per say. I work for the U.S. government. Weren't you told about this?"

"All I was told was to come here, clear an LZ, and wait for a Mr. Larson, he'd give me the rest."

"The mission details are on a need to know basis. Right now, all you need to know is that you and your APCs are to take me and my people to where I tell you to take us."

"That's pretty thin."

"That's all I can give you right now."

Mitchell didn't like it. He didn't like it when Captain Tice first told him and he was liking it less now. But he had been given his orders and he always tried to follow orders if he could.

Mitchell shouted out, "I need one man off of each track, here on the double!"

Paul responded from One-Two, Sanchez from One-Three, Keith from One-Four, and Frank came running over.

"Keith," Mitchell ordered, "You help Spec 5 Black with his gear. Take him with you."

"Right, Sarge," Keith answered.

"Sergeant Goldman, Sanchez will help you, you'll be on One-Three, and Nash, you go with Paul to One-Two. Mr. Larson, I figured you'd be riding with me."

"Good," Larson said.

In five minutes the equipment was loaded up and everyone was on their tracks. Larson took out his map and laid it in front of Mitchell. "I need you to take us here, coordinate 334362."

Mitchell stared at the map for twenty seconds and then looked up at Larson, "That's over ten miles inside of Laos."

"Yes it is. I was told you have been in Laos before."

"We've been over a couple of times, but never that deep."

"That's our destination and we need to get there as soon as possible."

Frank had been listening to the conversation, "Shit! I knew I wasn't gonna like this."

Mitchell glanced at Frank and then back to Larson, "I don't think we can make it by dark."

Larson weighed the implications of Mitchell's statement. Things had been happening so fast he hadn't considered that possibility.

"We can't be moving after dark, not in unknown terrain," Mitchell said.

Larson thought for a moment, then finally said, "Right, the work we have to do once we get there is going to take two or three hours and we'll need daylight to get it done. Take us in as far as you can go before dark and find a place to hide for the night."

"It ain't easy to hide four APCs." Mitchell said.

"It's imperative that we're not discovered," Larson said, "Not on the way in."

"No shit, Sherlock!" Frank added.

Larson gave him a look that didn't hide his disapproval.

"I know a place, we were at it about two weeks ago. It's about halfway to your coordinate." Mitchell looked to the west. The sky was filling with dense, fluffy, flat based clouds, cumulus clouds, usually formed by the onset of a thermally unstable air mass. "With any luck, maybe we'll get rain."

"How is that a good thing?" Larson asked.

"If you're getting a down pour at night, even Charlie tends to hunker down. The more it rains, the less he moves. The less he moves, the less chance he'll stumble onto us."

Larson's first impression of Mitchell was that he was just a kid, they all were just a bunch of kids. And of course they were just kids, nineteen, twenty, twenty-one year olds, but no longer like their peers back home. The war, the time they had spent in the boonies had aged them, made them much wiser than their years. Especially Mitchell, he didn't think or act like a twenty-one year old. He had gained experiences and learned skills that you wouldn't think possible by looking at his young face. Larson was beginning to understand that, beginning to realize that Mitchell knew more about how to survive in the boonies than he did.

"Lead the way," Larson said.

The Scout Section rolled off the ridge, through the little valley, and on into Laos. Mitchell was heading for a small plateau. It rose above the adjacent land and was moderately wooded on top. When they had been there before, there were no signs of activity. It was not part of any natural corridor or pathway. You would only go there if the plateau was where you wanted to be. The easy routes of travel would bypass it. Mitchell's hope was to spend the night there undetected.

An hour later, the four APCs climbed up the north side of the small mesa and stopped amid the woods on top of the flat upland. Mitchell got down on foot and guided the tracks into a tight cross formation. The backs of each APC were only a few feet apart.

The clouds had darkened, they had built vertically, extremely dense with a hazy outline and a glaciated top. They were charged with electricity, a flash of lightning followed by a single sharp crash of thunder. The smell of rain was in the air, it just wasn't falling yet. Normally Mitchell hated the rain, it was miserable to stand watch in, but tonight he was praying for it.

Mitchell called his TCs together. "We're going to stay here for the night. Button up your tracks, get ready for the rain. Keep someone in the turret all night. Any questions?"

"Yeah, what the hell are we doing?" Brian asked. That was the question on all their minds. The first drops of rain started to fall.

"What's with these Air Force guys?" Leroy asked.

"Our orders are to take them to coordinate 334362, beyond that I'm as much in the dark as you. Get buttoned up and stay quiet. Let's go!" Mitchell ordered.

The rainfall intensified.

Back on top of One-One, Frank had closed the hatch on the driver's hole and was working on the turret hatch. He had his poncho on, as did Country and Paganini. They were working on closing the main hatch. Country tossed Mitchell his poncho. By now, the rain was coming hard. Mitchell slipped it over his head and it draped down around him. Larson was standing on top the APC and was getting soaked by the driving rain. He didn't have a poncho, none of his people had ponchos or any other field gear for that matter.

"Get inside, Mr. Larson," Mitchell said and then turned his eyes to Country. "I'll take first watch, somebody relieve me in a hour."

"Right, Sarge," Country said. "Come on Mr. Larson, let's get inside."

Larson, Paganini, and Country dropped through the main hatch and closed it behind them. Mitchell climbed in the turret and sat down, draping the front panel of his poncho over the breach and trigger assembly of the fifty caliber.

The storm had brought the night on suddenly, compressing the normal half an hour transition time from dusk to dark, to a few minutes. Mitchell peered out before him, the visibility with the woods and the rain was thirty feet at best. He was beginning to realize that this mission was put together in a hurry. He had the feeling it was being made up on the go. Larson and his people were obviously unprepared for the boonies. Hell, the two Air Force Techs were wearing starched uniforms, for Christ sake. A blind man could tell they weren't combat personnel. No, something had happened, something unexpected, something serious and it had the big wigs' asses in a knot.

"What the hell have I gotten into now?" Mitchell whispered and stared into the darkness.

The hour passed slowly. By the time Paganini came up to relieve Mitchell, his legs had gone to sleep, his butt numb. He hadn't move at all the whole hour. His poncho was draped in a way that was keeping him relatively dry and he didn't want to jeopardize that. He climbed out of the turret and Paganini took his place. "Stay alert!" Mitchell said.

"Sure, if I don't fuckin' drown!"

Mitchell entered the APC through the rear ramp hatch, got out of his poncho and crawled to the front right corner.

"Pretty fuckin' bad out there," Frank said as he handed him a box of C's.

"Yeah, it's really coming down. If it keeps this up, I don't think we'll have to worry about Charlie," Mitchell answered.

"We gonna rotate watch every hour?" Frank asked.

"I think so, a hour at a time is long enough to be out there. Frank, you go next, then Country."

"I'll pull a turn," Larson said.

Mitchell didn't answer for a few seconds, "We'll see. So, how are we getting along down here?"

"Oh real good," Frank said. "We ask questions and Mr. Larson, here, answers with a line of bullshit."

Larson looked up, zeroing is eyes in on Frank. "I've already told your Sergeant that I'm not at liberty to discuss the details of the mission."

"Okay, you can't tell us the details, but surely you can say more than take me to coordinate 334362," Mitchell insisted.

"Like I said to your men, this mission is very important to further our efforts to win the war."

Mitchell rolled his eyes and took in a deep breathe, letting it out slowly. "Cut the crap, Larson. You need to think about who you're talking to. Me, Frank, and Country there, we've been in this shit hole for ten months now. We may not be smart enough to understand the big picture, the government's grand plan, but one thing we all understand, is that we're not, I repeat, not, trying to win this war. Shit if that was the case, we would have long ago bombed the North to holy hell, line up the 500,000 soldiers we have here and marched across the fuckin' DMZ!"

Larson didn't say anything. Mitchell lowered his tone and began again, "Look Larson, I'm as patriotic as the next guy, more than most, but we're out here every day with our asses on the line. We operate on trust, we have to trust each other and we have to believe the mission is worth the risk."

Larson spoke, "Are you saying, you might disobey orders?"

"No," Mitchell answered. "I'm saying, you can't accomplish the mission without us and we can't accomplish the mission without knowing what it is."

"You can't or you won't?" Larson asked.

"In this case, I'd say they were the same thing," Larson looked hard and long at Mitchell. No one spoke for a half a minute. "Trust us, Mr. Larson," Mitchell said. "Let us know what's going on. If it is as important as you say, that will give us the best chance of pulling it off."

"You're probably right," Larson finally said. "I work for the CIA, but I guess you already figured that out." Mitchell just nodded his head. "This morning, a reconnaissance plane went down. It was flying a photo mission over the Ho Chi Minh Trail and something happened. Anyway, it's down and the Air Force has placed it at 334362." Larson thought for a moment, "Have any of you ever heard of the U-2?"

"I have," Mitchell said. "It's a spy plane. One of them got shot down over Russia a few years ago. It caused a big stink. Was this a U-2?"

"No," Larson answered. "This one is top secret, only a handful of people knows of its existence. I hadn't ever heard of it myself, before this morning. This is not an ordinary plane." The seriousness was etched on Larson's face. "The word I got was that it is so advanced, it makes the U-2 look like a crop duster. We can't let it fall in the hands of the Soviets. It's more than the war effort, it involves our entire national defense. Nash and Goldman are from Kadena Air Force Base on Okinawa. They're here to remove some of the most secret equipment and to show Black where to place the charges to blow up the rest. That's it, Mitchell, we've got to get to that plane before it's found by the NVA."

It was quiet for a few seconds, then Mitchell said, "Early today, you said that it was imperative that we not be discovered, not on the way in. That bothered me. What did you mean, not on the way in?"

"If we get in trouble before we get to the plane and get the secrets off of it, I don't think we can count on any help. But, once we have that stuff, I think they would send your whole squadron to save our ass."

"So, I guess we better not get caught," Mitchell said.

Larson could see that Mitchell and the others were satisfied. All they needed was to know the truth.

"So, you some kinda' spy, like James Bond or something?" Frank said with a dry smile and a sparkle in his eyes.

"I wish it was like James Bond," Larson smiled. "I've been working for the CIA for twelve years and I haven't seen a Honey Ryder or a Pussy Galore, yet."

CHAPTER TWENTY-SEVEN

The dawn brought with it a feeling of renewal, invigoration. The earth looked and smelled clean. The vegetation looked and smelled clean. The APCs looked and smelled clean. The rain had stopped at 0400 hours, but before it did, it had washed the dust and grim from all things.

The morale of the Scout Section had also been invigorated. Larson had told them the facts about the mission and to a man, they were ready to go. In a strange way they were looking forward to it, after all, this involved spies and intrigue.

The first appearance of daylight saw the four APCs rolling off the mesa heading southwest. Mitchell's best estimate put 334362 just over nine klicks away. As they continued southwest the terrain became more and more inhospitable for vehicular travel. The M113A-1 could go almost anywhere, but the speed at which they traveled was determined for the most part by the terrain. The long flat ridges and small valleys that were predominate along the border were giving way to more rugged slopes. Small narrow canyons with steep rocky sides enclosed between well-defined hills. More often than not, the straightest route to their target was impossible to take. Mitchell was having to navigate a course of alternating directions, bypassing the natural obstacles that were slowing down their progress.

Few men could handle a map, a compass, and recognize terrain like Mitchell. When it came to ground navigation, he was the best A Troop had. That's why he was scout section leader. The zig-zag course he was being forced to follow had left Larson without a clue of where they were. Larson was nervously looking at his map, then at the surrounding landmarks and back at the map. He was hopelessly lost.

Giving up, Larson said "I hope you know where the hell you're going!" as he folded his map and placed it back into his shirt.

"Don't sweat it," Mitchell insured. "I'll get you to 334362. I just hope nobody has got there first."

"How far away do you make it?"

"About a klick and a half," Mitchell pointed as he spoke, "Over that big hill."

Twenty minutes, a zig and a zag later, they pulled up to the edge of a deep narrow cleft in the earth's surface.

"Hold up, Frank," Mitchell said over the intercom. He studied his map and then the surrounding land features.

"Is this it?" Larson asked.

"Close," Mitchell answered, "This should be real close."

There was no wreckage to be seen. Mitchell keyed the intercom, "Follow the ravine to the east."

Frank pulled back on the left steering lever and accelerated. They followed along the north side of the ravine for a little over a quarter of a mile.

"Are you sure we're in the right place?" Larson asked. The concern showed in his voice.

"I put us a little east of 334362," Mitchell said.

"Are you sure?" Larson said again.

"Down there!" Paganini shouted, "Bottom of the canyon!" He was pointing, excited, the kind of excitement a ten year old might have on Christmas morning.

"Hold it, Frank," Mitchell said into his intercom. He and Larson, both stood to get a better look into the ravine. A big piece of one of the SR-71's large vertical tails was visible, tangled in with the trees and ground cover. It's black paint blending it in well with the deep green foliage in the shaded bottom of the ravine.

"Is that it?" Mitchell asked.

"It must be," Larson replied.

"Ease forward," Mitchell said to Frank, "Slow."

"Look for more wreckage," Larson said to Paganini and Country.

The APCs moved along the rim, not much faster than a man could walk, everyone's eyes searching the ravine. They traveled less than one hundred and fifty meters when a twenty foot piece of what once was the fuselage was spotted.

"Hold up, Frank," Mitchell said into his intercom.

"This is it," Larson said. "We got to get down there."

Mitchell stood up in the turret, scanning the surrounding area a full 360 degrees. He keyed his radio, "Scout One to all Scout units. Set up here. Scout Three and Scout Four, face south. Scout Two, you face west. This is Scout One, stand by." Mitchell stopped transmitting and looked at Larson. "How do you want to do this?"

"I'll take my people down, get them looking for whatever they are supposed to be looking for. What do you think about security?"

"The tracks can cover things pretty well from here. I was thinking, I'd take my ambush team and go down in the bottom with you. Help out and add a little security down there."

"Sounds like a plan," Larson said.

Mitchell keyed the radio, "This is Scout One. Black, Nash, Goldman get your equipment unloaded. Ambush team report to One-Four with all your gear. This is Scout One, out."

In five minutes, Larson's people and the ambush team were at One-Four, ready to go. Mitchell looked up to the top of One-Four track. "Leroy, you'll be in charge up here. Keep an eye out in every direction. Charlie could show up from anywhere, but really watch the other side of the ravine. My gut is telling me if they come it will probably be from there."

The four APCs were set up on the north rim of the ravine. It was seventy-five to one hundred feet down to the bottom and over two hundred meters across. The north bank was steep and rocky, the south side a smoother inclining slope. The ravine ran east to west for at least a mile. One-One was covering the east end of the security line, One-Two the west. One-Three and One-Four were in the middle. The tracks were about forty meters apart and parked at angles that allowed them to cover in all directions.

Mitchell turned his attention to his ambush team, "You guys help with some of their equipment." He was

411

referring to the large amount of gear Larson's people had to take down. They began to load up the extra gear.

Larson took Mitchell aside and handed him a small slip of paper. "On this is a radio frequency. If anything happens to me and you're having to pull out, set you PRC-77 on this frequency and contact Wolfpack. Your call sign will be Bulldog. Tell them to commence Firestorm."

"What's Firestorm?" Mitchell asked.

"After we get the detail work done here, the Navy is going to blow this place to hell and gone. Now remember, call Wolfpack, you're Bulldog. Tell them to commence Firestorm."

"I got it." Mitchell answered.

Mitchell lead the way as the seven man ambush team along with Larson, Black, Nash, and Goldman started working their way down the bank of the ravine. As they got to the bottom more debris became visible. The Blackbird was broken up into hundreds of pieces, some no larger than a beer can. A quick fifteen minute search showed that the wreckage was contained in a relatively small area, no more than three hundred meters. Only six pieces large enough to be easily identified were found. The vertical tail that Paganini first saw, a twenty-five foot chunk of wing complete with one of the huge Pratt and Whitney J58 engines. The other turbo-ramjet was found eighty meters away buried in some low trees. Two sections of the fuselage and half of the cockpit minus the nose section were scattered over a one hundred and fifty meters.

Mitchell noticed there was no sign of fire. He thought that was strange. Most plane crashes result in fire. He didn't know that the SR-71's engines ran on a special fuel, JP-7, it was very stable with an extremely high flash point.

Goldman went to work on one of the large chunks of fuselage. It contained one of the camera compartments. He was looking for the powerful lenses and super sensitive film that made these cameras the most technically advanced reconnaissance systems in the world.

Nash was looking for some of the electronic sensors and side-looking radar components. Black was setting C-4 charges in the J58 engines. They had survived relatively in tack and they had to be destroyed.

Larson had gone to what was left of the cockpit. The canopies were missing and there was a gaping hole ripped out of one side. He found the RSO dead, still buckled in. Larson called out to Mitchell, "I need a hand over here."

Mitchell hurried over.

"Help me get him out," Larson said.

The RSO was wearing a fully sealed and pressurized space suit, silver in color, complete with sealed boots, gloves, and a helmet with a gold tinted face visor. This was not the normal flight suit a jet jockey wore. The only time Mitchell had ever seen something like this was on television. The Mercury and Gemini astronauts wore pressure suits just like this.

"This guy is wearing a space suit!" Mitchell said, his surprise was apparent in his tone.

"He sure the hell is."

"You were right, Larson. This wasn't an ordinary plane."

"No it wasn't," Larson said.

They pulled the dead man out of the wreckage and Larson said, "There suppose to be another crewman, the pilot, I think. See if you can find him, he must have been thrown free."

"Yeah," Mitchell said, "We need to take them back."

One of the most abiding rules of a combat soldier was that no one gets left behind. Men would die trying to recover the bodies of their fallen brothers in arms. It wasn't just the Americans that felt that way. The NVA, the VC, would always, if possible, remove their dead from the battlefield. It was universal, a warrior's duty. Those who had fallen in battle were to be honored, not forgotten.

Mitchell made a quick look around the immediate area, but found nothing. He called Frank over and the two of them expanded the search. Larson went to work on placing a C-4 charge in the cockpit.

After ten minutes, Frank called out, "Over here!" He had found the pilot's body about seventy-five meters away from the cockpit, in a clump of bushes, partly covered by a three foot triangular shaped piece of the titanium skin from the SR-71.

Mitchell came running, "You found him?"

"Yeah, at least most of him." The pilot was missing his left arm. It had been completely ripped away at the shoulder.

"Shit!" Mitchell said, "Let's see if we can find his arm, it's has to be around here some place."

Frank looked at Mitchell, as if to ask why, but didn't. The two men began to search. They found twisted pieces of metal, looms of electrical wire, but no arm.

Scraps of insulation, pieces of rubber hose, one of the Blackbird's tires that was impregnated with powder aluminum, but no arm. They looked for another fifteen minutes and finally Frank walked back to Mitchell, "I can't find that fuckin' arm."

"I just want to bring all of him back, not just parts," Mitchell said.

"I know Sarge, but how much time do we have for this? Hell, we don't know if he ever had two arms."

"I'd say that bloody stump from his shoulder is a pretty good clue," Mitchell said. "That, and have you ever seen an one-armed astronaut?"

"Good point!" Frank said.

"But you're right," Mitchell conceded. "We don't have much time. We have to get their bodies up to the tracks."

"That's a good point, too!" Frank said.

Their joking had not been meant as disrespect, it was their minds safety net doing its job.

Both the pilot and RSO were in full rigor mortis. They had been dead for twenty-four hours and rigor would probably last for another twelve to twenty-four hours. Their skeletal muscle fibers had ran out of adenosine triphosphate. Without the ATP, the skeletal muscles throughout the body becomes locked in a contracted position. Because all the skeletal muscles are involved their bodies became stiff as boards. This actually made the bodies easier to carry. A lifeless body is hard to handle, they bend and curve into angular shapes. Every unsupported part of the mass drooping limply. But in a state of rigor, they were stiff like a solid object and much easier to handle. The odd thing was that the RSO had died in a sitting position and was now locked in that position. It didn't make him any harder to carry, but it was a little unnerving to Mitchell and his men. None of them had had any experience with bodies in rigor mortis.

The space suits added forty pounds to their body weight. It took three men to carry each body up the steep bank. Mitchell, Frank, and Paul struggled with the pilot, while Keith, Sanchez, and Brian brought up the RSO. Mike stayed at the bottom with the radio to maintain communications with the APCs.

Leroy's eyes were as big as silver dollars when he saw the two bodies sealed in their space suits. "What the fucks that?" He said.

"Space men," Keith answered.

"Put them inside," Mitchell ordered.

"I don't want that shit in my track!" Leroy said.

"They're Air Force pilots, Leroy. They're wearing pressurized suits because of the high altitude that the plane flew at."

"You sure, Mitchell? I don't want no alien shit in my track."

Keith was having a good laugh about Leroy being spooked.

"Shut up, Keith!" Mitchell barked. "They're not aliens, Leroy."

They loaded the two bodies into One-Four and immediately returned to the bottom of the ravine.

"How much longer?" Mitchell asked Larson.

"Black is working on the last charge. Nash and Goldman have got all they could find," Larson said.

When the two Air Force techs left Kadena, they had a list of eleven items to retrieve, destroy, or confirm destroyed. They had found three and retrieved them. Four more they could confirm destroyed. The remaining four they saw no sign of, they assumed there wasn't enough left to be identified.

"Shit! Holy shit!" Paganini said. "There, Country!" He was pointing to the southeast. "Over there on the other side of the canyon!"

Country was in the turret, he grabbed the binoculars that was kept there. He looked through and focused them. He keyed his radio, "One-Four, this is One-One Golf, over."

"This is One-Four, over."

"One-Four, we've spotted gooks on the other side of canyon, moving this way, over."

Leroy scanned the other side of the ravine and was about to ask Country where, when he spotted them. "Roger One-One Golf, I see them, out."

"Rightfield, this is Scout Four, over!"

"This is Rightfield, over," Mike answered.

"Rightfield, did you roger One-One Golf's sighting?"

"Roger Scout Four, stand by."

Mike had signaled for Mitchell to come to the radio.

"This is Scout One, what do you got Scout Four? Over."

"This is Scout Four, we got gooks other side of the ravine, over."

"This is Scout One, how many and how far? Over."

"This is Scout Four, maybe ten to twelve guys in two small trucks about two hundred meters on the other side of ravine, over."

"This is Scout One, roger, stand by."

"We're out of time," Mitchell said to Larson.

Leroy's frantic voice crackled over the radio, "Scout One! Scout One! I think they've spotted us....Oh yeah, definitely, they've spotted us, over."

"This is Scout One, open fire, pin them down. Don't let them get to the ravine!"

"Scout Four to all units, fire! Fire!"

The chorus of fifty caliber machine gun fire rang out. All four APCs had open fire on the target. The red tracers were flashing across the ravine seventy-five feet above Mitchell's head. The mechanical, rhythmic explosions of machine guns echoing through the ravine. Black had finished placing the last C-4 charge and was running back over to Larson and Mitchell.

"Are you ready?" Larson asked as soon as Black got to them.

"Yes, all five charges are set."

"We got to get out of here!" Mitchell urged.

"What do you need to blow the charges?" Larson asked Black.

"They're on three minute delays. I was going to blow them, one at a time."

"We can't hang around here that long," Mitchell said.

"No, Black we got to blow them all at once," Larson said.

"Okay, I'll need four men to help me. I'll set up a signal and we can do them all at the same time."

Larson looked to Mitchell, "I need three of your men."

"Brian, Frank, you stay with me. The rest of you get up to your tracks." Mitchell shouted to his team.

"Nash, you and Goldman get back to the APC," Larson yelled.

The gooks had not expected to make contact. They were used to traveling unimpeded, without fear of attack on this side of the border. Seeing the Americans, shocked them. They were hesitant, not knowing what to do. Then the hail of fifty caliber lead flying their way gave them instant clarity. They turned and was heading for the cover of a small hill behind them.

Black pulled out another electronic timed detonator and about a half a pound chunk of C-4. Brian, Frank, Larson, and Mitchell were watching. "The detonators are all preset for three minutes, all you have to do is push the start button. I'll set this charge for thirty seconds. We each take one of the main charges. I'll set off this signal charge, when you hear it blow, push the start button and run like hell."

Each of the five men were given a charge to blow, Larson, the cockpit, Brian one of the fuselage pieces. Black took the other chunk of fuselage located approximately in the middle of the debris field. Mitchell and Frank took the two engines. In a minute and a half they were all in position. All the while, the machine guns continued to blast away above them.

Black started the signal charge timing and ran back to his main charge a hundred feet away. Thirty seconds later the half pound of C-4 exploded. It's concussion ringing through the ravine. All five men pushed their start buttons, turned and ran for the north bank of the ravine. They had climbed almost to the top when the five explosions went off in a chain reaction lasting less than one second. The five men topped the rim of the canyon and ran for their APCs. Leroy ordered the scout section to cease fire. The gooks showed no sign of wanting to engage.

Back at One-One, Mitchell climbed into the turret, Frank down in the driver's hole.

Larson set the PRC-77 to his frequency and keyed the radio. "Wolfpack! Wolfpack, this is Bulldog, over!" He waited only two seconds before calling again, "Wolfpack, this is Bulldog, over."

"Bulldog, this is Wolfpack, over."

Larson smiled with relief. "Wolfpack, this is Bulldog. Commence Firestorm. I say again, commence Firestorm, over."

"Roger Bulldog, commence Firestorm, Wolfpack out."

Within a minute, the code word had been flashed from Eagle to Da Nang to a aircraft carrier off the coast. Four McDonnell Douglas F-4 Phantom fighter-bombers, fully fueled and loaded with bombs, were standing by on ready alert. Their pilots and radar officers on board ready to go at a minute's notice. They had been waiting in their planes for the last hour.

The Phantoms were hooked to the catapult and launched one at a time. In two minutes, all four Phantoms were airborne and on their way to the target, 334362. The carrier was one hundred and fifteen miles from the downed Blackbird. It would take the F-4s twelve minutes to get there.

Mitchell keyed his radio, "This is Scout One to all scout units, let's get out of here. I'll take the lead, Scout One out."

One-One turned and headed northeast, the other APCs close behind. Mitchell and Frank were back tracking the same route they had come in on. It was fresh in their minds, that and a new sense of urgency after being detected had them traveling at a considerable faster speed leaving.

The gooks saw the Americans leave. After five minutes they moved up to the ravine and discovered the wreckage. The young NVA officer, that was in charge of the unit, ordered six of his people to investigate. He assumed that it must be important for the Americans to have crossed the border and of course, he was right. It was important and he was doing the right thing, but he was doing it at the wrong time. He had no way of knowing that Firestorm was about to consume them.

The F-4s came from the west, flying low and had slowed to 250 knots. Their first pass was for a visual target identification. The gooks scrambled for cover. The Phantoms banked, circled and forty-five seconds later started their bombing run. One at a time, they roared up the ravine, each plane dropping eight 500 pound bombs. They banked, circled and came again. This time the first two F-4s dropped eight cluster bombs each. A cluster bomb is designed to open up and scatter a hundred small bomblets. The floor of the ravine was saturated with explosions.

Almost every square meter was hit by these bomblets. The last two Phantoms dropped pods of napalm, filling the ravine with boiling fire. Firestorm had reduced the remains of the SR-71 to a point where it was no longer a security concern. It had also killed six NVA.

By noon, the scout section was back across the border and had rendezvous with a CH-47 helicopter. Larson, Black, Nash, and Goldman loaded their equipment and the bodies of the SR-71's crew onto the CH-47. Brigadier General James Clarke was there. He ordered Mitchell and his men not to discuss the events of the last day; not now, not ever, not even among themselves.

The men of A Troop knew something had happened and thought it had something to do with the CIA. For the next couple of months, it became a running joke. The scouts would be asked about it and would only say, "I could tell you, but then I would have to kill you."

CHAPTER TWENTY-EIGHT

A Troop continued to operate in the A Shau Valley for the next eight weeks. They engaged their elusive enemy on eleven occasions during that time, all having been relatively small firefights. Although they hadn't fought any major battles, they had under gone some big changes. At least it seemed that way to Mitchell.

The men of the Armored Cavalry lived together in a very close environment. The hardships and dangers they faced formed a bond, a brotherhood between them. Individuals would come and go, because of casualties or completion of tours, but when someone left it wasn't a faceless, nameless person; it was a friend.

That eight weeks saw some changes in the leadership positions of First Platoon and for the troop. The first to go was Sergeant O'Shea, the TC of One-Two. He was pulled from the field and sent home early because of the Sullivan Act, or what was sometimes called the sole-surviving son act.

During WWII, there were five brothers, George, Francis, Joseph, Madison, and Albert Sullivan of Waterloo, Iowa. They all died when their ship, the cruiser Juneau was sunk on November 14, 1942, during the battle for Guadalcanal. The Navy's policy was to separate members of the same family in wartime service, but the brothers had enlisted with the provision that they not be separated.

Consequently, their loss was probably the greatest ever suffered by a single family in American military history. From that time on the military would no longer permit the last surviving son of a family to be in combat.

Sergeant O'Shea's older brother had been killed in 1966 serving in the 11th Armored Cavalry near Xuan Loc. His younger brother was also in the Army, serving as a clerk-typist at Fort Carson, Colorado. On the night of April 25th, during a late spring snow storm, he was killed in a car wreck on Interstate 25 just outside of Colorado Springs. The death of his younger brother made O'Shea the sole surviving son of his family. Before he left he told Mitchell that he felt guilty for leaving his crew. Mitchell told him that was crap, he had given enough, his family had given enough, go home, get out of this shit hole while he could. Paul Bonds took over as TC of One-Two.

It was 1745 hours and A Troop had set up its NDP four klicks southeast of Firebase Destiny. Mitchell had received word to report to Captain Tice's CP for a briefing along with the platoon leaders, Lieutenants Neilley, Ross, and Parker.

Tice began by saying, "Gentlemen, this will be my last night as commanding officer of A Troop. Tomorrow I'll be leaving to return to the states." Holding up two pieces of paper in his hand he continued, "I have two orders here. First, from the Department of the Army, Headquarters 9th Infantry Division, General Orders Number 5325. Be it known that First Lieutenant Jeffrey D. Neilley is to be promoted to the rank of Captain as of 12 May 1969, et cetera, et cetera. Congratulations, Jeffrey!" Tice said holding out his hand to Neilley.

"Thank you, Sir." Neilley said, a faint smile formed on his lips, the light of pride burned in his eyes. Neilley was a good combat officer, a soldier's soldier. He never let his own ambitions supersede the welfare of his men, but the Army was his career, his life, he took great pride in this promotion. Ross, Parker, and Mitchell took turns congratulating him.

"Second," Tice said. "From the Department of the Army, Headquarters 9th Infantry Division, General Orders Number 5367. Be it known that Captain Jeffrey D. Neilley is to assume command of Troop A, 3rd Squadron, 5th Cavalry, 9th Infantry Division on 0800 hours 13 May 1969, et cetera."

It had been expected. Neilley had extended his tour for six months primarily because he was promised command of A Troop when Captain Tice's tour ended. This made it official and everyone congratulated him again.

Tice pulled a small blue box out of his pocket and opened it. "These were my first Captain's bars. I'd like you to have them, Jeffrey. I think they brought me pretty good luck this last year, maybe they will for you, too."

Neilley took the box, "Thank you, Sir. I'd be honored."

"Gentlemen," Tice said, "It has been a great privilege to serve as your commanding officer. Whatever success Alpha Troop has had, is in no small part because of you. All of you have served with professionalism and honor. I thank you. Because I consider you my friends, I'd like to tell you a few things that are on my mind. First, I want to tell you I have decided to leave the Army."

That hadn't been expected. It shocked Neilley, Ross, Parker, and Mitchell. They had no idea he was getting out.

"You're resigning your commission, Sir?" Neilley asked.

"Yes, I am."

"But why?"

Tice didn't answer for a few seconds. "I'll try to explain it. This last year has convinced me that the civilian leadership of our military has prosecuted this war in a manner that borders on criminal. It seems to me that their only commitment is to their own political futures. They make military decisions on the size and the violence or peacefulness of the last protest. Hell, the rules of engagement that they have placed on us makes it almost impossible to even defend ourselves, much less have any hope of winning this war."

"You got that shit right, Captain!" Mitchell spoke up.

"I don't want to impose my feelings on any of you," Tice said. "It's just the way I feel. I believe it is unconscionable to send soldiers to die for some ill-conceived political agenda. I believe it's more than unconscionable, it's fucking criminal. American soldiers should only be committed to battle if the goal is to win. It is apparent to me that our goal is not to win and therefore I am honor bound not to be a part of it."

Neilley, Ross, and Parker stood quietly, but not Mitchell.

"You're not imposing shit on me, Sir. I've been thinking that for a long time." Hearing it coming from his

CO, an officer and gentleman by act of Congress, made Mitchell think. "Maybe, I'm not the only one who thinks the whole world is upside down."

In three days, Tice was back stateside. He resigned his commission, ending his seven year career as an officer in the U.S. Army. He returned home to his wife and two daughters in Davenport, Iowa and took a job with his father-in-law, selling insurance.

First Platoon operated without an officer as platoon leader for the next ten days. During that time, Mitchell was acting platoon leader and Brian Banks took over the Scout Section.

On May 23rd, Lieutenant Allen Riggs was assigned command of First Platoon. He arrived by helicopter. The Huey set down in the middle of A Troop's perimeter, about fifty meters from Captain Neilley's track.

After getting directions to the CP, Riggs strode up to Neilley and said, "Lieutenant Allen Riggs reporting for duty, Sir," snapping off a book-perfect salute.

Neilley didn't return the salute. Instead he said, "That's not needed out here Lieutenant. In fact, it's frowned upon."

Riggs looked puzzled.

"The salute, we don't do that out here. You see, if a sniper was watching us right now and saw you salute me that would tell him I was a higher ranking person, someone in a leadership role. It's kinda like painting a target on my back."

Riggs dropped his hand to his side. "I'm sorry sir, I should have known better." Riggs said, embarrassed by the fact that he'd only been in the field for two minutes and had already screwed up.

"Well, it's just a little thing, Riggs. Don't sweat it. You're going to find that there are a lot of things that are done differently out here."

"Riggs was tall, at least 6'6". He was slender, but not skinny. His body was put together with long lean muscles, hard with natural strength. He was enthusiastic about his first combat assignment. He didn't have boonie smarts, but no cherry did. He did have a good head on his shoulders and in time could learn.

Mitchell met him for the first time at 0820 hours that morning. He had gotten a call to report to Rattlesnake's CP. The commanding officer of a Cavalry troop could pick his own call sign. Neilley had chosen to keep Rattlesnake, out of respect for Captain Tice. When Mitchell arrived, Ross and Parker were just leaving. He saw the tall, lean Lieutenant in his new, clean fatigues towering over Neilley. Mitchell guessed who he was.

"Mitchell," Neilley said, "This is Lieutenant Allen Riggs. He's the new First Platoon leader. This is Staff Sergeant Robert Mitchell, TC of One-One and Scout Section leader."

"Sir," Mitchell said holding out his hand.

Riggs noted that Mitchell didn't salute. "Good to meet you, Sergeant Mitchell," he said shaking Mitchell's hand.

"Mitchell is one of the most experienced NCO's in the troop. If you have any doubts about what you should do or when to do it, consult Mitchell. I have on many occasions myself." Neilley said. "Take his advice, he knows what's going on."

"Yes Sir, I'll do that." Riggs then turned his eyes to Mitchell. "If you see me screwing up Sergeant, don't wait for me to ask."

"You can count on it, Sir."

Neilley smiled, knowing that coming from Mitchell it was an understatement.

The next nineteen days, A Troop encountered the enemy twice. Each time it had been a short running firefight, only lasting a few minutes and resulting in no body count for either side. The troop had settled in nicely with its new command structure. Captain Neilley was proving to be as good a CO as Tice had been. Riggs was learning fast. He was confident in his own abilities, but not cocky. He didn't shy away from responsibilities or let authority go to his head. He had asked for advice from Mitchell on more than one occasion and had gotten it, unsolicited on several more. Almost nightly, Captain Neilley would spend a hour or so with Riggs, one on one, giving him the benefit of his experience.

For Mitchell things seemed to be stable again, at least as immutable as things got in the boonies.

On June 20th, A Troop was ordered to pull out of the A Shau Valley and back to Camp Evans. They stayed there for ten days, the longest time they had ever spent in what they considered a rear area.

Being in a rear or forward area seemed to be a relative term in Vietnam. It was all a matter of perspective, depending on where you were stationed. For soldiers stationed in Cam Ranh Bay, Saigon was the rear. If they were in Da Nang, they considered Cam Ranh Bay the rear. Soldiers stationed at Camp Evans felt like they were forward and Da Nang was the rear. Nothing was more forward than the boonies and if you spent most of your time out there, like A Troop did, everything else was the rear.

On July 1st, A Troop left Camp Evans and headed north for its new AO, between Dong Ha and Phu Phu'o'ng, very near the DMZ. Mitchell hated to leave the relative safety of Evans. He was getting short, just twenty-five days and a wake up. His DEROS was July 27th. He could see the light at the end of the tunnel. He just hoped that the light wasn't a train named Phu Phu'o'ng.

"Just maybe, I'm going to get out of this alive," Mitchell thought.

CHAPTER TWENTY-NINE

Luck was always a factor on the battlefield, but more often than not, the dumb died first or at least those who are forced to deal with the dumb decisions made by their commanders.

B Troop, minus its third platoon that had been assigned as security at Firebase Alfa, had spent the day escorting a convoy. They rendezvoused with the large convoy of over sixty trucks at the junction of Highway One and Highway Nine, just outside of Quang Tri. Their destination was Fire Base Carroll. The trucks were delivering the supplies for a major buildup that Carroll was undergoing.

B Troop was at the highway junction on time at 1000 hours, but the convoy was completely disorganized and had no chance of leaving as scheduled. Word filtered down that the convoy would roll at 1130 hours. It came and passed. Then 1230 hours was to be the starting time that also came and passed. The convoy finally came to life and began moving west on Highway Nine at 1310 hours, over three hours late. That time could never be made up. In fact, other problems along the way slowed them even more. One truck had mechanical problems and another unexplainably ran off the road and overturned. The mission that should have ended by 1400 hours had kept B Troop tied up until 1815 hours. They were supposed to set up a NDP at grid coordinates 452296, but now found themselves over an hour away as day turned to night.

The sun was already dropping behind the mountains to the west. The yellow-orange sphere was half hidden by the horizon. Its rays shining on the undersides of the clouds, casting a reddish-pink hue across the sky. In five minutes the sun would be completely obscured by the blue gray mountain summit. Thirty minutes after that, darkness would cover the countryside like a menacing shroud.

B Troop should have stopped and set up a NDP where they were while it was light enough to clear its perimeter and set out proper defenses. They didn't. The decision to push on to the assigned NDP at 452296 was made by Captain Henry Peterson, the C.O. of B Troop. Captain Peterson was new in country and had been in command of B Troop for the last five weeks. He had commanded a cavalry troop in the states, but this was his first combat experience.

The convoy had been about as organized as a Haight Ashbury love-in. That was bad luck, but the decision to set up a NDP after dark was just dumb. There was no compelling reason for B Troop to be at coordinates 452296, only Captain Peterson's overzealous compulsion to complete his assigned mission. His decision was questioned by both of his platoon leaders, but Peterson pushed on over their objections.

It was 1940 hours and completely dark when B Troop arrived at its assigned NDP. It was a long wide ridge line with an uneven surface, covered with knee high grass and clumps of brush ranging from four to ten feet high. They formed their perimeter but made no attempt to clear the inside of the circle. It would have been a waste of time because of the darkness.

Four miles away at coordinates 350366, A Troop had established its NDP, after spending the day on an uneventful search and destroy mission.

"Here's to another good day," Mitchell said to his crew as he raised a can of warm Coke in his hand and took a drink.

"What's so good about it? We searched all day but didn't find shit to destroy," complained PFC Glen McKay, the newest member of One-One's crew. This had been his third day in the field; three days of combing the countryside from sun up to sun down, searching for the enemy, his bunker complexes and supply caches. Three days of searching and finding nothing, for McKay three days of dust, sweat, heat, and boredom.

Frank looked over at McKay, then turned away with a look of disgust on his face. "Ignorant ass cherry."

"What?" McKay asked, not knowing the reason for Frank's disgust. "What did I do?"

Frank didn't answer. Paganini spoke up. "Let me ask you something Glen. Did you see the crew of one of the other tracks get blown away because their radio antenna hit a trip-wire in the trees and set off a C-4 charge packed full of nails and glass today? Or did you see one of your buddy's head explode and his brains splatter all over your shirt?"

Glen looked puzzled, not answering.

"Well, did you?"

"No."

"Hell, for that matter did anyone even take a shot at your today?"

"No!" McKay answered defensively.

"Well, that's why this was a good day!"

McKay was new and could be forgiven for some things. Like most cherries, he understood the words that Paganini had said, but would only comprehend their meaning after he survived his first fire fight. "I don't want any of us to get hurt, but I wouldn't mind finding some gooks to kill."

"Let me tell you something Glen," Mitchell said with a scowl on his face. "Nine times out of ten, we don't find the gooks, they find us. And when they do it's never a good day. I don't want to ever hear you say you hope we find some gooks again. You understand me?" Mitchell's tone was unmistakable. That along with Frank's and Paganini's condemnation convinced McKay that he had said the wrong thing.

"Yeah, I understand," McKay answered.

McKay's scolding ended as Lieutenant Riggs came striding up to One-One. "Johnson, get your gear together, you're going home."

Frank's eyes widened. "Me, sir?"

"Yeah, you. Now get going and make sure you bring your personal M-16, the one you signed for. They'll be checking the serial number when you turn it in back at Evans. You've got five minutes to be on the resupply chopper. There's no time to waste."

"Right, L.T." Frank said with a smile.

Riggs turned and left.

"Home." Country said, his voice breaking out into a laugh. "You're going home."

Frank just continued smiling, his black eyes that normally showed no emotion were dancing with life. He quickly gathered his few personal items and was standing behind the APC with One-One's crew around him.

"You listen to the guys that's been here a while." He said to Glen.

"I will." Glen answered.

He turned his look towards Paganini. "Keep your shit together, Paganini." It was the only time Frank had ever pronounced his name correctly.

"Always." Paganini smiled broadly, he knew it meant he had earned Frank's respect.

"Country, it's been good having you as part of the crew this last year."

"You too, Frank." Country said, the grin on his face couldn't get any bigger.

Mitchell held Frank's M-16 out to him. Instead of taking the weapon, Frank did a very un-Frank like thing. He stepped up and put his arms around Mitchell, holding him for five or ten seconds. Turning him loose he just looked into his face not speaking.

Finally, Mitchell said, "It's been real."

Frank nodded, "Every fuckin' minute."

"Now, get out of here," Mitchell said. "Get on that chopper. This is one ride you don't want to miss."

Frank didn't speak, he just took the M-16, turned and walked away

*   *   *   *   *   *

It was 2255 hours and all was quiet at coordinates 452296. B Troop had settled in for the night. Most of the men were asleep with only one man per track on guard. Captain Peterson had made a dumb decision and now that dumb decision was going to be compounded by bad luck. They had no way of knowing that the southeast quadrant of their perimeter was sitting right on top of a NVA tunnel complex.

The NVA Major that was in command of the tunnel complex had been busy forming a plan to take advantage of the opportunity that was literally parked on top of him. He would have the majority of his men attack B Troop from outside of its perimeter. They would open fire from all sides. When B Troop was fully engaged and its attention focused away from the center of its perimeter, a second group of enemy soldiers would attack them from within. With the main attack coming from outside the perimeter, there was a good chance that the soldiers who sneaked inside would be able to throw a twenty pound satchel charge inside an APC, exploding it, destroying the track, and killing most of the crew. He assigned eight, two-men satchel teams to stay in the tunnel near the opening that was inside the perimeter. The NVA's main body left the complex using two different openings that were outside B Troop's perimeter and took up attack positions. The NVA Major had ten RPG launchers and over one hundred and fifty rockets at his disposal. He deployed them strategically to cover the perimeter from all points of the compass.

At 0015 hours the attack began. Automatic weapons fire and rocket propelled grenades poured in on the unsuspecting and unprepared B Troop. The first

436

vehicle to be hit was Bravo One-Three. An RPG round burned a hole through its right side, critically wounding the track commander and one gunner before either had had a chance to man their weapons. On the opposite side of the perimeter, Two-Two's left side gun shield was hit, destroying the M-60 machine gun. It's crew, except for one man in the turret had been lying inside asleep and had not yet gotten to their feet. They all escaped uninjured. Of the ten RPG teams that were positioned around B Troop, nine were successful in hitting their target on their first shot. However, once the Americans began to fight back their ninety percent accuracy started to drop. Within thirty seconds, B Troop was pouring a sea of fifty caliber and M-60 into the dark. The enemy manning the RPG launchers no longer had the luxury of exposing themselves for any length of time to take good aim. Their success rate quickly fell to under twenty-five percent.

Within one minute of the first shot being fired, the combat had erupted into a pitched battle. The night was a blaze of red tracers streaking out from B Troop's perimeter and hundreds more, mostly green, streaming back in. M-79 rounds being lobbed at the enemy were exploding into flaming balls of light. The ninety millimeter cannons on the tanks started firing canister rounds. This ammunition consisted of a metal cylinder filled with a large number of steel pellets which when fired, spread out in a wide cone. They were devastating as an anti-personnel weapon.

The first two minutes of the attack had hurt B Troop badly, but they now had enough suppressing fire going out at the enemy that the fight was evening out. At that time the eight satchel charge teams emerged from the tunnel and fanned out inside the perimeter. The first satchel charge to detonate had been tossed into One-Five. It exploded violently, killing all that was on board. The APC burst into flames which in turn started to explode the one hundred and ten boxes of ammo that she carried inside. Next the Two-Zero mortar track went up into a searing inferno and began to blow itself apart as the four point two inch mortar rounds she carried exploded in a chain reaction.

All battles are usually awash with confusion, this one even more so. At this point, nobody in B Troop had any idea that the enemy was inside their perimeter. Their people were being killed, their vehicles were being destroyed at an infelicitous rate and they didn't even know where the worst of it was coming from.

*   *   *   *   *

It was a minute or two before midnight and Mitchell had quietly moved up beside the turret where Country was sitting watch. Country was deep in thought and hadn't noticed Mitchell.

"What's on your mind?" Mitchell asked.

The voice had startled him a little and he jerked slightly and then grinned out of embarrassment. "Sarge, I didn't know you were there."

"It's time to relieve you. What were you thinking about? You looked like you were a million miles away."

Country shrugged, "It's dumb, you'd laugh."

"Maybe not. Try me. You looked happy, it must be something good."

"You won't laugh?"

"I won't laugh."

"Okay, I was thinking about cotton candy and snow cones," He smiled as he continued speaking, "About the midway rides at the state fair and pitching nickels trying to win fuzzy dice or maybe a teddy bear."

Now Mitchell was smiling too.

"I told you, you'd laugh."

"I wasn't laughing at you. I was just remembering doing the same thing."

"Really?"

"Yeah, really."

"So what do you miss about home?" Country asked. "I know you miss Maggie, but besides her, if you were home right now what would you like to be doing?"

Mitchell thought for a moment, his smile spread from his lips to his eyes. "I'd like to be cruising down Central on a Saturday night, wind up that big 389 GTO and lay rubber in all four gears."

"Yeah," Country said, nodding his head. "We should be getting to go home soon, don't you think Sarge?"

"Anyday, I expect." Mitchell answered.

"I can hardly wait. There was times I thought this year would never end."

"Yeah, me too. Climb on out of there, I'll take over."

Country got out of the turret and Mitchell took his place.

Country started to go down inside the APC then stopped and quietly said. "I'm going to miss it some."

Mitchell looked back over his shoulder. "You're going to miss this place?"

"No, not the place, I'm going to miss you. I'm going to miss Frank and Paganini, all the guys."

"Yeah, I'll miss them too." Mitchell said. "They're a good bunch of guys."

"They are good guys, good friends." Country said. "I've never had friends like this before. I think it's the one good thing about this place."

They both were quiet for a few seconds, then Country climbed down inside.

Mitchell settled into the turret for his two hour stint on night watch and now was sitting comfortably with his back leaning against the turret hatch cover, his right foot propped up on the fifty caliber gun shield. The sky was dark, but so far there had been only a few sprinkles. You could smell the rain more than feel it. His thoughts turned to Frank. Mitchell was happy that Frank had gotten pulled from the field today and would be on his way home in the next forty-eight hours. He and Country, both were due to be pulled out for D.E.R.O. and home any day now, themselves. Going home and being with Maggie, the thought brought a warm feeling. A smile crossed his face as single drop of rain landed on his right forearm.

Off in the northeast Mitchell saw a flash of light, faint, then quickly followed by two more. "Lightning," Mitchell first thought, but soon realized it was the flashes caused by small explosions. He straightened up and focused his concentration. He heard a boom, barely audible, then two more. It was coming from the general direction where B Troop's NDP should be located. Within half a minute, the horizon was lit up with bigger and brighter explosions. Mitchell could make out the popping

sounds of machine guns, then louder bangs as the big
ninety millimeter cannons began firing. "Jesus Christ!"
Mitchell said out loud to himself. He continued to watch
the action off in the distance. The warm feeling had left
him and was replaced by a churning tightness in his
stomach.

A long minute passed, then the radio came to life.
"Alert! Alert! All units get ready to roll, fast! This is an
emergency! Say again, get ready to roll. Alert! Alert!"

Country hadn't yet fallen asleep and was sitting up
as Mitchell turned and yelled down, "Everybody get up,
now! We gotta get rolling. Everyone up!"

Mitchell was putting his flak jacket on as Paganini,
Country, and Glen stood up through the main hatch.

"What's happening?" Country asked.

"That!" Mitchell answered, pointing to the fight off
in the distance.

"Shit! Oh, shit!" Country said.

"Country, you get in the driver's hole and get her
started up. Glen you're on the M-60. Get ready guys!"
Mitchell said as the tightness in his stomach turned into a
knot.

The radio cracked again, "All units there is no time
to pick up your night defenses, cut your claymores loose
and leave them. Report when you're ready to roll!"

Country had slid in the driver's seat and started up
One-One's diesel engine. Mitchell disconnected the
claymore lines from the three detonators and tossed them
aside. He looked over his shoulder at Paganini and Glen.
They had their steel pots and flak jackets on, manning their

guns. He keyed the transmitter button on the radio, "One-One, ready to roll."

*   *   *   *

A satchel team made its way to within twenty feet behind Bravo Two Three. One man pulled the fuse ignition cord that automatically lit the charge's fuse, the other flung it in Two-Three's direction and then they quickly retreated. The intent was to throw it up and through the APC's main hatch, but the satchel hit the right side gunner in the back and bounced off, landing on the ground at the right rear of Two-Three, exploding two seconds later. The blast rocked the APC, blowing both gunners off their feet. The concussion totally stunned the entire crew. Their ability to reason or react was gone, but otherwise, they were unhurt. The two gooks recognized that the charge had fallen short and ran back to Two-Three. Before the stunned crew regained their senses, the gooks had tossed two hand grenades up and in the APC through its open hatch. This blast and accompanying shrapnel killed the T.C. and both gunners. The driver was badly injured, but still alive. It took a little time for the shock of the blast to wear off, but as it did he became aware of pain. Burning pain in the small of his back, in his left arm, and in the back of his neck. Looking over his shoulder he saw his T.C. slumped over the gun shield. The driver keyed the intercom on his CVC helmet, but the radio and intercom system was inoperable, destroyed by the blast. Reaching between his legs, he pulled the lever lowering the driver's seat. It was when he tried to leave the driver's hole and crawl to the back that he realized his legs wouldn't move. In fact he had no feelings in his legs at all. He ran his hands over them, there was no sensation felt through the legs of being touched, but his hands felt warm and wet. He lifted his hands and looked at them. They were covered in blood. He could see the two gunners laying on the floor of the APC. He called to them, then he called again, and a third time. They didn't respond, they didn't move. The driver knew he was hurt bad, his legs wouldn't move. He had no feeling below the burning pain in the small of his back. "I've gotta get help or I'll die." He thought.

He reached up with his hands and grabbed hold of the top ring of the driver's hatch and began to pull himself up. It was difficult lifting his body up and through the hatch using just the strength of his arms, but he managed to do it and then rolled off the top of the APC, falling hard to the ground. The impact shot pain through his torso, stunning him momentarily. Regaining his resolve, he looked up and saw the Two-Two track in the near distance. Pulling himself with his arms, he headed in that direction.

*　*　*　*　*

Mitchell heard another radio transmission. "One-Eight, this is One-Six, you take point. All other units follow in order. We're running with lights. One-Eight, move out now."

"This is One-Eight, roger." Billy Dill answered.

The One-Eight tank had a twenty-four inch search light mounted above its main gun, the only track in First Platoon so equipped. This was the reasoning for it to take the lead. Surprise or stealth was of no concern. Getting to B Troop as fast as possible was all that mattered.

One-Eight pulled away, followed by One-One, in turn followed by the rest of A Troop. Flares began popping off as they ran over their own trip lines. Billy's search light was casting out a beam one eighth of a mile. All the tracks had their headlights on. Mitchell had been here for almost a year, and he had never once seen the Troop do this.

B Troop had found themselves in this disaster due to a series of unlucky events, compounded by a dumb decision made by their C.O. A Troop on the other hand was going to wind up in it because they were doing what the cavalry has always done; Charge to the rescue. B Troop was being massacred and A Troop was rolling right in to it, to do whatever they could to save them. For that, they too would pay a terrible price.

*   *   *   *

B-Troop's command track exploded into a conflagration, flames leaping twenty feet high. Captain Peterson, his RTO, and his gunner died instantly and were being consumed by the blaze. The track's driver somehow survived the blast and was half running, half stumbling away from the charring wreck, his clothes and hair on fire, screaming a loud cry of pain, shock, and terror. One of the two gooks that had satchel charged the APC fired off a burst of AK-47 rounds into him. He fell to the ground, the screaming stopped, but his body continued to burn.

Bravo Two-Three's driver had pulled himself about halfway to Two-Two's position. Shock and loss of blood had weakened him to the point he only moved an inch or so with each pull of his arms. He raised his head to measure the distance he still needed to travel before he could get help. Digging his fingers into the dirt, grabbing handfuls of

444

grass, he stubbornly fought his way closer and closer to Two-Two. It had been eight minutes since he had started his journey. He raised his head again looking for Two-Two, but this time he didn't see it. He didn't see anything, just blackness. Slipping into unconsciousness, he laid there for the next forty minutes, slowly bleeding to death.

Just twelve minutes after Mitchell saw the first explosions, he, his crew on One-One, and all of A Troop were charging through the enemy's lines and into B Troop's perimeter. The battle was absolute chaos. There were explosions outside the perimeter and explosions inside the perimeter. Countless numbers of machine gun rounds were pouring out at the enemy. Lead slugs were whistling through the air and red tracers streaking through the night. All this was being countered by hundreds of rounds pouring back in, screaming through the dark. B Troop was throwing everything they had at the NVA that surrounded them. The gooks were responding in kind. When A Troop rolled in, the chaos became insanity. As they broke through the enemy's lines, the risk of being hit by friendly fire was as great as getting hit by the gooks.

There were four APCs totally engulfed in flames. Those fires along with the flashes of the explosions and weapons was lighting the battlefield in a faint, jerky, almost strobe light way.

One-Eight had broken through the NVA's lines followed close by One-One. They were less than twenty-five meters from the perimeter when Mitchell saw gunfire flash just in front and to the left of One-One. He watched the tracers streaking towards One-Eight and then Billy Dill slumped over in the tank's turret. One of the bullets had hit him in the neck and almost ripped his head off his body. Mitchell leveled his fifty caliber on the shadow of a figure that had just killed Billy and opened fire. The first two rounds cut the gook in half, the next five turned him into a crowd.

Even with their T.C. dead, One-Eight led the troop into the perimeter. They began peeling off to take up alternating positions between B Troop's vehicles. About half of A Troop was inside when Brian, who was in the turret of his One-Three, saw someone on the ground, inside the perimeter, raise up and fire at the back of One-Two. The bullets whistled right by the ear of One-Two's left side gunner. Brian drew a bead on the NVA and ripped him apart with fifty caliber lead.

"One-Three to all units, there's gooks inside the perimeter!" Brian screamed over the radio. "I say again, there's fuckin' gooks inside the perimeter!"

Hearing Brian's warning, Mitchell looked back over his right shoulder and motioned to Paganini to come to him. "There's gooks inside the perimeter!" Mitchell shouted.

"Inside!" Paganini yelled back.

"Yeah, inside!" Mitchell then turned to his left and warned Glen.

At that instant Paganini saw something on the ground, a shadow, a flicker of an image. "Is it a man, a gook, or one of our guys?" All these thoughts were inundating his head. His hesitation was only a second or two, then a muzzle flash came from the shadowy image and hot lead and green tracers peppered One-One. Two rounds hit the side of the APC, another hit Paganini's gun mount, still others sung by the crews' heads. Paganini opened fire and so did Paul on top of One-Two. The lead and tracers of their two machine guns intercepted at the shadow. His muzzle flash and tracers turned down into the ground and then stopped.

A minute later all of A Troop had fought their way in and was taking up positions on the perimeter.

"Country," Mitchell said over the intercom. "Cut the lights, but keep the engine running. We don't know what we might have to do or how fast we'll have to do it."

"Right, Sarge." Country answered and turned off the APC's headlights.

The fight had suddenly entered into a lull. Combat is that way. It could be raging one moment and then be relatively quiet the next. Battles seem to have an ebb and flow about them. There was scattered gunfire in different parts of the perimeter but it paled in comparison to moments before. The smell of the battle hung heavy in the air. The smoke suspended in the atmosphere was being illuminated by the glare of the burning APCs, giving the battlefield the appearance of ground fog over an English moor. There was an eeriness about it, foreboding, almost supernatural.

Suddenly out of the ghostly fog, an RPG was screaming towards One-One. It hit the right front and exploded, burning a hole through the hull of the APC into the engine compartment, destroying the Detroit Diesel engine that powered One-One. The impact jolted the track and blunted the crew's senses. A heartbeat later a second RPG slashed through the night. This one hit directly in front of the driver's compartment, blowing through the hull. The molten metal cutting through Country's flak jacket like a hot knife through butter. Regaining his cognizance, Mitchell saw Country slumped down in the driver's hole. He sprayed the moors with sixty to seventy rounds of fifty caliber, then dropped down inside the APC and crawled to Country. He pulled him out of the driver's seat and back into the open space below the main hatch. Mitchell could see that his wounds were too numerous and gapping for there to be any hope. Country was going to die and nothing on this earth could stop it.

In a weak, bewailing whimper, Country cried, "Momma." His body was shaking, involuntary muscle contractions jerking his limbs. Again, "Momma," followed by a frail choking cough and blood splatter on his lips.

Mitchell held him and spoke his name, but Country didn't respond, for he was someplace else. Then with his life drained from him, he was still, his eyes were open looking up at Mitchell, his lips slightly apart as if he was trying to mouth momma one more time.

Leroy was caught in the open on top of One-Four, when the conflict erupted again. A deluge of enemy fire flooded in on the Americans. A red hot lead slug ripped into Leroy's left leg just above the knee. It passed completely through the leg, shattering the femur. The same slug that had been flattened by its first impact then collided with his right leg directly at the knee joint, disintegrating the patella. Leroy's legs collapsed under him. He screamed in pain as Mike pulled him from the top of the APC down inside.

"God, Oh God!" Leroy cried. "Holy Jesus! God!"

Mike was rubbing his hands over Leroy's back and chest, looking for wounds. "Where you hit?" He shouted. "Where you hit, man?"

"Oh shit!" Leroy uttered a long, loud, piercing cry of pain. "My legs, my legs!"

Looking at Leroy's legs, Mike saw that they were mangled and a flood of blood was flowing from the wounds. "Hang in there!" He said.

"Oh God, I'm hurt bad, Mike." Leroy yelled.

"Keith," Mike said. "We got to get him to the medic track or he'll bleed to death."

'Where is it?' Keith asked.

"Center of the perimeter, they can get him on a chopper."

"Mike," Leroy cried out again, his voice reverberating with pain. "You gotta take over, you gotta be T.C."

"I will man." Mike said.

"Oh God, it hurts Mike, it hurts bad."

"I'll carry him." Keith said.

"You sure you can?' Mike asked.

"Fuckin' A I can." Keith replied.

Keith opened the rear hatch and with Mike's help dragged Leroy out the back of One-Four. Keith picked him up and placed him over his shoulder. Leroy screamed in pain as Keith held him by his injured legs.

"Watch yourself!" Mike warned.

Keith didn't answer, he just turned and headed for the medic track. His adrenaline was flowing at one hundred and ten percent. Almost in a full run with the one hundred and ninety pound Leroy over his shoulder, he moved through the night.

A medivac helicopter was just setting down as Keith got to the center of the perimeter. He carried Leroy right up to the chopper and literally threw him into its open door.

"He's hurt bad, it's his legs!" Keith yelled before turning back towards One-Four.

He was about halfway back, passing by a large clump of elephant grass when he came face to face with a NVA soldier. They were less than ten feet apart. Time was suspended as neither man moved for a second nor two. Keith's mind was over loaded with conflicting thought and instinctual panic. He could see the young NVA's face, his eyes were wide and wild with fear. The two men stared at one another, trying to come to grips with their situation. Finally, almost in slow motion the gook started raising his AK-47 towards Keith's chest. Keith's hands were empty, the .45 automatic he carried as backup on ambushes was strapped on his right hip. His brain said reach for the gun, but his body never got the message, he just stood there frozen in time. The gook pulled the trigger. Keith heard a metallic click, but nothing happened. Either the NVA's weapon had misfired or the thirty round clip in it was empty.

At that moment for Keith, time resumed. He dropped to the ground and rolled as one should if his clothes were on fire. He came to rest on his stomach, the big .45 pistol held in both hands. The gook was frozen in place, kind of glazed over, like a boxer taking a standing eight count. Keith popped off two rounds, nailing the enemy in his abdomen and upper right chest. Falling straight backwards the gook laid on the ground face up. Keith crawled over to the convulsing NVA and fired one more round under the gook's chin that exploded out the top of his head.

The battle had been in another lull for the past ten minutes. Captain Neilley was trying to get a handle on the situation. B Troop's C.O. was dead, his command track destroyed, and half of Bravo's tracks were not responding to radio calls. Mitchell was instructed to send someone over to Bravo Two-Three and see what their status was.

Glen had gone to have a look. He came running back from Two-Three and climbed up the back of One-One.

"Well?" Mitchell asked. "Is there anyone over there?"

"They're there." Glen answered. "They're inside."

"What the hell are they doing?" Mitchell asked.

"I...I don't know. They're just inside, laying down, sleeping, I think."

What Glen said made no sense to Mitchell, it was inconceivable, then he looked close at Glen's face, into his eyes. They were wide open, but not focusing on anything. They seemed to drift around in their sockets with this blank, panic stare. Mitchell noticed Glen's pants were wet in the front and down one leg. He had pissed himself. That's when it dawned on him that Glen had lost it, reality for Glen no longer existed.

"Stay here." Mitchell ordered. "Paganini, are you still with me? You haven't lost it, have you?"

"I'm still fuckin'here." Paganini answered defiantly.

"Good. I'm going to have a look. You keep your heads down and your eyes open."

"Watch yourself, Sarge." Paganini warned.

Mitchell climbed off One-One, with his M-16 in his hands, he ran flat out towards Two-Three. He came up from behind and looked in through the open rear hatch. There was three men inside, but they weren't asleep, they were dead.

Mitchell was halfway back to One-One when the flaming sign of automatic weapons appeared outside the perimeter. He dropped to his stomach, then realized the firing was aimed at One-One.

For a reason only known to himself, Glen had decided to leave his M-60 and climb into the turret. In during so, he stood full upright on top of the APC. An NVA had seized the opportunity. One of the lead slugs from the AK-47 hit Glen in the left front forehead and exited through the right rear of his skull, taking a large part of his brain with it. Mitchell opened up on the gook killing him, although he didn't know it; he just knew the shooting had stopped. It became completely quiet again. Nothing moved, it was as still as death.

Mitchell stared out into the darkness at the eerie fog of the moors. Before his eyes it metamorphosis into a ghostly entity. An evil force coming for him, floating closer and closer, intent on consuming him, destroying him. It was death. It had taken Billy Dill. It had taken Country, but that wasn't enough. It had taken the crew of Bravo Two-Three, still not enough. It had taken Glen and now it was coming for Mitchell. He closed his eyes, buried his face into the dirt.

"Don't fuckin' lose it now, Bobby," he said to himself. "Get a fuckin' grip." After a few seconds he looked back up and saw the smoke of the battle hanging in the air.

"Cover me!" Mitchell shouted to Paganini. "Give me cover fire, now!"

Paganini opened up with his fifty caliber, raking the darkness in front of One-One in an ark, right to left and back again. Mitchell jumped to his feet and ran full speed back to One-One.

There was long lulls in the battle interrupted by sporadic fights around the perimeter.

At one point, Paul caught a gook trying to crawl up to One-Two with a satchel charge. He nailed him with a canister round from his M-79. His body had so many holes in it, it could have been used for a screen door. But, just to make sure, Paul reloaded the M-79 and from point blank range, blasted the gook again.

Another skirmish was when Lieutenant Riggs spotted two gooks running away from the perimeter. In tandem with one of his gunners, they mowed them down with a hail storm of fifty caliber and M-60 machine gun fire.

The rest of the night passed in much the same manner.

CHAPTER THIRTY

It had been quiet for a good thirty minutes and by all appearances the fight was over. Fifteen minutes earlier a detail had come by and picked up the bodies of Country and Glen. Mitchell stared out into the dark that had in the last few minutes showed signs of graying. The dawn was off in the distance, weak but building. In another fifteen minutes it would give birth to a new day.

He glanced to his left at the unmanned Two-Three track of B Troop and then to his right where Bravo Two-Five was. He knew Two-Five was still manned by someone, because there had been firing coming from it during the last round of violence. He took a quick look over his right shoulder at Paganini, who looked stunned or scared, probably both. "What the hell happened?" Mitchell thought.

Less than twelve hours earlier, he was set up in a NDP commanding an APC with a full crew of five. An APC that for the past three hundred and fifty-two days had been his home, his anchor, an umbilical cord to any sense of security he had. Now it was all but destroyed. Two direct RPG hits assured that One-One had fought her last battle. And as for his crew, Paganini and himself was all that was left. Frank was gone, pulled from the field only hours before this disaster. Mitchell was grateful that Frank was safe, but he missed him.

Over the past year they had almost became one entity; with two sets of eyes to see the danger, two sets of skills to fight them off, and twice the courage to endure it all. His absence left Mitchell feeling somewhat fractional. Less than one hundred hours in the boonies and the war had taken Glen's life. There hadn't been time for Mitchell to get to know him but he was part of One-One and Mitchell's responsibility. Now he was dead. And the worst of all, Country was gone. He and Mitchell had been together from the very first day they set foot in Nam. They were together on every mission, together in every firefight; but now he was dead and Mitchell was still alive. For that, Mitchell felt guilty, it made no sense, but the feeling was strong in his gut.

This one hellish night had taken away everything that had given Mitchell any purpose this last year. He had felt an honor bound duty to keep the men in his charge safe and now they were gone. Mitchell felt he had failed, the whole last year had been for nothing, emotionally crushed he began to cry openly. It wasn't an audible cry, but the tears that filled his eyes were now spilling out and trickling down his cheeks.

"Mitchell, Sergeant Mitchell."

Mitchell was startled by Captain Neilley calling him from behind. He instinctively wiped the tears off his face before turning around to answer.

"Yes, sir." Mitchell said.

Neilley was showing the effects of anxiety
and fatigue. His face was drawn and haggard.
There was a large blood stain on the front of his
shirt. It was left there by a crew member of his
command track that had died in his arms, two hours
earlier.

"You're going home." Neilley said. "You
and Macintosh." Neilley's eyes were scanning
One-One. "Where's Macintosh?"

Mitchell didn't answer, he just stared at
Neilley, unable to get his head around the irony.

"Where's Macintosh?"

Paganini finally spoke up, "He's dead, sir."

Neilley's already haggard face was engulfed
with sadness. When he spoke again his voice was
hollow with despair. "You need to get your things
together, Mitchell. There's a chopper on the way.
You have to be on it when it leaves."

Mitchell still didn't say anything. He didn't
move, just stared at Neilley.

"Mitchell, you have to get it together now.
Do you hear me?"

"What about my track?" Mitchell asked.
"What about Paganini?"

"I'll take care of them. You just need to get
your gear together and be on that chopper." As he
spoke the CH-47 Chinook was descending to land.

Five minutes later, Mitchell walked up the
back loading ramp of the helicopter, placing his
duffel bag and M-16 inside. He turned and stood in
the doorway, surveying the battlefield before him,

the destruction, the death. "Life is precious and should not be wasted," Mitchell thought. That night it was used up in a gluttonous manner that could only bring shame on mankind. Tears filled his eyes, "The whole damn world is upside down!"

EPILOGUE

It was July 14, 1989, Mitchell was standing in front of the Vietnam Memorial in Washington DC. He was gently rubbing his fingertips over one of the more than 58,000 names that were carved into the black granite wall. The tears in his eyes blurred his vision a little, but he could see his reflection looking back at him from deep inside the black granite. Maggie's reflection was there too, as was Brian's with his arm around his mother's shoulders, standing a few feet behind Mitchell. Tears had filled their eyes also, as it does to almost everyone who visits this place.

Mitchell was deep in thought, his hand resting on the name of Hollis C. Macintosh, remembering Country, the way he had lived and the night he died. He had been there for two or three minutes, when he became aware of another reflection next to his staring back out of the wall. A chill shot through him as he turned to face the man he saw in the wall. It was Frank, twenty years older and thirty pounds heavier, but without a doubt, it was Frank.

"Frank!" Mitchell said, his voice sounding of surprise and excitement.

"Sarge!" Frank answered as he wrapped Mitchell up in a big bear hug.

"Man, it's good to see you." Mitchell said as they broke the hug. "What are you doing here?"

"I came to pay my respects to Country," Frank said. "It was twenty years ago today it happened."

"Yeah, me too." Mitchell answered. "I just felt like I had to be here. I can't believe we both showed up at the same time."

"Yeah, it's amazing." Frank said.

Mitchell saw Maggie and Brian, "Oh, what am I thinking," he turned and raised his arm towards them. "I want you to meet Maggie."

"How are you, Maggie?" Frank said. "You're still as pretty as I remember you in your pictures twenty years ago."

"I don't know about that," Maggie smiled, "but it's wonderful to meet you."

"And this is my son Brian." Mitchell said.

Frank offered his hand and Brian took it. "That would be Brian with an I." Frank said, smiling from ear to ear.

"Yes, sir." Brian answered.

"You know, it was me that talked your father into naming you Brian."

"No sir, I didn't know that."

"You bet it was." Frank answered. "I worked on him for over a month. Brian with an 'I', I kept telling him. It's a good, strong manly name, I'd say."

www.ingramcontent.com/pod-product-compliance
Lightning Source LLC
Chambersburg PA
CBHW051431260626
47162CB00001B/39